Out of Arizona

Roderick Robinson

I0628364

Racing House

ISBN 978-1-84327-939-6

The Racing House Press
20 Cambridge Drive
London SE12 8AJ, UK

Printed and bound by Lightning Source

MOST atlases will confirm that Bayonne (France), Prague
(Czech Republic), Genoa (Italy) and even Slapout (Oklahoma,
USA) – all mentioned here – actually exist. None of the characters, conversations or educational practices does or did. No
such flights took off or landed and only fancy has flown. No
ATC regulations alluded to were broken but it is true, despite
contrary evidence, that Pineau de Charentes is regarded as an
apéritif in France.

CHAPTER ONE

Change of address

"TELL YOU WHAT," said Jana. "Why don't I drive? Then I don't have to sit on this." She poked at the worn passenger seat.

Dirk ignored her, simply opened the driver's door.

Jana stepped up into the van. "Of course, it's our own fault. We turned this seat into a hammock. All that space in back yet I always put small parcels here. The sagging holds them like a shopping bag. A pity it doesn't do the same for my butt."

Dirk turned the ignition key. "In two hours' time you need never sit there again."

"Two hours, but that's 180 k of pain. Look, I'm grateful, you understand. Giving me your half of the van. But why Bordeaux?"

"To save me dough. Bordeaux to Montreal at a hundred-and-ten bucks. You can't beat that."

"With a direct flight to Phoenix?"

Dirk shrugged. "Can't have everything. There's half-a-day stopover in Montreal. But I'd rather kill time eating burgers than croissants."

"Phoenix," said Jana. "Phoenix, Arizona.

They were quickly on to the autoroute, travelling north. The noisy vehicle fell short of the 130 kph limit and the bodywork drummed metallically. Dirk said, "What you must remember – it needs a new fan belt. If the old one goes now you'll be walking away from this tin can. A new engine won't make cash sense."

Jana nodded. "I changed the belt on a Peugeot that was older. Hope to God things have moved on. Reaching the rad was a real bastard: I had to unhitch the drive shaft and loosen the engine mountings."

"This one's got more space at the front."

Dirk steered the van into the middle lane to pass a milk tanker. Jana hated being a passenger and was only making the trip to bring the van back. But Dirk made things bearable with smooth, planned driving as if he were flying the Cessna. Showing off he took the gear-change up into top without touching the clutch. "You realise I had to say yes to Westair when they offered me this job," he said.

"Of course. And it's a big, big step up. So long as you're sure it's your thing."

"My thing?"

Jana gestured. "Little planes versus big planes. You have to admit, south-west France fits your image. Grass strips as well as tarmac. Being in charge; a dream in militaries and aviator shades. Won't a Boeing 737 cramp your style? There's the dough, of course, that should help."

"France came at the right time. I was doing OK in Tucson and that part-time contract paid big bucks. But it was hell to organise. Too many people wanted the same time-slots. That's why I slipped you the double bookings. Even then I was still stacking shelves at Safeway. Then I met Jean-Claude at Cessna in Wichita. Gascon Air sounded like a vacation – and that's how it's been. But it's time to move on; GA's too weeny and Westair's big jets won't be a problem. It's the technicals that turn me on: the systems, the back-ups, the gee-whiz avionics. Facing all that a single engine doesn't rate. In the end, I'm just a big kid."

"One thing, Westair are solid. You won't be driving to work in a van. And you'll be playing at home."

"I speak the language," Dirk said, grinning. "No more ATC hassles."

"I try to imagine you. 'This is your pilot speaking.' Saying that, wearing a tie."

"Shit, I could use some dignity. But there's you. You're here in France because I asked you. It's as if I'm dumping you."

"You dug me out of an emotional hole. I had to get out of the States. And let's not talk dumping. Straight off I'll no longer be

Jerry to your Tom. With you away I'll fly longer routes, use the Seneca more, take over your students. All of it fun. No apologies necessary."

"Me out of the way? Sounds as if you won't miss me." His voice sounded petulant.

"Hey, we weren't exactly joined at the hip. I wasn't one of the local girls; I know your conquering hero looks. The clincher is I'm too old for your harem."

"Too old? We're about the same age."

"Right! Which makes me too old," said Jana.

"What's that supposed to mean?"

"Well, Madeleine's nineteen isn't she?"

None of this seemed to please him. Then the van's speed dropped away on an incline and he nodded at the mirror. "One thing I won't miss. A Frenchman glued to my back fender. Say I lifted the gas…" An irritated horn sounded to the rear and Dirk waved a hand through the open window. "Stay out of my lap, Jacques! Course he won't. I'll get more reaction when I lift next time."

"Just what you need. Pulled over by a gendarme and missing your cheapo to Montreal." She glanced at her wristwatch to check when she'd be back in Arcanques.

"Ah, Jana. Soul of sweet reason. How about an Orangina."

She passed him the flask-shaped bottle. He said, "Here's something I will miss. This taste, this crazy bottle."

"Did you know? They add mandarin juice."

"That right? Too subtle for KMart."

"Well Kraft own Orangina. At least they own Cadbury and Cadbury own Schweppes, who own…"

"Who own froggie Orangina. No shit! How do you know this stuff?

"I read the papers."

They were on the flat now and the Nissan Micra that had struggled behind them on the incline overtook the van. The driver described circles with his left index finger and Dirk laughed. "Haven't seen that before, sure as hell it's an insult. Yeah, the papers. But then your French is better than mine."

"Far better."

"Why's that?"

"Women talk to their landlady, guys don't."

"I make myself understood."

"Oh sure: altitude, bearing, flight path. Checking out girls with your drinking buddies. But not when it comes to laundry, or what's good at the charcuterie, or gossip. Then you're mute."

Dirk glanced across. "Madame le Lannic tells you what's happening?"

"How do you imagine I find out things? When I can't stand my room I watch TV with her. She's a widow; she gossips."

"Do I figure?"

Jana nodded.

"What way?"

"In March they all thought you were serious about Madeleine. But I guess Madame knows the answer to that one, by now."

"Anything else?"

"Oh sure. Cleverer than you might think. In the village they say, you can tell France doesn't interest him, just listen to the way he speaks. But he's passionate to fly. Why not in Afghanistan?"

"So what did you say?"

"Me! I'd no idea."

"No way I'd've joined the flyboys. Whereas you…"

Jana said nothing despite his waiting look. He said, "Shit, you're good enough."

She turned to the window.

At the airport he surprised her by ignoring the *Déchargement* signs and making for short-term parking. "Let's grab a coffee," he said. She'd imagined they'd just change seats, nothing more.

He loaded his tightly packed flight bags on to a trolley. "There's a coffee bar that looks on to the runway."

Still puzzled she sat at a table in front of the canted window; watched an Air Maroc Airbus lumber past to a stand on the right. Without asking Dirk had gone to the counter and now put a latte in front of her. Frowning he unpeeled his sugar cubes and stirred them into his black coffee.

"Lot of the time I can't figure what you're thinking," he said.

"Does that matter?"

"Mostly, no. Just now it does." He scratched his chin.

"You going to open up?" Jana asked.

He laughed. "Sort of. More a couple of questions. Questions I should have asked way back."

"Sounds heavy."

He sipped his coffee while her latte remained untouched. Said, "You're what they call a stoic."

Her reaction was to say no, to resist being typed. She was too complicated for a single word. But the more she thought the more she agreed. "I suppose."

As he stared out at the airport's messiness she noticed yet again his good looks. The tanned, delicate – almost feminine – face. Light brown hair in engaging curls. Terrific ears. Easy to see what Madeleine had seen. Dirk was no blue-cheeked Mediterranean local. None of that sculpted hair styling.

"So I'm not dumping you?" he asked.

"I just said. You got a thing about that?"

"I wanted to be sure. You might have got me wrong."

"Got you wrong? Gascon wanted a pilot. US trained with US flying hours. I wanted to leave Arizona. What's to get wrong?"

He smiled speculatively. "You never once asked: why you?"

"I didn't have to."

"No?" He was alert, interested.

"Come on, Dirk. You were recommending; your head was on the block. It had to be a pilot you could trust. As I say, what's to get wrong?"

"How many flyers do you think I know in Arizona?"

She paused. "Tons. You're saying there was some other reason?"

"What do you think?"

Jana sipped her cold latte, giving herself time. "We're not talking movie plots, are we? With you it's always pretty basic;

mainly a question of ass. But with me that doesn't arise so what else is there?"

He turned to watch a Lufthansa Boeing accelerate down the runway. As if it were important, as if it fascinated him. When he turned back his expression was warmer, less predatory. "Quite a compliment? Me asking you?"

"Doubt it. You may know a bunch of flyers round Tucson but France wouldn't tempt them. France would scare them."

"It didn't scare you. Were you desperate?"

Jana shook her head. "Keen, not desperate. France seemed like a place where things might change."

"And did they change?"

She stared him out "Yes."

"Yet you want to go back."

"Eventually, perhaps." She said. "But only for professional reasons."

"Socially then - "

" – it's better here," she said flatly.

"You don't mind being on your own."

"I've never been alone. Not talking about the Denver Broncos isn't being alone. In any case Les Bleus are a good trade."

"Les Bleus?"

"Shit, Dirk,"

"I know, I know," he grinned. "Girls in US grade schools play soccer, I can't take it seriously."

"You lost out in France. What's it been? You should have worked harder on the language. They use it differently. Big words. They'd have liked you more."

"Madeleine's English made me lazy. I let her do the talking."

"The ugly American - the kind of tracks most of us leave," said Jana. "No style. Did you give her the thumbs down in French or English?"

Dirk sniggered. "She's tough, that one. When I told her – in English – she shrugged. If I'm honest, I didn't get it. We'd been close. I expected more…" He spoke the word reluctantly. "… more emotion."

"You sound disappointed."

"Relieved. But surprised," he said.

Jana was irritated. "You just don't understand the French. What did you want: preppy tears? Madeleine's adult. You sure you gave her the heave-ho, or was it the other way round?"

Dirk said nothing, looked down at his empty cup.

"Don't worry," said Jana. "Hearts break easier in The Copper State."

But Dirk wasn't interested in Arizona for the moment. "You see me as some kind of shit?"

Usually he could take this sort of thing. His sulkiness was odd. She said, "Just a good looking guy who doesn't waste too much time on the women he boffs. No crime in that."

"Hardly house-trained?"

"Look, I didn't say that. You ride a wave, always have. Glamour job, a face like Johnny Depp. No reason you should spend nights picking lint out of your belly button. Anyone slates you it's likely to be jealousy."

But he was preoccupied and she wasn't getting through. Then she remembered. He'd arranged this coffee klatsch and she still didn't know why. "You've got something on your mind," she said.

"Forget it."

"Well I will." She got up. "See you around. Give me the keys. I've no idea why you wanted this long goodbye."

"Siddown."

She didn't want to because his sulk was in full flow and it could be a powerful weapon. But she was curious. Sitting down, she said, "This is a sour note, Dirk. You know I'm grateful. And we get along. Madeleine can look after herself and, plus side, you raised her stock in the village. What I said now was just girl and guy talk. Let's start again. Hey?"

"Another latte?"

"Sure. Why not?"

When he served her she started in immediately. "So I never asked: why me?"

He laughed. "Ancient history. Worse, a bad ego-trip. But, what the heck. I'm just about to put five thousand miles between us. We'll soon have our feelings to ourselves. You're right. I was never going to palm a doozie on Gascon. It had to be someone solid, easy with sea mists and the Pyrenees. But, remember, when I called it was still early days for me in Biarritz. My French was bad, my social life zilch. I asked myself why not good old Jana?"

Although she'd started to guess it sounded unreal out in the open. "You could have fooled me," she said carefully. "You did fool me."

"It gets worse."

"I can't think how."

"I thought I could take advantage," he said. "You wanted France, or at least anywhere that wasn't Arizona. You were eager. I figured the rest would follow. I put down the phone and went for a beer at the Bar Sport."

"And what happened then? Did an angel perch on your shoulder?"

He laughed. "Two sips and I saw it was such a bad idea! Pure male Hollywood. Expecting tit for tat. But I wasn't finished. A second beer and I had Plan B. I'd hold off and act the good friend from way out west. I'd offer to take you round the village, do the introductions, tell you about the opening times. Go out for a few drinks, play the long game, plenty of time to… get familiar. And then, well, why not… fool around."

Jana said nothing, imagined the plan, imagined it working.

Dirk shook his head. "Another bad idea. Me, with my French, doing the introductions!" He mimed outrageousness. "But even if I'd been fluent overnight you stymied me. First you preferred Arcanques to Ahetze. And I knew no one in Arcanques. A week passed and you were as busy as I was, hopping locals down to Bilbao or whatever. No time for evening beers or cosy talk. You were in flight."

"I didn't… I had no idea… Honest."

"So I noticed," he said. "You put it well ten minutes ago: 'With you it's usually a question of ass.' Should I have played to my strengths? Not held back?"

"I'm not used to… having my ass fought over."

"So you'd have been easy meat?"

That sickened her. "Probably not. I am suspicious by nature."

He pointed. "That's another latte you've let go cold. But neither of us should grumble; things came out right. We went our own ways. Madeleine showed up for me and I take it you get to practice your French with Eliazar. And your Spanish."

"Hey, this was your problem, not mine."

"You're right. I should have stayed shtumm. I told you this was an ego-trip. The sort of itch men like to scratch. And you've done well. People like you. Jean-Claude says your *baptemes de l'air* convert well."

They talked stiffly about Gascon Air, burying what had gone before. Then it was time for him to check in. Although she was keen to be away she offered to wait in the queue with him but he was processed quickly and they stood awkwardly at the international departures gate. He moved slightly and she thought he might kiss her.

"Just one thing," Dirk said. "I didn't know you had a nickname."

"Neither did I. Who uses it?"

"Madame le Lannic."

"First I knew."

"Yesterday. I called in to say I'd gassed up the van. You weren't there. Madame asked her daughter: where's Mademoiselle Griotte?"

Jana felt the hotness in her cheeks. "Oh that. Just a private joke."

He was close enough to notice her distress. "Except it isn't a joke, is it? OK, it's something lousy."

It had been some time now. And France had been good to her. This was unexpected. Hating herself she needed his brief sympathy. "*Une griotte* is a Morello cherry."

At first he was adrift but reacted quickly. "Ah, shit." Kissed her – there.

SITTING in the van she wound down the window to examine her face in the door mirror, tracing an outline above her jaw. A modern languages freshman at Arizona State had likened it to Bulgaria. ("See this little peninsula in the north-west. That's home to Vidin on the Danube, just up the road from Mihajlovgrad.") He'd worn glasses with thick lenses and claimed to be colour blind. She hadn't believed that.

Her mind churned and she knew this made the area stand out as a deeper red. When the specialist told her parents it was a port-wine stain she had been too young to know what port wine was.

The van engine started with a shudder and she followed signs to the autoroute. Rumbling along on the inside lane she switched on the radio, tuning away from Dirk's pop station to rolling news. While flying she would never do this. Background noise dulled important sounds. But the van was all background noise.

Quickly the news bulletins gave way to a forum where a group of Frenchmen mauled over the Afghan war in cranky-toned voices. The views were familiar but that didn't matter, Jana listened instead to the vocabulary, five-dollar words like *moralité, rebarbatif*. So different from the illiterate questions on Phoenix radio where the host had to coax callers into making sense. Here the arguers rephrased loose ideas without regard for anyone else's feelings.

Someone had just labelled American public opinion *éphèmère* and she laughed aloud. Laughed again at *tire de son propre camp* and its failure to capture the English sarcasm of friendly fire.

Friendly fire was today's talk-show topic. It followed hard on a disaster in which a US pilot had mistakenly attacked and de-stroyed a vehicle carrying European troops. Transmissions be-tween the US aircrew were played and replayed by the French host who translated exultant jargon that faded into doubt and arrived at awful certainty.

The studio group talked about problems of youth, the godlike status of military pilots, national irresponsibility, an incapacity to understand another country's point of view. Repetition set in and Jana turned off the radio.

She imagined flying that mission. Envisaged the F/A-18 Hornet with its big V-tail, loaded with tackle that characterises the modern fighter jet, the shadowy target bracketed by tight symbols on the gunsight, the decisive moment, the explosion with its excess of light on the screen. And the sequel.

She had a personal interest. Her career in the US Air Force had ground to a halt during the simulation of just such an attack. The report canning her had come at the end of a weapons course but surely not because she'd failed to master the systems, fly the patterns or deliver the plane. Technicalities were her meat and drink. Which meant it must have been defective behaviour or a character flaw. Had her instructor, with incredible prescience, looked ahead, imagined a friendly fire disaster and guessed Jana would crack under the Calvary the Hornet pilot was presently undergoing? And from this decide that aerial combat had been a psychologically unsound decision from the start?

The urge to fly dated back to her troubled youth and had then evolved into looking for the toughest job on offer. Mere transportation wasn't enough and by age sixteen her ultimate goal consisted of slipping an air-to-ground missile down the throat of a two-metre target. She'd even sorted out the morality, reassured that training would equip her with a professional pride, a knowledge (admittedly limited) of international politics and an adult form of patriotism. But everything depended on military correctness: a legitimate target identified and destroyed. Without that clarity the comfort and purpose of military flying disappeared.

No course and no tutor had prepared her for accidentally killing one of her own, for letting loose friendly fire, even though this could happen in aerial attacks. Her ability to survive such a foul-up would have depended on how her instructor had measured her innate qualities. Had Major Sondergard seen this weakness in her? Had her flying added up to no more than manual skills, without any mental toughness? If so why had the discovery come so late in her training?

Unless, of course, she had failed for some quite different reason.

ARCANQUES was only a couple of kilometres off the autoroute to the south of Biarritz and when Jana parked the van on the street Mme le Lannic was hanging out washing, a daily, sometimes twice daily, event. She turned her gaunt face towards the vehicle and Jana saw the resentment. Perhaps Jana should have tried the driveway. That way her landlady could have enjoyed telling her this privilege wasn't available.

"M. Boonhausen has gone?"

Dirk's mis-pronounced surname was a le Lannic touchstone, a refusal to adapt. Her distortions, at first amusing, quickly became wearisome. They were impervious to correction because Mme le Lannic preferred being wrong. Very soon, Jana told herself grimly, this wouldn't matter. Mme le Lannic would have her perversity to herself.

"He has gone."

"And the *camionette* is now yours?"

"It is."

Mme le Lannic continued to stare at the van, as if deciding whether she was entitled – anyway – to warn Jana about the driveway. Warning for warning's sake. Then a happy thought occurred. She nodded at the van, "It will be useful."

"Doubtless," said Jana, extracting full ambiguity from that flexible French term. During the drive back from Bordeaux she'd prepared for what would follow, knowing it wouldn't be pleasant. But why had she gone on accepting her landlady's strictures all this time? "I must change my clothes."

"Dinner is at seven." Dinner had been at seven for the last two years but tonight would be the dinner not taken. Should she warn Mme le Lannic? Jana decided not.

Upstairs she changed from her jeans into a summer dress and drove off in the van. As she arrived at Ahetze she was reminded it was not nearly so pretty as Arcanques which had won awards for "floweriness". She hardened her heart against this.

Dirk's landlady, Mme Chauvelet, was by turns welcoming, confused and then suspicious as Jana explained she wanted to take over Dirk's now vacant room. Sheets were referred to vaguely as if using the barely cooled bed were indecent. But resistance melted when Jana offered a further week's rent to move in that evening, adding to the payment Dirk had made in lieu of notice. With Mme Chauvelet now in a sunny mood Jana was able to confirm a further, symbolic prize. Dirk had parked the van on the house's driveway and this right now passed to Jana..

Jana's only twinge of guilt occurred when she re-entered Mme le Lannic's and smelt the rabbit cooking. In the US rabbit was regarded as vermin and therefore unfit for eating; it had taken the French to reveal that special aromatic gravy. Despite this rich temptation she went directly into the kitchen to pass on the bad news and to watch its effect. Gauntness turned to slackness as Mme le Lannic's voice rose in half-phrased protestations that echoed and re-echoed "*Impossible*". Each time Jana stonewalled: it was a private decision and there was no alternative.

"But tonight!"

"I have my reasons," said Jana.

The driveway tyrant would have previously demanded what these were. Not now.

"And you will live at...?"

"Ahetze."

"At Mme Chauvelet's?"

Jana nodded.

"Is Mme Chauvelet less expensive? We could discuss - "

"That is not the reason."

After this response silenced Mme le Lannic fear replaced shock. Left her reviewing her financial practices, assessing their legality, wondering how much Jana knew. A sum of money, all in cash, transformed her silence into mere dumbness and Jana turned away. The petty autocrat had become a lonely widow.

Arriving in France Jana had two large suitcases which travelled free and a third on which there were excess charges. That little world had grown and spread out and she knelt to gather up huge ring-binders, most second-hand, on aviation law, pilot instructions for the Cessna 172, a directory of airports in south-west France together with a monster Collins-Robert dictionary, a DVD course on advanced conversational French, tax law for foreigners, maps of northern Spain and northern Italy. Plus scuffed paperbacks to while away time as she waited to fly back from Hyères, Clermont-Ferrand or Grenoble. In her haste to leave Mme. le Lannic she had forgotten to call at the supermarket for empty cartons and now faced taking her belongings downstairs in penny-numbers.

On her sixth trip Ghislaine was sitting on her bed.

"You could have been kinder to my mother, Mlle Nordmeyer." Previously it had been Jana. The tone was formal, cool.

No one expected nuances in a second language. "*Alors,*" Jana replied.

Ghislaine shrugged. "There is such a thing as politeness, you know. Don't Americans practice politeness?"

"For us politeness is synonymous with equality."

Baffled by this hasty epigram Ghislaine would have died rather than ask for an explanation. Instead she took the offensive: "You are saying my mother is not your equal?"

"Not at all." And Jana left the room carrying a tottery pile of large-scale maps of the Pyrenees.

Clothing was next and Ghislaine watched interestedly as Jana took jackets and trousers off hangers. Because she'd been limited in what she could bring to France Jana had discarded much of her US wardrobe imagining it would be easy to replace. In fact the French equivalent of casual, durable US aviation wear was inferior and more expensive. Arguably it was more fashionable.

With the clothes stowed in the van she faced an even more intractable task. Mme le Lannic had provided dinners Monday to Friday but not at weekends. Jana had bought saucepans and a skillet reluctantly after she discovered eating out regularly was expensive and carried the stigma of being seen alone in restaurants. The kitchen implements were awkwardly shaped and not easy to gather up. As she pondered the answer Ghislaine surprised her by starting to collect the pans. "You know Mme Chauvelet does not cook as well as mother."

"I know. I can smell the rabbit."

Ghislaine giggled as she went downstairs. "A moment," she said, turned left into the kitchen and emerged with copies of the newspaper Sud Ouest. "These will stop the rattling."

From then on Ghislaine helped Jana transfer the rest of her belongings after which they both sat on the van's tailgate, the doors open, their feet dangling, enjoying the sun.

"I think you were somehow hurt," Ghislaine said.

"That's true."

"My mother, no doubt?"

Jana nodded.

"You prefer not to explain?"

"You might say I was over-sensitive."

"I think not," said Ghislaine gloomily. "Remember the le Lannics are farmers, my mother's family too. Not rich farmers. In agriculture feelings are a luxury and are not discussed. My mother knew something of the war, a bad time to have feelings. Those memories stayed with her."

"A hard life I'm sure."

"I'm sorry you are leaving."

The sentiment was unexpected. Ghislaine's angular face was a precursor to her mother's, twenty years in arrears

"Sorry. Why sorry?" Jana asked.

"I am French. We have our prejudices. You are American."

Jana recalled those early weeks: the relentless scrutiny, the austere and formal answers to her questions, the endless pettifogging about anything to do with ablutions. A family that needed her rent and perhaps resented the fact.

Jana smiled. "You are still French and I am still North American."

"But not the one we feared."

"What changed?"

"The language. It's always the language," said Ghislaine.

"Hardly surprising. I needed French at work."

"That meant nothing to us. One evening, after dinner, we were talking. I realised I knew the names of your parents, where they lived, what they did. The way you got your certificate – your licence. That you voted for the… the other party, I have forgotten the name. You were no longer a fantasy figure from the cinema."

"Well, I'm… glad."

"You became almost exotic. All those names, so difficult to pronounce. Touson not Tuxon. You had been everywhere: Alaska. New Orleans, but not our Orléans. I learned how to say Orleens. We have lived in Arcanques for ever and you have flown a plane to Ciudad Juarez. You are a pilot and I am a *pharmacienne*. A dull life but through you I lived vicariously."

Jana smiled at the five-dollar adverb. "Working in a pharmacy isn't dull. Your pharmacy helped teach me French. The regulations, the products, the ailments, the behaviour of customers. More useful than aviation."

Like her mother Ghislaine rarely smiled but did so now, briefly. "One responds to questions asked in French."

"I got to know Arcanques and you got to know Phoenix."

Another brief smile. "I know you must move. But perhaps we could meet."

"I would like that."

"You could speak English to me. Improve my English."

Jana's eyebrows rose. "You speak English?"

Ghislaine raised her voice a little as she changed language. "Of course. I have what I think you call – the English call – a distinction. Once I won a prize: a very difficult *roman* – what is *roman*, ah, a novel - by the author, Faulknaire. Requiem for a Nun. You know that novel?"

Jana resumed in French. "Faulkner is difficult. But here you are, you speak English."

"My mother said I must never reveal it.. She was afraid you might never speak French again and she would not be able to… follow."

"I was very proud of my French. Still am. I like showing it off."

"But you are not ostentatious"

"I chose the wrong word there. I mean I enjoy using French. In any case it seems polite.

"Ah, polite. I too like speaking English. What I do not like is being forced to speak English."

"Or American."

"You understand. I shall miss you. But you are agreed? We will meet?"

The repetition worried Jana. "Of course. But you have…"

"A boyfriend? No longer."

No surprise. The references over the dinner table had been infrequent with no hint at any sort of passion.

Ghislaine apparently foresaw the two of them sipping gloomy rouges at some bar. "Something healthy, I think. At the *salle polyvalente*. Do you play badminton?"

Yes, that would be less defeatist. "You could teach me – in English."

And Ghislaine smiled a third time.

MOVING her possessions from Mme Chauvelet's driveway into the new room took a mere half hour. Jana had deliberately re-fused the evening meal and used the van to drive into Bayonne, looking for an impersonal place to eat. McDonalds would do.

The Golden Arches, just off the Avenue du Grand Basque, was populated mainly by teenagers. Plus one comatose tramp. Did French youths regard McDonalds as chic? They looked enthusiastic enough, bumping against each other at the counter, flipping up their sweat-shirt hoods and flipping them back, shouting their orders, wolfing down the food while standing on the forecourt outside. A US teenager would have recognised the place but not the enlarged photographs of *crudités* and *salades*. Not that the French lads had gone for any of these options; all had called for Beeg Macs.

Jana ate her Chicken McNuggets placidly. Two years ago she would have avoided McDonalds and sought out *blanquette de veau* as proof she understood French culture. But after a while she accepted hers was a Yankee metabolism. With time to spare and with someone to talk to she was perfectly capable of enjoying a meal lasting an hour and a half. Alone she preferred fast food and saw this wasn't a French skill. A hamburger on a length of baguette missed the point twice over: it lacked symmetry and the crisp bread required so much effort to chew that the meat patty either disintegrated or fell on the floor.

She read a discarded copy of L'Equipe wrestling with sports slang that appeared to change from day to day. Discarding the empty Sprite can she took the paper with her, walked south until she found an empty bench overlooking the Adour and applied herself, educationally, to a long speculative article about the prospects for the French football team re-formed after a comic series of implosions during the recent World Cup.

Having finished this stern exercise she remembered Dirk had nagged the Chauvelets into installing a shower. The skin on her shoulders crinkled in anticipation. Mme le Lannic could only provide a bath from which Jana always emerged feeling slightly tarnished. She got up and walked back to the parked van.

Purified by a shower and wearing a clean tee-shirt she lay on her bed flicking through *Avions de Chasse Moderns*, picked up out of pure nostalgia in the Bayonne street market. She stopped at a page showing variants of the F-18 Hornet and considered the friendly fire incident again. She hadn't flown the Hornet but had more than an idea of how it would handle. Her training had included nearly thirty hours on the Talon jet trainer, time enough to appreciate its manoeuvrability and its exhilarating rate of climb. The Hornet, weighing three times as much, was more of a mobile weapon than the nimble Talon but Jana sympathised with the *Gott mit uns* conviction the Hornet pilot must have felt as he closed on the target that was to betray him.

Would he still be flying? France's TF1 news had said it was "likely" but Jana thought this was speculation. If it were true it would play into the hands of the USA's critics as proof that US forces were insensitive to foreign opinion, too powerful to be influenced. Not that Jana cared for any of that. Her interest lay solely with the individual who made a mistake in the middle of a warlike attack.

For months her whole life had centred on becoming a fighter pilot. She tried to imagine being free to engage in combat and then having that prize taken away in an atmosphere of public condemnation.

Outside her room the stairs creaked as the Chauvelets – whom she was now required to call Sylvie and Hugues – made their way to bed. Seeing light beneath her door Hugues whispered to his wife, albeit audibly, "You were lucky with the lodger." using the idiom "falling into luck" that so delighted Jana. His wife's reply was less extrovert and only the surname le Lannic was unmistakable.

Jana recalled her former landlady's face - skin drawn tightly over the temples and round the nostrils - receiving the bad news. Losing the rental would be a harsh blow. But Morello cherries had a knowing ring to it, and sounded intentional. Jana touched her jawline and turned out the light.

She knew she wouldn't sleep. She lay on her right side, her left hand passive between her thighs and thought about Dirk at Bordeaux airport. Absurd to say she'd somehow become inaccessible to him. They saw each other daily and had even eaten out on occasions. If he'd wanted to "fool around" he could simply have asked. And he'd never been shy about that. The way he told it made it seem she was a prize, a modest one but ultimately desirable. Utter nonsense. A more likely reason for his reticence would be that of the practised philanderer: one didn't have casual affairs – and with Dirk all affairs were casual – with colleagues at work. In any case he hadn't been short of alternatives. There'd been a steady flow of French women keen to test rumours about the pretty-faced US *aviateur*.

As to putting forward her name at Gascon Air, she'd simply been the best available. Any other pilot in and around Arizona, male or female, with her skills would have worked for an interstate airline at a salary Gascon couldn't have matched. But why this almost naive admission about her body? Other than the final benediction there'd never been anything physical between them.

Which left pity. Yet that surely wasn't Dirk.

Jana tossed the light duvet to one side, feeling a sheen of perspiration along her arms and in the small of her back. There remained the final fantasy. How would she have responded, had he done what he set out to do? It all seemed quite unlikely yet erratic sex had left her a connoisseur of casual affairs and why men flout traditional rules when choosing female partners.

In many cases the cause was desperation, born out of low self-esteem and a terror of the future. Characteristically this led to a shrill first encounter and often ended in something dangerous and pathological.

Curiosity was a frequent failing with over-weening Frenchmen. It took the form of a test: have I the power to pick any woman – even one others have discarded – and temporarily enrich her miserable life?

And then the Sexual Good Samaritans who hadn't thought it through and whose charity ran out after two dates.

None of these variants fitted Dirk but it was as well to remind herself that his good looks might be a delusion. Handsome men were often spoilt, the result of receiving more than they handed out. But this was pure theory and in the end he was good to look at and she supposed she would have accepted him. Brief sex was better than no sex and with Dirk there would at least be cheerfulness and a lack of introspection. After which he'd probably roll away, pull out Sports Illustrated and start discussing the Knicks.

And then there was Eliazar but he was more cult than lover and Jana didn't care to define him.

CHAPTER TWO

Flight to Montauban

GASCON Air's tiny administration office faced south-east and Jana could see dawn breaking at the far end of the runway. A tug pulling baggage cages jingled past, briefly shutting out the view then re-revealing the gilded tarmac.

Ginette's early-morning face was clogged with sleep as she sat at the computer and handed over scribbled met notes. Jana constructed a benign outdoor world from Wind N 8 k, lt cum 3000 m, gnd 20 C. "Flying for the sheer fun of it," she said but Ginette shivered despite the warmth and mumbled about the early shift.

Looking over Ginette's shoulder she checked the screen and the flight-plan template slots already keyed in: departure Biarritz-Anglet-Bayonne (BIQ), destination Montauban (XMW), estimated flight 1 hr 58 min. From her own notes she dictated the remainder.

"Forgive the strip-tease," she said as she took off her jeans and hung them in her locker, emerging with a red tie knotted round the collar of her white blouse and wearing a work-polished Gascon Air uniform in dark blue polyester with wrist stripes stitched on in yellow tape. "A Chad Air outfit," Dirk had called it.

Company rules demanded it be worn on all flights although the cap – synthetic, unstiffened – was only for welcoming passengers and saying goodbye. During some hastily grabbed snack the billowy white top of Jana's cap had brushed against ketchup and a faint residue still remained, defying the most aggressive stain-remover. Her briefcase dating back to Arizona was at least leather, unlike the company issue which would have disgraced a Bobigny schoolchild.

"You'll finish at one?" Jana asked.

Ginette shook her head. "Armelle has woman's problems. I'm here until you're back."

"It's out of my hands. The Toulouse stopover is open-ended. I'll amend the flight-plan there."

Ginette nodded.

"Can I get you a couple of croissants before I leave?"

Ginette's face softened "That's kind."

"I have the van now. I'll drive over and bang on the back door of the bakery."

"But you're a pilot. All this trouble."

"Pilots are human," said Jana.

"One male pilot thought I was dirt."

"*Croissants* or *pain au chocolat*?"

"One of each, please. You're a star."

A fifteen-minute round trip but Jana had time enough. From day one she had cultivated the two women who were her direct link with the company when she was flying and they had returned the favours. It was something Dirk had never appreciated. Time after time he would ask Ginette or Armelle to phone Madeleine about flight delays and they implacably rebuffed him with company rules. "They're both drag-arses," he had told Jana but by then he and they were incorrigible.

When Jana handed over the warm paper bags Ginette said, "Leave me your other locker key. I'll take home those wretched garments and improve them in some way."

Outside the sun was steaming the dew away from F-SDR and from the glittering hardstanding. Long ago Jana had memorised the exterior checks for a Cessna 172 but as ever she took out the laminated sheet. When she arrived at the insistent "CHECK VISUALLY the fuel level in BOTH tanks" she reached for a wood billet stored under the pilot's seat, stepped up on the stirrup, opened the filler cap and used the billet as a dipstick. If anyone had asked her she might have parroted her primary USAF flight instructor as he introduced her to the Texan trainer for the first time. "The checklist doesn't change. It's printed. What's in your head can change. And it changes for good in a

Fox 5." She'd guessed the slang and was amused to learn that Fox 5 was gallows arithmetic which attached a Kill Factor of 1 to Planet Earth.

One check was personal. All nose wheel tyres had received her undivided attention ever since hers had burst landing an advanced jet trainer at Randolph AFB. An unpleasant event with a worse sequel. The enquiry made nothing of her skills in bringing the plane to a safe halt, concentrating nigglingly on whether the tyre's weakness might have been detected during the pre-flight. Spats on the Cessna's three fixed undercarriage wheels prolonged the job but Jana had learned to be patient.

Many exterior checks required judgements; inside, the options were binary on-off or designated states: rotating beacon (on), elevator trim (take-off). Finally the day's business could begin.

"Biarritz Tower, Foxtrot - Sierra Delta Romeo, radio check 118.725."

"Foxtrot - Sierra Delta Romeo, Biarritz Tower, readability 5." Two years ago she'd had problems with the Midi-Pyrénées accent which swallowed the middle syllable of readability in a gargle of saliva. Now it had become one of the sounds of home.

Jana slouched into her seat, into her kingdom. Here she was boss and her disfigured other moved over to the passenger side.

Turning the ignition switch to Start she watched the propeller groan into reluctant movement, jerk unnervingly, flick, then - with a puff of blue smoke - turn into a blur. Pointers on gauges swung round and the eggshell fuselage vibrated and hummed. Jana waited, watching sources of information approach and achieve familiar values.

"Foxtrot – Sierra, request departure information."

A longer reply from the tower, this time. Plenty of opportunities to savour the "ing" sound which came out "enn" here in the south-west.

Taxi-ing never varied since the parked Cessna always stood north of the end of runway 09 and the route was inevitable. From boredom and perversity the ATC controller occasionally tested foreign pilots by varying the instructions but here there was no scope. Parking brake unset, throttle opened, the Cessna rumbled on to the tarmac taxiway, stopped at the holding point, received clearance and turned on to runway 09.

Parking brake set, engine throttled down to 1000 rpm, Jana announced herself again:.

"Foxtrot – Sierra cleared for take-off, wind 190 four."

Maximum throttle, brakes off and the Cessna moved eagerly down the wide runway. In the approved fashion Jana held the uprights of the W-shaped yoke in both hands but her grip was gentle, her touch alert to the plane's tiniest movement. Her eyes saw an indicated 65 knots at which she drew the yoke back slowly, felt the undercarriage lose contact with the runway and, seconds later, adjusted the climb speed to an optimum 73 knots. The plane flew.

Mechanically she looked left, above and right; three seconds later she did all this again. Climbing now on a course between the river and the A65 autoroute east to Toulouse, towards the rising sun.

THE CESSNA was twelve years old, two years younger than Jana's flying career. While at high-school in Flagstaff she had worked evenings at Dunkin Donuts, accumulating the cash for flying lessons but hiding the reason from her parents. They, meanwhile, had been saving towards her advanced education, aiming at something more elevated than her father's job as distribution manager at the Purina depot. An attorney, perhaps. Or heavy science, if her inclinations went that way.

Although the money they saved was real enough, their hopes for Jana were qualified. The port wine stain, which they preferred to call *naevus flammeus* because not everyone recognised the medical term, had been a nightmare at grade school and they prayed her social life at least would improve at high school. But the stain which had started out pink and confined increased in area and deepened in colour and their prayers took an ironic twist. Jana's passage through high school was stable enough, mainly because she had little social life to speak of. On top of this the Nordmeyers later learned that treatment was mostly ineffective and that the disfigurement could well increase in later life. Make-up was said to be the only useful compromise.

Both parents had been born into hardworking blue-collar families where long conversations were rare. Bringing up Jana quickly broke that tradition for shared talk proved to be the only way of easing the heart-break of their daughter's troubled passage through school. Discussion based on what Geoff and Lisa heard from teachers and neighbours since they learned nothing from their long-suffering daughter.

Soon after grade school they had talked about further education but only vaguely. Neither side of the family had gone to college and tuition fees were frightening. Things might well have died the death if, one evening, Geoff Nordmeyer hadn't helped Jana prepare for an English test. A labour of love since his only inheritance from his self-taught father had been a handful of poetry anthologies which he often opened rather than wait for Lisa to finish Flagstaff's Daily Sun. Sure, he could say he was widening Jana's horizons but secretly he had a vice for reading verse aloud.

The work was wide-ranging and Geoff covered the waterfront with quotations from close to two dozen poets. Getting the cadences right left him unaware of a growing pattern which Lisa started to notice. Halfway she touched his arm and whispered. After then it was only a matter of keeping half an ear open as Pope's "beauty draws us with a single hair", Emerson's "to die for beauty, than live for bread", Byron's "walks in beauty like the night" plus Dickinson and Keats seemed to conspire in a plot to undermine their daughter.

"Do you think she noticed?" Geoff asked when Jana had gone to bed.

Lisa shook her head. "She protects herself by not noticing. There are worse things. The way the kids formed that circle in the playground..."

Geoff said, "She does well in English which means she'll never be far away from ideas about beauty. 'Beauty is truth, truth beauty,' as Keats says. Course it's nothing like the taunting

but there's going to be pain there, definitely. She could feel poets are against her. Imagine if she went to college: three years
being reminded week after week. But what can we do?"

Lisa thought. "We've got to stop pussy-footing. She must go
to college and we must start saving for the fees. We've talked
about it before, but here's the difference. The pile we save must
be a big one; enough to major in whatever she wants. It can't be
Dogpatch U, just because the fees are less. And we don't want
to be taking out loans."

Their parents had passed through the Depression. Debt was
more terrifying than disease.

From then on the Chevy wagon wasn't replaced, the week in
Florida was abandoned and three out of four credit cards were
scissored to death. They worried Jana might notice these
economies but then laughed at themselves. Jana was after all a
kid and cash was an adult thing.

As they'd expected there was no let-up in Jana's persecution
at school and they were reluctant even to raise the subject of a
career. It didn't help that relations, neighbours and friends
tended to discuss Jana evasively, suggesting that their daughter
would need strength of character to enter employment undamaged. One thing was certain: Jana would have to make the decision. But when they finally found the confidence to raise the
subject their daughter surprised them.

Preparations for that discussion were elaborate. Geoff Nordmeyer hired an aluminium boat with an outboard and they
drove 30 miles south of Flagstaff to Mormon Lake. The idea,
barely articulated, was that the lake's tranquillity and lack of
eavesdroppers would ease what had to be done. Watching her
father hitch the boat to the station wagon Jana had been silently
astonished but she delayed comment until she had their full attention.

Inexperienced in boat launching, Geoff Nordmeyer paddled
in foot-deep water in his brogues before calling on two bikini-
clad sun-bathers. Yanking the starter rope he failed to catch the
stuttering outboard, flooded the carburettor and was forced to
wait, immobilised, a yard or two from the shore, until the excess

fuel evaporated. Even simple tasks like opening the coolie chest and distributing sandwiches were fraught when the flat-bottomed craft proved unexpectedly sensitive. Only the efforts of Lisa Nordmeyer to treat each disaster as comical kept frustration and even fear at bay.

"So," said Jana, opening a Dr Pepper, "what exactly are you guys playing at?"

Her mother, who was unable to face Jana without uncontrollable affection, said, "Why so snitty, angel? Your dad and I were thinking of taking up boats big time."

Even Jana laughed.

Her father put down his sandwich and wrung out his socks yet again. "It might not look it but we reckoned we'd be more peaceful here than back at the ranch. Talking about the future."

"The future? Uh-uh."

"Your future."

"Yeh, I sort of guessed that."

The two adults checked to see who would now start the discussion. Geoff Nordmeyer, diminished by his rolled-up trousers, knew he should have worn shorts. Knew too this was a minor matter. "Your ma and I feel school's been tough on you. Isn't that the case?"

Jana said nothing, simply looked fixedly at a small peninsula jutting out from the shore and host to two Ponderosa pines. The adults waited, familiar with teenage silences. Wary too. Previously they had only offered comfort; today they were addressing prime causes for the first time.

Both misread Jana's silence. At grade school she had suffered jeering and pointing, more recently whispering and a humiliating apartheid. But like most children she had accepted the hurt as part of a normal life. Less an acute state, more a chronic ailment. Left alone she concentrated on solitary benefits, on fantasies beyond her classmates, on the ironies of being a spectator. Asked to comment her instinct was to refuse; she saw no profit in questioning fate.

"Angel, we don't want to pry."

Jana frowned then turned to her mother. "Tough? I suppose."

Despite her maternal feelings Lisa Nordmeyer laughed breathlessly. "You don't have to hold back for us, angel. We know. It's been tough."

Jana shrugged, "So what?"

Geoff Nordmeyer took his daughter's hand. "What we're saying is it needn't always be like that. We can't change the world but things could be different at college. What matters is you choose your future, not us. Go for an easier ride."

Jana raised her hand. "Are undergrads going to be easier on this?"

Her father sighed. "Probably not. But go to college anyway. And pick a major you genuinely like. Don't feel it has to be high society. Whatever's best. We've been knee-jerk like most parents. A doctor'd be nice, that kind of thing. But you're what matters. Enjoy yourself at U, see what makes sense."

"We don't expect you to make up your mind now," said her mother. "Most kids find it difficult. Heck you've plenty of time to think things out. And you don't have to do us any favours. The cash is being put by."

Jana gnawed her lip and turned to look again at the two pine trees.

Her father spoke quietly. "It could be dress design for all I care. If you'd like that. But it doesn't have to be classy or even feminine. Look at me: a mechanical engineer. My first job I ran four lathes in an engine shop. Dirty work, man's work. But if you felt comfortable…" He paused, worrying about showing his hand, painting a life where Jana might effectively hide herself.

"Anything?" Jana asked sharply.

They looked at each other, startled. "Sure," they said in unison, a wavering octave apart.

She addressed them both. "Don't get me wrong. I'm grateful for the cash and the freedom. But I have thought about this myself. A face like mine gives you time for that."

"Angel!"

"I have to say things out loud, ma. Otherwise I'd go mad. I looked at college and what happens after. Took the first step four months ago."

"Four months?" Geoff Nordmeyer stared. "Dunkin Donuts?"

"You never asked. I'd've told you if you had. I'll tell you now."

"Donuts was weird. I didn't like to ask," said her mother. "You said you wouldn't wear the make-up, but there you were, using it every night."

"Couldn't risk scaring the doughnut lovers. Dunkin's part of the plan. Haven't spent a dime of what I've taken and won't for another year and a half." Jana looked deep into both their faces. "Then it'll go on flying lessons. Another part of the plan."

"And the rest?"

"A USAF degree at Arizona, Then pilot training. The civilian licence will give me a leg-up. Not officially of course but I'll be ahead in basic training."

Perhaps the jargon made them pause, strange words from a world they had never suspected. They said nothing. Jana would have preferred to leave it at that and field questions. But she felt forced to go on.

"You were on track, Dad. That talk about workshops, where my face wouldn't be a problem. Bent over a lathe. But as you said it's a man's world. I'd be low man, probably for years. And it's no fun working with males who have the drop on you."

They nodded, trapped by their earlier open-mindedness. Aware too of the privations they'd inflicted on themselves doing the saving. Jana's decisiveness had turned their plan into something quite ordinary.

Jana continued. "I need a job which judges me on merit. The Air Force claims that but they could be lying. Perhaps I'll need to be pretty even there. But I should get a better shake than teaching college or dogging it as an attorney. In the meantime I get to fly."

"And this is what you really want?" Her mother sounded distant. "You never gave us any hints."

"More than anything. Flying's important, something everyone can recognise. A real existence."

"I'm impressed," said her father but it was clear he couldn't add anything for the moment. Or possibly in the months to come. Already the saving had been heroic and he'd looked forward to playing the father's role, guiding Jana from a position of strength. Now that had been taken out of his hands. The money would simply be spent.

"Ma?"

"Angel, I'm just taken aback. You'll have to forgive me. I'm happy you know what you want. And… we'll support you. We said we would. But there are risks."

That evening Lisa came up to her room and sat beside Jana on the bed. She looked closely at the bookshelves. "I've been a poor mother," she said.

"Rats. You've always been there for me."

"I love you, angel. But on its own love's not worth much. Loving should mean caring and knowing. If I'd taken stock of these books, what you said today wouldn't have come as a shock."

"Was it such a shock?"

"I'm proud of you. You're an adult, almost beyond me. But I'm scared too."

Jana hadn't mentioned her long-term goal of fighter pilot, there'd been enough revelation and she'd leave that until later. Had her mother guessed? But when she looked hard she noticed her mother's fears were on a more primitive level.

"It is risky, isn't it?"

Jana nodded. "It's difficult, so there has to be a price. But most pilots get to collect their retirement."

"I'll try not to be stupid," Lisa smiled fleetingly. "I managed when you learnt to drive and this is something like that."

Her mother spoke slowly, almost stammering. "Just one thing. I'm not sure you'll tell me the truth anyway but I need to ask. Flying's risky, we all know that. But is risk… what tempts you? You've suffered terribly. Is flying a way of… ending that"

Jana kissed her mother. "I'm telling the truth. I promise. I need to get away from what I've been dealt. I need a skill that doesn't say I've got to be pretty. But there's more. Flying itself. The joy of it."

AND THIS was that type of joy, wasn't it? A carpet of southwest France at three thousand feet. Clumps of trees like tight green sponge, orange roof tiles, cars idling along narrow roads like iridescent beetles. A seat of privilege in a well-found vehicle she could trust, linked to like minds who spoke the same pared-down language.

"Auch approach. Foxtrot-Sierra Delta Romeo, Cessna 172, from Biarritz to Montauban, 20 miles west of Auch, altitude 3000 ft, VFR tracking to Fleurance."

Jana acknowledged the compressed code of aviation: this is where I am; moving towards you; afterwards I will move towards somewhere else. So specific, so clear, so formal.

It was not the elite triumph she had planned as a teenager, the fighter plane. But it met one need she hadn't then foreseen: making the best of her own company. Being alone was the essence of her life, not simply its burden. Flying was self-reliance, a source of mild awe among civilians and a form of hard-won protection against the second glance, the surprised look and the averted gaze.

The Lycoming droned like the heart-beat of her life. Head up she glanced left and right, then down. Not an easy place for an emergency landing, too many trees, too many small farms with small fields. But suppose it had to be, suppose it was now! A two-kilometre glide which meant... where? There! That field with the discouraging stone walls and the cattle. Tighten the seat belt. Maintain height for what was lost would never be regained. Drop over the nearest boundary wall, over the gate if possible, nose up, full flaps, stall and fall.

But already the plane had flown beyond that field to a new field. Hey, why don't I just fly the plane, enjoy the joy.

WAITING to start the first semester at Arizona State, she had received a phone call at home.

"Brewin, Dave Brewin. You remember."

She didn't.

"High school, for Pete's sake."

Brewin? Jana recited the class register to herself. Brewin? Brewin? Oh him. Parents had a ranch-style on Old Walnut Canyon Road. In his last year he'd driven an Alfa Romeo to school.

"What can I do for you, Dave?" Had they spoken to each other? Ever?

"Jana." He sounded as if he was trying out her name - probably was. "You've had some great news. Heard you solo-ed last week."

"That's true."

"Mind me asking? How many hours?"

Brewin's face was coming into focus. Blue jowls, must have started shaving two years ago. And no, they'd never exchanged a word.

"Nine hours," she said.

"Nine hours! That's terrific! I'm taking a lesson at Wiseman on Thursday."

"Well… good luck."

"See, I'm wondering if we could meet. Coffee somewhere. You could tell me what to expect."

"Meet?" You're speaking to Jana Nordmeyer. The girl everyone ignores.

"Hey, just to talk flying. Nothing funny. Run me through things."

"Your instructor will do that," Jana pointed out.

"Yeh, but that would be official. Technical."

"Most of it is technical… Dave."

"But you could ease me in." The wheedling said it all. This was a different Dave Brewin from the one she remembered - noisy in class, pathetically pleased to be place kicker on the school football team.

"You really want to fly?"

"Oh sure."

Well, why not? "If you think I can help."

She was reassured when he suggested a shabby mall of shops two miles out of town. Oh yes, he wanted to talk to her but not with others watching.

When he arrived – late, despite his pleas - he positioned himself on the banquette to avoid her cheek. But Jana was used to that. And, although he seemed unaware of them, his naïve and insulting questions could have been predicted. Soloing after nine hours was taken as the yardstick: if she could do it, he could do it. And this mattered. He'd asked around and was astonished that some students had taken thirty-five hours' instruction spread over five or six years. He'd be old, for Chrissake.

So why the urgency? There was vague talk of an uncle who had access to a twin-engine Piper but Brewin hadn't come to talk about the whys. He was convinced there was a trick to going solo, that Jana knew this trick and that high school loyalty demanded she pass on the details. When Jana explained how student pilots were assessed he became disturbed and shouted rudely at the waitress for another Diet Coke.

"When did you know you'd got it?" he asked, hunching forward over the table, intent, pleading even.

"It's kind of vague. I wasn't exactly sure."

"Yeh, yeh." This was the trick; the device which would absolve him from… What?

"When I found myself liking it. When I could feel the plane."

He wanted more. This wasn't the trick.

And then Jana realised what she was seeing. Apprehension. She asked about his instructor and he didn't want to talk about that. She tried to make things easier by explaining the theoretical stuff, the introductory walk round the plane, but he remained impatient. He wanted to be beyond instruction. Being forced to face his first lesson frightened him.

For her, flying had not only been serious, it came with a sort of honour code. Brewin's state of mind offended that code. Some kind of warning was obligatory and she listed her doubts if only to save him from humiliation. But she stopped short of telling him that if she could interpret his wide eyes and the perspiration above his upper lip, his instructor would react similarly and even more swiftly.

She couldn't reach him. He insisted he was "up for it", even "excited". And in the end she recognised her worries were groundless. She could pretend to share his manufactured excitement since it was clear he would never command any plane.

"As I say, good luck. Flying's fun."

"Fun, yeh," he said, his voice almost desperate.

She gathered her purse, but he wasn't finished. In a parody of the butt-slapping, arm-wrestling senior at high school he reached towards her hand but stopped short. "We could drive down."

"Down where?"

"Wiseman. Just for that first lesson."

I'm his magic charm. He's hoping what I've got will rub off on him.

This surely was payback time for all that classroom exclusion she had suffered; Brewin would make an ideal sacrificial goat. But she couldn't remember any occasion when he himself had sniggered or pointed; punishing him would only be symbolic, not truly justified. Besides, following Brewin to the bitter end, seeing him excluded from her fiercely defined world, would confirm her rigorous beliefs about flying. On that basis and as a grimly detached observer she agreed to let him drive her to Wiseman.

And so it happened. Two days later the world of aviation rejected Brewin. Soon after entering the cockpit for initial familiarisation he vomited up a copious and ill-judged breakfast of waffles and was guided back to Wiseman's offices for medical attention. Having to clear up the mess the instructor sought out Jana, Brewin's presumed girl-friend, and asked angry questions.

"I'm not his girl-friend," Jana insisted.

"OK, OK. But you're with him. Why's that?"

"I'm his lucky rabbit's paw. Not so lucky, it seems."

The instructor looked at Jana more carefully. "You must be that kid that went solo in under ten hours. What's the story? Is he trying to go one better?"

"We were at the same high school. He wanted my advice on learning to fly."

The instructor grinned. "Didn't you tell him that's my job?"

"He had this idea I knew the easy way."

"Ah, a crazy. But then he was half right. You solo-ed quicker than I did. Only by one hour, but quicker. Nine hours wasn't it? I hated going into double figures. Perhaps you'd better tell me how you did it."

"I love flying."

He laughed. "Me too. You had Mike Brubaker, didn't you? A hard man to convince. You must be good. What are you going to do with the licence?"

"Air Force. The licence will be my rabbit's foot through basic training."

"I guess you won't need it. Wanna help me clean up the sick?"

Jana pondered. "Why not? There'll be something to learn there."

"Hon, you'll make a damn fine pilot."

She would have driven Brewin home but taking the wheel of his Alfa might have left him with permanent scars. Instead she turned away as he repeatedly mistimed gearchanges on the car's close-ratio box. Eventually, when even he couldn't ignore his incompetence he pulled off the highway.

"You aren't going to tell anyone, are you?" he asked warily.

"Who would I tell?"

He looked surprised. "Classmates, who else?"

"You aren't very observant."

"What do you mean?"

"Forget it. Tell me, why did you think flying was such a great idea?"

He tried to pout as when she'd asked him before. Then he shrugged. "Bad grades. Math, science. Flying seemed a way out. After all, you learned."

Again the unconscious sneer. But Jana no longer needed any reassurances. "So you get the licence. Then what?"

"Air Force, of course."

She sighed. "You haven't gone into this at all. USAF pilots have degrees."

A new door had just closed in his face. "Ah shit."

"What does your dad do?"

"Insurance."

"I take it he was paying for the lessons."

"He… wanted me out of his hair."

"Yeh. Time to talk to him again."

BREWIN'S instructor had been right; she was, by most standards, a damn fine pilot. But not fine enough. Jana checked the
oil pressure, the magnetos, the bearing and thought about Afghanistan. Yesterday's Sud Ouest had a piece about drones.
Risk-free, the headline had said. Supposedly an al Qaeda lieu-
tenant had been taken out on the Pakistan border (some collat-
eral damage) by a drone controlled from a base near Las Vegas.
Jana considered "risk-free" and compared it strategically with
the role of a fighter pilot. Was there much difference between a
drone and an airborne missile launched ten kilometres away
from the target?

Her wristwatch showed she was still twenty minutes away
from Montauban. Checking her part of the sky she saw only a
glider, way below, hugging the ground to the north, close to the
amusingly named Condom. In recalling Dave Brewin's humiliation (A month or two afterwards Lisa, her mother, reported seeing him at Safeway wearing a Trainee Manager tag) she was
reminded of her own failure. Had it been a delusion? The Air
Force encouraged trainees to regard fighter pilots as top of the
tree. Yet, hitching a ride from Florida to Phoenix in a C-5 Gal-
axy, she spoke to the pilot of this gigantic enterprise, lolling at
the controls as the auto-pilot guided them over the beige Texas
plains.

He laughed. "Sure, I was sucked in by all that Top Gun crap.
But even before they told me I couldn't take 8G turns I was suspicious. There's only one reason for flying a fighter and that's
aerial combat. But what are the chances? I started looking at
flying differently. The truly great pilots are those who handle
lousy weather in places where there's no friendly ground radar
and only a pile of rocks below. Or the ocean."

At the time Jana's seat in a fighter was still a possibility. When that was taken away the disappointment was too intense for other flying options and she left the Air Force. But here she was, hopping from place to place in a foreign country, practising the self-reliance she had seen as her only saviour. Away from critical eyes.

There were worse ways of earning a living, said Dirk, one of the few good pilots who had never been tempted by single-seater jets.

Below France celebrated *la vie sauvage*, a huge stretch of the Gers criss-crossed by tiny roads and dotted by clusters of houses that hardly qualified as hamlets. Jana knew from experience that a car on such roads might expect to travel sixty kilometres in an hour whereas the Cessna continued to cruise at 220 kph. France, her mother had said, why live there? Isn't it backward? If it was then a plane made sense.

US and French forms of loneliness were different. Here it had been briefer, simply a matter of getting used to the terrain. She'd made acquaintances at the airport, over shop counters, at the *mairie*. In her home country loneliness was directly related to her imperfection. In France imperfections – physical and mental – attracted less discrimination. Two of Mme le Lannic's neighbours had daughters with Downs syndrome and when their families met other families in the village Jana noticed that the children were not ignored but drawn into the conversation. *Griotte* had caught her unawares.

"Montauban Tower, Foxtrot-Sierra Delta Romeo, overhead, joining for runway 32"

Even civilians recognised landing as the greater skill. Power alone, plus a few instinctive adjustments of the controls, took the plane into the air. Exchanging air for ground was another matter. Flying slowly, but not too slowly, deliberately sacrificing the plane's aerodynamics – these things created their own dangers, required their own judgements. By now Jana's ears were attuned to the engine note of a 60 knots landing speed and her whole body anticipated the audacity of slowing the plane to a 87 kph stall as a means of lowering it that final metre on to the tarmac. And there it was: a good stress-free professional landing at Montauban, the sort of thing she was paid to do.

A landing that recalled Mesa. "Goddamn perfect," said Mike Brubaker, her Texan instructor, as the undercarriage struts compressed and the stall horn sounded simultaneously. Her first landing in fact and confirmation she was doing the right thing.

At Montauban her landing had the economy and grace all pilots looked for in returning to earth, the plane's weight easing from the main wheels to the nose wheel

"Foxtrot – Sierra Delta, taxi to apron, via taxiway Kilo."

Jana parked the Cessna in front of the *météo* shed, went quickly through the checks, switched the mixture to idle cut-off and flipped the master switch. Picked up her wretched cap.

Her two passengers were sitting on a bench seat outside the airport's marginal café enjoying the morning sun. At this distance they looked like twins: radiant Mediterranean complexions, carefully styled dark hair, conservatively cut navy blue suits, polished lace-up shoes. No brief cases, these days: Apple laptops in Vuitton carry bags. Senior executives working for an acronym based in Lyons; more specifically property developers

It was still early and there were few people about. They recognised she was their pilot and both sat up in unison, assessing her hips, her height, her urchin cut. Experience told her there would be a further assessment.

Jana saluted as Gascon Air protocol demanded, albeit in the casual USAF style. "Messieurs. Jana Nordmeyer, Gascon Air. At your disposal."

They were standing now, barely matching her height, extending their hands, both looking where she expected them to look, confirming their national stereotype. Americans and Brits looked away quickly, Germans stared hard as if exercising a right, Italians often smiled. But French males – or at least the predators - examined what they saw, working out what effect the stain had on Jana and how it would influence their performance were they briefly to become her lover.

Jana took off her cap. Fairly sure of their response she asked if they would like coffee since there was time. They glanced quickly at each other and nodded. In the café they took a four-seater booth where they sat opposite her, their view uninterrupted.

"Mademoiselle is... American? Your French is good."

It was an approach most Frenchman regarded as irresistible.

CHAPTER THREE

Hands-on with Seneca

GASCON Air's three chairs were all now occupied. Jean-Claude the owner creaked uneasily on his then stood up, irritated. "Let's do this at the *brasserie*. There's room to breathe there."

"And who'll carry the files and the laptop? And come back for the stuff we forget? And how will Ginette call up those people you'll need to call up," said Jana

Jean-Claude offered another option. "I could check you out on the Seneca."

"That's my afternoon treat. Come on J-C, bite on the bullet." For fun she translated the idiom literally but Jean-Claude, like most pilots, had good English and smiled faintly at her teasing.

"I'm told balls means rubbish in English. But back in the eighteenth-century a ball was a bullet. They moved on we didn't. Very clever, Jana. Why am I not allowed to hesitate?"

"Because it's a bad habit in the Seneca – or any other plane."

He laughed good-humouredly. "As your M. Thurber has said memorably, *Touché*. But Jana, I admit we are not Académie Francaise but let's all talk French. Standards have slipped, I admit. We had to make concessions for Dirk but we know it's not necessary with you. Yet you taunt us. We're simple Third World residents."

Jana had never had a better boss. A superb all-weather pilot, imperturbable in crises whether in the air or at the bank. A man who didn't care for US politics yet loved to employ pilots trained there. Who had left a high-paying job with one of France's multi-nationals to follow his love of flying and take on the commercial terrors of a mini-airline.

Jana laughed. "Why not start with an agenda? You were a businessman once, J-C. Isn't that the way meetings start?"

"Don't remind me. Agendas. The sun going down and we're still on item three. Please spare me the agenda."

Jana got up and poured coffee for herself, J-C and Ginette - something she had sworn she would never do if there was a man close at hand.

"What we need to discuss is simple enough." she said.

Jean-Claude leant back in his chair and looked at Jana with something close to affection.

"We know why you're dragging your feet, J-C. You're facing two or three lousy decisions, none of them fun."

"No secrets at Gascon Air."

"How could there be?" said Ginette. Her feelings for her boss had probably overstepped a self-defined mark a year or two ago. Now she tended to address him snappishly.

"Nor would I want any," he said smoothly. "The floor recognises Mlle Nordmeyer."

"I don't want to make things difficult."

"That isn't your style. Proceed."

Jana said, "You're not going to replace Dirk, at least for the moment. There isn't the money."

"That's true."

Jana's French was fluent but not wholly idiomatic. As she talked literal translations slid into and out of her consciousness and conversation was still full of simple pleasures, Jean-Claude's "Well heard." being typical.

"That leaves two planes and two pilots," she continued. "Given our cash flow you need to be out doing your famous marketing. That in its turn brings two more lousy decisions: a Seneca stuck on the tarmac and a proprietor who finds himself back in the harness he hated at Elf Oil."

"You should be in charge, *chérie*."

"No I shouldn't. You're Gascon Air. But logically I should take over the Bordeaux – Paris contract."

"Pouf to your weekends. Jana you must have some leisure."

Jana said, "If Gascon Air fails I'll have all the leisure I need. Not that things are that tight. If I take on the run it frees you up for gladhanding and lets you cherry-pick the rest of the work.

You've got to fly, J-C. Otherwise your sacrifices don't make sense. And you'll be irritable round the place."

That last bit wasn't entirely true. He had never been a romantic about his company and had borne its hand-to-mouth existence gracefully. But Jana hated to see him earth-bound.

"A kind suggestion, Jana. I will consider it."

"You'll accept it," said Jana and gestured to Ginette who'd been watching them, waiting to contribute.

Ginette's snappishness died away when it mattered. "You must, Jean-Claude. Please."

Jana added, "And the Cessna's vacuum filter has only twenty-six hours left, just about a week. We need to schedule Eliazar." In booking Eliazar for Gascon Air she would, in effect, be booking him and his motorhome for herself. This left her slightly uneasy and a shriving gesture seemed necessary. "Now the van's all mine I can throw that into the pot as a freight carrier."

"My God, my airline and I are becoming a charity," said Jean-Claude.

"I'll even paint a lousy d'Artagnan on the side."

"You always hated my sweet logo. I never understood. Gascony, d'Artagnan: what could be more logical?"

"A guy with a big feather in his hat. And a sword. Not much aviation logic there."

"But," said Jean-Claude winningly, "everybody remembers it."

"Like they remember a dose of clap."

"Ah *chérie*, how would you know? But I must earn some *sous*. This enquiry by the man who grows asparagus and avocados. My immediate reaction was no: where's the profit in flying vegetables to Bordeaux? But I'm told white asparagus sells for more than green and that restaurants now print Picked Today in Pyrénées-Atlantique on their menus. I need to haggle with him. I'll be back at three for our flight of delight."

Dirk's former students were detailed in a folder marked Jana – It's All Yours in confident felt-tip script. She picked up the phone.

"May I speak to M. Daoust, M Matthieu Daoust."

"Matthieu Daoust here."

"You've been taking flying lessons with M. Boonhausen, I believe." Try as she might Jana had never got across Dirk's surname satisfactorily for the French.

The pause was inevitable. "That is M. Dirk, I suppose."

"Indeed. I'll call him Dirk from now on. As you know he returned to the United States and I am taking over his schedule. My name is Mlle. Nordmeyer, Jana Nordmeyer, and I have worked with Gascon Air for two years."

"You are American, of course."

"Congratulations on getting the accent."

Daoust now regretted his briskness. "The accent is not so… strong. And your French is very good."

Long ago Jana had learned to discount that compliment. With etiquette stripped away it conveyed no more than faint surprise.

"At least air traffic control understands me these days."

"That is important for both of us."

Jana permitted herself a light laugh. "You paid in advance for your instruction. I assume you wish to continue?"

"But of course."

"Will you accept me as your instructor?"

"But of course." There was no way Daoust was going to refuse this intriguing development.

"Of course you have not met me. I was trained in the United States by civilian and USAF instructors. I am CFI – that is to say Certificated Flight Instructor – and my qualification has been verified here in France. I - "

"Mademoiselle, there is no need. I was impressed by M. Dirk and I know Jean-Claude well. Gascon Air is small but has high standards. I shall present myself on Saturday morning as usual."

"I look forward to that. First here's the number of my mobile phone. Also, Jean-Claude says I should add thirty minutes – without charge – to your lesson to review what Dirk has taught you. Please understand, this is not an examination. We will get to know each other and I expect your good progress to con-

tinue." The latter was not strictly true. Daoust had received fifteen hours instruction and, according to Dirk, a solo flight was
still many hours away.

"I hope you will be proud of me," said Daoust voluptuously.

Three more transfers were made. The first two – both men –
mirrored Daoust's interest in Jana's gender. The third was a
woman and the tone was cooler. Jana was asked to explain her
pilot training in full and the woman came as close as she dared
to asking Jana her age. Understandable perhaps given that she
had made rapid progress with Dirk and might soon solo.

There remained the call to Eliazar which Jana preferred to
make outside Ginette's hearing. "I'll take a quick lunch, Nette.
Be back in less than thirty minutes to take over the phone."

"Quick lunch! This is France, do I have to remind you?" But
Jana was out of the door.

She bought a cheese salad baguette at the Taste 'n' Fly in the
departure lounge of the airport then found an ugly bench near
one of the car parks.

"Eliazar, it's Jana."

"I can tell. You breathe a certain way before you speak."

"Where are you now?"

"Enac flying club, near Toulouse. Rebuilding – recreating! - a
Lycoming 320 for a careless owner. What are you looking for?
The obvious?"

"Yeh, that too. But first we need a filter for the Cessna's vacuum system."

"How many hours it done?"

"Four-seven-four hours."

"Next Thursday?"

"That's perfect."

"We say morning, heh? And in the afternoon we…?"

"'Fraid not. Make it early evening. Dirk's back in the States.
We're short a pilot."

"You limit me," Eliazar complained. "Weeks have passed. I
will be inventive."

"Goes without saying."

"In Spanish we say *ingenioso*. No, that's something else."

"You're that too, Eliazar. Thursday, then."

"*Adiós anglosajón.*"

"*Adiós.*"

Jana ate her baguette reflecting on Flagstaff's Greenlaw Baptist Church whose congregation her mother had recently joined. Why Baptist? Why a church? The unexplained news had arrived as a PS to Lisa Nordmeyer's weekly letter which she continued to send despite Jana's pleas for emails. Jana, a child of her times, was more or less incapable of using a pen and always replied to Lisa by phone. But the phone was too direct for intimate enquiries and the Baptist church might well be intimate. Before he died her father had cheerfully – daringly – admitted to a low-grade, non-proselytising atheism and Lisa had obediently followed him. Now something had changed and Jana needed a sufficiently delicate approach to find out why. At least her mother would never meet Eliazar, she told herself comfortingly.

Having finished her baguette she re-entered the terminal via a metal-framed greenhouse that served as entrance to the modernistic structure. The flat, dispirited buildings associated with flying had always depressed her. Once, landing at a primitive strip in Mexico, she noticed that part of the admin building lacked a roof. Desks and filing cabinets visible to the open sky, perhaps the result of a tornado. Her passenger, a Mexican, laughed at such national incompetence but Jana had found it more forgivable than the ugly ducting and fan units that encrusted the roofs of most US airports.

Ginette looked up. "Back so soon? You must take care of your stomach."

"I'm Arizonan, I thrive on fast food."

"And die from it. Where is my bandeau?"

"You don't have to bike home for lunch. Take the van."

Ginette paused in her fussing. "Dirk used to say that. 'Take my car.' A Frenchman would never offer that."

"We're kind of casual that way. I mean, what the heck's a van?"

"And yet Dirk was never polite."

Jana said, "Never added 'If you please.' Didn't mean a damn to him but I can see why it wasn't easy to take."

Ginette positioned the Alice band in her hair. "You care for Jean-Claude. I mean - "

"I know what you mean. He's a great boss. Even more important, a great pilot. I could never work for a bad pilot."

"I suppose not."

"In flying we have to look after each other. Trouble is, bad pilots continue to take off and when we see that happening we need to tell the DGAC. We need to keep our eyes open, check that no one's getting a little - I don't know the French word – sloppy with it."

"Sloppee? I think *négligé* perhaps."

"That's it. J-C's never *négligé*."

Ginette nodded. "And you are keen to help with his finances. I can see it."

"I'm keen to help."

Ginette left and Jana took down the Piper Seneca IV Information Manual. A redesigned engine gave better cruising, she read. And how long did it take for the company to figure out the need for that?

"**THERE'S** a Bendix King autopilot, I see. That would be a first for me. OK if I use it?"

"You have the plane," said Jean-Claude.

"Ah, there we go. The LEDs make things really simple. I read it up back in the office. GPS roll steering. Works with a multi-leg plan. You ever switch it on?"

"Guess."

Jana saw his grin. "Your face tells me no."

"I am old-fashioned. I have used it on longer flights and when I'm discussing things with a passenger. But rarely. It's not turning on an auto-pilot that disturbs me, but turning it off. When you disable M. Bendix King it's a voyage from one state of mind to another. I'm transformed, I feel more lively, more professional - but that shouldn't happen. I should be equally lively, equally professional when M. Bendix King is in charge."

Jana nodded. "But today I'm here to show you I can fly the Seneca. And that includes the systems - one day I may need Old BK. So let's give him a work-out. I'll pick a waypoint ten kilometres ahead with a new bearing and let's see if he's to be trusted. Watch me J-C: here's distance as time and, yes, it shows on the screen. The new bearing is 035. That checks. And now he takes over."

Neither spoke. It was as if another person had entered the cockpit, someone to whom they'd not been introduced, someone who inhibited their conversation. Then in three minutes the Piper swung smoothly starboard twenty degrees on to the new bearing.

Jana flipped off the autopilot, laughing. "Meet Mlle Nordmeyer again. Your pilot,"

Jean-Claude smiled, "This is an utterly pointless flight, you know."

"Aviation routine is never pointless."

"Pointless but pleasant. I enjoy watching you fly but the only thing that matters is your landing. Before that we can theorise. Imagine, I am a sheikh from a sandpit filthy with oil. Rich beyond the dreams of avarice. You must indulge me, I am influential. OK?"

"OK, Your Oiliness," said Jana.

"You moved from Mme le Lannic?"

"Dirk's old room is better."

"But that was not the real reason."

Mme le Lannic had passed into history, but the name alone revived certain sensations for Jana. She was also surprised. Jean-Claude lived almost fifty kilometres away from Arcanques and would hardly be *au fait* with local gossip there. Would there in fact be local gossip? Foolish question. There was always local gossip.

"A minor matter. Personal."

"Personal, yes. But not minor," said Jean-Claude.

"I'm trying to make it minor."

"That goes without saying. Tell me, Jana."

"I'm not sure it shows me in a good light."

Jean-Claude sighed and she glanced across at him, slightly alien in the right-hand passenger's seat. Relaxed but authoritative. Crinkly brown hair going grey, combed back. Square fifty-ish face. He was the person she liked most, trusted most. And she realised he knew all or part of the answer to his question.

"Jana, I could say I am entitled to ask. As your *patron*. But how can I be your *patron*? You are not some *mignonne*. You do what I do; we're equals. I ask as your friend."

She told him and he nodded. He had known. How?

"An unpleasant time," he said. Despite the tension she relished his phrase: a bad quarter of an hour.

He added, "I am sorry it happened. Here in France."

"No, not that. France has been OK, honest. Perhaps that's why it hit me. I wasn't expecting it. But perhaps I over-reacted."

"How can that be?"

Jana said, "Losing my rent must have been a disaster."

"Hardly your problem. I want to think about this. Why not show me stall and recovery."

"Stall or stall/spin?"

Jean-Claude roared with laughter. "I wonder how old you were when I recovered – for the first and last time – from an induced spin. That is: any spin. Just a stall, *chérie*."

"And you're OK with 4800 ft altitude?"

"Are you?"

"Oh sure."

"Then go ahead."

Jana reduced the power and increased the angle of attack, nose up, felt the Piper lurch as it squelched in its pocket of air, heard the horn sound. Endured this awfulness for two or three seconds, reduced the elevator angle, gently adjusted the speed and applied the rudder. Jean-Claude looked at the altimeter and blocked it from Jana's view with his hand. "How much height do you think you lost?"

"Waddya mean - think? I know how much: 260 ft."

He looked out through the side window, over the Gascony National Park towards Mont-de-Marsan. "Perhaps it's as well I'm happily married and a good Catholic," he said wryly.

"It cost a lot to train me, J-C. But outside this cockpit I'm pretty ordinary."

"My wife says invite Jana for dinner. I say I can't: she'll think I pity her. I wish I could explain to Adélie about the altimeter."

"I'd love to come. But let's hope there's more to talk about than stalls."

Jean-Claude nodded. "No doubt. Let's fast forward. It's January, the carburettor on the port engine has iced up and the engine's cut out. The starboard engine is misfiring. What are you going to do?"

"Throttle back, shallow incline, carburettor heaters on, peel my eyes."

"Let's start by killing the port engine."

The sound of wind sighing over the fuselage was more evident and Jana experimented with the throttle until the clumsily balanced plane achieved some kind of equilibrium. Throughout, she combined quick glances at the instruments with slightly longer glances at the gradually nearing terrain below. "At a thousand feet I'll make a probable decision."

At twelve hundred feet there was nothing – just dense woods and occasional white boulders. Although she hadn't time to look she was conscious of his calm scrutiny.

"Unmade access road, bearing 040. Probably not wide enough but that's it! Whatever! I'm making a gentle – ve-e-ry gentle - turn to starboard. Now we've got five hundred metres straight ahead. Gonna be hairy. Full flaps two hundred metres short, then cut starboard power"

Jean-Claud laughed shortly. "Re-start the port engine."

They were back at five thousand feet. "Would we have survived?" he asked.

"The key was whether I managed to hold five degrees nose up and keep the plane dead centre on the access road. But I'm satisfied with the percentages."

"So am I."

He was silent for several minutes then spoke slowly. "You deserve more. For your abilities and as compensation for the careless way the world seems to treat you. I have influence in

French aviation and I could recommend you for something better. Should I do that?"

Her throat contracted. "So I'd fly bigger planes. But not necessarily with better people. Sometime, I'll look for work back in the States. For professional reasons. But not for a while. Not after that."

FOUR people sat down for dinner at the Chauvelets, the newcomer being their eight-year-old grandson Octavien whose looks reminded Jana of a puzzle she had never come close to resolving. Animated moist eyes, *crème brulée* complexion, dark curls overhanging his forehead as if from a vine and a mouth that despite his tender years was disturbingly kissable. Into what black hole would all these glorious features disappear before Octavien emerged as the average self-regarding adult Frenchman?

"Good evening, mademoiselle," he said gravely and Jana, imagining herself licking his seductive cheeks, felt obliged to match his seriousness.

"Good evening Octavien."

"Mlle Nordmeyer is from the USA like Dirk. She too is a pilot."

"Do you enjoy living in France?" he asked.

"It's a beautiful country. Even more beautiful when you see it, as I do, from the air."

"My father says this is 'a good corner'. Perhaps you do not understand."

"I agree with your father. But then France is full of many good corners."

Old beyond his years, he smiled his approval. Now he took the dish of creamed spinach and held it so that Jana could serve herself.

Hugues Chauvelet noticed Jana's surprise. "Octavien is well behaved, *hein*?"

Jana laughed. "I didn't want to embarrass him by saying so. In any case my opinion is not so valuable. Our kids are not famous for their good behaviour. How long is Octavien staying?"

"Just three nights," said Mme Chauvelet. "Our son is in Paris for business and he has taken his wife. A short visit. But we would not mind if it were weeks. Octavien is good company."

"I can see that."

The boy appeared to be modestly avoiding all this. Jana asked, "Octavien, do planes interest you?"

"Technology interests me. I hope to be an engineer like Papa."

"I have to return to the airport this evening. To make two phone calls, that's all. Perhaps you would like to see my plane if your grandparents would permit that."

Controlled he was, but this tested him.

"I think I can say yes on my grandson's behalf," said Sylvie Chauvelet, laughing.

As Jana and Octavien drove over to the airport in the otherwise empty van she apologised for its well-worn interior. "In English we would say it's a working vehicle but that's not good French."

"I understand." He paused, then smiled. "So it must be good French. This was M. Dirk's van wasn't it?"

"We shared it. When he went back he gave me his half. Very generous. Except I will have to replace the cam-belt. A tedious job."

"You will do that, yourself?" he asked.

"Are you surprised? Because I'm a woman?"

"Oh no," he said. To be thought sexist appeared to irritate him. "I thought pilots are... what is the word? Too grand?"

This made her laugh. "Some pilots are too grand. But Gascon Air is a very small airline. We are all quite humble."

He thought for a while. "I would like to watch you do that replacement. The belt, you know."

"Would you really?"

"To learn the names."

"I can't do it while you are with your grandparents," said Jana. "Later. But you aren't too far away. I will discuss it."

He nodded carefully.

At the Gascon Air office she emailed a modification to a parts order sent earlier in the day then looked at her watch. "A little too early. I want to telephone my mama but she lives in the USA and she will still be shopping. She lives in a town with a strange name for French people: Flagstaff the same as flagpole."

"Which *département*?"

"You understand the United States. Arizona."

A longing passed over Octavien's face.

"Now, I'll show you the Cessna."

"The plane. Yes. Please spell the name."

And Jana did so.

They sat together in the cockpit, he in the pilot's seat so that the instrument orientation was more immediate. "The big dials are the most important," said Jana. "These three are directly in front of the pilot. Can you guess what this one measures?"

He drew closer. "The word is ALTI. There's a French word like that. Height?"

"Correct. And this one? Quite easy. There are numbers and these four letters: N, E, S, W. Almost the same as the words in French."

"They have this on boats. The direction."

"Correct again. The compass. This one is slightly harder. Notice the little shape in the middle. It's a plane. When the plane moves sideways, it moves."

Frustrated, he tapped his fingers on the yoke. She explained turn-and-bank and he looked avid for more explanation.

They worked their way through the others until Jana looked again at her watch. "We must go now, now. I need to phone mama."

"Could you leave me here? I will simply look. Not touch anything. I swear."

Palpable yearning. "I cannot do that. Aviation has many rules and pilots agree to obey them - even when there are no 'policeman' and when there is almost no risk. Obeying the rules makes flying less dangerous. But you and I may come back again. And I will talk to your grandparents – I mean your parents – to see whether you can fly with me."

"Fly!"

Jana now used the office phone to call her mother after J-C pointed out the horrendous costs of doing this on the mobile. As ever her mother responded with unforced affection, but when asked about recent developments her tone changed. "It's really nothing, angel. Just something we can talk about face to face."

"Face to face?"

"I was thinking of a visit. Not Biarritz, of course. That's too awkward. Paris perhaps. Can you get to Paris?"

"I can get anywhere," said Jana. "But how about you? Do you have a passport, even?"

"A passport. Will I need one? Then I suppose I will have to check that out."

Jana was about to leave it at that but then couldn't. "Would you mind if I guessed what this is all about?"

"You don't have to. It's stupid of me to hold back. And it's so obvious. When your dad died, after all that agony, I needed re-assurance. I didn't have his strength of mind and I started going to church. I didn't tell you because I know you're not a church-goer. Like dad, you don't need it. I wish I had that strength. I met somebody, a widower. We talked about Paris and it seemed romantic. Now, as I talk, it sounds like a bad movie."

"No, no. Come to Paris."

"Do you approve?"

"Of course I do. As Dad would have done. Did he encourage you to...? Oh, I'm sure he did."

"As a matter of fact he did. Told me not to be sentimental. That's your dad, isn't it?"

Jana said, "All over. Don't tell me any more. Or in your letters. Let's talk over champagne and linen tablecloths. The way it should be done."

"Angel... I'm so lucky. Now please, tell me some good news from your side."

"Dirk's back in the States so there's more flying for me. I moved into his room so I'll need to give you my new address." Jana glanced across the office at Octavien who was trying to pretend he wasn't listening. "And I've got a new pal. Octavien, he's eight. Says he's studying technology and truly likes planes."

"The perfect pal. Give him my love. Do they do that in France?"

"They do."

"Oh, angel... Look, it's your dime. Dave – that's his name, he's a widower – and I will do some planning. Fix up a flight."

Jana put the phone down. "How good's your English?" she asked Octavien, smiling.

"I didn't..."

"I know you didn't. My mother sends you her best wishes. No, stronger than that – her love."

"I am honoured. I think your father died. Your mother... will marry? And you are happy for her."

"Brilliant. Gosh, it's dark already. I must get you home."

With Octavien in bed Jana explained what had happened to the Chauvelets. "His interest is like most kids - fascinated. He asked to watch me fix the van. That's quite a dull job which must mean he's keen. Perhaps you could speak to his mother about it, ask her to check things out with Octavien."

"You like our grandson?" Sylvie asked.

"Oh sure. Who wouldn't"

Undressing in her room Jana realised that the bookshelves there must have been put up by Dirk. Astonishing he should find the need, more so that he had been prepared to handle the DIY. But ever since Bordeaux Dirk had proved more complex than she had thought.

Still ruminating she switched off the light and found her thoughts turning to Octavien. Suddenly she was was alarmed. She, an unattached woman, foreign, socially disadvantaged, he a bright attractive kid. The first kid she had ever noticed. Those eyes! That complexion! Would the world draw these facts together and arrive at a sordid conclusion? Could she be sure it wasn't sordid? She tried to remember Sylvie's tone of voice: You like our grandson?

Over breakfast she modified her previous generosity, insisting she had no desire to interfere with Octavien's family, that things had "just happened" and that Octavien was a good kid. But the subtleties would have tested her in English and, as she wrestled, she then realised she ran the risk of seeming to have changed her mind.

"Octavien's mother must be sure about this. In this day and age one cannot be too careful about children," Jana said, regretting it immediately, envisaging even more horrifying implications. But the Chauvelets in their innocence merely nodded.

Jana had a free morning but was determined not to linger at the house. Alone she drove the van down into Biarritz, crossed the Adour, parked, and committed herself to a deliberately exhausting walk up the Atlantic coast. In the afternoon she was thankfully employed, picking up marine electronic kit from Toulouse, unloading at Biarritz and delivering it by van to a yachtsman at the St-Jean-de-Luz marina. Inventing busy work she delayed her return home until Octavien had gone to bed. She showered feeling perturbed, a failure.

CHAPTER FOUR

Ghislaine meets Boyce

BADMINTON at the Arcanques *salle polyvalente* was a messy affair. A complete novice, Jana found it hard to follow the decelerating flight of the shuttlecock and Ghislaine was disinclined to rein in her competitiveness. A further disadvantage was that the hall had been divided into two courts, the other occupied by a more expert couple of teenage girls both of whom shrieked piercingly, covered a wide area and constantly came to a squeaking halt on their rubber soles just as Jana was about to serve.

Ghislaine's reservations came later in the evening when she regarded the Tuesday night jazz audience at l'Hibou in Bayonne.

"Who are these people?" she asked suspiciously.

"Specialised tastes. They detest pop and are bored by symphonies."

"So many men wearing black leather jackets. Even suits. Chic, I suppose, but strange."

"I'd never noticed."

"Is this very *vieux jeu* to you?"

"Yes and no. They say France is keener on jazz than America is. In Arizona it's definitely minority music. This group are playing mainstream, twenty years out of date, Ben Webster, Coleman Hawkins, all my heroes. The really modern stuff is hard to take. Very industrial."

Ghislaine laughed nervously. "You found l'Hibou by yourself? Very brave."

"It was the other way round. Most bars have televisions playing game shows." Jana paused significantly. "Other bars are also better lit."

Ghislaine picked up the reference. "Ah, yes. Your... But does that matter?"

During a lifetime of evasive and insincere reactions Jana had rarely heard such directness, such dismissiveness. She said, "In France it matters less. Where it does matter is where I come from."

A drum solo broke in and Ghislaine looked on, bemused by a perspiring Algerian and his exaggerated stick waving. When a legato clarinet took up the next chorus she leant over and said, "Surely, that banging noise was meaningless."

Jana, never a fan of drum solos, laughed aloud.

Encouraged, Ghislaine said, "You were saying, in the USA..."

"Not a country for imperfect women."

"And the wonder machine – the laser – does nothing?"

Not many knew about the laser treatment and Jana was surprised. But then Ghislaine, on the fringe of medicine, had had two years to consider her former lodger.

Ghislaine added, "I suppose you know about the special make-up. We sell it at the pharmacy. I assume..."

Jana sighed. "To hide my face from my passengers I'd have to wear make-up all day. And re-do it regularly. I fly planes I don't model clothes. As to my love-life make-up would simply delay things. Eventually I'd be exposed. Better to start out from square one."

"I agree. Pharmacies sell cosmetics and perfume and I'm supposed to prove the point. My face can feel as stiff as a meringue."

As if on cue a tenor sax player who could easily have been an Afro-American stood up and blew a husky and beguilingly slow My Funny Valentine verse. Ghislaine noticed the response on Jana's face and became silent. Afterwards she asked, "A good song but it mocks women?"

"Not really. Love can overcome mediocre looks."

"Ah, I had not realised. It could be my song, then."

Jana was outraged. "But you are not..."

"I am my mother's daughter."

The band had taken a break and a waiter, shirt hanging loosely, jeans secured with a six-inch-wide belt, looked at their empty wine glasses.

"He wonders if we're from a certain Greek island," said Ghislaine. "I've forgotten the name."

"We could prove we're not."

"Work before pleasure," said the lad. "Your drinks, mademoiselles."

"Something a little better."

"We have just opened a three-year-old Madiran."

"Two glasses of that, then."

As they sipped their wine Ghislaine looked around. "A serious lot, these jazz enthusiasts. I think most are here for the music."

"I can't complain. That's why I'm here.

"And have there been...?"

Jana said, "I've been approached. Salesmen showing off their English. A man in his forties who asked me how the US visa system works. A well-dressed Belgian who offered me a ride in his BMW. But when asked couldn't say which model. And, ah yes, a physics undergrad from Lyons who seemed homesick and who I accommodated."

"What exactly do you want, *minette*?"

"Not to be embarrassed, not to be disappointed. And you?"

"Reality. On both sides."

The Madiran, at 14 per cent, worked on them, relaxing them into confidences. "It's been some months," said Ghislaine whose angular face profited from contemplation. "He sold cough syrup, just cough syrup. Something the British mysteriously call an ethical product. Do you know that word?"

Jana shook her head.

"Bought without prescription. Handsome enough and no desire to bore me with soccer. A champion in archery."

An unfamiliar word which Jana needed translating. Ghislaine giggled. "You know, Cupid. There were little jokes about arrows and hearts. Rather too well practised. But oh the problems of accommodation. He was staying at a *logis* at Cambo-les-Bains. I couldn't go there. The *patronne* went to school with Maman and it was far too cold to do it under the skies. Luckily he had a station wagon but things did not go smoothly." Ghislaine giggled again. "To prepare for our passion he had to move the boxes. Of cough syrup."

A similar story from Jana seemed in order. "Accommodation is not my problem. He lives in a motor caravan and his wife – there is always a wife, isn't there? – remains in Bilbao. It is very physical. Like our game of badminton but with a score that's... more obvious. Passion without passion. No hearts, no arrows."

"How can that be?"

Jana shook her head slowly. "It's hard to explain."

"No, do not tell me. I want us to become friends. There are limits."

"But you told your little story amusingly, with panache."

Ghislaine said, "Because it was unimportant. This is important. I can tell. Let's talk of something else."

"Nah, that's shitty." Inadvertently, because of the wine, Jana had reverted to English and saw Ghislaine's eyebrows rise. "Sorry. How weird those foreign words sounded. We are friends and I'm behaving like a teenager. My lover – not the exact word but it will have to do – my lover is drawn to the stain. It excites him. He's clever and full of energy and he is good for my body. But that's all."

"Crazy! My dear Jana, I think... I think you should take notes." And they both collapsed in laughter followed, quite soon, by streaming eyes. At which a broad-shouldered black man, head shaven and shining, dressed in black jeans and black polo-neck, drew a chair over to their table. "Bin watching the pair of you," he said in American-accented English. "So, solemn, so-o-o solemn. Then all these high spirits. Seemed like a good time to butt in. Course honkie chicks could be scared by a black man, even when he's as good looking as I. But check out the odds: two to one. And heck I'm witty. You'd be fools not to let me stay."

Jana glanced at Ghislaine who nodded, still wiping her eyes. Jana said, "But ditch the collard greens and talk normally. Princeton, at a guess."

"Columbia to be precise. Not sure I could have kept that up any longer. The trick is to use the jive stuff as an entrée and then go broad church."

"And there's another ground rule," said Jana. "Ghislaine has some English but it's rusty. Either you talk like Mister Rogers or you do the decent thing."

"I'm Boyce and you are Jana," he said switching to formal but serviceable French. "Overheard your name from your friend. Worked out where you were born from that 'Nah' you said. Before I order more of this great Madiran let's hang on to that fascinating confession you were making."

Jana tensed then subsided. It was Ghislaine who intervened. "That was intimate."

"I agree," said Boyce easily. "But I've something in common with Jana. And mine is bigger. Covers my whole body in fact."

Jana flapped her hand. "OK, you've booked your seat. But make mine a Perrier with a slice of lime. I've got a van to drive."

When he went to the bar, Jana asked Ghislaine: "Are you happy with him?"

"My dear. I could take that ebony head and…"

"Better than badminton?"

"Much better."

As they sat together again, Boyce said, "Cards on the table. I'm with SocleSoft France and I begged to work over here. I like jazz which means I like France. Not French jazz you understand; Stephane Grapelli's violin is just as squeaky as Ray Nance's. But the French looked after Sidney Bechet and made more out of Dexter Gordon and Bud Powell than the home crowd. Never mind. We were talking about sex. And our defects. There is one bonus, isn't there?"

"If rather rare."

"What bonus?" asked Ghislaine.

"Oddity can be attractive. Can be a fantasy. I know it's a cli-ché but women have been known to size up Afro-Am Columbia graduates."

"Ah, I understand. How does that work, Boyce? asked Jana.

"It's a great ice-breaker.," He smiled devastatingly, the white of his teeth an arc of pure happiness. "I've no complaints. So what do you both do?"

Jana was reluctant to respond, not wanting to encourage his interest in her. But after acknowledging flying was cool and continuing to keep Jana in the loop, Boyce started addressing himself mostly to Ghislaine.

"See, the pharmacy's like a sociological laboratory," he said and it was clear he knew France and was keen to know more. Were customers secretive about prescriptions? Not at all, said Ghislaine, some boasted about the number of drugs they took. Did this confirm France's notorious hypochondria? A stereotype invented by the Brits. What advice was Ghislaine entitled to hand out? "Many questions, many innocuous answers."

And Ghislaine blossomed. Her mouth which tended to be lipless in repose became animate and gay. She teased Boyce and he took it good-naturedly. Jana looked on, vicariously happy, noting that when they said their goodbyes in the car-park Boyce asked for the exact name of the pharmacy. It came as no surprise to hear he had called the following day and asked her to dinner.

Ghislaine said apologetically over the phone. "It wouldn't have happened without you. And he is, after all, American."

"For goodness sake, I've spent time with all three-hundred-million of them. Go for it, girl. And don't forget his hidden asset. The fantasy feature."

"Jana! If my mother were to hear."

But then Jana had an appointment in a motor caravan the following evening.

SHE wasn't in the best of moods. It rained the whole day, all across France, from the Cote d'Aquitaine to the Rhone. Since Eliazar was working on the Cessna Jana took the Piper. She'd been warned that the antiques she would pick up in Avignon were in large cardboard boxes stuffed with packing: not heavy but bulky. That meant removing the rear passenger seats, finding a cover big enough to protect them from the rain in windy conditions, and trolleying them awkwardly, one by one, to temporary storage in the hangar. Visibility as she flew east was dull, almost monochrome, with sky and horizon occasionally merging. Not difficult but depressing. As she entered Provence the rain became heavier, almost tropical, and when she opened the plane door in Avignon huge raindrops were hitting the tarmac causing a ground-level mist. She cursed herself for forgetting to bring the waterproof cover but the boxes were, happily, shrink-wrapped.

It had been an early start and she was hungry but didn't care to waste time on the meal she would have liked. Sustained only by a coffee and a brioche she taxied to the east and watched a Comanche speed off down the runway, disappear into a wall of particularly heavy rain and then think better of it. The aborted take-off took some minutes to clear and the subsequent visibility report from the tower at 100 metres left her with something of a judgement call.

The tower said rain intensity was varying, typical of summer storms, and allowed a three-minute delay for her take-off. Within thirty seconds the rain appeared to switch off completely and piercing blue sky was visible between towers of black cloud. An alert traffic controller quickly cleared her and she was off, pools of runway water dulling the plane's feel, taking away its lightness under power and prolonging by 150 metres the point at which she normally took off.

At the much larger Toulouse airport a Boeing had contrived to roll its front wheel off the tarmac when turning from the runway to the taxiway – probably trying too hard to take advantage of a short break in the weather when landing. Holding patterns had to be observed for a quarter of an hour. And when Jana finally reached the apron, got out of the plane and opened the waiting room door there was no one about. This was annoying since the consignors had stressed the value of the antiques and insisted their representative be present at the unloading.

After ten minutes a door opened in the offices opposite and a discouraged man in a business suit peered out. Fumbling, he erected an umbrella and stepped out, only to see the umbrella stripped of its fabric. Impatiently Jana ran into the rain towards the man, still standing indecisively holding the umbrella wreckage. As she ran she stripped off her windproof jacket and hung it on his shoulders. "We need a trolley," she shouted.

He reacted as if she'd asked for a JCB. She added, "I'll bring the boxes to this office door. Is that OK? No need for both of us to get wet."

The four boxes each required a round-trip of 50 metres and the man gestured helplessly each time Jana stepped over the threshold. Finally she offered him the receipt to sign and he hadn't got a pen. She reached inside her windproof, still on his shoulders, and took a ballpoint out of the pocket. As he signed his hand shook and she realised dyed hair made him look younger than he was.

"Mademoiselle, I was completely helpless and now you are virtually drowned. What can I do for you?"

"Is there someone in this building who can help you?"

"Oh yes. My driver has – ironically – gone for a coffee. But Mademoiselle is not French. American?"

Jana nodded.

"That is remarkable. I ask again: what can I do for you."

"Always use Gascon Air for your air transport. Keep me flying."

He laughed at her hard-nosed reply. "I will, I promise. Ah you are a veritable naiad with your hair like romantic seaweed over your temples. If you were French I would take advantage of you and ask if I could kiss your face. But perhaps Old World courtesies are unacceptable."

"I'm guessing at that word seaweed. As to courtesies, the New World swaps things round." And she kissed his withered cheek.

It was the last pleasant moment of the working day. Sitting in the plane's empty interior she peeled off her uniform jacket, then surreptitiously removed her bra in an attempt to sop up moisture with paper towels. Only to find herself overseen by an audience from the second floor of the office. She waved dismissively.

As she checked the instruments and started the engine the windproof felt rough against her skin but at least it was dry. By now the taxiway looked like O'Hare on Friday night and it took twenty minutes before Jana was cleared for take-off. As a further irritation she was required to accept an unexplained heading for Bordeaux, held for twenty kilometres, before turning west to Biarritz. The rain eased and visibility improved, allowing her to guess that her uniform trousers, tight round her thighs, were drying out. On her body. That seemed unhealthy.

After parking the plane on the Biarritz hardstanding there were the seats to replace. Then phone calls to make and emails to send as her need for a shower became more and more obsessive. But when she got home one of the Chauvelets was uncharacteristically using the bathroom and humming pleasurably, apparently in for the long haul. Eliazar's motor caravan had a tiny shower and that would have to do. Only as she drove over cart tracks to the familiar secluded spot above the Adour could she finally adjust herself what lay ahead.

THEY stood naked in front of the miniature built-in wardrobe, bodies touching lightly, his engraved with whorls of black hair, hers a faint *café au lait*, chest against breast, stomach to stomach, brushing teasingly from side to side. With his unfailing instinct he had gently turned her head so that his mouth engaged her jawline, not merely kissing her defect but speaking to it: "Jana *carino, carino*."

She moved as if in readiness.

"Not yet," he whispered. "For me it is a gift."

"But I'm… unclean."

"Pah. I can smell a bar of *savon de Marseille* any time. This is you."

"It's not womanly."

"Not in your country," he said. "But this I can taste." His tongue ran along the ridge of her shoulder, presumably cleaning a path through the dried sweat, her delight mingling with mild horror

As she arched back his square fingers slid softly up to her shoulders and began kneading the muscles. "*Carino* you are tired, I feel it here."

He'd recognised her fatigue as she stepped through the door. Flying was her joy but it was a demanding joy and hours of concentration had left a twitter in her eyelids. She buried her face against his so that wiry curls scratched her skin.

"Lie down on the bed, face down," he said and he knelt beside her, working on the junction between her neck and shoulders, drawing away the tightness, relaxing her spine.

"I may fall asleep," she said, her voice muffled by the duvet.

"Then I will finish the tortilla. Read a little. Then wake you with Casals."

Astonishing that he - the supposedly impulsive Latin - was able to curb himself during these attentions, mingling physiotherapy with arousal, relaxing some muscles and stimulating others. Most remarkable of all, silencing her near-desperate demands for a shower. In answer he had said nothing and simply slid the palms of his hands down her body over the inward curve of her waist and the outward curve of her hips. That alone charmed her. He did it again, this time checking left and right like a sculptor appraising the surface of something he had just smoothed.

How had he known? Once, at Arizona State, Jana had risen at six to complete an essay on high-level order picking, slipped off the tee-shirt she wore as a night-dress and caught an indirect reflection of her hips in the wardrobe mirror. Still a fresher and still reluctant custodian of her virginity she was pleased by what she saw. Student wisdom then said boobs were the only shapes that mattered but she had other ideas.. Although her breasts were acceptably sleek she believed that hips, and hers in particular, were sexually more significant, harder to fake or to rearrange and could, if wielded intelligently, project sex appeal at a distance. If poverty ever forced her to choose between a well-fitted pair of jeans or a bra, it had to be the jeans. The theory was never tested at college but Eliazar had artfully confirmed it and his hands were celebrating those hard contours to good effect.

Jana rolled on to her back and found him standing over her, hands dangling, still paying silent homage. This unheroic almost comic Spaniard with his stumpy body, slightly bowed legs and ragged Pancho Villa moustache, an effortlessly skilled plane mechanic moving to and fro in France's south-west, sending his earnings back to his wife in Bilbao who mothered an unspecified (thought to be large) brood of children, a great Bach enthusiast and a master of intelligent love-making.

"My hips," she said.

His French vocabulary and syntax were patchy; he didn't know the noun but recognised the emphasis. "*Acabado*," he said casually. Jana had taken Spanish as a minor for a couple of semesters and remembered the word had links with "perfect" but had never bothered about the distinction.

"Sounds nice. What does it mean?"

"*Consumado*," he said, grinning.

"That is nice. *Por favor*, sit down close." One incidental delight had been the ease with which she'd adapted to the Spanish *tu*.

He had an attentive look which said he was out to please. Using the back of his fingers he rippled over her breast.

"Skilled hands," she said dreamily.

"Mechanic's hands."

Those same hands had attracted her the day they met. The Cessna had been grounded with a tachometer failure just before an urgent and profitable flight that afternoon. Dirk had called in Eliazar and she'd mentioned her deadline to the Spaniard, not in a hectoring way, simply to let him know.

His closeness told her he found her attractive. There was, he said, an official way of replacing the tachometer which involved removing a panel. It took time but it was easy. And there was an unofficial way. Go unofficial, she'd said. Unemployed until the plane was serviceable she watched him thread his way through the cat's cradle of cabling behind the bulkhead. It took him less than an hour.

"Those hands knew what they were doing," she said as she ran up the engine to test the gauge, he sitting beside her in the passenger seat.

"They have other uses," he said quietly. His eyes were almost black, deep set into his skull and they were watching her at work as she had watched him earlier. He added, "Most Yankees like *paella*."

Thus it had started.

Beneath the washboard of his fingers her nipple stirred but his attentiveness affected her even more. His was a face that shut out the history and geography of her life, making her feel important. Again he turned her head to the right to kiss her cheek, then her neck.

"I plan badly," he said in mock apology, getting up. "*Senor 'vativo* is elsewhere."

That shortened word dated back to the first time in his motorhome. He had stroked her face: "There must be protection. Perhaps I am not alone, perhaps you are not alone." Which was just as well. Unbedded for several months, she'd been dangerously close to accepting whatever he proposed. Afterwards, she realised it had been a polite way of admitting he had other lovers. So polite she'd accepted it without resentment.

He lay on her and she knew he preferred there to be no assistance. "It is my way. I am sorry." That too she had accepted. It allowed her to close her eyes and follow his guidance.

An hour later he prepared a green salad, heated the tortilla and they sat side by side at the narrow plank resurrected at the side of the bed to create a dining table. "This is a strange affair," she said affectionately.

"Because I am always... *el jefe*?"

"Because I don't mind. I want you to be the boss."

"If I hurt you, if you are unhappy I will change."

"I know."

He took the plates to the sink, folded up the table and switched on the CD player. Casals played one of the Bach cello suites, groaning his own accompaniment. "You have your shower now, perhaps."

"I had forgotten," she laughed. "How powerful you are."

In the narrow shower stall each move had to be planned and her calves and feet were beyond her reach. The soap she noted was *savon de Marseille*, probably a consensus among those who took their pleasure near airfields. As she stepped out he was waiting with the towel and a brisk series of drying strokes. The towel thrown to the floor he held her against the wardrobe door. The chrome handle, although recessed, pressed hard against the small of her back and her gasp, when it came, arrived for several reasons.

"Upright. That was different," she said as they lay upon the bed.

She saw perspiration in his moustache. "Different, yes. It was…" he struggled for the French word then gave in and used Spanish which she recognised.

"Selfish! Oh no." she said. "But was it enjoyable?"

"Then, yes. Now, perhaps not."

"That saddens me."

The gulf of language was too wide and he stared up at the air vent, lost in critical contemplation, until she started to put on her jeans and trainers. "Jana." He used her name rarely and yet, Spanish-accented, it had a lingering sweetness. "You are Yankee. I am sorry."

"That's ridiculous. We made love. I came here to make love."

He shook his head. "You are Yankee. You understand that this…" He gestured, perhaps at the bed, unable to complete the sentence.

"I understand, I promise." She kissed him, ensuring he felt her breasts against his chest. "These are just flashes of happiness."

The florid phrase reached him and he smiled.

She got up ready to leave, then stopped. "And this?" she touched her jaw.

He rubbed his chin. "That is not Yankee."

ELIAZAR had parked close to the river bank on the edge of a field. To avoid over-running the thick waving grass Jana followed three sides of the rectangle to reach the gate, conscious of the motor caravan's diminishing blur, seeing the light go off in the bedroom and on in the kitchen, deluding herself she could still hear Casals. The track was rutted and wet. Driven slowly the van still fishtailed and bounced painfully, into and out of puddles which threw up sheets of red muddy water. Old though the van was she ached at its mistreatment and at the sense of anti-climax. Early tomorrow the caravan would be on the road to Pau where Eliazar had a week's work. Then, who knew? Perhaps even into Italy. The after-effects were dying away more quickly than usual.

She had invented "flashes of happiness" for his sake not hers. His way of life had always been evident and it would be foolish to complain. Except that the intensity and direction of his love-making made the abrupt endings more difficult to endure. She'd been proud of her self-reliance over the years, built a career on it. But once again the emotional loneliness bore in on her.

Now on a tarmac road she took out her mobile and switched it on, feeling it shiver in her hand. A text message, surely from the network. But no, someone with a longish surname. She held the phone to the lighted speedometer and read: Chauvelet. This had to be an emergency and she slowed, stopped and reversed into a farm access road. "Please ring up until 11." Signed not H for Hugues or, even less likely, S for Sylvie. But an unknown Y. Her watch showed quarter to eleven. It had to be one of Octavien's parents.

His mother, in fact, who tartly introduced herself as Yvonne. "With a profession like yours I'm surprised you switch off your phone, Mlle Nordmeyer."

This wasn't going to be pleasant. Nordmeyer had been pronounced impeccably and that was ominous.

"Sorry about that. A… social evening."

"No doubt. Well, Mlle Nordmeyer, you appear to have made a singular impression on my son."

"I take it you're not pleased?"

Yvonne Chauvelet laughed harshly. "Admirably frank, mademoiselle. Good. Perhaps you would like to tell me – precisely – what you said to Octavien."

"You mean in response to what he said to me?"

"Just answer the question. Precisely, please."

Jana was tempted to accept this aggressive ping-pong game but Octavien's interests needed protecting. Somewhere along the line it sounded as if he were being misrepresented. "Let's not fight, Mme Chauvelet. It isn't good for any of us. I enjoyed Octavien's company and I'd hate to betray him. Let me tell you briefly what happened. Then I'll answer anything you want."

"You are persuasive mademoiselle. I see how he was influenced."

"Nevertheless…"

Jana summarised quickly. How the visit to the airport had been made with the agreement of his grandparents. How he had responded intelligently to the cockpit tour. And how his request to watch the van repair arose quite casually. "Then there was the possibility of a flight. I suggested he discussed that with you and his father. I had in mind some kind of discount. I was truly astonished when he wanted to watch the repair. It won't be a spectacle in any sense but he did ask twice."

"However you put these opportunities before him."

"In the course of conversation, yes."

"And you persisted. Why was that?"

Jana's fear of betraying Octavien had not been a ploy. It was possible the child had offered his own views - he was intelligent enough - and Jana didn't want to hand over a weapon that could be used against him. But she recalled Octavien's reasoning which had concerned his father. There couldn't be any danger there.

"He said he was generally interested in technology and hoped to be an engineer, like his father."

And Mme. Chauvelet uttered a low-volume scream of triumph. "Ah there we have it. I think your so-called profession took over at some point. This is quite untrue. Octavien will study history as his grandfather did. That is my father. This is all arranged. He will not mire himself in technicalities."

Tough on Octavien. Mother and father at each other's throats over his future and, judging from this conversation, it would be foolish to bet against the mother. "In that case I apologise for any trouble. Forget the invitation. My best wishes to your son, madame. He is a remarkable boy and I'm sure he will be successful in any career. I bid - "

But Yvonne's triumph had come too quickly; she was not ready to put down the phone. "So you will see, mademoiselle, how dangerous - "

"I do indeed."

"A family is society's vital unit."

"Indeed."

"You do not, of course, have a family."

"True. But I am part of a family. I bid you goodnight."

Jana leant back in her seat expecting palpitations. But exhilaration was closer to the mark - successfully returning machine-gun bursts of French (speeded up deliberately she was sure), protecting Octavien and opting for a tactical defeat. She understood how the gifted child had become a miniature adult so quickly and regretted he was now lost to her.

But that wasn't the end. As she pulled into her driveway the lights were on *chez Chauvelet, grandpère et grandmère,* and the front door opened to admit her. How well the French administered a shrug, she thought as she followed them into the salon.

Hugues pushed forward a glass, one of three on the low table, and took the cork from a bottle of *pineau de charentes*. The shrug and then the booze: I like France.

"Our daughter-in-law insisted we give her your mobile number," said Hugues, paying lip-service to a toast as he raised the glass.

"It was unfair of her," added his wife.

"I have already spoken to Mme. Yvonne. It seems I misunderstood things. My bad French, doubtless. Octavien will become a historian not an engineer." She looked to see whether they grasped the irony. "A mistake anyone could make."

A split second passed when she thought she'd missed the target then both broke into relieved laughter.

"The English say you should not wash dirty linen," said Hugues from his easy chair. "I'm told it means we shouldn't criticise our family in front of strangers."

Jana nodded, surprised. Hugues was a former *petit fonctionnaire* retired from an ill-defined post at the Hotel de Ville in Bayonne. Previously, his entrenched Frenchness had seemed proof against anything foreign.

Sylvie resumed what sounded like a rehearsed statement. "But we do not think of you as a stranger. You were kind to Octavien. That pleased us."

"But Mme Yvonne is his mother. It was wrong of me to discuss things without consulting her first."

The Chauvelets looked at each other with great delicacy. "His mother, yes. But he also has a father. Vincent, our son. There are… difficulties. Vincent may wish to speak to you about Octavien."

"Of course. But for the moment Octavien is my only responsibility. If I can help I will. Otherwise I will stay silent."

Recorking the ritual bottle Hugues said, "That is all we ask. Thank you mademoiselle… no, thank you Jana."

Jana's animation lasted through her toothbrushing, undressing, laundry sorting and even a few pages of an early Gavin Lyall with an aviation background. She looked back warmly on Octavien glad of her manoeuvres and of the Chauvelets' greater trust. But once the light was out her handled body recalled the earlier part of the evening. Eliazar was a wraith now, a light presence like the pressure of the duvet, forgotten the moment she fell asleep.

CHAPTER FIVE

Octavien's worried father

ARMELLE made better coffee than Ginette but was in her forties and lagged behind the atmosphere at Gascon Air. She had the perfect voice for phoning bereaved relations and was a schoolfriend of Jean-Claude's wife, Adélie. Jana had wondered whether she kept an eye on the wealthy women who took impromptu flights to Bordeaux or the Cote d'Azur with J-C at the yoke. If so it had to be unrewarding work; no man was more married than J-C.

Armelle was also unnervingly formal. "M. Grosmont has found it necessary to go the bank. He begs you to forgive him and asks if you could examine the insurance contract for the Piper Seneca and then telephone the broker. There is the possibility of a reduced premium, I understand."

A slangy response, though tempting, would have been cruel and counter-productive. Armelle was well organised and reliable. Jana took the thick document, "He's very trusting. I hope I can understand this stodge."

"We both regard your powers as infinite."

"Armelle! Don't tease."

"I never tease."

"Then you're very sweet. I was going to wash down the Cessna. This at least will be different."

When Jana called anyone new there were always preliminaries. Entranced by her accent and her job the insurance broker babbled freely and seemed on the verge of a dinner invitation. She waited him out patiently.

Since she would regularly fly the Seneca he needed to know her qualifications. Such ecstasy.

"Nine hours! The United States Air Force. Formidable."

She read extracts from her log book, thrilling him still further. He said, "So many famous destinations. Plus O'Hare, Chicago! Still the busiest airport in the world?"

"Certainly it's busy. That's no problem, though. They have the experience."

"They do not love fools there, I suppose?"

"Neither does ATC here at Biarritz. "

He put down the phone reluctantly, promising an email within the hour.

Armelle couldn't avoid hearing. "Is it strange to be American working in France?"

Jana refilled her mug with *café filtré*. "It's strange to think back. The way Arizonans warned me about France. That the French hated Yanks. That they made things difficult. The terrible bureaucracy." She held up her mug, smiling. "The terrible coffee. The national inferiority, the brusqueness. I'd be back in three months, they said."

"But aren't some of those things true? – Not the coffee, of course. We are not the easiest people."

"OK, in the early days there was some *froideur*. People were wary, waiting for a torrent of English or, worse still, American. But then my terrible French told them I was learning the language. They corrected me; I expected that. What pleased me was being encouraged."

"You learned while you flew. Wasn't that difficult? Dangerous?"

"Things were tougher in the *boulangerie*. Flying's vocabulary is limited with lots of almost-English words. No syntax; mostly notes, messages. Also I'm lucky. English is the primary language in aviation. Over the RT the controllers usually help. Once I'd straightened out your crazy numbers I was safe enough. The hairdresser took far longer, as did the dinner table."

"And France is now… ?"

"France is my home." Jana glanced at Armelle, so proper in her twinset, tidy and motherly. "France is also kinder than the USA."

Armelle nodded. "Ah yes."

The email from the broker arrived. Jana turned it into a memo for Jean-Claude and left it on his desk. "Anyone wants me I'm washing down the Cessna. I have my mobile."

"I will tell Jean-Claude you are 'attending' to the Cessna."

This was the closest Armelle had come to a joke. "You follow office politics," said Jana.

"He doesn't like you washing the planes. You make him guilty. Not a job for a *patron*, I suppose."

"He is the boss and has to show authority. But we're small. When passengers see me doing humble work it proves we look after the details."

Secretly Jana quite enjoyed the twenty minutes it took to clean a plane - the *Americaine* who'd gone native. A Vanns, two up, with Aeroclub Basque marking ambled past on the taxiway as she used the hose. The instructor not only waved but pointed out her devotion to his pupil. A bowser driver smiled. Jane worked on until the Cessna shone virtuously in the morning sun and she switched to collecting road grit from the footwells. Her mobile rang.

"Good morning Mlle Nordmeyer. Vincent Chauvelet. Octavien's father."

As predicted. "M. Chauvelet. How can I help?"

"First, an apology. Family squabbles aren't pleasant."

"My mistake. I needed Mme. Chauvelet's permission."

He spoke impatiently. "You did our over-cared-for son a favour. Don't apologise."

"Your wife wasn't happy."

"She's often unhappy - for many reasons. But put that to one side. Could you do me a great favour? Could I see you for half an hour? I could come to the airport."

"I'm not sure I - " Was this a battlezone?

"To discuss Octavien. You seem to understand him."

"Your wife… "

Vincent Chauvelet sighed. "I see, of course. You'd rather not risk another of Yvonne's phone calls. Obviously I shall not tell her. Alas, I can't guarantee she won't find out."

"A problem for Octavien…"

"This is not your *salade*. But no one else is familiar with my son. Yvonne has seen to that. My parents tell me you have the boy's interest at heart. I can see… "

He sounded utterly defeated. She said, "I think he enjoyed my company, more important what I do. I suppose that helps. OK, a brief talk then. Twelve-thirty at the airport. The bar. It's called the Belharra. But I could be called away; the nature of my job."

"Leave a message at the bar. I'm sincerely grateful."

Jean-Claude was looking intently at his laptop screen where Jana saw thumbnail pictures of light planes. "You can't afford them. Or perhaps you can. You've just been to the bank."

"I'm concerned with range. Today I refused a booking for the Czech Republic. Would a Beechcraft Baron be better than the Seneca?"

"Anyone else ever ask for Czecho?"

"Never," said Jean-Claude, grinning shyly. "But we have no tradition. These things can accumulate. Or am I being optimistic?"

Jana said, "You've got to be; you're an entrepreneur. But cash flow's the key. What's the market for Senecas? How long to offload it? Sell it first and get a better idea."

"The wings of an angel and the soul of a huckster."

"What's a huckster?"

Jean-Claude told her.

"I like that. Is it OK if I dash out for half an hour?"

"Lunch? You! I hope it's a man."

"It is."

"Who may need a plane?"

"Just possible. Two seats even. What's our policy on children? An eight-year-old to be precise."

Jean-Claude's mouth turned down. "A man with a child? Not encouraging."

"He has problems."

"Let's hope they're marital. Go out of course. I wish you went out more often."

They discussed insurance terms for the Seneca, looked for the disadvantages. "This broker is a débutante," said Jean-Claude. "No doubt he tries harder. Was he thrilled by your accent?"

"Enthralled."

"A Gascon Air asset. You could do a website video: the joys of flying, sing the Marseillaise. If only you played a tenor sax."

THE TWEED jacket gave him away. Old-fashioned chic: it would match any pair of trousers. The sign of an engineer who'd taken over a department but couldn't abide a suit. Alone at a small table, face resigned, feet stretched out, a small glass in front of him. She too must have been obvious since he stood up immediately.

"Mlle Nordmeyer," he said extending a hand.

"It's Jana."

"Vincent." He gestured at his glass then shook his head. "I suppose not. Something non-alcoholic?"

Dirk's face flitted. "An Orangina, please."

"Tell me about my son."

"Look, mine's a man's world and children haven't figured much. Octavien changed that. He's polite, intelligent, hardly a child. Something told me he would be good company. I invited him out of self-interest – for me rather than for him."

Vincent nodded.

"I asked him to guess the cockpit dials. He did well except for turn-and-bank and that irritated him. Making him even brighter than I thought. When I had to make a phone call he asked to stay in the cockpit; promised not to touch. I explained the safety rules and he understood perfectly. No complaints."

"That pleases me."

"As it should. I mentioned needing to change the cam-belt on my old van. He was surprised; thought pilots were 'too grand'. He asked if he could watch, if I could 'point out the names of the parts'."

Vincent smiled distantly.

Would her private reactions be useful? "Of course I went too far. Outsiders are more interesting than parents; they don't do the discipline. I insisted he discussed everything first. With you and your wife."

She paused. "Talking to his mother I did a boo-boo. I mentioned what Octavien had said; that he wanted to be an engineer 'like Papa'. She had different ideas and I came between you and Mme. Chauvelet."

"A minor matter given our other problems," he grunted. Abruptly he tossed off his glass and snapped his fingers at the woman behind the bar. With a *grand* in front of him he leant back. "As you guessed there are disagreements. Octavien – her choice of name, you realise – must act the diplomat. He smiles when Yvonne mentions history; covers up his feelings about other matters.

"I'm head of electrical systems at GEC-Alsthom in Bayonne. Developing brake systems for the TGV. Octavien asks questions constantly when his mother is away. Responds politely to her fantasies. They are fantasies."

Vincent sipped at what Jana realised was cognac.

"I try to hide the real Octavien from his mother. Eventually she and I will confront each other. Our marriage was a mistake and Octavian must not suffer. Suffer now, I mean. Later he will suffer but getting older may help."

He pushed his glass away irritatedly. "Mlle N - that is, Jana - you see why I needed to talk. Away from an unsavoury domestic atmosphere, since the real subject is Octavien. I care for him a great deal. But I may not make the right decisions."

"I have no useful experience," said Jana. "But I'm happy to listen."

"Happy despite all this gloom. You helped me in one sense. You responded to Octavien's personality; that was encouraging."

Inadvertently Jana glanced at her watch. Vincent said,. "I mustn't keep you. You are too qualified to be a simple sounding board."

Jana smiled. "A new phrase."

"Really! Your French is so good I haven't made any concessions. A sounding board is a panel of wood to reflect sound effectively. I talked figuratively: exercising my opinions. Was it your French that brought you to France?"

"Problems in Arizona. There was work here and I needed a change."

"Has it worked? Are the problems now history?"

"They are."

"Was it just the change? Or was it France?"

"It was France."

For the first time Vincent smiled properly. "I know and like America. Particularly the reality of the suburbs. I worked in Massachusetts for six months. I am glad France has harboured a charming American citizen." This time his smile was more roguish. "So France has a secret appeal?"

His transformation was a relief. "France is more tolerant about this," she said, touching her jaw.

"Tolerant! One tolerates a failing. That is not a failing. It is merely… a difference."

"In the USA it is better not to be different."

Now he slumped back, his newly-found delight leaking away. "Was this… difference at the heart of the problem?"

"It was." Jana felt the mobile vibrating against her hip.

"Jean-Claude here. A million apologies. If I were God I would allow you the whole afternoon with your Frenchman. But I am poverty-stricken J-C Grosmont and in ten minutes I am taking the Seneca to Nice. While you – I hope – will perform a *bapteme de l'air* for… M. Yves Jument. Who waits for you impatiently."

"I may have to refuel the Cessna."

"A fascinating step in M. Jument's instruction."

"Give me five minutes."

Jana closed the mobile. "Sorry. A *bapteme de l'air*, they usually happen about this time. One reason I rarely plan lunch."

"An introduction to flying, I take it?"

"Which might convert to lessons."

"Perhaps I need to be baptised. I could monopolise your conversation."

"You buy time in the plane, not my chat. Baptisms are serious."

"And I would be a most serious student. You must go, obviously. I would like Octavien to see your famous cam-belt. Would you agree to a small deception? For Yvonne I pretend to take Octavien to the beach but we make a detour, a technical detour."

She stood up. "Octavien would have to share the deception. Would you be happy with that? I'm not sure I would."

"How clear-sighted. *Bonne route*! No that surely should be *Bon vol*."

JANA waited as Ghislaine set the pharmacy alarm then locked and re-locked the doors. Jana said, "You haven't scrubbed your face. This is the first time I've seen you in full warpaint. You look impossibly glamorous."

"It even hides my mother's jaw bones. All thanks to Boyce. He came to spy on me, buying bath salts of all things. Since he can't change the colour of his daytime face I'm not allowed to either."

"So… Boyce continues?"

"He does and I change," said Ghislaine. "You see that dusty Clio on the other side of the road? That is mine. And very necessary. Guess why."

"I'm not sure I dare. You once accused me of being unkind to your mama. I don't want that to happen again."

"Bravo! Obviously Boyce cannot knock on my front door. My mother is aware of him, of course. There are no secrets in Arcanques but she is happier if she cannot see him."

"And Boyce accepts that?"

Ghislaine stopped, poised and dramatic, on the pavement. Eye shadow too, Jana noticed. "It saddens him. But not for the usual reasons. Do you know why he enjoys meeting me?"

"You're attractive, lively, the rest."

Ghislaine shook her head. "Not at all. And I dispute those qualities. No, it's because I'm French. Apparently that makes me glow. He would like to increase my Frenchness by meeting my mother and – for all I know – my neighbours."

"And you. How do you feel?" asked Jana.

"Well of course I find him quite thrilling. His hands – black on one side, parchment on the other. And that shining confident head. Then there is the Boyce effect. When women over fifty see us together, arm in arm in the street, they want to hate the very idea. Then they look again – at him – and they see part of what I see."

"You're having fun?" said Jana.

"Fun? It's more complex than that. I will tell you inside."

The frontage woodwork of la Bonne Femme looked worn but not neglected. It had not apparently been cited in any of the gastronomy guides whose stickers decorate the jambs of suaver restaurants. And the easel on the pavement announced merely Plat du jour, €9.50. The tables inside were bare scrubbed wood, and the diners – including several families with children – had the comfortable look of long-time customers. Conversation embraced the high-pitched chivvying tone that Jana had heard in neighbourhood restaurants on the outskirts of French towns.

"*Mlle la Pharmacienne,*" said a red-faced woman who looked like the proprietor or the proprietor's wife.

"*Mme la Patronne,*" replied Ghislaine, and they were escorted to a table for two fenced in with substantial panels which hid their heads once they were seated.

"Flying tomorrow?" asked Ghislaine.

"Tomorrow's Saturday, the day students take to the air. But I could risk a couple of beers."

"Why not a Leffe?" suggested the *patronne*. "A stronger taste. It lasts longer than a blonde."

"Perfect."

They ordered oysters and then *magrets*. Ghislaine apologised for the latter. "I know, they're inescapable in this region. But here they're done with cherries and they're not as heavy."

"Tell me about complex Boyce," Francine said. And there it was, a small relaxation at the mouth corners.

Ghislaine said, "You remember when we first met? He said he liked France. It seemed like mere politeness. But no, he is truly *francophil*. He has read books – modern books not just Balzac and Zola. He understands our politics. Watches TF1 news. Asks questions, many questions."

"And you enjoy being interviewed?"

"He is serious."

"Too serious?" asked Jana.

Ghislaine slid an oyster over her heavily coloured lower lip. "How clever you are to ask. He doesn't wish to be seen as US. A friend not a conqueror is how he puts it."

"A friend!"

Ghislaine laughed so loud one of the other diners angled his head to see into their booth. "You are such a cynic, my dear Jana. But I told you things are complex. The first night he kissed my cheeks; two nights later finally my mouth. Just once my mouth. I felt confused.

"There were two more dinners and more ambiguous kissing. I did not mind. I felt somehow it was a tactic. I would wait. Last week we went to l'Hibou again. We drank wine and he said: the best way to understand jazz is to dance to it, do you agree? Notice his method: I am invited to agree to this theory. I am not asked if I care to dance."

"Very subtle. So subtle you had to agree."

And Ghislaine laughed again, though more quietly. "I did agree. Dancing is not one of my skills but he dances like an angel. Proving what racists say! He absorbed me, guided me. Made me happy to be dancing."

"Perhaps I could borrow him for one evening. I dance like a defensive end."

"Whatever a defensive end is." Ghislaine's eyes glistened. "But that was not all. As he danced he communicated himself. There was no mistake."

Jana waited.

"Our valedictions in the car were more passionate. He said in English: 'Ghislaine. Great name, great girl.' Then in his stiff French he asked if I recognised his feelings. I was careful, I said: perhaps. I looked into those eyes that are so white because they are surrounded by dark skin. 'I would like to make love to you,' he said. 'But I would never ask tonight. There is too much happiness. I will only ask after we've had a – What is the English word? Lousy! – a lousy meal and we've walked back to the car in the rain. When we're both low. When it would be easier for you to refuse if you wanted.'"

"Hmmm," said Jana. "I'd have to think. But that's what's so clever. He's saying he won't take advantage of you. Yet he does just that. He's saying you're civilised, that you'll make the right decision. And will you?"

"Why not?" said Ghislaine neutrally. "And now, as Mme la Patronne serves our *magrets*, tell me about the life of Jana Nordmeyer."

She had never told Ghislaine the full Eliazar story and was tempted to exchange frankness for frankness. Decorum held her back. What she had just enjoyed was a narrative in which feelings and words between two people had evolved. A minor love story. With Eliazar there was no narrative, just a hermetic sexual event. No preliminaries and no future. Instead she told Ghislaine about Octavien, culminating in the meeting with Vincent at the airport.

"The excuse is he wants to guard the child's future. And I accept that. But there are two objections. His wife will interpret things differently if she finds he's met another women, even if Octavien is present. Second, Octavien will be part of the deception and I'm not sure we should do that to him."

"You say this Vincent was becoming suggestive," said Ghislaine

"There was talk of taking flying lessons. That sort of thing."

"And is he attractive?"

"Hard to say. He's in turmoil. Mood swings."

"Presentable?"

"Chunky. A man's man, I suppose." Jana thought. "But I hardly know anything about him. Octavien has been our world."

They drank coffee. "You need a male friend," Ghislaine said suddenly.

"Don't we all?"

Ghislaine laughed. "Not just between your legs. To get another view of the world. A different conversation. A new concern. Boyce talks about his work, his vulnerabilities. Being black and trying to ignore the discrimination. This evening he is at a conference in Berlin. A stupid subject he calls IT. He and a white colleague will speak: one as spokesman for the company, one on some minor technical developments. 'Guess who gets to speak on what,' he asks me. As he talks he holds my hand. In his frustration he gestures with my hand as well as his own. I find it easy to become enraged by his difficulties."

Ghislaine pushed her empty cup away neatly. "Just imagine. Knowing Boyce I am taking sides in a struggle I never knew existed. Arguing immediate justice for him. This is all new for me. In Arcanques and here on the edge of Bayonne my life was slowly contracting. Now I am peering into a different world. He likes my being angry for him. 'But stay French. Because that's what I like most of all.'. A small matter perhaps."

"Oh, no."

"It is different for you, *chérie*. Your life is wider, you have authority and skill. But even so…"

Jana shook her head. "Flying is my life. But long ago I accepted it was a limited life."

"Oh *merde*. Have I been boasting?"

"You have and I'm happy for you. Very happy." Jana smiled mischievously. "And on that day when it rains and the meal is lousy I think I can guess your answer."

"He is American. Americans always go back."

"Perhaps. But I doubt he is thinking about that. Buy Nina Simone CDs and play them for him. They are eloquent on a homeland rejected."

Ghislaine said, "Nina Simone? Surely Boyce must be made to love Johnny Hallyday if he is to understand the true France."

"Now that would test his francophilia."

CHAPTER SIX

Two flying lessons

MATTHIEU Daoust was twenty minutes late for his 9.30 am lesson.

Jana's civilian training had been at Mesa, south of Phoenix, 160 miles from Flagstaff. Like many trainee pilots she'd been forced to book weekend slots when instructors' schedules were most crowded. Delays were deducted from time in the cockpit. It was fortunate she'd solo-ed quickly; the family station wagon had racked up 115,000 miles and might not have survived many more lessons.

Here at Gascon Air Daoust would be indulged (They needed his money) and Jana spent the time re-reading Dirk's notes about Daoust's uncertain progress. To some extent the free time added to today's nominal hour was already part of his routine. Dirk's debriefings and classroom sessions had added up to far more than the fifteen hours on Daoust's log book. More significant, Dirk hadn't trusted him to take off the Cessna until the thirteenth session. Jana's familiarisation would need to be painstaking.

She sat in the tiny reception-cum-classroom space where students were received and looked out to the car park. A Mercedes coupé was easing through the airport gateway and something told her this was Daoust. As the car got nearer she noticed the driver was accompanied by a woman.

Neither of them hurried. Daoust, if it was him, not only removed his lightweight linen suit jacket but his tie and shirt. Apparently he believed flying demanded he wear a pale green Lacoste and a beige wind-breaker. Jana imagined her own instructor's reaction to this leisurely scene. Mike Brubaker, as Texan as a horntoad, was both laconic and, on the ground, short-tempered. Quite capable of opening the door and shouting that the plane was losing dough.

Daoust's sun-glasses were hooked into the cleavage of his Lacoste shirt. Of course they were Ray Bans. "Mlle Nordmeyer, you are now more than a voice on the phone. Today I am shepherded by my fiancée Laure."

They shook hands and Jana knew she was under extra-professional scrutiny. Laure wasn't about to hand over her Mercedes owner willy-nilly. Not that scrutiny took more than a few seconds. "It's Jana by the way. Takes less RT time."

"And I, of course, am Matthieu." Laure was presently reaching up and rearranging Daoust's expensively cut hair, ruffled when he changed shirts. Jana suspected he would have kept it ruffled. More pilot-ish.

"Are you familiar with the airport, Laure? There is a bar and a restaurant. If you mention you are with someone taking a flying lesson they will give you a table overlooking the runway."

Laure waved dismissively. "Matthieu is free to play his little boy's games. I shall retire to the car and listen to the radio."

Matthieu looked disappointed, had hoped for an admiring audience. Whereas Laure had issued a judgment: the female instructor was not considered a threat.

Once inside the cockpit Matthieu discarded his airs and provided the take-off running commentary Jana had asked for – matching the gyro and runway headings, forecasting the point when the airspeed indicator became active and the speed at which the yoke could be eased back. Jana took a north-easterly course aiming at a thinly populated area bounded by the Adour as it changed direction and ran north to south. At 5000 ft she handed control to Matthieu asking him to maintain that altitude and a bearing of 067.

After minor undulations and one quite perceptible yaw he held the altimeter and gyro readings to within acceptable limits.

"You were pleased with my commentary?" he asked.

"It's a useful exercise. Predicting my take-off is slightly different from processing your own data. And, yes, I was pleased."

His smile was almost endearing. Jana said, "I'm asking for a medium bank to starboard – say 30 deg. Take her all the way round and resume your present heading." Deliberately, she did not warn him what to look out for; it was time to find out what he had learned during his hours with Dirk.

There was no need for her to call out "Height." Seconds into the bank Daoust remembered his altimeter – perhaps even sensed the height loss - and made the correction with a whispered *merde*. But it dis-oriented him and after the full 360 degrees he'd forgotten the original bearing.

"067," she said in an intentionally calm voice. "OK, climb to 5500 ft, maintain the bearing for a minute, descend back to 5000 ft and then immediately repeat the bank." This time everything went well.

His fingers drummed on the yoke. "But doing it a second time is not good enough."

"It was a test with no warnings. We know what went wrong; now tell me what went right."

He looked sulky. "Nothing went right."

"Matthieu, think! Why did you lose height?"

"I didn't check the altimeter."

"Why not?"

"I was… searching the sky."

"And that's a good thing."

"But… "

"Yes, the altimeter would have been nice. But you only lost 400 ft and you checked the height before I asked you. Did you remember the altimeter or did the plane – shall we say – tell you?"

"I think I knew something was wrong."

Jana said "Then that's good news. If there's a choice it's more important to look outside the plane than be glued to the instruments. A quick glance that's all; remember the shape the needles make; at 5000 ft it's like six-o'clock, a straight line. Now, would you like to do some slow flying?"

"Slow?" He smiled in recognition. "Ah. Preparation for landing."

She was careful not to confirm his guess. Dirk's notes were pessimistic, suggesting Matthieu froze slightly as the runway loomed. However his priorities during the banking exercise encouraged her, as did his willingness to listen.

Controlling the Cessna at slow speeds consisted mainly of tiny adjustments to power, trim and pitch and Matthieu already knew enough for Jana to keep her instructions to single words. Dirk's comments combined with Matthieu's playboy arrival at the airport hadn't exactly raised her hopes but his slow flying was better news. As Mike, Jana's instructor at Mesa, had put it: "A wash-out comes after two hours' lessons, tops. Fear grabs their balls and it's all a big blur. They're back into their Caddie and looking to buy a power boat. But if they stick instruction for five hours it's short odds there's something there. Something you can teach. But you need to sneak up on 'em. Blindside 'em."

Despite the plane's awkwardness Matthieu was applying himself. True the altimeter flickered but he corrected quickly. Also, he divided his attention more effectively. Within a few minutes the need for instruction dropped away.

"OK, let's have some fun. Here's the chart and there's the Adour. Find an identifiable point on the river, take a bearing for Grenade-sur-l'Adour, fly there and fly back. I'll give you the wind corrections."

Another Brubaker theory. "Give them drills – all that repeated stuff - for forty minutes; grind their asses. Then perk 'em up. Let them just fly. Prove that the hard work's worth it."

Faced with getting from A to B and back, Matthieu was seized with boyish enthusiasm. Some of his movements were almost intuitive. Re-approaching his departure point – a jetty with a dinghy moored alongside – he learned how easy it was to mistake a landmark from a different direction but Jana downplayed this. "We all do it – once!"

Returning to Biarritz she decided to take advantage of his new abilities and confidence. Alerting the tower she landed the plane then brought it to a halt on the runway. "You have the plane," she said to Matthieu, "but spend ten seconds in deep thought."

In fact the take-off and the cross-wind leg were competent but flying at 1000 ft seemed to unnerve him and he continually allowed the nose to rise. Jana completed the pattern herself, glad to see him reflecting on what had gone well. As she finally switched off the engine he remained seated, in no hurry to open the cockpit door.

"I was used to Dirk," he said. "Learning to fly is a strange world and I wondered if I would behave differently – stupidly – with a woman. A Frenchman's question perhaps. You encouraged me cleverly, I could see that."

"Part of the job."

"You reminded me why I wanted to learn."

"That's what it's all about."

But when she opened her door a strange weariness attacked her. For a moment, standing on the tarmac, her legs wobbled. Blood sugar, she told herself.

Despite her aloofness Laure had not spent the ninety minutes listening to the Mercedes' radio but was waiting at Gascon Air reception. Matthieu wanted to talk about his progress but the details were opaque to her and in any case she wasn't listening. She was there for a purpose and Jana was that purpose. "You are American Mlle Nordmeyer," she said. "Isn't our part of the world too rural, too bucolic?"

"No more than Arizona where I was born."

"And may I enquire what brought you here?" asked Laure.

"I needed a change of air."

"Air, you say. I'm surprised you found France attractive. Our so-called socialism can hardly be to your taste. Aren't we cheese-eaters? Aren't we monkeys?"

"I hope I can look further than the cartoons," said Jana neutrally.

"A free spirit. Good to know. I sincerely hope France made you welcome."

Jana took ironic interest in *sincèrement* pronounced to mean exactly the opposite. "Better than I could have imagined."

Laure looked round at the shabby sofa and leather chair. "And the new air you wished to breathe?"

By now Matthieu had noticed the edginess. "Time to leave, Laure?"

"I like the country and the people," said Jana.

"Well, then." Laure turned to leave, causing her expensive print dress to swing out aristocratically.

Jana entered the office and said to Ginette, "May I beg a cigarette."

"You? Smoke? Was the Countess over-protective about her fiancé?"

"A little. It's not that. Teaching people to fly is hard work."

She smoked outside the office, leaning against the brick wall, fifty metres away from the Cessna. Her last cigarette had been over a decade ago with the USAF and a tingling palate brought back that tensely competitive part of her life. Someone on the course, name forgotten, who had dropped out two weeks later, had started to smoke openly despite Air Force disapproval. Half of the course copied him, defiant of the regime, intent on insisting they were not robots and that they would relax in their own way. At the time Jana had never smoked and going along with this small insurrection had been an uncharacteristic, almost fearful, decision. But then, as she told herself, the life she was leading was hardly normal.

There was no great pleasure in smoking now, in responding to an almost forgotten addiction. Teaching had not affected her this way before. She had gained an instructor's licence soon after leaving the Air Force, an essential asset in her line of business, and a natural extension of being a pilot. Subsequently she had taught without problems in Arizona and had then stood in for Dirk here in France when he was overbooked, albeit to tightly defined guidelines.

The session with Matthieu had been different. That morning, for the first time, she had noticed how her language fluency differed from that of a native. In instruction, nuance, tone, emphasis and choice of word took on extra significance in the cockpit where facial clues and pointers tend to be lost. If there'd ever been communication problems flying alone she'd worked them out within seconds. But such gaps were more noticeable acting on behalf of a student pilot.

The difficulties weren't insurmountable. She was justifiably proud of her French and constantly looked for improvement. Concentration solved most things. But something more insidious had also arisen as she worked to re-establish Matthieu's abilities and belief. In the plane he was her complete responsibility, a much broader obligation than teaching him manoeuvres and how to interpret data. For safety's sake she needed to predict where he might fail. And she needed to know quite clearly what was going on in his mind.

Teaching flying in Arizona had been more instinctive, more light-hearted and had profited from native rapport. Here in France, cultural slippage widened the gap between teacher and taught and her instincts were less effective.

As a result she inhaled needfully on her cigarette. Flying nourished her and provided a legitimate reason for being solitary. The loneliness of the cockpit was a refuge which was unaffected by carrying passengers or being test-flighted by Jean-Claude. But having to take care of a trainee pilot who didn't respond to English was like mothering a succubus. Was there enough of Jana to go around?

And now the link between Matthieu's lesson and the cigarette between her fingers became clear. Mike Brubaker, her Texan instructor, had been on her mind throughout the morning. His sayings, his laidback yet skilled view of aviation, his authority and (provided you did what he ordered) his friendliness. He smoked. He'd been smoking that day when, as an eighteen-year-old, she'd arrived for her first lesson at Falcon Field in Mesa. Jana had been fifteen minutes early.

"Y'all from?" Mike said.

"Flagstaff."

"Shoot. That's two-and-a-half hours." He grinned, blowing smoke away from her as they stood on a raised porch overlooking perhaps four dozen planes parked on the far side of the runway. "Course, I could act stupid and ask why you druv all that way."

"Yes, that would be stupid."

He laughed wheezily. "How do you come by mah name?"

"Banging on doors, mingling with Flagstaff pilots, asking questions."

"Well, you're paying top dollar. Shoulda said 'paid'. You handed us a heap of cash up front. But are you just pissing it away?"

"Hope not. That's a big slice of my life wasted at Dunkin Donuts if I am. For the record I've read books, worn out Flight Simulator and nagged people to death. None of it worth much if I weren't so damn sure I wanted to fly, needed to fly."

His glance swept over her face without expression. "What do you know?"

"Try me."

"See that Comanche over there?"

"I see it."

"Gimme the registration."

She read it out and he grunted. "So you know a Comanche. OK, when I've finished this smoke you and I are going to walk over there and… what?"

"You'll pre-flight the plane."

"Keerection. You'll pre-flight it. That worry you?"

"No."

"You're sure full of confidence. Course, it could be something else you're full of. So, pre-flight's done, prop's turning, gauges say there's a chance of life. What next?"

"Busy airfield. You'll need clearance from the tower and a bearing."

"Won't try you on RT, you've probably got all that figured out. All the usual bull. But there's something extra I'll be saying to the tower."

Jana flushed with irritation, slurred her feet on the floor. "Oh shit, oh shit. Ah! That you've got me aboard!"

And he reached out and shook her hand.

In the air his requests and guidance were almost monosyllabic and it was all she needed. Two or three equally curt questions and she flew straight and dead level at 5000 ft, banked, climbed, watched him induce a stall and recover ("Remember all that for next week."). Then they flew out towards the Mogoller Rim where he found a deserted strip in the desert and had her fly "slow and dirty" down to 500 ft, lining up the runway with his wind corrections.

After a third repeat she looked at her wristwatch. "We've been gone way over an hour."

"I'm having fun. Aren't you?"

"It's… fucking marvellous. But why's it fun for you?"

"Don't often get a natural." He turned and smiled beatifically. "'S'allright. You can give me a big sloppy kiss if you've a mind to."

She did.

The following week she flew the Comanche off Falcon Field and her approach at the deserted strip was down to 200 ft. Later he had to rescue her from her first stall recovery and he pretended to be disappointed. On the way back he rehearsed her in RT procedure and had her relay the transmissions until they were half a mile downwind from the Falcon runway.

In some respects the first day she flew the whole lesson from take-off to landing was more intimate, more personal than going solo. His relaxed approval at her side flooded her with well-being and promised a future that would blot out her history.

"You know when you're at your best?" she asked.

He rolled his eyes comically. "When ah shet mah mouff."

After the solo he took her for a beer despite a waiting customer ("Danged advertising exec. Wears an earth magnet.") He ordered but did not touch a shot of bourbon explaining it wouldn't be a celebration without a drink on the bar for him.

He knew about her plans and why she'd paid for her own lessons. "Jana, you know you fly real well. Don't need me to say so. The Air Force is another bucket of shit. There it's going to be more than just flying. If you find yourself in an F-18, fine. Forget what I've said."

He paused and she looked at him, startled. He said quietly, "I tried. Didn't make it."

She supposed not many knew this. Pilots who'd been trained by him would have found it hard to believe. "Mike, I can't…"

"I just said, it's more than just flying. It could happen to you. It shouldn't, but it could. If it does, well, you're tough enough. I know that and I damn well know why. After? Fly for an airline and make regular dough. Fly single engines and have some fun. As we did. You'll be disappointed about USAF but you'll get over it. Just one point: if you end up hedge-hopping Cessnas you'll have to teach people flying if you want to eat meat on Fridays. It won't feel like consolation. But keep going, keep looking. You could end up like me. Feeling as I do - today. Good."

She dropped the butt on the ground and crushed it with a suede boot, one of a pair she'd been forced to buy in from the USA. The French equivalent had looked terrific but had lasted three weeks.

As to Mike's final advice she'd not rejected it, merely filed it away. At the time she couldn't afford any point of view that didn't include becoming a fighter pilot. Later, still very young, she'd taught equally young Arizonans to fly in a spirit of banter, undeterred by sharing a cockpit and the risks to her solitude. Today, at thirty-eight, getting to grips with Daoust whom she didn't really care for had left her drained. Yes, there'd been professional rewards from charting his mind, deciding what he could do, testing him with the unexpected. Blindsiding him, in fact. But when it was finished she was only too conscious of the emotional energy she'd consumed. Flying for two rather than one.

At the Gascon Air office she poured coffee for herself. Ginette asked coyly, "Another cigarette, perhaps?"

Being teased was a comfort. "A brief lapse. A first and last."

Jean-Claude looked up from the innumerable forms he was required to fill in for the bank. "Smoking, Jana? Not like you. Was it that hideous woman?"

"I've met worse in bars."

"Was it that wretched Matthieu? I've never liked him."

"He improves when given his head. But he's not satisfactory. He still comes apart below 1000 ft. Matthieu was my first real student and I had to think it out from square one. There's also the language. I've really got to speak more carefully to students."

"Pah. Your French is superb. You were more disturbed by that virago than you know. Say the word and we give Matthieu his cash back and say goodbye."

Jana shook her head, smiling. "Suicidal, J-C. Think of the bank. I can stand the hassle, I promise."

Jean-Claude grinned back. "Just one of my foolish gestures. But what about a stratagem? She wasn't interested in his lesson yet she was out there, watching, before it ended. Why not take her with you the next time? Challenge her – politely, of course. There's nothing like a flight in a small plane to clear away stubbornness."

"Good point. In the meantime I need to up my blood sugar."

"Blood sugar? What is that? Do you know, Ginette? No, I thought not. We French have no blood sugar."

Rather than hide herself out in the car park she ate her chicken salad baguette at a table in the restaurant, ordered an Orangina as a toast to Dirk, and added sugar to her latte. Visitors to France using the summer airline services glanced briefly, then looked away in that familiar guilty way. An old conundrum: she tried to imagine what these strangers saw and what, say, Jean-Claude and Ginette saw. Did the stain fade, become invisible or turn into something the eye simply missed? Merely a difference, as Vincent Chauvelet had said, in a moment of casual pragmatism.

Walking across the hardstanding to check the Cessna's fuel she experienced the – admittedly faint – urge to smoke. She had supposed this morning's cigarette was simply a gesture towards memory. But it was a trap set in the past like most traps.

THE AFTERNOON lesson belonged to the student who had passed effortlessly through Dirk's tutelage, looked like a sleek Parisienne with a name to match (Dieudonné Labossière - "But please, please call me Didi.") and who casually emphasised her confidence by tossing expensive stilettos into the back of her Porsche Carrera and slipping on ballerina pumps. On the phone she had sounded over-brisk and censorious but she approached Jana smiling.

"Mlle Nordmeyer, I owe you an apology," she said, shaking hands firmly. "I was unbearably rude when we spoke. I think it was pure superstition. I'd done well with your colleague, M. Boonhausen, and I saw his departure as an omen. An end to progress! What's more I seem to retain some old-fashioned ideas about women. I've passed through several glass ceilings myself and I should have known better. I spoke to Jean-Claude about you and it turns out I was even stupider than I imagined. Please forgive me."

Jana laughed. "American accents aren't always welcome."

"There at least I am unprejudiced. I am a corporate lawyer with an international practice and I regularly work in the USA. Unlike my political countrymen I enjoy Americans. I'd offer to speak English for our lesson if that didn't suggest I was criticising your excellent French."

"I'm grateful for the offer. However, I had my butt kicked while instructing another student this morning. My French needs to be better, especially with students who lack your shining re-cord."

"Shining record, indeed! We are starting off well. I am but-tered with flattery. Now, I know Gascon Air has excellent coffee and M. Boonhausen always offered it. But to tell the truth I can-not wait to get into my dear little Cessna."

"Neither can I."

Outside the plane, Jana handed over the laminated pre-flight checklist. Didi made a mock bow. "A gentle damper on my gushing. Bringing me down to earth."

Inside the cockpit, as the engine warmed up, Didi said, "Mlle Nordmeyer I've already talked too much. Students should listen not talk. But I must explain. Twenty years ago ski-ing looked graceful and I became a good skier. Superficially flying has the same kind of appeal but flying is much more important to me - I will eventually buy my own plane. I intend to be become a good pilot. But is aesthetics a fanciful reason for wanting to fly?"

"Done well flying is beautiful to watch. At least to educated viewers. A good yardstick."

"Good, I'd hate to be thought fanciful. From now on I will do exactly what you say. However Gascon Air is graciously giving me an extra half hour of flying and I can afford to be profligate. I would love to watch you take off, climb to 1500 ft, do the box, sweep down and round to the runway, touch down, then off again. You've done it thousands of times and I myself several dozen. The English unromantically call it 'circuits and bumps'. Would you indulge me please?"

"With commentary?"

"I think not."

"Not even at the moment of beauty?"

Didi raised both hands. "You *do* understand. Yes, some words then. But not the jargon. I think I understand what is required technically. Just… say whatever you wish."

Jana flew three-quarters of the pattern in silence. Then: "You need to know where you are in space. Not from the instruments - visually. There are four phases: flying straight and level upwind, taking the banked descending turn to starboard, arriving at the correct altitude, and touchdown. If I'm lucky no one will know exactly when one phase becomes the next."

Didi nodded but said nothing. Jana touched down and was now climbing away from the runway. She said, "You have the plane."

Sitting upright, alert, Didi fractionally drew back on the yoke so that the ASI showed the optimum speed for climbing. Didi said, "You said 'If I am lucky…' and yet there was nothing lucky about what you did."

"Just approved procedure. Approved because it cuts out the risks we know about. Up here we're in alien territory. There are risks we can't always foresee. But let's forget about them for the moment. At 5000 ft turn to port on your own bearing for Moliet-et-Maa. From Moliet fly 012 using the coast as reference and making your own wind adjustments. At the southernmost tip of Etang-de-Biscarosse turn to starboard and fly 167 for Labouheyre."

Jana spoke slowly and clearly. Immediately Didi took the hint and wrote the figures in a notebook clipped to the centre of the yoke. The transition towards the coast was smoothly done and Didi settled on course checking her wristwatch. "Ah, beautiful but oh-so-familiar France," she said. "Tell me about an exotic flight, Mlle – No! After watching your approach I request the intimacy of calling you Jana."

"Didn't you call M. Boonhausen Dirk?"

"He was so pretty, so confident, so American I enjoyed the frisson of being formal. But with your permission I prefer informality."

"Sure. I'm Jana. An exotic flight, then? My friend Ghislaine who works at a pharmacy was thrilled when I mentioned Ciudad Juarez."

"In Mexico, isn't it? The most criminal town in the country."

"Armed soldiers round the perimeter. Half-tracks in front of the airport. Two security lowbrows with Uzis if you wanted to go downtown. It took a long time to get there. I started in Tucson and landed at a private airstrip in the Texas Panhandle to pick up – I assume – a trio of spooks. All wearing shades, carrying grips that weighed a ton."

Didi laughed. "Jana being Jana went downtown."

"Hey, I hate risk."

"But you went downtown."

Jana said, "I had to get tourist stuff for my mother. The goons were poor protection. I was nearly a head taller, and much paler."

Down below, to the left, white rollers played along the barren, anonymous line of this part of the Cote d'Aquitaine. Jana noticed Didi inspecting them too, then clicking a met report on her Iphone. "You OK?" Jana asked.

"The minute you said 'making your own wind adjustments' I went on tiptoes. Knew there would be a reason. Gusts to 25 kph but variable. Why can't the physical world be consistent?"

"Because a consistent world would be full of planes flown by idiots."

"What is that marvellous English phrase: does not suffer fools gladly. The first quality of a flying instructor. Have you ever refused a student?"

"Just the one" said Jana. "An academic high-flyer, daughter of old money living out in Catalina Foothills, the swanky end of Tucson. And for a really silly reason. She couldn't tell left from right. Imagine! I tried everything: a scarf round her wrist, coloured dots, told her about port and starboard. Nothing. Each time she needed to check her writing hand. But that took time and I could never, ever, see her landing a plane. Her parents were furious, so was the guy I rented the plane from."

Didi was now approaching the lake at Biscarosse for her change of direction and needed to concentrate. Summer's sun had dried up the southern shallows – as Jana well knew – and visual information was ambiguous. Didi over-flew, box-turned back and re-approached 1000 ft lower. Finally satisfied she climbed to starboard, up to 5000 ft and settled on 167. She glanced at Jana with raised eyebrows.

"Don't worry," said Jana. "That's what I hoped – expected – you'd do. Go to the top of the class." And Didi's breasts rose as she breathed in more fully.

"That was cruel."

"So's the world, Didi."

This lesson was much more restful than that with Matthieu. Jana sensed Didi would have asked more but held back, not wanting to appear curious. Especially about the usual subject. Knowing nothing about the habits of corporate lawyers Jana pushed out a few sallies but realised they were too simplistic.

"I take it corporate lawyers are ambitious?"

"All of us are mini-Napoleons."

"And what's your ambition?" Jana asked.

"You're part of it. I want the plane I buy to be a perfectly justifiable expense."

"The flying advocate."

"Just so," said Didi. "But your ambition must be more complicated. If I had your skills I'd want to fly for the rest of my life. A bigger plane? A jet? Surely you'd hate to run an airline?"

"Once I wanted to be a fighter pilot. I was very naïve. Somehow I separated what I wanted from the reasons fighter planes exist. In the end I failed."

"I can't believe that."

"Combat flying requires a peculiar kind of person. I wasn't that kind. Failing was almost the end of my life. Now, I like this gentler stuff."

"What do you want from life?"

Jana had often pondered this herself but was still no nearer an answer. "This is going to sound pathetic. Less transience. A stable domestic existence."

Didi was sharp enough to recognise the euphemism, intelligent enough not to push further. "The stability is already there, surely?"

"In the air, yes. I wouldn't step into a plane if it wasn't. Elsewhere... I suppose I'm less sure of myself."

And Didi merely nodded. Scanned the space round the Cessna – left, right, forwards – and let her eyes slip back to the instruments. Jana looked unobtrusively at her profile, absorbed its austere beauty, its cleaving sense of achievement. The pair of them flew on, alternating hard-eyed observation with inner reflection.

Didi asked, "We're approaching Labouheyre. Do I hover over the centre?"

"No backchat, student. What I ask for will be a leetle difficult. Find a bearing which intersects the BIQ flight path half a kilometre from the end of the runway. Five kilometres out tell the tower about your approach and aim to swing down straight on to the flight path, exactly half a kilometre out, landing as if your tyres were duck eggs."

"Why duck eggs?"

"Larger and prettier than hens' eggs. Two things to consider. What do you reckon?"

Didi, having time, took her time which was the third, unspoken, consideration Jana wanted her to grapple with. Didi was smiling now. "I imagined we were friends and perhaps we are. But it is your job, as a friend, to torture me."

"I say, hand on heart, it's for your own good."

And Didi laughed aloud. "You perfect Jesuit. So, your two considerations! You've contrived a route back to Bayonne I've never taken before. For my 'beautiful descending turn' there'll be no known visual references. Second I suspect the tower will report a stronger crosswind and I'll have to offset the descending approach. Congratulations, friend."

"Didi, look at me."

And Didi did so, slightly startled.

"Dirk could have solo-ed you. I could have solo-ed you and I will do so, next lesson. But what's a solo? Fly the pattern, land on the tarmac with your undercarriage still intact. Compared with what you've already done it's nothing. What I'm asking for is one of those moves which bring together all your experiences into something new. This is the start of real flying."

"My dear…"

"Long ago you learnt the manual and technical skills. What I needed to know was whether you have the temperament to use them calmly and logically. You may not feel sure that you can but I am sure – on your behalf. Also, you can rely on what I'm saying. My hands will be at rest, a long way off the yoke."

As she flew the chosen course Didi remained alert, perhaps a little too alert. Jana said softly, "You're an attractive woman Didi. A husband, perhaps, or a partner. I never asked. Certainly hordes of admirers."

Didi giggled which is what Jana wanted. "If they could see you now they would all sign away their freedom."

And Didi, a corporate lawyer with an international practice, drawn to flying because of its aesthetics, struggled against another giggle.

The tower reported 17 kph from the north and Didi, head swinging almost rhythmically left and right, offset the Cessna two plane widths to the north, descended on a trajectory that needed no yoke movement, reduced the power at 200 metres and lowered the flaps, flew tranquilly on a line where the plane's nose and the runway centreline coincided at a height of 50 ft, then gently pushed the throttle to idle. The oleos sighed as the plane's weight was once again supported by Mother Earth.

Jana said nothing as Didi attended to the comparative trivia of getting the Cessna to the Gascon Air stand. Nor did she speak when the engine was switched off. Didi looked serenely out through the windscreen. Without turning her head she said, "Jana you're an angel."

Lisa Nordmeyer's term of affection for her daughter. Jana said, "I wish I was. But it was no great risk and took no great knowledge. If you're really surprised I'm disappointed. Pilots should know themselves and you may need to work on that."

"But we've only been together for less than two hours."

"A cockpit's a small world. I didn't need to understand those big deals in New York. You're stripped to the bone here. I saw all I needed to see."

Didi reached on to the rear seat for her chic black handbag. "I realised going solo isn't a final achievement. I shall be renting a plane and building up the hours. Also, I shall require you to pass me out on the Seneca."

"Jean-Claude will do that."

"Jana, I want you."

"A few weeks ago you wanted Dirk. It's emotion talking, Didi. Jean-Claude has many more hours on the Seneca than I have."

Didi wiped perspiration from her forehead. "I've never exactly understood the word but I believe you are what Americans call cool."

"I am and it's kept me alive. I want you to be cool too, Didi."

They walked to the parked Porsche and Jana smiled as Didi put on her stilettos. "Power shoes," Jana said.

"I suppose so," replied Didi. "Well, my expert instructor, we have at least one more lesson. After my famous solo – which I am now compelled to achieve – would you at least have dinner with me? Plus champagne."

"Champagne!" Jana raised her hands in mock horror. "I could be flying the following day."

"Oh Jana, don't be so difficult."

"Just teasing. Of course I'll come and drink your champagne."

A moment's awkward silence as Didi considered the propriety of an embrace rather than a handshake. Jana took her hands. "And there's that question which kindness prevented you asking. It's as you guessed. It's the reason why I fly. And why I am good at it."

"And there's another question."

"That will have to wait, Perhaps for the champagne."

And now they were able to embrace without awkwardness.

TIRED again, but more pleasantly than before, Jana walked back to the office to report Didi's lesson to Jean-Claude, and found him chatting to Vincent Chauvelet. Vincent said, "Mlle Nordmeyer. You must think I'm pursuing you. But your mobile wasn't switched on."

"I switch it off during flying lessons."

"Of course. I saw your van and waited. But please, you have business with M. Grosmont. I will wait outside."

Jean-Claude had watched these exchanges distantly. When they were alone he said, "I fear M. Chauvelet is inclined to reveal his private life. And it seems to concern you. I hope I haven't told him any of your secrets."

"He has problems with his wife and their son's future. I let the son see the Cessna; that didn't go down well with the wife. I apologised and tried to back off. But Vincent wants me to continue being involved with his son."

"Welcome to the suburbs. My lips are sealed. How did things go with the blessed Dieudonné?"

"She prefers Didi. She's ready to solo. I tested her good and hard and I have no doubts at all."

"Details please."

Jana explained and Jean-Claude smiled, almost to himself. "I wonder how well I'd have done that for you."

"Don't be silly, J-C. You'd have flown it blindfold. She's very pleased with herself and, of course, grateful. Wants me to pass her out on the Seneca. Complete nonsense, you're the one with Seneca hours."

Jean-Claude stared at her. "You look quite tired."

"Instruction takes me that way. But don't worry. I enjoy it. And I made progress with M. Daoust. I won't waste too much time with Chauvelet."

Who was leaning against the side of her van. "I will not keep you tonight. You have had a busy day. However, I am visiting my parents – alone – tomorrow afternoon and perhaps we could speak then."

Jana said, "It would be wrong to arrange anything hidden from your wife. My advice is that you tell her what you have in mind, even invite her. Otherwise she may misunderstand your reasons."

"Or, perhaps, understand them," he said enigmatically. "We will talk about this tomorrow."

When Jana arrived home Claire Chazal was starting to unfold the TF1 eight o'clock news with further horrible revelations about Afghanistan. Jana hesitated in front of the Chauvelets' screen and was urged to sit down. Five minutes later Sylvie handed her a bowl of warmed-up soup, later a slice of tarte ta-tin. Jana had been out of touch with the war for a week or so and struggled to keep up with a report from TF1's political correspondent. The sentences seemed to get longer and more abstract.

Abruptly she shuddered and woke up in the darkened living room. Someone had draped a rug over her shoulders and her wristwatch showed 3.41. Shamefaced she hurried upstairs to her own room, removed only her windproof and her suede boots and fell asleep again on top of the duvet.

CHAPTER SEVEN

French Sunday lunch

ABRADED by her outdoor clothes she woke again at six. Strong sun through uncurtained windows warmed her face and she dreamed of floating away, seeing herself from above – a mere object, much reduced in importance. Fearful, she rolled away from the glare, trying to re-establish what thirty-eight years had achieved.

Jana, she had learned, was a corrupt form of Diana but that meant little since she'd never been drawn to mythology. Her mother had seen the name in a child's story about female timber wolves and had dismissed her father's preferences that went no further than greetings cards. Once Jana was old enough she approved the choice and fancied she heard the she-wolf howling her name in the northern forests.

Because the USA prefers to be literal she had to fight to have the j pronounced as y. Simultaneously she insisted on spelling the name with a j instead of a y. Written out, Yana looked weak, over-feminine, a long way from her hard schooling. As to her surname the ill-informed imagined it was a seventeenth-century byblow whereas it dated back only to the early twentieth. Her grandfather's trawler had gone down fishing off the Grand Banks and Hans-Georg Nordmeyer had opted, like other immigrant Germans, to switch to farming and mew himself up in the anonymous central states of the USA.

On Sundays the Chauvelets got up an hour later, thus it was too early for Jana to shower. As she took off her slept-in jeans she remembered Ginette pointing to them and asking whether she'd been a *garcon manqué* when young. It took time to translate "failed youth" as tomboy but it wasn't the first time the point had been raised. Even in high school there'd been accusations and it had been easier to say yes rather than no. To pretend to fictitious vandalism as a way of avoiding further jeering. The matter had re-surfaced at college since flying was often seen as a tomboy occupation. But it was only in the air force, when she met women who were true tomboys, that she knew she didn't belong in that sexual halfway house.

At thirty-eight, did typecasting matter? Labouring jobs were inevitable with a small airline. Loading freight and washing down planes might be seen as tomboyish. But when Ginette put the question Jana wanted to protest. Wanted to bring in the allusive, teasing conversations with Ghislaine. So, so superior to Dirk's casual chat which typed her as a competitor or merely a woman denied her oats through an administrative error.

She sighed. Being solitary sometimes meant subduing feminine traits and sometimes accepting them. On her rare forays into what passed for society Jana Nordmeyer needed to be a natural, unexaggerated woman - just as capable of rejecting male overtures as being friendly. As to slow-moving Vincent Chauvelet, surely all he really wanted was a nanny figure for Octavien as his tenuous marriage fell apart. Nothing more.

In any case she could now leave her bedroom. She had a plan to blot out the image of the ageing acquaintance who fell asleep before her hosts' television.

Wearing her cotton bathrobe, she collected her laundry and stripped her bed (normally Sylvie's task), taking the pile downstairs and feeding the washing machine. Since she would later be part of the French Sunday lunch her first (unauthorised) contribution was to peel potatoes and leave them under water in a pan on the stove.

Next she returned to her room, put on new jeans and walked down to the village to buy croissants and three baguettes at the boulangerie. At a temporary stall that appeared in the church square only on Sunday mornings she bought a bunch of freesias.

Back at the house Sylvie appeared in the driveway.

"Jana, what are you doing?" Almost an accusation.

"Jana breaks her routine and the earth moves. Here's bread and croissants with flowers for grandmother's grave. I hope flowers bought by me are acceptable."

"Of course. But there is no need…"

"No need? I was ashamed; it was kind of you to let me sleep."

"My dear, don't concern yourself. You work so hard."

"My bed linen is washing with my laundry."

"My dear… " Sylvie wasn't pleased by these disruptions but Jana didn't care. Falling asleep needed atonement: something out of the ordinary.

Hugues joined them and they had their breakfast in silence broken finally by Jana. "If I could put the meat in the oven, do the vegetables, whatever, while you are in church I would be more than pleased." But Sylvie had no intention of handing over an expensive joint to someone whose skills as a cook were un-known. She shook her head and uttered a sh-ing sound which French women reserve for events beyond contemplation.

The Chauvelets left in clothes reserved for churchgoing: a flowered dress bought for 15 euros in the Thursday street market and, in Hugues' case, a smooth fabric jacket so tight that it must have dated back twenty years. Neither was poor but clothing was thought unimportant. In any case cheap shabbiness would be a commonplace in the congregation.

Jana set the table for five since, from time immemorial, the next-door Piaillers were expected. After a long – US length – shower she went back to her room to prepare her final surprise. Her ash blonde urchin cut was still wet as she combed it into two arcs bracketing the sides of her face. With the fingers of her left hand as a scissor-like guide she edged round the extremities with real scissors, removing a precise 17 mm. Heat from the hair dryer caused the edges to curl inwards.

The hair styling wasn't parsimony, rather self-defence. A se-ries of French stylists had insisted on creating an angled slash of hair which bisected her face diagonally, giving her a menacing thirties Berlin look. This she could do without. The parentheses on either side added a briskness that might pass for efficiency,

What the Chauvelets had not seen before was a tan gaberdine skirt tight enough to render her rump and thighs as an enlarged wine goblet. This she now examined, turning one way and the other at the wardrobe mirror, telling herself that the hobbling of her knees was a price worth paying. The skirt had been bought for a Gascon Air open day when J-C demanded a garment more feminine than trousers. But the fabric was susceptible to spilt wine and the skirt had remained on a hanger ever since.

As a final detail she opened her blouse neck by one extra button and filled the gap with a dark green tulle foulard.

In her wardrobe she had a single bottle of California zinfandel, bought in a Toulouse supermarket for an aborted party. Jana knew little about wine. Even so she knew more than the Chauvelets who were governed by a blind faith in cheap, tannic drenches labelled baldly Bordeaux. Would the lunchers reject her zinfandel out of hand? Perhaps not, if the bottle were already open and she downplayed it as "an experiment."

As she heard the hall door being opened she slipped on her only pair of brown court shoes and went down to meet everyone. The reaction was gratifying. Even the male Piailler, who resisted everything transatlantic, uttered a small, high pitched grunt. Hugues went further with "Charming."

After the greetings the two men resumed an argument that must have started soon after the freesias had been laid on Grandmother Chauvelet's tombstone (a rectangle of granite polished to such high gloss it looked like black plastic). Hugues, it seemed, had incautiously admitted to admiring Christine Lagarde, then finance minister in France. The male Piailler, whose first name nobody, not even his mouse-like wife, used growled that Lagarde looked "suspicious". Asked to enlarge he damned her in bursts of south-west France patois from which shallow, flighty and "a tease" were just about detectable.

Jana who saw Christine Lagarde as the most stylish, witty and persuasive politician in the world, and who nursed a secret ambition to look like her when she reached that age, decided it was time to enter the discussion. She knew she would never be invited to contribute but would be tolerated if she did. She knew too that her attempts to undermine M. Piailler's sexism had taken on a certain piquancy. That, deep down, he rather enjoyed these disputes provided she stuck by certain rules never completely articulated.

"In fact, Christine Lagarde is a woman," Jana said brightly.

"Ah, Mlle l'Aviatrice. That is true. A new trend, you could say. Not only a woman but a beginner, lacking experience."

"Unlike those deeply skilled statesmen – with their enormous moustaches – who directed France so expertly in 1914 and in 1939."

Hugues looked on uneasily. He was better educated than his neighbour, a retired carpenter who had worked only in wood, "never this wretched PVC and alu." But he lacked M. Piailler's zestful cunning and his tendency to disagree. Besides, M. Piailler needed no one to defend him.

"I doubt those statesmen's wives would have done any better. And surely mademoiselle you cannot quarrel with the destiny the Good Lord has set out for women. Perhaps they might become statesmen – better even than men – but there is one skill in which they are quite superior. Always will be. To compete, a man needs a laboratory. Whereas a woman only needs herself."

The reference to the Good Lord touched on one of those ill-defined rules whereby M. Piailler, spraying the ground like a dog out for a walk, defined his no-go territories. To keep on playing Jana would have to make a detour.

"But M. Piailler some women can do two things simultaneously. Ségolène Royal has four children and has led a party. Her successor, Martine Aubry, is at least married."

He contorted his face comically. "But they are Socialists, mademoiselle."

Riskily, Jana replied, "In my father's house there are many mansions." wondering whether chateaux would pass as mansions.

"I am enchanted you are not beyond the influence of Mother Church."

At this point Hugues' resolve cracked and he insisted his neighbour came out into the garden to examine "a matter of some pride". Hugues' indifferent skills as a gardener were well known and the contestants smiled good-naturedly at this thinly disguised diversion. Since Sylvie was occupied in the kitchen this left only Mme Piailler who had never, to Jana's knowledge, initiated a conversation. Jana had often found herself in similar *tetes à tete*, Mme le Lannic being one early colloquist. The fodder was dull but not entirely a dead loss. Having discussed the weather, past, present and future, with a selection of maiden aunts and widows over the months, Jana now treasured a vocabulary and phraseography that lay outside daily life at Gascon Air. The *Je vous en prie* mode, as Jean-Claude explained, in which even the commonest requests and observations were hedged about by extreme expressions of politeness. Working her slot machine, Jana prodded Mme Piailler into a string of these elocutions until lunch was announced. By then Jana had modified her presentation of the zinfandel. "Regard this as a Franco-US experience. Half glasses only. If no one likes it I will be more than happy to pour it down the sink."

Anti-US opinion might have told against the wine had Hugues not admitted - fatally - he had never heard of zinfandel and wondered if it was expensive. When Jana mentioned a figure four times that of the normal lunchtime bottle everyone demanded full glasses. And since the zinfandel was the exception and a bitter *petit-chateau* Bordeaux the rule, a bottle of the latter was also opened.

M. Piailler became uncharacteristically genial. "I was impressed, mademoiselle, by your robust defence of modern women," he said with twinkling insincerity.

"It's obligatory, m'sieu. Given the option men would insist I wasn't fitted to fly a plane. *Kinder, Küche und Kirche*, as the Germans say."

Few provincial French admitted to German and there was no answer. However Jana's profession often seemed a puzzle to rural Frenchmen and Hugues asked her whether flying was difficult to learn.

She said, "The qualifications are simple. But the student must want to fly. If, for instance M. Piailler expressed that wish I am sure I could teach him."

M. Piailler suspected he was being teased. "Perhaps you are the exception, mademoiselle; you know machines. And you are, after all, American. But I see women driving cars carelessly. Is flying a plane… natural?"

"Not at all. Otherwise the Good Lord would have given us wings. Despite that many French women fly planes. Yesterday I gave a last lesson to a French woman who is a superb pilot. Who learned very quickly how to fly."

Since Jana's student had to be local Hugues asked her name and the table recognised it immediately. Both men appeared cast down. Dieudonné – God-given in more ways than one. Already successful in one arcane field, Didi had branched out.

"She intends to buy a plane – with two engines! – and practice her law all over the country."

This news proved so depressing that post-lunch talk lurched to a halt and the Piaillers departed sullenly soon after. Although Sylvie protested Jana insisted on helping with the washing-up and she was still holding the tea-towel when Vincent – whose plans she had completely forgotten – arrived. His fixed expression looked serious and when Jana moved towards the stairs she was asked to stay "on behalf of Octavien".

Sylvie timidly proposed opening another bottle but a male hand waved dismissively. It was agreed they would remain indoors rather than risk being overheard on the patio.

"Mlle Nordmeyer is already involved," said Vincent. "But from the best of motives."

Solemn nods from the parents.

Vincent appeared to be ticking off a checklist. "I should say the disagreement between Yvonne and myself is wider than a fracas about a simple car repair. She insists Octavien should follow his grandfather. I want him to make up his own mind. He may have done just that. Engineering seems to fascinate him."

More nods.

"Some say he is too young to know his mind. But a counter-vailing argument says he is too young to have a future thrust upon him."

The mixture of zinfandel and cheap Bordeaux had lowered Jana's resistance to Vincent's excesses. But she stirred slightly at "countervailing".

"Some say he's more intelligent than his years. I suppose this disposes of the previous two arguments." Pleased by this circular conclusion Vincent allowed himself a mirthless smile.

He continued, "How could watching this procedure harm Octavien? Yvonne thought it outrageous, as if we were corrupting him. Perhaps Mlle Nordmeyer's gender played a part." Vincent turned to Jana. "I hope all this is not too embarrassing."

Time to show she was still awake. "Things have been harder for you."

"Indeed." He turned to his parents. "And now another problem. I did make an immoral suggestion to Mlle. Nordmeyer. I bitterly regret that."

Even Jana's eyes widened. "A deception so that Octavien could watch the repair." Vincent's face, pinched till now, relaxed. "I'm sorry Mama. Let me explain. I mention this repair, this procedure, as if it were a heart transplant. But it's quite simple and will take less than two hours. It is a measure of Octavien's innocence he thinks it so important. Is that not so, Mlle Nordmeyer?"

"I am not a God-given mechanic," said Jana.

"God-given?" The word didn't fit Vincent's plain talk. "I rather doubt that. However Mlle Nordmeyer points out the deception could harm Octavien. Very stupid of me. Mlle Nordmeyer had a better suggestion. That I should invite Yvonne to watch the repair too."

The faces of the elder Chauvelets were tense. It wouldn't have been their choice

Vincent shrugged. "I tried yesterday. It didn't go well. For Yvonne it was an ultimatum and I was accused of many things. Ours has been an unhappy marriage and we now have what lawyers call a *casus belli* with Octavien as the battleground. If I agree to a separation I may see my son twice a month. The alternative is Yvonne will petition a court saying I am unfit to be Octavien's father."

Jana stood up. "I appreciate the background. But surely this is now between you and your parents."

Vincent looked up, his face wearied and troubled, real signs of how much Octavian meant to him. "There is not much more but it does concern you. Please stay for a few moments. The fact is I must move out of my home. Eventually I will find somewhere to live. A hotel perhaps…"

"Oh no," said Vincent's parents, appalled at such domestic disintegration.

"You must stay here. I can easily move," said Jana. A horrible prospect but Vincent's beaten look had touched her. The other three faces shone with relief, then, immediately, with guilt.

"Jana," cried Sylvie, and began to sob. Hugues was frozen and incapable and Jana reached over awkwardly to take Sylvie's arm.

"*Merde!*" said Vincent and Jana liked him the more for that. "Always these consequences. I cannot ask you for this… Jana."

"There is the linen room," said Hugues vaguely.

It was as if someone had said "You have the plane." Jana reacted sharply. "Far too small. Vincent needs space for Octavien. We can improvise. I take the linen room and move if things become impossible."

The room was indeed small. A single bed occupied half the floorspace leaving only a narrow surrounding footpath. Jana's wardrobe sat uneasily out on the landing, forcing everyone to push past it. At each ugly rearrangement Sylvie's head dropped and she sobbed again. Jana put an arm round her shoulders, "Think of Octavien… and Vincent. Have an early night. Let Hugues comfort you." Retiring at seven in the evening was unheard of but eventually the elderly pair decided to shuffle upstairs.

Denied cognac Vincent made do with *pineau des charentes* and lay exhausted on a lounger on the patio. "You are very generous, Mlle Nordmeyer – that is Jana."

"Two syllables rather than five. Much more efficient." Jana accepted a glass of sticky fortified drink the French unaccountably call an aperitif and sat on an upright plastic chair.

He laughed weakly and gazed out at the other houses on the estate, orange tinted walls, roofed in heavy undulating tiles. "You see me as the eternal engineer. Jean-Claude said you trained in the USAF. Doesn't that require a technical degree?"

"It could have been basket-weaving. My father was in distribution and suggested logistics science as an easy option. It meant nothing to the USAF. They were more impressed I'd paid for flying lessons as a civilian."

"And you wanted to fly - what are they called? – planes of war? So why are you not in Afghanistan?"

Jana said, "I didn't make the grade."

Vincent swallowed *pineau* and winced at the sweetness. "You don't look like a failure."

"USAF fails more pilots than it passes."

"And yet war seems simple: kill or be killed. I suppose I'm glad you didn't make the grade. I had another reason for coming here today."

Jana stiffened.

"Of no consequence to you but it is to me. It occurred to me I'd taken a narrow view of my son. Pushing him into some form of engineering. But if I had seen him respond to Yvonne – to history – I'd have been happy. I read history for pleasure. Not just the Albigensian heresy which fascinates so many in this part of France. Ancient history, Bismarck's integration of Germany, post-independence USA, anything. I don't know why I'm telling you this but somehow it seems necessary. Should I recite the kings of England to prove my point?"

Jana relaxed. "I wouldn't know if you'd got them in order.

"How about US presidents?"

"Same again. I stop at Millard Fillmore. But you needn't do any of this. I'm the one who's mono-culture. In any case it doesn't matter. What does matter is that Octavien means a lot to you."

"A matter of self-defence," he sighed. "Yvonne comes from a family of academics. Her parents were *professeurs* in Paris – the liberal arts, of course, as the Anglos say. She herself was engaged to a *maître de conferences* in archaeology at Lyons who broke things off very close to the wedding. I think she never really recovered. She had a *licence* in central European languages and worked for GEC-Alsthom where I met her. Impressive, confident. So much so I didn't notice how eager she was to marry. But what a terrible mistake afterwards. How dominant she was – and is. We live in a house she chose, take holidays in Hungary and Romania, spend many weekends in Paris with her parents. The hardest blow was when she stopped visiting my parents; they bored her, she said."

Jana recalled the dictatorial voice on her mobile.

Vincent continued. "I'm a rather poor Catholic but I do believe in marriage. Or did. When Octavien was born I transferred my battered affections to him. Yvonne allowed this but anything to do with his education was her province. Even my enthusiasm for history – his supposed goal in life – didn't count. I was told not to interfere. My approach was not 'structured'."

Jana wondered whether she would meet Yvonne. She hoped so. Dragons have a special appeal.

"I didn't immediately give in. There were arguments, bitter arguments. Our fights affected Octavien but Yvonne either didn't notice or didn't care. Nothing mattered than that she should prevail. Rather as it was in the Viet Nam war. Oh, my God! How tactless. I had forgotten your nationality." He smiled wistfully. "Your French is too good."

"Don't worry. At least you didn't accuse me of lynching blacks."

"Who did?"

"Some PCF gook in a Perpignan bar. Go on."

Vincent reached out for the bottle of *pineau* on the floor, thought better and withdrew his hand. "You may think I've been feeble accepting Yvonne's terms but things will not rest there. I shall take legal advice as soon as I can. There'll be support for me once a court has heard Yvonne in full song."

Jana dangled her sticky empty glass. "A beer? I know Hugues has some. I'll get another pack on the way home tomorrow."

"I'm hardly a blessing on this house. I dispossess you, subject you to misery and forget my duties as a host. Also I prefer 'ardent spirits'. Perhaps because I want to get drunk."

Jana cleared her throat suggestively. "Hugues does have cognac on the premises. I know where he keeps it. But it's sort of secret. He's not entirely..."

Vincent roared with laughter. "... not entirely generous with it. My father is a great and good man but not open-handed. I've never known why. Tell me where it is and I'll explain I found it by accident."

Jana took a Kronenbourg from the fridge and Vincent returned to the patio with an alarmingly full glass. "I shall make this last, I promise. Let me offer you this sole lounger."

Jana shook her head. "It doesn't go with my New World character."

Ha laughed again. "I believe you said you were unmarried. But that doesn't always mean a lot these days."

"Unpartnered, then."

"Really? And you left the USA because of... no, I apologise, but there is a reason for asking. In our rare moments alone Octavien continues to ask about you. Not only about the cam-belt but whether he will see you again. You can understand why. He has not met many women who have mastered engines. I know your work is demanding but would you consider speaking to him occasionally. I think we can safely discount more attacks – physical or verbal – by Yvonne."

"I'd be delighted."

As she tried to make herself comfortable that evening in her tiny cabin of a room it was hard to avoid thinking about Octavien. As a pawn between adults he was still in play. On the other hand, Vincent wasn't devoid of stolid, honourable attractions and an evening out – with or without Octavien – would carry a low level of emotional risk.

CHAPTER EIGHT

New cam-belt

MORE sacrifices were demanded the following morning. Jana got up in good time to avoid hogging the bathroom but not before Vincent who could be heard singing Bewitched – seemingly in French - under the shower. Usually she left the house too early for breakfast but the Chauvelets were incapable of letting Vincent leave unfuelled. Hugues had even collected baguettes. By the time she had showered and dressed the kitchen smelt of coffee and it seemed churlish not to sit at the table.

Vincent had just finished explaining how he had come upon Hugues' "well hidden" cognac which he promised to replace. Now he complimented Jana robustly on her freshness.

"We need your logistics skills," he added. "The driveway has become – literally – a critical path. Our vehicles need sequencing."

"My hours are irregular. I'll park on the street," she said, but Vincent wouldn't have it.

"No more mortification Mlle Nordmeyer, that is, Jana. I slept badly last night, my thoughts on you in that tiny room. I may have a solution. I'll speak to a colleague at work."

As Jana drove to the airport she couldn't help feeling Vincent was more like a man celebrating liberation than a father on the brink of breaking a decade-long marriage. After a kilometre it began to drizzle and she switched on the windscreen wipers; for some reason the rain was significant but she couldn't think why.

This was one of Armelle's mornings and her quiet efficiency replaced Ginette's chattering. Jean-Claude was presently on the return leg of the regular Bordeaux – Paris contract flight and would fly to Tarbes to discuss a marketing venture with the Hotel de Ville. If these proposed trans-Pyrenean tourist flights succeeded Gascon Air might well need both another plane and another pilot.

Jana had nothing to do. Once this might have meant lolling at her desk, tossing balls of paper into the waste basket and trying to egg Armelle into indiscretions. But the Internet had changed all that and there were at least two dozen websites she could usefully trawl, varying from Cessna's technical updates to blogs run by professional pilots and, especially, flying instructors. Half an hour spent in this way was pleasant enough but not sufficiently absorbing to shut out the realities of the airfield. Jana was lucky enough that the office's single window did not overlook Gascon Air's hardstanding and a nagging view of the stationary Cessna.

In the Air Force economics had been a distant theory. In civil aviation it was everything. Not just accountancy data but a grinding awareness of what it cost to own and operate a plane. Never more apparent than when she left the USAF's cocoon.

Almost immediately she found it impossible to make a living from her parents' house in Flagstaff. Northern Arizona demographics were against her. Despite the town's well-educated population there was none of the disposable income that goes with flying light planes, let alone owning them. Phoenix, on the other hand, was too large and had attracted a huge cluster of aviation companies not merely in the state capital but throughout nearby Glendale, Scottsdale and Chandler. Phoenix would be worth another look once she'd become established. Tucson, five to six hours drive from Flagstaff, was the logical base. But working there meant living there.

In Tucson "living" took on another meaning. Having somewhere to sleep, cook and wash during those early months was an ill-defined experience and quite often the car provided all three services. That same Chevy wagon she'd used to get to Mesa Field for basic instruction and which her father had finally discarded with a quarter of a million miles on the odometer. If she flew rarely then she had plenty of chances to practise her cunning especially when it came to tranquil nights. Places she could sleep the night away in the back of her car existed but they weren't immediately obvious. Car parks were a no-no as solitary vehicles were investigated by the law and those who broke it. Unexplained cars were also regarded as suspicious in rural or semi-rural surroundings. Far better the squalor of an industrial zone so long as she rose early and departed.

Even less bearable was the financial nightmare of renting a plane and looking for business equipped solely with a mobile phone. When a family of three finally called her, needing to attend a wedding at Lake Havasu City, she felt physically sick after the call ended. The suicidally low rates she had quoted wouldn't cover costs and her personal hygiene was at such a low ebb she drove through the night to Flagstaff to shower and to borrow a summer dress from her mother. Why all the fuss? Lisa had asked. Because she worried she might ruin the day for the wedding party. Lisa had opened a tiny purse symbolically too small to contain much money and slipped twenty dollars into her hand.

By this time her father had retired from Purina with cancer that would soon kill him. He was upstairs, sitting on his bed, when she kissed him goodbye and he awkwardly tucked thirty bucks into her pocket whispering "Don't tell your mother." As she started to leave he continued to hold her. "There's a book down there with a marker. You can reach it easier than me."

When she tried to hand it over he shook his shining head, bald from the chemo. "You keep it."

"It's one of your poetry books."

"I know, but I'm making a bet. Remember the lit. course work I helped you with? I always thought there was a chance you might show an interest."

She didn't ask about the marker, didn't dare. Driving south on I17 towards Phoenix, round about Camp Verde, she reached back for the heavy book and rested it on her thighs against the steering wheel. Opened it at the marker and, five seconds at a time on the empty road, read Christina Rossetti in snatched lines:

> *And dreaming through the twilight*
> *That doth not rise nor set,*
> *Haply I may remember,*
> *And haply may forget.*

Late that evening, back from Lake Havasu City with her passengers, she drove straight to the timber products company and took over the forklift on the night shift. At two in the morning she checked out a fifteen-minute break, bought coffee at the vending machine and walked over to her locker to allow herself the luxury of reading the poem in one pass. Even as she turned the key she remembered she'd had to dash to make the time clock and had left her shoulder bag on the back seat of the Chevy. Anyone could have opened that rickety old car with a folded sheet of notepaper and someone had.

Her father died ten days later and, irony of ironies, she had a flight on the day of the funeral. It was the worst day of her life and from then on her father's death was inextricably linked in her memory with the horrors of extreme poverty. Using the money she'd have spent on gas getting to Flagstaff she mailed lilies and a transcription of the Rossetti looked up in a cyber-cafe. With the battery capacity of her mobile waning, she called her mother from a supermarket car park, well away from the sight and smell of light aircraft. "I want to come home and live with you," she said.

"Angel, that's plain foolishness."

A few days later she found a second-hand copy of the anthology at a Phoenix bookshop. It was a bittersweet moment to discover that it qualified as a rare volume and the asking price was fifty dollars. She could live a week on that. That evening, on the edge of running out of airtime, serving behind a bar at Ryan Airfield, she met Dirk.

He bent to look at her name tag. "Nordmeyer. Why does that ring a bell?"

"Ask my bank manager."

"That shirt says you fly."

"In a limited kind of way."

"Gimme a Rochefort Trappiste, the bottle, no glass." And this gorgeous – rather too gorgeous – young man shuffled over to a group of his siblings, no doubt to pass out of Jana's life forever. Except that in three minutes he was back.

"Hey Nordmeyer, suppose I said nine hours."

"I'd say fluke. I peaked early."

"Don't believe a word of it. Now listen up."

He'd been through it all, just as she had, and was sympathetic. Eighteen months in all. Now he was an independent pilot on and off the books of a medium sized airline, following what his less handsome male friends called the Ski Instructor Route - leisure flights for Tucson's outdoor women. He also had a favourable theory about women pilots.

In standing in for him when he was over-booked Jana began - as he predicted - to make a marginal living from a sub-set of Dirk's clientele; women who preferred a pilot of their own gender, providing she had no pretentions towards glamour. At the time Jana owned two pairs of jeans.

When Dirk left for France some clients transferred to Jana on his recommendation. She was thus able to buy a second-hand trailer in which she often showered three times a day. And to lease a twenty-year-old Comanche. As part of the community of Tucson pilots, all of whom had known Dirk, she occasionally drank soft drinks to their beers and made wry jokes about flyers dying broke. But those early days, waking up at five in, say, the truck park of a steel stockholder, were an acid reminder of how bad things could get. And that the so-called good times were never free from paradox – impoverished pilots at the command of wealthy passengers – that marked the fragility of aviation economics.

Now, sitting unproductively at her Gascon Air desk, she was continuously aware that the (thankfully unseen) Cessna 172R out there, bought for 120,000 euros, ate up 450 euros a month without even taking to the air. Sure, it was Jean-Claude's ultimate responsibility but flying was her life.

What was it about rain she needed to remember? The answer arrived late in the morning.

Armelle picked up the phone and announced the company in well-modulated if unnecessarily sympathetic tones. Then said to Jana, "A Mr Willis, I think originally from the USA."

The name meant nothing but a burst of slangy American English clarified things. "Doubt you even know my last name. I'm Boyce; remember, at the Bayonne jazz club?"

Ghislaine's discovery. The SocleSoft functionary who believed love was best tested during discouraging weather.

"Hi there. How's Ghislaine?"

"More and more fascinating. So French! I know that must sound damn stupid but it's what races my motor. She insists I read Romain Gary, that I make my 'ing' more nasal. And she's trying to make me buy a C5."

"What's that?"

"Jana, you've been here two years and you know nothing. It's a Citroen. Which is a car."

"She's good company. We eat out and she makes me laugh."

"Me too. Anyway I've got a trip planned and you could help. A buddie with SocleSoft Italy has an apartment in Genoa. He's away for a week and says we're welcome to it for a coupla days. Driving there would use up too much time. How about you fly us? But it's got to be tomorrow?"

"Can you start early? I have a freight run in the afternoon."

"Dawn'd be romantic."

"Say seven am. That's early enough. But I must warn you, have you ever been to Genoa before?"

"Never."

"The air strip runs east to west on reclaimed land out in the Med. Steep slopes north drop straight into the sea and there's a hellish downdraft. The approach is mostly from the west and even civil airlines slip and slide a lot. The Cessna will jump like a ping-pong ball. I'm sure you've flown a lot but I promise you'll find it scary."

"Shit! Can you handle it?"

Jana laughed. "I can. Can you? Or will you shoot your cookies? And what about your French cookie?"

Boyce laughed back. "It'll be a nationality thing. Ghislaine would rather slit her wrists than vomit in front of me. And vice versa. I'll pass on the details the way you passed them on."

"Once you're down – and you've cleaned up anything you've left on the deck – you'll have a great time. Genoa's a proper city."

"Tell the truth I'd have a great time even if it was Hackensack, Noo Joisey."

"Happy about that, Boyce."

Jana reflected on the day she'd left Mme. le Lannic's house. Ghislaine, a peripheral figure, had wanted to be friends. She'd seemed provincial, slightly gaunt and slightly reticent. Deserving of charity. Now, paired off with a black US executive with glittering shaven head and a tailored suit she had taken on her own glitter. But was Boyce perhaps too fashionable? And was his potential US bolthole something to worry about? Jana cared very much that Ghislaine remained unhurt. There was nothing she could do personally but she was comforted by Boyce's fascination with Ghislaine's Frenchness, the feature that made her a rare collectable.

Jana explained the itinerary to Armelle who entered the details into the booking log. Faced with a round trip of 1700 km and a fuel range of 1200 km she used the laptop to check aviation fuel prices in Italy but they dead-heated with France. She then scrolled through the Defence Ministry's website for the new co-ordinates of an enlarged military no-fly zone in Alpes de Haute Provence. Had a preliminary look at tomorrow's weather system. Pre-flighted the Cessna and trundled over to the re-fuelling pumps. Finally she re-read the regulations at Christoforo Columbo airport for any changes since her last flight.

By which time Jean-Claude was back from his marketing trip to Tarbes which had left him cautiously optimistic.

"If we need another pilot, have you got anyone in mind?" Jana asked.

"Perhaps I will contact Dirk."

She smiled. "You do flatter the Yanks."

"They're more professional. Even the amateurs."

She told him about Boyce's booking. "Is his credit card strong?"

"He works for SocleSoft."

Jean-Claude said, "You warned him about Christoforo Columbo? Ah yes, you must have. You've flown there yourself. And you've checked that no-fly zone near Barcelonette? They've increased... Why am I asking? I don't need to."

"Because I won't be offended."

"The perfect answer," He scratched his nose. "My wife asks me if I'm in love with you. It's a joke when I mention you once too often. When are we ever going to find time for you to have lunch with us?"

"When the Tarbes thing comes off."

"You say 'when' not 'if'."

"That's right."

At the Chauvelets there was champagne on the table, courtesy Vincent. "My dear Jana, your selflessness is at an end. I am lent a caravan and it will be installed this evening at the side of the house. Take a long, long shower and I will move your belongings back."

The evening meal was a convivial affair for Hugues and Sylvie also. Both had faced the gloomy likelihood that Jana's rent would have to be reduced. And since Vincent had delivered the compensatory Courvoisier, the elderly couple permitted themselves digestifs. There seemed little regret that Yvonne had passed out of their family circle but perhaps this wasn't surprising given that they bored their daughter-in-law.

"Another bonus," said Vincent. "Yvonne will see her parents in Paris this weekend and she thought it better not to take Octavien. So he will caravan with me. May we arrange that strange treat he so desires."

"But Jana should not spend her little free time doing repairs for entertainment," said Hugues. "When you were younger and poorer, Vincent, you spent many Saturday afternoons underneath that terrible old Renault."

"I would volunteer, but I believe Octavien would be disappointed."

Jana nodded. "Octavien has an exaggerated view of pilots. Doesn't believe their finger nails should get filthy. But he has never seen me checking the oil or ass up in the footwell looking for a pencil I've dropped. I should have time on Sunday; I already have the replacement belt."

Vincent asked, "Will the audience be only juvenile?"

"No, of course not."

Translated to a new level of generosity, Hugues held up the Courvoisier but Jana shook her head. "I have an early start tomorrow. Flying to Genoa."

Sylvie misheard. "In Switzerland?"

"Not quite that far, That's Geneva. Genoa's in Italy."

"You will need your passport."

"I will indeed." She hadn't told them that one passenger would be the daughter of her former landlady, or the even more fascinating identity of the other. But they probably wouldn't have been surprised. Ahetze was only eight kilometres from Arcanques where Ghislaine and her mother lived, and everyone in both villages would know about Boyce. Happily Ghislaine didn't seem threatened.

Jana had intended to make an early night in her old bedroom. But had first to wait for the elder Chauvelets to clear the bathroom and then brace herself for Vincent.

He picked up the empty champagne bottle and put it in a plastic bin outside the side door. Sat down at the kitchen table and said, "I need to apologise for a very French fault."

She waited, eyebrows cocked.

"You allowed me to use your first name. But here, with my parents, I'm terribly formal. Accidentally I say Mlle. Nordmeyer. I hope this doesn't sound like one of those specialised Gallic insults."

Jana laughed. "French social life's a nightmare. Whenever I get things right I remember the blunders."

"Of course your French isn't perfect but it needn't be. The tiny faults – and they are tiny – add to your charm. Is that patronising? – I hope not. Most French people enjoy hearing an Anglo making an effort."

"Especially a Yank?"

"A Yank! I would never say that."

"A US complication. But simpler than *tutoyer*."

"Almost everything is," said Jana.

He looked at his empty brandy coaster, picked it up, put it down again. "You must know I was grateful about the room. Impressed too; you were so decisive. You recognised what was wrong then spoke – irresistibly."

"Hesitant pilots die young."

Vincent said, "Flying informs your life, I think."

"Flying is my life. Otherwise I'd be mere *néantisme*."

Vincent tested the French word. "What is that in English? Nothingness? I cannot agree."

"But you believe those who fly have special qualities."

"Perhaps. But I do not want to embarrass you."

Her reaction was to deny him the opportunity. But again he'd seen her face as "a difference", a view that seemed to crystallise France. He didn't deserve stifling.

"A risk we both take," she said.

"Embarrassment is two-edged," he said. "In a superficial world you have suffered. Perhaps you'll always suffer. But you are not bitter."

"Flying helps."

"Yet I calculate – engineers always calculate – you spend more time outside the plane. Be objective. How would Sylvie or Hugues judge you? What would Octavien say? Ignore my opinion, I'm biased."

She said nothing.

He said, "I return to Octavien. You do not know children yet you set out to please him. When Yvonne attacked you thought of his feelings. You stepped back, even blamed yourself. You saw my foolish suggestion from the boy's side. In your place I would have argued; instead you protected my son. I'm grateful. But I confess, I'm not objective."

He spoke without emotion, careful not to look at her, allowing her time to notice his Julius Caesar nose, his tired hooded eyes. She said, "Much depends on this wretched cam-belt. Thank God I don't have to rebuild the gearbox."

"That would be a complete rock concert for Octavien."

THEY CAME in two cars since Boyce lived well north of Bayonne. The clothes he wore reminded Jana of the US – bum-hugging whites, a fine-striped shirt good for the office or the promenade, and a golf jacket intended to hang loose. Why couldn't the French do casual clothes? Boyce hugged Jana cheek-to-cheek. "Hi Lindberg. What's the weather? Will my *cocotte* see the sights?"

"Solid cloud at 10,000 feet. Steely light with high contrast. Good detail. Wind north-westerly."

"Gahhd, I love the talk."

Ghislaine was obviously spending more time in the salon - the highlighting must have taken two hours. Her long tan jacket held by a slackly tied belt was very new. Boyce greeted her with an excavatory kiss.

"One thing," he said, handing over two holdalls, "I'm out of the loop the first hour. I'll take a back seat to catch up on bedtime. Won't wear my earphones so you can gossip your asses off."

He was snoring by the time the plane reached the runway. Jana confirmed her clearance and inspected the airspace ahead.

"May I say things as you do this?" Ghislaine asked.

Jana opened the throttle. "Of course. But you may hear me talking to the tower. Wait till I've finished then say again."

"We're moving! This is exciting, my friend is driving this thing. Before it was theory; now you do clever things, examine this *horlogerie*, supervise this little universe. I admire what you do, I expected that. But not this sort of love. Am I fantastical? Do you mind me loving you – only as a pilot, you understand."

Jana said, "A love that will die away quickly I fear. Now everything is new and mysterious. In half an hour you will start to recognise the repetition. Familiar old Jana again."

Ghislaine raised her hand in protest, "Don't say that. This is a romantic journey and you are part of the romance."

"You sound happy."

"I think I am. But tell me, what must I look out for?"

Jana pointed. "To your right. That winding silver strip is the A64 autoroute to Toulouse. From 5000 feet it's almost pretty."

Ghislaine clapped her hands. "You're playing my game. Maintaining the magic." She paused. "Is it still magical for you?"

"Last night I told someone flying is my whole life. He pointed out how little time I spend here in the cockpit. So I'm assuming other things keep me entertained as well. Come out of your romantic bubble for a moment: what kind of woman am I?"

"What was this man's view?"

"That I wasn't bitter."

"Bitter? Of course not. Ah, I understand. Some people might expect that. Happily you disappoint them. What kind of woman? Slightly secretive. Capable of listening. Of being a friend – to me at least. At times you are stern but with reason." Ghislaine gestured round the cockpit. "And then this skill which I – an otherwise serious *pharmacienne* - find worthy of love. Does the man mean anything?"

"He's decent and honourable. Until recently he was persecuted by his wife."

"But could you kiss him?" asked Ghislaine

"No, I think not."

"Would you allow him to kiss you?"

Jana thought. "Perhaps."

Ghislaine sat back. The provincialism had almost disappeared. Her make-up was subtler, it absorbed the angularities rather than highlighting them. Previously she'd worn pendant earrings, now she wore studs. Had she decided the changes or Boyce? Was the will to change more important than knowing what to change?

"Wild France," Ghislaine murmured, looking through the side window.

"The town of Auch at two o'clock."

"Two o'clock? Of course, how clever, how concise. Auch is a hundred kilometres from Bayonne but I have never been there. I shall fly over it, treat it as a carpet. A day of change."

"It rained yesterday," Jana said significantly.

"Yes it did. You listen to me, remember everything - the mark of a friend. And Boyce is like that too. He telephoned me at the pharmacy and said he wanted to talk about the weather. And I knew."

"You *are* happy."

"Realistic I hope. I may be a mere episode. An episode I could never have expected. I shall be 41 in November. Do you like Boyce?"

Jana said, "He is perfect company. I cannot believe he sees you as an episode."

"Really?"

"You are more than he expected."

Ghislaine looked at her manicured hands. "Tell me what is happening in this *bolide*, what will happen."

Jana gestured. "The information is there on the watches and clocks you mentioned. We are suspended five kilometres above wild France. We are not flying as fast as we can, we cruise at 222 kph to save fuel and preserve the engine. In twenty minutes you will start to see Toulouse and we will pass it on the south. Near Toulouse I must listen to ATC – the policemen of the skies. Toulouse is busier than Biarritz; ATC may ask me to change my direction or my altitude to avoid large planes."

Ghislaine nodded. "The non-emotional environment pleases me. The language is numerical; condensed, abrupt. I wanted to study mathematics at university but I wasn't sure I could then earn a living. Here we are on the fringe of mathematics: its efficiency, its directness. And you – my friend - have mastered this world."

"Numbers suppress emotions. Up here emotion must be controlled."

"For pilots, yes. But not for passengers," said Ghislaine.

"Passengers sign on for the emotion." Boyce must have woken and put on his headset without either of them noticing.

"Hi Boyce," said Jana. "There's a musette under the seat. Thermos of coffee, half a dozen croissants. Why don't you hand them round?"

Boyce opened the vacuum flask, filled the screw-on mug. In English, he said, "Here hon, give this to the pilot. Jana should get first sip."

Jana hadn't heard "hon" for a long time. Was it sign of contentment? She glanced to her right and saw them looking at each other. Turned away to avoid intruding

Toulouse ATC confirmed the Cessna's altitude and bearing without correction. Away from that busier airspace they crossed the Parc du Haut Languedoc with its textured green humps undulating out to the horizon. Then over the Rhone. Jana showed them the Garmin GPS. Explained the newly extended military no-fly zone and showed how GPS headings took them safely round. "Now we are in Italy. To be pedantic, Italian airspace."

Boyce rested his hand on Ghislaine's shoulder; she laid her hands over his. Jana looked straight ahead.

Twenty kilometres out she announced her approach to Christoforo Columbo. Wind speed 27 knots from the north.

"Always from the north. Those damn mountains. Boyce, could you pack up the musette and shove it under the seat. Both of you check your seat belts. Wedge your bodies if you can."

At five kilometres out she maintained a higher speed than usual, holding the plane against a wind that wanted to push them out into the Mediterranean. When the speed was finally throttled back the plane dropped a hundred feet, bucked its port wing up, then its starboard wing, dropped another 100 feet, bucked again. A year ago the violence had disturbed her and following the rules too closely made things worse. This time she was ready and landed perfectly, nose slightly up, power down to idle, the hydraulics compressing.

"Holy shit!" said Boyce. She'd forgotten them both for fifteen seconds. Turning on to the taxiway she glanced quickly at Ghislaine and saw her smiling faintly. "Jana, you knew it would be like that."

"My second landing here. This one was better. I'm glad I was alone for the first."

Boyce said. "I honestly thought I was going to die. The only comfort was I was in very good company."

"Flatterer," said Ghislaine.

In Mediterranean sunshine, they walked across the hard-standing to the terminal extension that handled the *douane* for incoming private flights.

"Have a bite with us," said Boyce. "So I can repeat how grateful I am you saved my life. And that of my *cocotte*."

"The *cocotte* agrees."

Jana shook her head. "I have that parking spot for forty minutes only, then I'm hit for big fees. I need to grab a sandwich, gas up and be on my way."

"Into that wind?" asked Boyce, frowning.

"Taking off's easier. In any case it's what I'm paid for. Zero crosswind's no fun at all."

He hugged her as he had when they met that morning. "Gotta speak mah native tongue. Out there I wuz proud to be a US citizen."

Ghislaine took Jana's hands. "These emotional Anglos. How about a cool Gallic farewell?" Her hands reached for Jana's neck. "But not today. A good start to our little holiday. Having our lives saved."

They walked down a hallway to the taxi rank while Jana made her way to a newsagent's kiosk with three shelves of snacks. On impulse Jana turned again to look down the hall-way. They were approaching the outer door where strong sun-shine shrank their silhouettes to blurred triangles, he carrying the two holdalls, she with her arm round his waist. The door opened automatically and they went out into the glare.

Jana bought salami on ciabatta and imitation Orangina, sat down at an all-aluminium table and stripped away clingfilm, realising as she did so the discs of sausage would be beyond her. Her throat felt in spasm. She re-wrapped the film and took small sips of chemically flavoured drink straight from the bottle, trying to understand why Ghislaine's happiness moved her. Perhaps it went back to that moment when Ghislaine picked up a frying pan and a casserole and carried them downstairs. Breaking off to gather newspaper that would stop the vessels rattling in the van. Guessing that her mother's insensitivity had hurt Jana. Announcing rather than suggesting they should meet.

Two nationalities involved but with the traditional roles reversed; as if Boyce were somehow acting on Jana's behalf in a shadowplay yet to be resolved. Jana imagined them making love, black skin against southern France tan, he murmuring French words as part of the love-making, she holding back to guard against "an episode". She giving in, being possessed. He...?

Don't be a bastard, Boyce. Don't be a US bastard.

A LATE *bapteme* and Jana phoned Sylvie Chauvelet to duck out of Sunday lunch. When she arrived mid-afternoon Octavien was sitting on the garden wall, patient and composed. Since their previous meeting much had happened, their relationship must surely have evolved. How for instance should she greet him?

In fact he greeted her, holding out his hand, "Mlle, Nordmeyer, I am happy to meet you again."

"Octavien, I am happy too," she said. "But were we so formal? I can't remember. I'd rather be Jana."

"Mlle Jana?"

"We must ask your father. A subtle point. Too subtle for a foreigner."

By this time Vincent, his parents and even the Piaillers had emerged from the front door. Jana waved in their general direction, knowing etiquette demanded more hand-shaking. "Already we have a problem," she said. "If Octavien's calls me Jana will that ruin his manners, M. Piailler?"

"There is no option. Until Octavien is eighteen he must call you Mlle Nordmeyer, that is the rule. But you will be married by then and he must learn to call you Mme Ix."

"I believe your crystal ball is cracked." Jana turned to Octavien and spread her hands. Had he followed the joshing? "You were right."

He had. "But secretly, Mlle Nordmeyer, you will be Jana. No, that is too familiar. Mlle Jana."

The rest brought chairs from the patio. "Perhaps it should be *Son et Lumière*. Perhaps I should sell tickets. Please get comfortable. I must put on old clothes."

Laying out her tools reminded her of Eliazar. Four days ago a text in execrable French had said La Spezia was now "half official" and he had a six-month contract. This made him simultaneously happy and sorry. Jana put Eliazar out of her mind for the moment.

She tapped the cover at the front of the engine. "Cam-belt, timing belt. What does it do, M. Octavien?"

Opens and closes the engine valves in the "prescribed" order.

"You have done your homework. Why are we changing it?"

Because the synthetic material is old and may break. That would damage the engine. Expensively.

Jana concentrated on removing the cover, explaining how an inline engine was easier to work on than a transverse engine. She pointed at the exposed belt, stretched it to show how flabby it had become, slackened the tensioner, stressed the need to maintain the pulley positions. Octavien answered every question she posed. A quick, casual glance confirmed Vincent Chauvelet was watching her rather than his son. The others had settled into languid positions on their chairs, relaxing while someone else worked.

With the new belt in place Jana had Octavien reposition the tensioner which he accomplished easily. Despite smaller fingers he was less agile when replacing small screws that held the cover in place. With the work complete, he was told to turn the ignition key and start the engine.

The older viewers clapped ironically; Vincent's clapping was fiercest. Sylvie brought out beer and soft drinks and Hugues another garden chair.

"Are you teaching our grandson to be a garage mechanic?" Hugues asked.

"He wants to be an engineer. Identifying engine components can help."

"And you. Repairing aeroplanes is not your *métier*. Why did you learn?"

Jana said, "To save money. I was very poor when I started flying. A car was essential but I could only afford an old one. Besides there is a pride in not depending on others."

Vincent had eased his way over. "Is that an American attitude?" he asked.

"It's a US tradition," said Jana. Each allusion to the USA reminded her of Boyce. He and Ghislaine were returning from Genoa this evening by train. Blissful days perhaps but what next? She went on, "Yanks are thought wasteful but that's old hat. My parents' neighbours repaired their cars and their homes. Some did large projects – adding extensions, building vacation cottages."

Jana watched Octavien politely answering M. Piailler's rough-hewn questions about school and soccer. Vincent noticed this too. "Another trip to the airport perhaps? He'd like that. Especially just the two of you."

Just the two of you. But not always the same two, Jana imagined. What more natural than that Papa might make three? And that Octavien might on occasion be subtracted. But then engineers tended to think strategically.

Jana said, "I need to telephone my mother again. It's an arrangement I have with Jean-Claude to save money with the mobile. I hate to take Octavien away from his grand-parents. And his father. "

Hugues and Vincent looked at each other. "We can spare him for an hour," said Hugues. Vincent, playing the long game, smiled.

This time Jana and Octavien sat inside the Seneca and she noted his enthusiasm had if anything increased. His eyes were intent. "This plane is bigger. I think it will fly further."

"The Cessna's range is 1300 kilometres. The Seneca can fly 1600 kilometres. From here almost to Prague in the Czech Republic."

"How long would that take?"

"Almost seven hours."

"You often fly alone?" he said.

"I do."

"Are you lonely?"

She said, "I have the plane to manage. The route to Prague is over developed countries; I'd be talking to traffic controllers much of the way."

"Are you ever lonely?"

"From time to time. Why do you ask?"

He looked straight ahead. "Mama and Papa do not live in the same house. I may become lonely."

"Are you afraid?"

"I am not sure" He pointed to a gauge. Jana said, "Revolutions per minute, port engine."

"You speak to me differently. Not like M. Piailler."

"Anything else?" asked Jana.

"Many people say I try to be too clever. Mama's friend said I made her shudder. It was a joke, I think. I asked Papa if I could marry you."

"Why would you want to marry me?"

"Because I'd discover things."

Jana locked up the Seneca and they walked to the office. Jana said, "I will call my mother again - in English. Listen if you like. Practice your languages."

"Angel!" said Lisa Nordmeyer.

"When are you coming to Paris?"

"I need to talk about that. I'm sorry, really I am…"

Jana comforted her. "It's OK. It's a costly hop."

"Dave says Paris would be a mite showy on the threshold of a new life." The words were strained, not typical. Jana presumed she was quoting. "Instead, we've fixed the wedding date. No point waiting, Dave says. Two weeks today. I'll understand if you can't make it. "

"Whoa, there. I'll make it. You know that."

Lisa said, "Sorry, angel. I couldn't be sure you approved. Your dad and me, now someone else. "

"Mum, it's your life. I'll be there, give you my blessing. If I'm entitled."

An indeterminate sound with Lisa adding, "And there's Dave."

Jana spoke briskly. "He only has to please you, mum. That gets my blessing. But I'll be there and back. Gascon Air isn't United. I'm half the workforce."

This time a sound that was definitely a sob. "That should be good news, but it isn't. I'm selling the house and we're moving into an apartment. Your room will be gone."

Jana said. "You don't want me in tears. I'm your faraway daughter, home on a flying visit. Don't wreck your schedule for me. Give me the date, the time, your new address and your new landline number. I'll see you in church."

After she'd put down the phone she sat for a moment. The new developments had to be due to Dave; it seemed likely she wouldn't get on with him. And he, no doubt, disapproved of her. How did one hand over one's mother? The idea shocked her. Disturbed by the silence Octavien moved his feet slightly.

"Got that?" she asked.

"There was only one voice."

"My mother's a widow and is remarrying in two weeks' time. I'm attending the wedding."

His eyes widened. "All the way to the USA."

"Flagstaff, Arizona, which will be even trickier."

As they walked to the van Octavien asked, "Why do people get married?"

Jana replied offhandedly, "Because they enjoy each other's company." Then realised the question had nothing to do with Lisa Nordmeyer and everything to do with Octavien.

Over soup at the kitchen table the Chauvelet trio questioned her about Octavien, forcing her to be evasive. Fantasy weddings and loneliness were too raw for discussion and she majored instead – in boring detail – on the comparative ranges of the two planes.

As Sylvie and Hugues were on tenterhooks about a TV programme Jana insisted they move into the lounge leaving her to wash up. Accompanied of course by Vincent. "I suspect Octavien was embarrassing," he said quietly.

"Innocence like that gets to me."

"You are his hero but that role could be a burden. I'll restrain him - gently."

It sounded like an attempt to gain sympathy. But he still looked beaten and depressed. "There are far worse things," she said.

He put down the bowl he'd been drying as if he distrusted his hands. "I've used Octavien to enjoy your company. Even this afternoon." He bowed his head. "Men make awful assumptions about single women."

There was no doubting his pain. She said quietly, "I repeat: I've known worse things."

"But we'll be sharing this house, our meals."

"Your concern has always been Octavien. I could forgive an awful lot for that. Not that there's anything to forgive. You're a father not a roué."

"You trust me?" he asked.

"What's the alternative. Insist you don't look at my boobs and my ankles? Or make suggestive remarks?"

He turned away to face the sink.

CHAPTER NINE

Didi solos and dines

"GIVE me five minutes," said Jana, opening the door of the Cessna and jumping down on to the tarmac. Pilots didn't scamper but she didn't care, relishing the quick run to Gascon Air's office and the rail where Ginette's bike was shackled. Followed by three hundred metres of wobbly cycling over the cracked concrete slabs to the rear of the main terminal. This was the gloomier utilitarian area which the tourists never saw, protected by tubes of razor wire and plastered with warning signs about unauthorised personnel. She showed the scribbled note to the gate guard, chained the bike to a fence and took the lift to a door where yellow and black signs were even more menacing. Inside, and for the first time, she oversaw the runway from the privileged interior of the air-traffic control tower – a modernistic protuberance like the prow of a ship built into a corner of the terminal.

"Thanks a thousand times," she said, handing over a carton of Camels. The ATC officer, tanned almost black despite his artificial working environment, nodded wryly at his forbidden bribe.

"Not a word, of course," he said in that Pyrenean voice Jana had heard so often in her earphones.

"I understand."

From the huge in-sloping window she picked up the Cessna, its rotating propeller flickering in the morning sun. Seconds later she heard Didi's calm voice over the tower's loudspeaker: "Foxtrot – Sierra Delta Romeo, request departure information."

Liturgical responses were exchanged and the Cessna moved off the apron on to the taxiway, paused at the holding point and emerged between the two white-painted rectangles that marked the runway's operative end. Final clearance and the propeller became a blur. Off with the brakes, two hundred metres down the strip and the nosewheel lifted, then the undercarriage. Jana who didn't easily retain poetry murmured the one line that had stuck:

Oh! I have slipped the surly bonds of earth.

The Cessna rose at an angle prescribed by the plane's aero-dynamics while its prophet watched, breathing consciously, subject to a welter of ideas about what constituted beauty. Tiny now, the plane turned smoothly to starboard beyond the tower's visual arc. Jana walked to the other side of the jutting glass cor-ner, counted the seconds, saw the Cessna appear, flying straight and level downwind. Saw the shallow bank merge into the de-scent, saw the bank straighten out and align with the runway, saw the plane - confidently level, nose up - touch the metalled surface at exactly the same point it had left.

The controller, at Jana's side, picked a microphone from a plastic holster and handed it to Jana. "Tower to Foxtrot – Sierra Delta. *Tu as les ailes. Tu es ange.*"

Unhurriedly the response arrived, "Foxtrot – Sierra Delta to Tower. *A cause de toi.*"

The controller reached for Jana's far shoulder and briefly hugged her to his side.

Away from Gascon Air's shabby reception area the two women leant against the warm metal body of Didi's Porsche. "You encouraged me to be blasé," said Didi. "And you were right. But it is quite, quite different. To be alone."

"Alone but not lonely," said Jana, thinking of Octavien.

"Not at all lonely. There is this newly trained self. But the greatest novelty is self-reliance. I consider myself a superior lawyer but legal self-reliance arrives gradually and is tested bit by bit. In the air self-reliance arrives as a single entity. Good-ness, how French I sound."

"The St-Ex of our times."

Didi shuddered. "I promised I wouldn't be romantic about flying. I suspect it's a dangerous fault. But... When we met I admired that quality in you. I couldn't help seeing you as distinct. Americans often seem that way to the impressionable French. That wasn't it. You were good at something I wanted to be good at, I suppose I was envious. Today I realised this other quality. You have always depended on yourself, possibly even as a child. You have taught yourself not to fear fear."

Didi stamped impatiently. "But this requires time and a meal. I was going to insist you have dinner with me tonight. Instead I am begging. Also that you allow yourself a little wine so we may talk freely. If necessary I will pay for a lesson tomorrow morning which neither of us will take. So that you may return gracefully and soberly to the world of fallible mortals."

Jana laughed at Didi's passion. "I'd love that. You're not the only one celebrating. I'd forgotten the thrill of watching a student solo-ing."

Walking back to the office Jana checked her mobiles for texts but found nothing. Inside she said to Ginette, "Thanks for the loan of the bike. I made the tower on time. No calls, I assume?"

There were none. Four days had passed since Ghislaine had returned from Genoa but there'd been silence.

Compared with the morning, the afternoon would be anticlimactic: a revisionary lesson with Matthieu. But before that she needed to squeeze in a quick drive to the flying club at Oloron-Sainte-Marie to deliver a Lycoming starter motor which Jean-Claude had picked up from Paris. The flying club had its own strip and J-C had urged her to use the Cessna. Jana had, however, finger-wagged him a stern lesson on the economics of a round flight totalling less than 80 kilometres.

"How unglamorous, driving a van down the autoroute," he said, teasing.

"You'd prefer chatting about bankruptcy with the accountants?"

"Aren't Americans optimists?"

"Except about money."

The drive was dull enough until she left the A64 and took an N-road backdropped by the Pyrenees. A challenging place for a flying club but the dogsbody who signed for the starter motor claimed operations had been accident-free.

"It's the Vendée students who crash. They're not used to contours. Our students have this magnificent aide mémoire."

She was back in time for a reflective mug of coffee and to re-live watching Didi's solo from the tower. Ginette, ever the real-ist, reminded her of the work in hand. "Are you going to tell Matthieu the truth?"

Jana sighed. "I have a plan. If it fails I may have to be brutal."

"And his fiancée?"

"She flew with us last time but I'm not sure it did any good. She ignored the scenery and had her eyes glued to the altimeter. Called out every deviation."

Uncharacteristically the couple arrived early and were wait-ing – collectively nervous - in the reception room. Jana assumed they'd talked to other students and had come to their own con-clusions about the time tuition was taking. Both had a desperate look and she knew they would exaggerate anything positive she told them.

Jana took the wooden kitchen chair which kept her higher. There was no way this could be misinterpreted. One bonus was that Laure's anti-US tendencies had been shelved; Jana was seen as Matthieu's only saviour.

Jana shook hands and formed her mouth into what she hoped was a placatory tone. "Two lessons ago Matthieu made some mistakes but he also made progress. When Laure joined us I felt we could go forward. We did steep banked turns. Mat-thieu showed promise but when we repeated the box flights he had problems maintaining 1500 feet."

Both nodded.

"Now I could continue to divide the lessons: half an hour on new techniques, half an hour on revision. But I don't think this is a good idea. Can you see why?"

It was Laure who spoke first. "Altitude is fundamental."

Matthieu blew breath from a sulky mouth and said nothing.

Jana said. "If we don't resolve altitude it's a waste of time looking ahead. Let's spend three-quarters of an hour maintaining height and then relax for fifteen minutes. But... " Leaving the sentence incomplete emphasised the penalties of failure.

Matthieu sighed and for the first time he had Jana's sympathy. He hadn't approached flying in a laddish or unplanned way; he'd read a couple of books, brought Flight Simulator, ridden through setbacks with Dirk and accepted the repetitions. But the last four lessons had shown no measurable progress and doubt was now tangible.

"Mlle Nordmeyer, am I the problem?" Matthieu asked.

Jana softened her voice. "In one sense, yes. You are uncomfortable at low altitudes. But you're not the first. I have manoeuvres which may help."

The gloom remained. "Do I have the ability? Am I wasting my time?"

"And money," added Laure tartly.

Jana drummed fingers on her thigh. "That may be the wrong question. Do you still want to learn? That's vital."

Matthieu spread his hands. "Desire depends on progress."

"Excuse me while I speak to Jean-Claude."

J-C appeared to be negotiating on the phone with the Tarbes Office du Tourisme but had boasted in the past he could conduct two conversations simultaneously. "One moment. M. Traille," he said, putting his hand over the mouthpiece. "What's your assessment?"

Jana said, "I'm not sure he's going to make it."

Jean-Claude nodded. "M. Traille, suppose you guaranteed only three flights a day?" Again the hand slid on to the mouthpiece. "But you want something?"

"Make this a free lesson. So he's not harassed. That takes away one hang-up. Or, if you like, cut the cost by half."

Jana could hear the attenuated voice of M. Traille buzzing like a wasp. "Make it completely free," said Jean-Claude, as she knew he would.

Back in reception Jana lowered her voice. "This is a difficult time and we've no wish to take advantage of you M. Daoust. J-C says we will not charge for this lesson. So we can both be entirely honest with each other."

This dispersed some of the gloom. Daoust said, "Mlle Nordmeyer I wasn't accusing you of exploiting me. I would prefer to pay."

"Let's discuss things after the lesson."

Jana flew the plane east to a deserted area of woodland between Blaudos and the Adour. "Our box circuits won't disturb anyone here," she said. "But let's try and settle your mind about low altitude. Watch me closely. I'm flying at 1500 ft. I turn slightly, using opposite aileron and rudder, and the plane sideslips to starboard. Yes, we're going down but nowhere near as fast as if we were in a dive. Still descending, still descending as you see on the altimeter. Still descending, still descending. Here we are at 500 feet and it's time to straighten out the plane, increase the power and climb."

Jana turned reassuringly. "I'm not going to ask you to sideslip – not yet, anyway. But I'll ask our passenger a question. How long were we descending, Laure?"

The virago on the ground was a most tranquil passenger. "Oh, perhaps fifteen seconds."

"Those would be very quick seconds. Without practice, it's hard to judge. I cheated and kept an eye on my watch and it took seven or eight seconds. At a rate of 130 feet a second. I sideslipped intentionally but you, Matthieu, might do it accidentally. This obviously worries you. The point I'm making is it's easy to correct as I've shown. Even more important, there's plenty of time. Seven or eight seconds is an eternity. If anything happened at 1500 feet, you wouldn't be hassled. I'd have time to tell you long before I had to take over. You understand? Now, let's fly some boxes."

In making turns after each two-kilometre side of the box Matthieu added power. Thereafter he couldn't bring himself to reduce power, the nose rose and the plane started to climb. His instinct was understandable; he was making himself "safer". But Jana required him to fly straight and level. The problem was not so much now but in the future when he needed to lose power to land.

Fear rather than forgetfulness was the reason. Jana had shown him his fear was baseless. This time his turn was smooth, the throttle was worked back and the altimeter remained steady. Jana said nothing nor as he approached the next turn a minute later. Second and third turns were perfect.

Jana said, "Excellent, Matthieu. Go on flying boxes until I say stop. I shan't watch the turns. I'll look out of the window at all this wonder." Ostentatiously she turned in her seat. For six minutes the engine droned, roared slightly in the turn, dropped back to a drone.

Still looking out of the window Jana said, "Same thing at 1000 feet." Which, bar an initial shaky turn, he did.

After two complete boxes she smiled. "Take the plane up to 5000 feet, pick a destination – any destination within about ten minutes – check your present location visually, take a rough bearing and go there. Telling Laure why you want to fly."

The tenseness in the cockpit became a festival of feeling. "Why? Why?" said Matthieu, close to exultancy. "Because of the beauty – in what we see, and the way we move."

"Not because you want to show off?" said Laure, teasingly.

"Of course. Showing off, yes. But technically. Cautiously."

It was as if the plane sensed the change in Matthieut. Taking advantage, Jana used the Adour as a reference, gave him a new bearing for a point five kilometres downwind of the runway, provided RT announcements on Matthieu's behalf, had him progressively reduce altitude, instructed him to turn on to the approach at 1500 feet where she finally took control.

"You were reluctant to hand over," she said.

"For ten minutes I was half a pilot."

"Better than that. Seventy-five per cent."

And Matthieu laughed delightedly.

At the Cessna's stand Matthieu handed down Laure from the plane then hugged her. Waited until Jana had locked the cockpit door and – more circumspectly – hugged her. "How did you do it?" he asked.

"Instructor's magic."

"May I pay double?"

"You may not. This was free, remember?"

"Oh no, for this one I must pay."

Alone, Jana went to the toilet, locked the door and sat on the closed seat, running the cold tap and splashing water over her face. She would have stayed longer had she not switched on her mobile and seen three missed incoming calls. All from Ghislaine.

"You were flying, of course."

Jana replied, "A lesson I wasn't looking forward to. Worked out better than expected."

"And now you are, where?"

"Sitting on the toilet. Splashing water on my face."

"You are ill?"

"Flying for two. In France. It's like a difficult love affair. But what about you? You didn't call. I feared the worst but didn't dare disturb you."

"Feared the worst. What is the worst?" Ghislaine asked. "I've been playing the teenager and I apologise. What happened was the one thing I didn't expect. I was ready to be exploited. To respond cynically. To be adult. To be a short-time whore. But sympathy and talk of the future came as a surprise. I tried to be sceptical but what type of deceiver talks until four in the morning about persuading my mother to accept him?"

"Ghislaine!"

"I should have rung. I had this fantasy you were some kind of catalyst. But I told myself everything was fragile, that I needed to consider and re-consider. Besides it seemed impossible to repeat what he had said, the tones, the nuances, the insistence on my importance. Even now it feels risky putting it into words that the rest of the world can hear."

Jana said, "And you? Without misgivings. How do you feel?"

"Oh, I am in love. There is no doubt. But it's a state I need to handle carefully. Perhaps I too should sit on the toilet and splash myself with cold water. If you wish… "

"Tonight I'm dining with a student who just solo-ed. It will be a state of unequivocal bliss."

"Quite different from love. Tell me, dear Jana, is love an absence of uncertainty?"

Jana said, "Not for me."

"Was there fear?"

"Indeed."

"Otherwise it would be unbelievable," said Ghislaine. "Bah, I should simply give in. There's always the asp if I am deceived.

"There's always discussion before the asp. Let's meet."

"You will recognise me. I'll be the one who's confused."

ONCE AGAIN she took out the gaberdine skirt, the white blouse and the dark green foulard - her only options. Having now bought an inexpensive Pifco hair drier she flicked away with the hedgehog brush, looking into the mirror and dwelling on Ghislaine. A provincial in the best sense: endowed with hard patience, proof against being swept off her feet. That same quality Madeleine had shown when Dirk announced he was returning to the US without her: turning the threat of emotion into harsh wit.

Boyce had not played the US bastard, rather had gone to the other extreme. Willingly made himself vulnerable. Just how vulnerable would soon become apparent since Mme. le Lannic wasn't given to embraces. Was that a definition of love? Being prepared to bare one's soul? Jana tried to envisage discarding her own accumulated protection. Saw only darkness.

In the kitchen the family sat down to soup. Invariable soup. Reassured that Jana was meeting a woman Vincent offered to lend her his big Peugeot.

"And not arrive in the van?" Jana said. "The van will be my pumpkin."

But the Chauvelets didn't pick up the reference and there was a hiatus. After which, lumbering Cinderella jokes

The restaurant fashionably aped the USA, employing youths to park diners' cars in a cramped area at the rear. The system had its sceptics and a paterfamilias, wearing a navy blue blazer, watched angrily as his big Audi swept away in a cloud of grit thrown up by the hard-working front tyres.

The van aroused suspicion, as if a labourer was using the wrong entry. However, as Jana opened the door, showing a well-shaped ankle, she caused one car-jockey to double-take. Gravely she accepted a plastic token. "If I lost the token and said 'Van' there'd be no problem?" she asked. The lad was quicker than the Chauvelets: "Mademoiselle, I would bring it to you myself."

As Jana approached the main door it was opened by a uniformed lackey and from then on she was passed like a relay baton from one functionary to another until she arrived at Didi's table. Didi stood up. "Why can't I dress like that?" she asked crossly. "I must lack confidence. Why else this single bare shoulder, these folds, these crossovers, these breast enhancers?"

Jana stood back: "How can you say that isn't you?"

Didi reached forward impatiently and embraced Jana. "Perhaps it is me. I seem to need these extras; I can't get away with simplicity."

"You're a success. And that get-up proves it"

Didi shook her head. "Success with contracts, with court judgments – that's what the clothes say. But they say nothing about going solo in my darling old Cessna. Tonight I should have worn my trousers – the ones all flyers wear. I forget the name. I've dressed as if I wanted to outshine you and that's vulgar. Oh goodness, please sit down. On the banquette next to me so we can whisper our confessions. And why didn't I order them to pour out your champagne? Ah, I see I did. Someone read my mind. Things are finally going right."

Jana let bubbles fizz on her tongue. "These questions, they're all the same, just phrased differently."

"They are"

"A successful man may do as he pleases. But a woman who's made her way must always wave the flag. No one must under-value her."

"And you?"

Jana looked wry. "My successes are rather specialised. Not exactly a source of wealth."

Didi looked up, noticed a waiter trying to prove he was not eavesdropping. She said to Jana, "So, I must continue to be vulgar. And you must help me. I insist you order the most lavish dish." She addressed the waiter, "What is the most lavish thing you offer?"

He was boyish but socially skilled. "Lobster, but it is not the best. Try turbot."

"We want to celebrate vulgarly."

He smiled. "Celebrate with wine, then. The sommelier will help. But please protect me. I didn't say his bottles were vulgar."

Jana addressed Didi in quick American English. "This place has more style than you suspected."

But before Didi could reply the waiter, lowering his voice, said in impeccable English. "We are also demotic."

The two women laughed. Didi said, "In that case, as a demotic gesture, please choose my entire meal. And the wine"

"For me too," added Jana.

More relaxed, Didi sipped champagne pleasurably. "I expected everyone to be stiff but perhaps this evening will be fun. Perhaps it's time we introduced ourselves? I'm more than a customer, you know. And you! What do I know about you? Born in Arizona, you fly as you breathe. Surely there's more."

"Nothing that matters."

"Nonsense, you simply need encouraging. I shall summarise myself, shaming you into taking off the Arizona veil. It's odd, isn't it? - men would never do this."

"Do we need to?" asked Jana.

"Need? Yes, I think so, it's a matter of trust. Take the fact I am here unaccompanied. What does that say? Better that I tell you. I am not a lesbian, a divorcée, widow or a careerist. I am happily married and have two children, both girls, both at high school."

"You married young."

"How quick you are, Jana," laughed Didi. "There are more clichés. I was born in Rozay-en-Brie, twenty-five kilometres east of Paris. At primary school and high school I was very, very clever but finally not clever enough. In both schools one student was always superior, effortlessly superior. His first name was Luc and his second name was…?"

"Labossière."

"Yes, my dear Luc," Didi's affection was evident. "Academically wonderful but with another, greater, quality: a schoolteacher who wants to be nothing else. Can you complete this modern fairy tale?"

"Traditional roles are reversed. You earn more so he has amicably agreed to become what we Anglos call a househusband. Have the French come up with – found it necessary to come up with? - an equivalent?"

"How you slander us, Jana. Have you never heard of a *homme au foyer*?"

"Alas no. Apologise to Luc on my behalf."

Didi said, "I am determined you will meet him. He knows a lot about you. I continue. Freed from academe we married and discovered our professions are flexible. We may live wherever we wish in France. So we chose the south-west."

"The beautiful corner."

"Untarnished by the self-importance of Paris. We live in some splendour for the sake of ourselves and our daughters. They each have a horse and that, I believe, says everything. What more do you need to know?"

"I have a theory," said Jana. "Tell me your daughters' names."

"A theory based on my terrible given name, no doubt. My parents are devout Catholics, by the way, and my mother was forty-one when she gave birth to me, her sole child. After much trying. I have given our daughters a better start."

"By christening them beautifully. France specialises in beautiful names for women."

"Do you approve of Chantal and Céline? Luc and I adore the letter C it seems. But oh my God. Suppose you do not like them?"

"Then you could say I had a tin ear," said Jana. The phrase had no French equivalent and Jana offered it literally. Didi grasped the meaning, they laughed together and sipped more champagne.

A small plate of *amuse bouche* arrived and they both reached for the tiny brown shrimp in aspic. "You have it," said Jana. "You still aren't sure this place can and will be fun."

"Haute cuisine can be terribly pompous."

"But not when the waiter says 'demotic'."

"True." Didi turned on the banquette and faced Jana with shining dark eyes that required no make-up. "That's my predictable, comfortable life. How about your less predictable, less comfortable life. That is, if you care to. I admire your technical skills, of course. But also your easy, uncomplaining, very American philosophy. Can you talk about that?"

Jana popped a tiny slice of toast and caviar into her mouth. "Much of it was predictable."

"Was America a factor?"

"It was."

"But there was more?"

"There was."

Didi emptied her glass, turned her head and immediately attracted service. "If it's too personal we'll discuss other things."

"Not too personal." Jana's hand rose to her face. "That was a good word you used - uncomplaining. It became a habit, not complaining. If I'm to explain my life I might seem to be breaking that habit. But I was different when I was younger, more defensive. I would need to re-create that state of mind."

"Try me. I wasn't always a corporate lawyer. I've defended people in court." Didi smiled. "I have put words into others' mouths."

The scallops came with morels and were enhanced with a faintly citrous sauce. Jana said, "I had no childhood, as such. Persecution saw to that. So I set out to find a solution. Isn't that one definition of an adult?"

"Flying was the answer? Alone and away?"

"Didi, don't neglect your shell fish or I shall hate you. Mmm." Jana cut the scallop with the side of her fork. Elsewhere others were holding knives as well as forks, Anglo style. "Flying yes, but not flying Cessnas. I chose jets and aimed to kill people. Doesn't that reverse your sense of admiration?"

"But now you do fly a Cessna."

"Because I wasn't good enough for an F-18. Incidentally being prepared to kill is second only to the dirty deed itself. Should you be dining with me?"

"I repeat, you do fly a Cessna."

Jana mopped up clear sauce with a torn piece of baguette, knowing this was permitted. "You're defending me, saying flying was what mattered, not pressing the missile launcher. You may be right. I wanted to master a jet fighter because – to some crazies at least – it's the ultimate plane. If I had to shoot up people that was part of the price. It so happened I failed during weapons training so maybe my subconscious recognised I wasn't a natural born killer. That's a movie, by the way."

Did smiled. "I know. Directed by Oliver Stone."

"Can't match a French intellectual."

"My dear, dear Jana. Am I harassing you?"

Jana wiped her lips with a table napkin as thick as a curtain. "Ask away. It's the later part where I'll need to concentrate."

Unobtrusively another chill bucket had appeared. Didi tried to reach the neck of the bottle but was deftly forestalled. "Puligny Montrachet 2005, madame. Pierre Morey," said a different, non-demotic waiter.

"A little white burgundy, Jana? No obligation. Flying takes precedence."

"I'm not flying tomorrow morning. But did you hear this handsome young man? Of course you didn't, you're French and he's part of French life. There you sit, gorgeous, stylish, very expensive, no visible family burden, yet you're automatically madame. We're probably of an age yet the car jockey saw me as mademoiselle. Sign of a good restaurant."

They tried their rich yet astringent white wine. Didi said, "I knew about the USAF. But what happened afterwards? Flying is a difficult profession."

"Part of the US dream. Some nights I slept in my car which sounds character forming. There were times I ceased to be a woman; the squalor was just too masculine. Washing myself in a supermarket ladies room I yearned to use eye-liner, to wear a non-military shirt."

"The money, tell me about the money," said Didi.

"After USAF I had a few thousand and a single credit card. But flying – all of it – is expensive. When I had a job I rented a plane. I drove a forklift, pulled beer at the airfield café even though that's not a good idea; pilots need their status. By pure luck the bar work paid off. I met Dirk. My clothes told him what I really wanted to be doing. He held an imaginary yoke and asked: how many hours?"

"Pretty-faced M. Boonhausen. Perhaps just a bit too confident. I can't complain. You inherited what he created."

Jana continued. "I'd gone solo pretty quickly in Arizona and Dirk remembered my name. At the time his work schedule was out of balance and he needed someone to take over flights he couldn't handle. Better still, he had this theory about women who hire planes...."

Didi interrupted, "I wouldn't accept all his theories. He believed he understood women. Perhaps in the USA, but not in France."

The demotic waiter eased a plate in front of Jana. "Lamb from the foothills of the Pyrenees."

"And the wine?" asked Didi sharply.

"The sommelier is behind you madame."

The sommelier, otherwise the non-demotic waiter, inclined his head ten centimetres and whispered, "You were looking for opulence. This is a mere Montpeyroux, Coteaux de Languedoc of course. See what you think, I will take it away if it is not truly an experience."

Didi smiled at Jana. "You've got the lamb while I get the turbot. Interesting psycho-analysis. Taste the red and take M. le Sommelier's challenge."

And Jana went along with the ritual.

"So," said Didi. "Film-star Dirk's theory about women?"

"Some prefer to be flown – and instructed – by women pilots. Dirk let women know about the alternative and I stepped in. The theory worked and I am grateful; he saved my professional life."

"So I am not your first female admirer. I must be careful. That sounds Sapphic and yet I'm sure you're not of that persuasion."

Jana sighed. "It might have helped in the early days. As it was thanks to Dirk I leased a plane – a very old one – and acquired a home. In the form of a caravan."

"And entered a wider social life?"

"Of a sort. But yes, you are right. After all, sleeping in one's car one sleeps alone."

Didi paused, the glass of burgundy merely held aloft. "You talk of hard work. Lack of basic amenities. Were there also indignities?"

"I suppose I was prepared for those. In the Air Force and during those first months as an entrepreneur I couldn't afford to be a woman. Or it didn't seem so. I longed for my own shower but often I asked myself who exactly was I showering for?"

Didi put her glass down and rested her chin in her hands. "Was your country really so hard on your… individuality?"

"Only someone French would ask that question," said Jana, laughing. "Don't forget I'd conditioned myself. I was hardly outgoing. With my peers there was cameraderie, some solace. Man to man, if you like. Sometimes man to woman in a dark bedroom. But beyond that being social hardly seemed worth the effort. Better a half-cocked reason for breaking it off."

"I'm beginning to hate this."

"Not yet. I haven't sung for my supper."

Didi asked, "Am I prurient? Unpleasantly curious? I felt I had to know. You're far more than the Jana who sits in the left seat. But am I entitled?"

Jana drank a third of her Montpeyroux. "You are entitled. On your own behalf and the other French people I've met. The cure I needed probably started here. French people have raised this same subject of my face and then gone on to something else. Most have been casual, some dismissive. One Frenchman said it was my 'difference'. France deserves my frankness."

Didi breathed out audibly. "Finish your Basque lamb. Then tell me."

CHAPTER TEN

Interlude: Roy

THE TRAILER had survived the Arizona winter but looked too feeble for another. Jana doubted she could afford an apartment but it was time to look at what Tucson offered. She tried a cyber café which served good latte but was discouraged by one of the larger websites which divided property types into Single Family, Townhouse, Condo and Manufactured, none of which seemed to fit her needs. Since she was flying from Ryan Field she revised her search to nearby Valencia West. Saw studio rentals ranging from $400 to $600, decided she was an internet innocent, and went downtown to speak to a human being.

Some realtors had open-plan offices as big as bowling alleys and these she avoided. Instead she made for a smaller frontage claiming to be family-run, flagging the slogan: Coffee and Sympathy (Tea's for Sissies). At the door a tall grey-haired man in a much-scuffed suede jacket courteously stepped back and allowed her to enter first. She smiled back at him hurriedly and took this to be an augury.

What she imagined would be a ten-minute chat took three-quarters of an hour. "We need to get a handle on you." said Penny, having brought Jana her second latte of the day.

"Think bottom of the pole."

Penny shook her head. "Nope. Students have that sewn up. We could look at listings near the college but I'm betting you're up a notch. That you're in paid employment."

"Only just! I'm a civilian pilot. Fake status, no dough."

Penny needed persuading about freelance flyers. When Jana mentioned a studio, Penny looked up, made what seemed like an appraisal based on age and suggested an efficiency. "Bigger than a studio. Two rooms, usually a separate kitchen. Here's a couple on this flyer."

Penny offered the keys to a studio and an efficiency and Jana, now enmeshed, surrendered details about herself as security. They discussed various suburbs, none of which Jana had visited and she even found herself solemnly considering whether a pool attached to one development might be a deal-breaker.

Guided out of the office by Penny she passed by an adjacent interview in which a scuffed suede jacket looked familiar. The man raised his lined face and asked, "Got something good?" The accent was east coast, possibly New England. Jana waved vaguely.

Both residences were a great improvement on the trailer. A square room was more life-enhancing than an aluminium tunnel, studio doors closed solidly instead of trembling on their hinges, and kitchens were more than a niche for a microwave. She drove back to the trailer park and entered her home of the past two years, noticing how temporary it looked. But then trailers didn't get repainted. From her accounts book she assessed what sort of a hole a $450 monthly rent would make. Pretty enormous.

As she juggled the figures her mobile rang. An infrequent event; caller unknown.

"Hi, my name's Roy Teague but that won't mean anything to you. We were both in Mullard's the realtor this morning."

"Suede jacket?"

"I'm glad I wore it. Most of my clothes are anonymous."

"Say Bar Harbour."

"No need, I confess: I'm from the Bay State."

"A rare accent in Tucson. What can I do for you, Mr Teague?"

"I have a business proposition. There I've said it, and it sounds just as ambiguous as I expected. Not the approach any woman wants from an unknown man." He laughed shakily. "I'll start again. I'm Roy Teague and I'm keen to appear legitimate. Prove I am legitimate, damnit. I've called Mullard's and told the agent I spoke to – Melanie, by the way - if Jana Nordmeyer asks for details from my folder she's to be given them. Does that make me less threatening?"

Jana closed her account book. "Assume I've spoken to Melanie and you're Mandela and Jimmy Carter rolled into one. What's the proposition?"

"First, I need your pardon for sneaking your name. I suppose we both chose Mullard's because they're cosy. A tad too cosy, I'd say. I overheard all you told Penny without trying. Am I forgiven?"

"Make my future golden and I'll forgive you."

"How about a silver or cupro-nickel future?"

Jana said, "I've no secrets from you. If you heard all I said you know I'm a marginal member of society. Poor if not poverty-stricken. I take it you need a pilot. You're on record at Mullard's so it won't be Kalashnikovs into Mexico or bringing in Muslims who want to fly Boeings. Yup, I'm available."

"Good. OK, I'm a vet. That's veterinarian not Veteran of Foreign Wars. I specialise in cattle, pregnant ones in particular. I do business in New Mexico, Oklahoma and the Panhandle. A plane makes sense. A plane leased by a pilot that's hungry for business makes even more sense. I've checked you out and I know you're good at what you do – kinda famous, even – and that you're reliable. How about a retainer so I have priority call on your services. Six months, see how it goes."

This caused Jana to re-open her accounts book and read casually through notes that might now be outdated. "A dream job, Mr Teague. But I'd be failing if I didn't tell you there's a cheaper option."

"You mean fly my own plane? That's very straight of you Miss Nordmeyer. But before that I need a feel for using a plane. I'll aim to retain you for six months anyway. If I decide to take lessons that period would be extended. Look, my offices are out east at Tanque Verde. Why don't you call my secretary and fix an appointment."

Jana put down the phone and wondered how many dollars added up to a retainer. Enough to move out of the trailer? To exchange the rented Comanche for a plane with more range? Enough for both?

Good times. But why had he been visiting Mullard's?

The first two questions were quickly answered. Teague's office proved there was money in pregnant cows and the retainer would cover both her immediate ambitions. Office hardly described it. To the rear were labs and parking for a dozen cars.

Teague explained: "Bovine pregnancy has a fashion side, especially when a prize bull's done the impregnating. That's a big hit all round. With some owners ranching is a hobby or a tax deduction and they fly in from the east or west coast. When they come here that's when I need some show. The desk is sapele, but what would I know?"

She mentioned the replacement plane. "A thousand mile range and a higher cruising speed gives you a better deal." She gestured at the spacious office. "All this was bought through fat fees. Fees relate to time. Save time and use it to charge more fees."

He was amused. "People are soft-hearted about vets. Furry animals and all. You're hard-nosed. I like that"

"You know why I'm hard-nosed."

Now he was contrite. "I'm ashamed about spying. I hope it's coming up roses now."

"Lots of roses. And here's a possible bonus. I'm operating out of Ryan Field but I don't have to. You'll be my biggest customer. I take it you live outside Tucson; could I move to a field that's nearer?"

"Yes, but..." He looked away. "I wasn't at Mullard's by accident. My wife's leaving. She'll get the ranch. I need something temporary. I could start looking over by Ryan Field."

"Sorry about that," Jana said conventionally. "You don't want a long drive after a long flight. One less hassle."

"Makes sense. Have you been...?"

"The only partner I ever had was the USAF; otherwise it's been a struggle to stay alive. Female Flying Dutchman. I was just guessing at what you're going through."

She suspected the split-up was his first; that it wasn't his fault. He'd turned away from her and, perhaps, from a future he was trying to shut out.

"So banal. Husband and wife separate in this day and age. No big deal. In fact, quite a big deal."

Silence.

Speaking gently, Jana said, "This is a great move for me but I hope you've thought it through. You and I will spend time alone together. We'll talk. Am I the right mother confessor?"

His eyes refocused. "Oh heck, yes. Back at Mullard's I wasn't just listening to your CV. I liked the way you put things." He paused as people often did before acknowledging the elephant. "You've seen tough times, I don't need to ask. This is the US, after all, world centre for quick judgments. I like the way you've survived. Sure we'll talk. I'll confess and maybe you'll confess, who knows? But try a slap across my chops if I'm too bluesy."

"A soft slap. And only once a day."

For the first time he laughed, then flicked the long quiff of grey hair away from his forehead. "One other thing. When Mary-Beth asked me to move out I sat back and thought about the world I was moving into. Nearly all men. I couldn't bear all that locker-room talk. Nature favours balance and that's what I need. I doubt I'd have chosen a guy for this. Is it OK?"

"Tell yourself you're paying for a pilot not a psycho-analyst. And I'm hardly a great example; I have big defects. Don't forget I signed up to fly jet fighters. Most people don't see that as normal."

"It'll be civilised talk about practical stuff ."

But of course it wasn't. His clients took advantage of the new, more mobile Roy Teague and often he went there and back three times when once would have been enough. The newly leased Cessna 182 Skylane was good for over a thousand miles, cruised at 167 mph and they spent long hours together.

Vet college at Cornell was quickly disposed of. Money hadn't been a problem there, given a father who regularly reaped Goldman Sachs bonuses, and Roy enjoyed the same financial tranquillity when it came to setting up a partnership at Cape Cod. Mary-Beth's parents lived in Marblehead, bred springer spaniels for fun and were one of his first customers. Within a couple of years he enjoyed local status and the marriage had jigsaw logic. He refused the Rotary despite fierce pressure from clients who, he suspected, wanted discounts on their shih-tzus and daughters' ponies. The Teagues moved to the peninsula coast, had two daughters and appeared to be facing a comfortable future.

"At thirty-five I asked myself: why did I become a vet?" he said as Jana eased the Cessna away from the municipal airport at Santa Fe. "Mostly the answer's knee-jerk – a love of animals. But for me there was more: I liked the technical side, the way the medical stuff was evolving. Speying tabbies didn't exactly cut it."

Jana levelled out at 6000 feet and tuned to the Tucson beacon.

Roy continued, "Putting a finger on it, the marriage started unravelling at the Class of 95 reunion. I needed conversation. Found myself talking to a guy who'd gone straight into cattle, started up this Tucson practice I now run, and was looking for a partner. In vet terms cattle are state of the art: there's research, papers get written, it's international and there's real money. Mary-Beth hated the idea. It had to be east coast, had to be Cape Cod. I had to promise the kids would go to Bryn Mawr, that there'd be ponies, that we'd have a ranch with a zillion bedrooms. But she was never happy."

It was enough for him that Jana flew the plane.

He talked on reflectively. "Crazy luck; my partner was badly injured diagnosing a Brahma bull. After that, he couldn't stay comfortable during the long drives. I bought him out and he settled for a sit-down life with a lab practice out in California. Mary-Beth saw right off I was here for life. Heck, she spent as much time in New England as she did in Arizona. Time enough for an affair with a CPA out there. Not out of lust nor love, more to prove she could. And to prove she didn't need me. I think she's wrong there but I'm not in a position to argue. The ranch is worth stacks and she'll sell in her own good time. Then move east."

"And the girls?"

Roy laughed harshly. "Elaine'll do what her mom wants but Debbie has notions to be a vet. I sure hope to hell Mary-Beth cuts her enough slack for that to happen. That she doesn't become a pawn. I can see Debbie moving back to Arizona. By then perhaps I'll have been kicked in the head by a Brahma bull. Who knows?"

"You still feel for your wife?" Jana asked.

"I sympathise. Cape Cod to Tucson – hell it isn't even Phoenix – was a culture shock. Mary-Beth's been a real mother. She got a top degree in medieval studies at Brown; it's something she's still interested in but she put it to one side when she married. We had ten good years. But I'm a vet. It's what I chose to do and it's paid off for my family. Except for the move. In the end I'm the bad guy because I broke the dream. But then I imagine myself, still cutting tabbies, looking out at the ocean from Falmouth, waiting for something to happen. Here in Tucson it has happened; I wake up wanting to do my job and I'm vet of choice for a hundred discerning farmers in three states. With lab services for a dozen other vets. Ah shit, tell me about yourself, Jana. You still sore you didn't make it in the Air Force?"

"Yes and no. There's a shooting war in Afghanistan. Perhaps the US should be there, perhaps not. It wouldn't be my decision. My aim was to fly planes well and if I were in Afghanistan with the Air Force – the US air force – the job would be tough but easy to understand. Jana Nordmeyer the person, the woman, would be out of the loop. I'd just be JN the pilot."

"But you can't not want to be a woman," he said, exasperated

"Why not? Being a woman hasn't been all that easy."

"But that's crap."

"You're leaving Mary-Beth. Do you understand that?"

The sun was setting out to port and the lights from the instruments created a green cast on both their faces. Roy opened his mouth to speak but was interrupted by an ATC request for confirmation audible in both their earphones. Jana responded in the emotionless voice she'd perfected over the years and after that there was silence for fifty miles.

Finally he said, "Sorry about that. None of my business."

"That's OK. Forget it." But she was still disturbed.

He stared out over the instruments, trying to understand the growing darkness ahead. "Don't you ever get scared? Alone, no reference points. Planes are so fragile."

"Being scared is natural. And a good thing. Keeps me safe. And it's there all the time, from the start. You walk round the plane before that first lesson and you say: who the hell says this thing'll fly? The answer is dull, but dull's a comfort. Procedures. You check the plane's OK, you get in and check some more, you do the things that keep you safe and – gee – the plane flies. After that all this stuff says the plane's flying properly. Nothing to be scared about."

"You trust the technology, I suppose."

"Yeh, but not blindly. The technology blends together, gives you the whole picture. The turn-and-bank says the plane is level even though I can see zilch, the radio tells me where Tucson is, the compass proves we're going there, and the ASI confirms we're flying at the right speed and won't fall out of the sky for running out of fuel. There's more."

"And you've done it all before."

Jana nodded. "You don't need a book when you tie off a tabby. You find your way round the tripes or whatever; a place that seems less certain to me than all this mechanical stuff."

He reached back for the musette and took out the vacuum flask. "Coffee?"

Jana smiled. "Sure. The pilot's friend."

He lingered on her smile for several seconds then opened the flask. The smell of the coffee was powerful between them.

He said, "You predicted all this, didn't you? Talk that becomes confession. Talk that can get bitchy. You warned me."

"The cockpit's a pressure cooker. I had to be sure we could get along."

"You were right. Vets are used to being in charge. But here I'm just a passenger."

"A passenger who pays the bills."

This observation didn't please him and he went silent again until the final approach at Ryan Field. The strings of landing lights caught his eye. "It's beautiful."

"Careful," said Jana, joking. "Think of the reason, not the pretty colours."

They parted in the car park, he to his Toyota SUV, she to the ten-year-old Chevy. He said, "Flying's good for me. Frees me from the chores.

As was her habit Jana ignored the ambiguity.

THE DAY before Good Friday. Jana had picked up two Denver U students and was delivering them to their parents' ranch on the eastern edge of the Sonoran Desert. They'd been good company during the flight chatting about the recession, the war and Obama's problems, even showing an interest in the plane. Looking down at the dirt strip a mile away from the big ranch building, one of them said, "Hey, that's mom in the Merc. We're honoured. Perhaps she's showing off her new wheels."

But it was merely to pass on a message. "A Mr Teague," said the woman as Jana unloaded her sons' rucksacks. "Can you call his landline after nine tonight."

The call had been relayed from a girl at Ryan Field who did reception for Jana when she was flying. Jana knew Roy had got back from a conference in California and that his daughters would be spending Easter with their mother. Previously he'd thought of going on to San Francisco, but then most of his leisure plans were tentative. Customers who could afford his high fees were by definition wealthy and tended to call him out at any time. Jana hoped this didn't involve yet another long flight into the Panhandle; she had hoped to see her mother in Flagstaff.

The indoor swimming pool at her apartment block was discouragingly crowded when she arrived home in the early evening and she reluctantly resorted to machinery in the gym. Portliness was an occupational hazard for pilots and her preferred solution was to swim lengths. The stepper was more punitive but she found it hard to take the twenty minutes' mindlessness. With that out of the way fifteen minutes of travelator were, by comparison, bearable. But the temptation to slump on the couch afterwards and eat a sandwich had to be resisted. Luckily she still had the makings of a chicken stir-fry.

Regular charters from Roy had allowed her to rent an efficiency just west of Drexel Heights, halfway between Ryan Field and Tucson's business district. Not since she'd lived at home had she enjoyed such luxury. From time to time she wandered from the kitchen, though the living room and into the bedroom savouring all that space. She'd furnished the rooms quickly and cheaply from garage sales. The bed, bought new, had caused a moment of indecision: single, double or king? Would the single be realistic? Would the king be tempting fate? The bigger bed, she told herself firmly, would be more comfortable.

Curtains, acquired a week ago, still had to be hung but that job at least could wait. Her wristwatch said ten past nine and she took out her mobile.

Roy's voice was subtly different, lacking its usual authority. "Good Denver trip?"

"Wouldn't recommend it. That grass strip near the college has a giant bump a hundred metres in. Hard on the oleos. How was California?"

"Trematode and nematode treatment. Otherwise flukes. What could be sexier? You working this weekend?"

"Late Sunday afternoon, picking up a fishing party from Snow Flake. You got a call-out?"

He paused. "I was thinking of switching off all my phones and taking a quick vacation. Lake Tahoe, somewhere like that."

She could fit that in with Flagstaff. "Early start tomorrow; pick you up Monday morning?"

"Er, more than that."

"More than what?"

Five or six seconds of nothing. He said, "Stupid. It won't work. It'll sound like amateur night. OK, what time tomorrow?"

"What won't work?"

"Just a lousy idea. What time?"

"How about six-thirty?"

"Six-thirty it is."

Jana trawled non-existent sound, the silent mobile pressed to her ear. Thought about the flap of grey hair across his forehead, the deep lines at the sides of his mouth. Stood up, walked to the window and looked down at the parking lot divided off with saplings ("Our way of adding zip to a forgotten feature," the brochure had said). Played I Wish That I Knew by Nina Simone.

He was waiting by the plane in the drab pre-dawn, his face arranged in a greeting. No apparent mysteries. "Low cloud, I see. Any problems?"

"Visibility's half a kilometre at Tahoe. But it varies and they're not optimistic. You still want to go?"

"If we can't make it, I'll try somewhere else. So long as it's quiet and there are trees. How about you?"

"Thought I'd spend the night at my mother's place."

"That's Flagstaff isn't it? No problems landing there?"

"They don't do cloud at Flagstaff."

He said, "I've never been. If Tahoe goes pear-shaped drop me off at a Flagstaff motel."

At 6000 feet they were out of the clouds and into the sun. "Tell you what," he said, "let's stay up here in all this light."

Between calls to the Tahoe tower she kept on glancing at him, trying to gauge what had been on his mind. But he was determinedly casual, as if the flight itself were part of the holiday.

An hour in and Tahoe visibility was down to 200 metres. She said, "I think we'd be wasting time and fuel if we continued. Do you want me to try Reno or Carson City?"

"No. I hate Nevada. Look, make tracks for Flagstaff. I've brought a handful of JAVMA mags I haven't read. I'll rely on you to recommend a burger joint where I won't be poisoned. That'll do fine."

"Sounds like a hell of a vacation. You were talking about quiet back there. You could stay with us. I guarantee quiet; no excitement whatsoever."

Was that a flash of interest?

He said, "I wouldn't want to get between you and your parents."

"My dad died some time ago. Mom's lonely. She'd be glad to cook for a man. But I just hope you have a high boredom threshold."

"You're sure, now?"

"Just let me switch the ADF to Flagstaff, turn on to – let's see - 131 and dig out my mobile."

Speaking to her mother she sensed him watching her. Then he reached across and asked for the mobile. "Mrs Nordmeyer, Roy Teague. Yep, yep. Look your daughter's flown me all over the southern central states on business – I'm a vet, by the way. No complaints either side. But my two nights in Tahoe are a no-go because of low cloud. Sad, eh. Yep, yep. I was resigned to a Flagstaff motel but Jana says you give shelter to animal strays. Is this true? Yep. I'll be as quiet as the proverbial... No, I don't want you driving out to the airport. I'll rent. Mighty grateful, ma'am. Looking forward to meeting you... to meeting you, Lisa."

He handed the mobile back. "Didn't want your ma embarrassed. Better she knows just exactly who you're bringing home. Saves you explaining"

Jana laughed. "And who am I bringing home?"

"Wealthy guy whose wife's just kicked him out. Dubious state of mind."

"Was that what yesterday was about?"

He nodded. "But today I'm back to normal. Following the turn-and-bank as I should."

"Good to know," she said, faintly disappointed. "But there's no need to rent a car. We're only twenty minutes from the airport."

"I have my reasons."

These included buying long-stem roses. When they arrived her mother hurried, almost stumbled, down the driveway and he stood back as they embraced. Then presented Lisa with the roses he had kept behind his back and kissed her on both cheeks. At first Jana admired his panache. Then she saw the heartening effect this had on her mother and her feelings migrated into personal warmth. She found herself, like her mother, simpering foolishly as Roy took control and ushered them into the house.

Etiquette was better managed inside. Since the phone call Lisa had worked with the strength of ten to transfer the femininity out of the main bedroom so that Roy had a characterless but identifiably male place in which to sleep. Jana thought the gesture excessive but saw the logic; his en suite bathroom would save them all from embarrassing encounters carrying toilet bags.

"You both got up so early," said Lisa, "I'm preparing a hearty brunch."

Jana said "I'm starving but let's eat in the kitchen. So we can talk."

Lisa smiled. "Beats me angel why we never turned that orphan dining room into an extra garage. Your dad never liked it either."

It was one reason why Jana had suggested the kitchen. More than that she needed to re-embrace the heart of the house. The room where she had been most protected. Nothing had changed. The ice box, almost thirty years old, had rounded contours where newer models had straight edges. On the sideboard was her mother's radio – permanently dusty from an explosion of baking flour a decade ago. Fish slices, a palette knife and other larger utensils sprouting like metal flowers from a glass jar Jana had decorated with acrylics at high school. What had the jar contained? Gherkins?

"Where are you now?" he asked. "Back in fifth grade?"

He'd been watching and she was pleased. She'd been worried about the house's shabbiness, not for her own sake but for the light it might cast on the family. A quick glance told her the house wasn't shabby – her mother wouldn't have allowed it – it was just a well-used home.

"It could have been any grade. Or high school. But the kitchen was always where I was happiest."

Her mother, busy with a skillet, turned on hearing this, her hand at her throat.

Roy looked around the room. "I guess I lost out. We used the dining room, my mother insisted. But never as a family. She sat in on kids' meals but had dinner when my father got home, usually pretty late. My mother said the dining room taught us good manners. I have no way of knowing. I'm sure you taught Jana good manners, Lisa, but I have the feeling you'd forgive me if I put my elbows on the table. Is that right?"

Lisa, still affected by Jana's memory of happiness, turned tremulously again from the range. "Just do it, Roy."

As they made their way through the mounds of scrambled eggs, link sausages and hash-browns Roy entertained the table with a monologue of veterinary stories, leaving them little need to contribute. This tactic became clear when he poured himself a second cup of coffee and stood up. "That was fantastic, Lisa. But now you need to be together, the pair of you. I'm off to another part of the house – perhaps even the orphan dining room – to drink my coffee, bring myself up to date with JAVMA, and perhaps doze."

As Lisa opened her mouth to protest, he raised his hand. "This way I get out of the washing up."

"He's good company," Jana said casually. "Good to work for, too."

"Indeed he is."

They stacked the dishwasher together. "This reminds me of Dad," said Jana deliberately. "Why did he hate the dishwasher so much? Why did he always wash up by hand?"

"I ask myself those kind of questions every waking day. Silly stuff. I suppose it's normal. I never took time off to ask why while he was alive, now it's too late and they become important."

"How are you bearing up?"

Lisa said, "The biggest loss is not having someone to talk to about you."

"Me!"

"Don't be surprised, angel. We got into the habit when you were young. Trying to figure out what was best. What we could do. Then seeing you take over your own life. Geoff was never over-emotional like me but he felt for you all the time."

Jana said, "I owe you both a lot. Not just the cash. The way you let me turn your world round. I know it worried the hell out of you, yet you let me go ahead. It was the only way and it has paid off, I promise."

"We both knew for sure when the Air Force slapped you down. You didn't stop for breath. Those first two years in Tucson must have been a nightmare. Proud of you, angel."

They hugged each other. Jana said, "Tell you what, this afternoon let's take a sentimental journey. Lake Mormon. It started out a disaster but it was what I needed. You and Dad were great. It's a nice drive and we can tell Roy both sides of the story."

As he had predicted the early start and the close JAVMA typeface had driven Roy to sleep. She stood over him trying to imagine Mary-Beth's state of mind - willingly dropping a husband over a disagreement about geography. As she pondered he woke up and their eyes met - without expression.

Jana explained what was planned. "Sure. You drive, I'll sit in the back with your ma."

"She'll like that."

"I haven't seen love like that in a long time," he said, levering himself out of the chair and inclining himself forward so that she couldn't see his face as he spoke.

The conversation behind Jana sounded lively enough on the short journey. A cruel wind scoured the ramp where the Nordmeyers had launched the boat and after a token half minute outdoors they retired to the car and reminisced about Geoff who had died a year earlier insisting he didn't want "Keystone Kops mullarkey" at the funeral.

"By which he meant?" asked Roy.

"A priest doing a eulogy about someone he'd never met," said Jana.

"One of the truck drivers at Purina volunteered," said Lisa. "I thought it would be bar-room jokes but I can feel the tears when I remember. 'Geoff Nordmeyer knew the business and knew the men. What else matters?' I tried to thank him afterwards, a young fellow, but he was away. Shy, the others said."

After dinner they tried to watch Fargo but even Jana – usually unaffected by long hours – fought to keep her eyes open. As she undressed in her old bedroom her mother came in and closed the door quietly.

Jana yawned. "A nice guy, isn't he? He likes you."

Her mother gripped her wrist. "It's you he likes. Make an excuse for me tomorrow; take him up to Grand Canyon or wherever. Talk."

"We've done nothing but talk. All those long flights."

"Angel, talk to him face to face."

On a grey morning they took the route north joking about their destination as if Grand Canyon were too portentous for a leisurely Saturday drive. With the last of the suburbs behind them, Roy said, "I take it your mother saw through me?"

"The too-perfect guest."

"Liking her made it a lot easier. I guess she helped you through the bad bits?"

"Both of them did."

Roy said, "I meant what I said about her love for you."

"Living away I forget. I shouldn't."

He looked forward toward the Coconino Plateau, sightlessly, as he often did from the passenger seat in the Cessna. "We don't have to say anything if it embarrasses you."

"Tell me what it was that wouldn't work."

He sighed. "I tried to make it sound innocent; damnit it was innocent. But perhaps innocence is too old-fashioned for the oughties. I wanted your company, just that. Socially, for a couple of days. Nothing more. "

"There's an obvious question."

"Was I sure that's all I wanted?" He laughed drily. "Of course I wasn't sure. But if that's how it worked out, so be it."

"Why not start over?"

"Why not? At Mullard's I wanted the way you looked, the way you talked. I still do. The problem was, after Mullard's I bought you. That's why it's difficult: how do you talk to an employee? It's high risk. Even if you turned me down, even if you hated my guts I'd still want you flying me. Perhaps I want to be dominated. Perhaps the left seat is symbolic. Now you know everything."

"Not exactly."

"Didn't think you'd go for anything that simple. I've tried to figure you out. There's a vulnerability I like but there's toughness too. Whether you want to be a woman or not doesn't matter. Despite the technology you're wrapped up in, your competitiveness and your willingness to shoot people out of the sky you can't escape being feminine. More so than Mary-Beth, say. The mark has affected you, directed your life. But I suspect you're more a woman with it than without it. Shit, I didn't think I could say all this."

"You could say we've had the social bit. What happens now?"

"We're at our best together in the Cessna. You doing your job, me doing mine. We could wait until Sunday."

"Don't forget the fishing party at Snow Flake."

"Shit."

"Why don't I pull off down this logging road?"

He smiled wanly. "Not until you've given it a bearing. You always do."

THEY became lovers a week later and on long flights she reflected on that bald transition. As if this new state were defined only by physical union, by minutes spent coupled rather than hours absorbed in moving from self-reliance to willing dependence. At first it had seemed impossible - a terrifying prospect of leaving herself exposed. The carapace was all she had. But the carapace was exactly what he demanded. As he put it bluntly,

"Oh sure, I want the pilot, but more than that I want the other Jana."

Had he tried to take away her protection she might have resisted. Instead he persuaded her to give it up. It didn't work immediately perhaps because she recognised the endearments and instinctive hands on her body were part of his medical baggage. She responded almost mechanically on that first occasion, in the hotel room, confident there'd been no frightening inroads.

He said nothing but the second encounter, an hour later, lasted longer and had artful pauses, "Come to me, Jana. Forget flying, take your hands off that goddamned yoke." She giggled at that and in giggling lost her fixation with the solemnities of sex. Saw the fun, saw the unity, gave into the calculated delays which proved to be both unendurable and irresistible. Felt grateful at the end and was careful to suppress saying so.

But this was a merely the start. Without knowing it she was exploring the frontier between sex and love-making, discovering that Roy's nature played on her nerve-endings even more effectively than his body did; that they were, in effect, still coupled out of bed - making chilli together, walking round Mission Manor Park ("like State freshmen") and sitting on the banks of the Santa Cruz wrapped up in their parkas. The wonder of this mutual possession was sealed officially when she picked up his ringing phone and found herself talking to Mary-Beth.

"Ah, I think I that may be Jana."

So Mary-Beth knew. Jana said, "Let's hope there aren't other options."

Mary-Beth laughed pleasantly. "If my word means anything I'd say no. Roy's a faithful soul. I was the tart, not him."

"Thank you for that. He'll only be a minute. He left his diary in the car."

"Talking to me could be a pain."

"Not so far.

"I need to say I didn't pry. He volunteered you during one of our endless meetings with the attorneys. He'd been generous about an investment – which wasn't at all necessary – and for the first time I apologised about bollixing things. He shrugged his shoulders in the way he does and said things had worked out. Said how you'd met. To me a plane cockpit sounds an ideal place to get to know someone. I said a pilot's licence would be a big improvement on PhD medieval studies and he gave me what I call his wry smile. He didn't deserve what happened and I wished him luck. And meant it."

"I appreciate all that. I can hear his key in the door. I'll hand you over."

Roy stood before her, eyebrows arched. "Mary-Beth," Jana mouthed, and he grabbed at her wrist. "No, it's not like that," Jana said, holding the phone out of reach. He looked dubious.

"Promise," she said, blowing a kiss and giving him the phone.

Returning the kiss he spoke calmly. "Sorry, M-B. Perhaps you heard some of that. I shot from the hip. But I understand the talk's been… what the heck, neighbourly. Good."

He went on to discuss his daughters' trust funds but Jana remained standing, looking at him. Seeing herself as part of a union, shared but not shared. Aware too of Roy's protection, of being surrounded.

When he put the phone down he noticed her, transfixed. He said, "I sort of over-reacted."

"I enjoyed being looked after."

Although she spent most nights in his hotel room and, later, his apartment she retained the efficiency, using it for early-morning flights with other clients. These were increasing. Dirk's theory about certain women preferring women pilots had flourished via word of mouth and occasionally it was difficult to fit everything in. Also, a new, well-endowed company, Executive Flights, which had invited her to stand in as instructor on several occasions, was closing on a nearly new twin-engine Beechcraft Baron and had asked about her regular availability. At a stroke this would mean a modern, medium-range plane without any of her previous financial burdens.

There were in fact few days in the month when she didn't fly. As an act of gratitude and affection Roy ordered a flight to Flagstaff so the two of them could take Lisa Nordmeyer out to dinner. Knowing Jana had such an extravagant protector led Lisa to buy an astrakhan coat, to tint her hair and to make late-night phone calls.

Without friends for guidance Jana moved blindly through what was her first sustained love affair: being interrupted in her smalls laundering and feeling the chill bathroom tiles against her back, taking car journeys which ended in unplanned rural obscurity, exchanging lewd whispers over supermarket trolleys. Aware somehow that the intensity would fall away and thus being able to prepare herself for a more measured tempo which actually added to the pleasure. When they lay, both tired, watching television, conscious of their bodies, letting desire accumulate and finally dealing with it in bed.

What was astonishing were his feelings of uncertainty, as if he were trespassing on territory she imagined to be hers. At three in the morning she found him gripping her arm and asking urgently about her reaction when they first met.

"You opened the door for me at Mullard's. A rare thing in the good old US and it forced me to look up at you; normally I keep my head down. You smiled and gestured which I found nicely pre-war even though you weren't remotely old enough. Inside Mullard's I lost you but what you did stayed with me."

He reconstructed. "You were in my line of sight when I sat down with Melanie. You weren't keeping your head down then. I bet I could draw the exact curves of your neck from memory. You looked rested but alert, as you do in the plane."

"You asked me as I was leaving. Had I found something good?"

"I wanted to slow you down. I'd been listening to you with the other realtor. I wanted to trick you into saying something. You replied but I didn't catch it. That was a bastard."

A week later they were leaving a grass strip near Amarillo following the unsuccessful confinement of a prize Charolais. He'd been thoughtful. "Looking back aren't you scared at the accidental way it happened with us?"

It was his most direct reference to their future. The harsh metallic tone of their earphones – conduit for vital but dispassionate information – nevertheless accented the yearning.

"I never thought that. Now I will," she said.

The dead earth of Texas, then Oklahoma, unrolled slowly beneath the wings of the plane. Next time he spoke his voice was husky. "Climbing, you ease the yoke back towards your breasts. Hard smooth plastic against all that softness. Erotic stuff for me. It shouldn't be allowed up here."

She wanted to joke but couldn't. Wanted to take his hand and put it against her breast but couldn't.

As Roy had said, his was a mainly male world. At social gatherings she met money men, attorneys, other vets and senior business executives; the wives clustered in groups away from the men. Roy drew her in with him, not wanting to be separated. Her face attracted familiar scrutiny but, for the first time, her discomfort became a shared experience. When he noticed the staring he offered to stop going out but she refused. This was chickenfeed, she said, nowhere near her ordeals at grade school.

Younger women held in tow might have been ignored but Jana's maturity brought questions about her occupation. Her answers caused confusion. She was thought modest, hiding the fact that she ran a mini-airline. Then Roy tended to catch her eye and wink; it was their secret.

To mark the three-month anniversary of that drive north from Flagstaff - always referred to as Grand Canyon Day, a destination never reached – Roy gave her a stainless steel vacuum flask to replace the glass flask she used for coffee and kept in the plane's musette. Etched on the side was the final verse of Burns' My Luve is Like a Red Red Rose:

> *And fare thee weel, my only Luve*
> *And fare thee weel awhile*
> *And I will come again, my Luve*
> *Tho' it were ten thousand mile.*

because, he said, the trouble with pilots was one was constantly having to bid them goodbye.

HAD she caused the affair to fail? That was what she told herself afterwards. But surely the blame – if that was the right word – was shared. The twin-engine Beechcraft had seduced her and had marked the beginning of the decline, but the decision wasn't taken independently. They'd recognised the risks, discussed them, and agreed the solution. Roy himself had urged her to accept Executive Flight's offer. Besides, neither could have foreseen the irony which forced them apart.

"Sticking with the Cessna is just stubborn," he said. "There's nothing romantic about a single-engine plane. The Baron will give you more experience, you'll land at bigger airports, and you'll use better technology."

"Listen to the aviation expert," she said fondly. "But you're more to me than the Baron. The fact is I just can't fly the whole of your schedule."

"So, fly what you can. I'll charter someone else for the rest. But that'll be temporary. It's now time for the cheaper DIY option. The one you mentioned so nobly when I phoned you after Mullard's. The option that would have put Jana Nordmeyer out of a job."

They had just finished a late evening meal at Todd's restaurant at Ryan Field after yet another long flight, this time from Slapout, Oklahoma. A new client, a banker-farmer who'd insisted on Roy and who'd agreed premium rates which reflected the distance. Jana reached across the table and touched his cheek. "I always wanted to fly you. But I had to be honest."

He caught her hand. "And yet you'd been starving a month before. Living in that wreck of a trailer. When I phoned, what I really wanted – wanted like hell – was to see your face full on. At Mullard's it had been the side and back of your head. A golden bell which was pretty good, but not good enough."

"Me and a Jersey cow. So you're going to learn to fly?"

"It makes sense, you said. But there's more. Being a vet's obscure. Being a pilot you could be proud of me."

"Proud? Does that matter?"

"Wrong word," he said. "How about proof? Proof I'm willing to let you guide me?"

"Not sure about that. What is true you've been free to choose."

He squeezed her hand. "Yeh, that's what counts. You chose too."

Actually she was proud of him. "Why are we here with the dirty plates? Why aren't we back at your place?"

And when they got back, despite their mutual need, they showered, threw clothes into the washing machine and even listened to the radio news, letting the pressure increase before lying down on his gigantic bed. As he entered her he said, "Here's the local news from Slapout, Oke. It's good news. Fees up seventeen per cent. Courtesy Miss Jana Nordmeyer. An asset to the practice."

"An asset to practise on. Are all vets like this?"

"You'll never know."

Her response was wetly muffled by his tongue. His greatest gift had been to show her that sex and laughter may be combined.

Afterwards she said, "You know it's better I don't teach you flying."

"I reckoned that would be the case."

"I'll find you someone good. Fella or female?"

"Fella. As ugly as you can make him."

The following month was chaotic. Jana texted Dirk in France and had him recommend an instructor. "Try Josh, he does nothing but," Dirk replied. She paid for a simulated lesson with this tranquil South Dakotan and after half an hour offered him the job as Roy's instructor and as her stand-in – with the Cessna – on days she couldn't fly Roy.

Her new employer, Executive Flights, operating from Tucson's international airport, booked her four days of transitional training for the Baron at a field close to Hawker Beechcraft's headquarters in Wichita after which she flew a twice weekly service from Tucson to Fort Worth. During thirty working days she flew Roy twice only, both of them short hops to Tuba City. Evenings together were rare; contemplative love-making a true luxury. Long trips forced Roy to cancel his two initial flying lessons although Josh let him handle the yoke as a taster.

"How many hundreds of miles have I watched you? Making it look easy," Roy said, beside her in bed, tracing her neckline. "Hardly touching the yoke. Calm and lovely. Whereas I… stare at the compass, at the altimeter, saw away sideways, feel the plane bump into fantasy waves. Suffer cramp in my hand."

Behind the light tone of voice she heard the disappointment. She kissed him, ran her tongue along his bottom lip. "Early days yet. Did you read the stuff?"

"Oh sure. It helps. I read it while Josh flew me, while he showed me what ten degrees of flap meant. I'm used to digging tough stuff out of print. It's my clumsy hands that let me down."

Her shoulders ached from the Fort Worth round trip but she guided him into the second bout of love-making, the bedside clock showing one o'clock, the alarm set four hours hence.

She stole away groggily the next morning, trying not to wake him, putting on her shoes in the hallway outside the apartment, driving away in a new Toyota that had replaced the aged Chevy, buoyed with anticipation despite the dark, despite the hours and the miles.

Cleaned up by Executive Flights since she last used it, the red E55 Baron gleamed under hardstanding lights. Like most pilots Jana tended to become sentimental about the planes she flew even those that hardly deserved it. But there were no doubts here. An Executive mechanic had told her it looked like a million dollars and this was literally true. New, it had cost well over seven figures although the company had bought it for much less at a fire sale. The performance statistics, especially the rate of climb, justified the price tag, but it was the aesthetics that pleased Jana. The streamlined nacelles, the long arrogant nose and the precisely raked dorsal antenna were part of a unified design proclaiming its sleekness and its aerodynamic efficiency. And, she told herself, it handles like a dream.

But how did they manage to design such a serious-looking cockpit?

As she touched the yoke, each tip studded with a multitude of buttons, she was reminded of Roy still unable to fly straight and level. Was she betraying him with the Baron? She considered the nature of love and was sure she loved him. Eventually he would share this part of her life. Had to.

She took off for Phoenix, picked up three suits who had oil business to attend to in Dallas, drew their attention to informal breakfast in the musette and explained the meaning of the Burns' verse on the flask.

"A love letter, then. Kinda permanent," said one of them.

"Let's not tempt fate," she said, laughing, confident fate was not being tempted.

But fate was tempted and sprang its trap during the next booking: flying a rock group round a series of gigs over territory that matched Roy's practice. The charter lasted three weeks during which she spent one night in Tucson; the other evenings she made phone calls, initially long, then shorter. Abruptly he told her that flying progress was slow.

"Josh says I have heavy hands," Roy said. "Don't know about that. They didn't show up in animal surgery. Whatever, the ailerons don't like them."

"I take it Josh has some answers?"

"Thumb and two fingers, both hands. Could be that my fingers aren't all that delicate either."

He spoke neutrally, whereas normally he mocked his own shortcomings.

She said, "One rocker offered me five-hundred bucks for the flask."

"Good to know I can do something right. Push him up to a grand and then take it. I can always have the etching redone."

"Oh Roy, I couldn't do that."

Two days later Roy tried a shallow descending turn and Josh had to take over the plane. "But there's a weekend coming and I'm free. I've asked Josh to give me four hours spread over the two days. See if continuity helps."

"Shit. I wish I was there to gee you up a bit."

He responded angrily. "I've got to work this out myself. We agreed. I don't want you tied to the Cessna for life. The Baron is progress and you've earned that."

"You're more important. I hate the pain you're going through."

"Hey, I'm a grown man."

Although it was pure torture she refrained from calling on the Saturday and Sunday of his extended lessons. When she did call, on Monday, his mobile was switched off. Unheard of. Tuesday too. She finally made contact at midday on Wednesday.

This time his voice was brisk and unnatural. "Yeh, sorry about that. I've been doing some thinking. And talking. Josh suggests I try a new instructor; he knows a guy who's good with problem cases. First lesson on Friday." He paused. "Perhaps we could cut down on these progress reports. They can be a bit of a hassle, you know."

She tried to envisage him five hundred miles away, holding the phone, talking in this disguised way. Thought randomly of his tanned neck, the result of never wearing a tie. The capable hands which had smoothed over her. Grey hair barbered rather than styled. None of it coalesced. She wanted to say that learning to fly was unimportant, that her new status was meaningless, that she needed nothing more than to work hard and be with him. When she spoke her voice too was different, stilted, as if she were passing on results from an AIDS clinic. "You're right, I've been a pest, it hasn't helped. I'll stay quiet and see you at the apartment on Saturday night." She tried to think of a word of affection but none worked.

The rock group were waiting in an SUV that would take them to the airfield where she would fly them to Albuquerque. She knew they'd watched her and as she opened the door the bass guitarist in the adjacent seat asked, "You OK, angel?"

It had been a mistake telling them her mother's salutation. All of them preferred it to Jana. She had last cried at primary school and she wasn't about to cry now. But the awful thing was she wanted to.

It was nearly ten in the evening when she got back to Tucson. As she let herself in he got up from the couch and took her in his arms. She tasted Scotch in his mouth, not beer, not wine, and then he drew her into the bedroom. As he undressed her it seemed strange he should be doing this. I am an unsophisticated lover, she told herself. Normally I undress myself and then lie down on my back, legs apart. Now it was as if she'd forgotten how. Covering her he strained to be inventive, pretended to be tender and exaggerated amateurishly. She saw through each contrivance; saw too what she had lost.

Afterwards he grinned and pretended to wipe sweat from his face. "It didn't work, the new instructor. He was full of new tricks but I was full of the old shit. Heavy hands." He slid a hand in between her sticky thighs. "Still good for some things though."

Futilely, hopelessly, she said: "I'm sorry, truly sorry. It's not the end of the world though. I can quit Executive, go back to the Cessna and be your loving chauffeur. Honestly I don't need two engines."

His eyes seemed to pity her. "The Baron's your reward. How would it be if I took that away?" He stroked her temple. "There is something you can do for me, though. But we'll talk about that tomorrow. Get some sleep, now. Poor babe, you look all stressed out."

While he was in the shower on Sunday morning she called Josh. "What's all this crap?" she asked in a terse voice.

"Oh shit. I'd rather it was anyone than you."

"Heavy hands?"

"I hope to hell I did the right thing. It's an excuse. Something to let him down lightly. To be kind."

"But why?"

"Because I didn't want to tell him the truth. His problem is fear. Once he has hold of the yoke he's scared."

And now Roy was scrambling eggs with something close to cheerful desperation. "Big favour, I know. But I think you need confirmation. A quick flip in the Cessna, somewhere over the desert at 5000 feet so I'm not a threat to anyone. I have the plane and you check out my incurable disease."

There was only one approach. She had to pretend the Cessna was a laboratory and Roy was an innocent white rat, duplicating Josh's teaching. Coolly and scientifically. Because she had devoted herself not just to mastering flight but observing its iron-clad rules she was able to say "You have the plane." then sit back and watch. Forewarned, she didn't have long to wait: obsessive eyes, mumbled mnemonics (seconds too late), jerky scrutiny of the airspace at ill-timed intervals, moments of alarm when instruments failed to show what he was hoping for.

She could have loved him for these failings, perhaps even more intensely. But she knew, ultimately, he wouldn't let her. Those terrified periods when he had part control of the plane had revealed flying to be something distant, beyond comprehension. Hindering Jana's progress as a pilot would be selfish and destructive. Jana must continue to fly with Executive and then move to something even grander. If the price was separation he would pay it.

Jana said, "I have the plane." and saw him sink with relief back into his seat. Now she wanted to lie, something she could never recall doing in a plane cockpit. She said, "I get Josh's drift. He called it heavy hands and I'd probably agree. One thing or the other it doesn't matter. I'm sorry you were forced into this. You were right: I'll stay with Executive and we'll share a bed whenever we can."

A realist would have foreseen what would happen, would have shrugged and looked for a form of escape. But Roy had been Jana's first love and she couldn't walk away from her memories of that elevated condition. Only when his infidelities became inescapable did she start – half-heartedly – to look elsewhere. In a final humiliation she accidentally picked up the landline phone in the apartment and overheard an unknown woman's voice referring to "your girlfriend with the make-up problem". She must have been gathering her belongings at the same time Dirk was telling Jean-Claude there was a pretty good pilot in Arizona. Bags packed, she was slipping on her wind-proof when her mobile vibrated. Advised by Dirk, she heard J-C's comfortingly accented voice for the first time: "Is that Mam-zelle Jana Nordmeyer?"

CHAPTER ELEVEN

Wedding in Flagstaff

THE WAITERS, demotic, autocratic or whatever, were gone leaving behind one lounge-suited man whose status was ill-defined. He had assumed a role played out in all truly good restaurants: distantly sitting at a desk, apparently entranced by a pile of receipts, never once looking in their direction. Didi paid for the meal and wine and Jana added a monster tip. Even the car jockeys had gone home and the lounge suit smiled as he handed over their keys. "You will have no problem leaving our unforgivably cramped car park."

Van and Porsche stood twenty-five metres apart in the open space, like mute characters in a Beckett play. Didi led and Jana followed until they finally swept between the wrought-iron gates of the Labossière house. Despite the lateness Luc rose from a table on which children's exercise books were scattered. He enfolded Jana's hands in his. "I hoped your evening would end here. I insist you stay the night. Sharing a house with Didi recently has been like living with a Catholic convert. I never met her earlier prophet but I wasn't going to miss you, my dear Jana. I'm off to bed now but I must sometime talk to the custodian of my wife's soul."

Jana slid her hands away and grasped his similarly. "You'll find Didi – should we say Dieudonné just this once? – is in possession of her own soul. My lesson was a formality. Your wife was born to fly."

Luc belatedly kissed his wife. "Born to fly, my dear. Nice to know that isn't just a metaphor. Did you raise my little request?"

Didi dropped her arms. "I forgot. In my defence Jana has told a poignant story which kept me silent. And it's not quite finished.".

"What request, M. Labossière?"

"Luc, please, Jana. Would you be prepared to describe your profession to my class."

"Better if they came to the airport. We could use the Cessna for show and tell."

"Show and tell," said Luc, quickly grasping the new idiom. "The difference between two nations. In France we resort to words. American teaching is more forceful, more vivid."

Dates were exchanged, Luc departed and Jana concluded her story. Didi, surprisingly, wept.

"Just a love affair that went bad," said Jana unconvincingly.

Didi smiled through glistening eyes. "Far far more. The two columns of your life: your profession and your need to love."

"Remember, I am always prepared for emotional disaster."

"Prepared to be destroyed? Or, at least, badly wounded?"

"France looks after me," said Jana.

"Bravo that France binds up your wounds. But has France provided a replacement?"

"Is that France's obligation?"

Didi flapped a hand. "Has France had the wit to deliver a man who can see further than your cheek?"

"I have – I think – an admirer."

"An admirer! That word! Is it someone old, young, timid, or damaged? Tell me."

Jana explained Vincent while Didi, tears wiped away, sat like a raptor on the edge of her easy chair. "You care more about the child."

"Possibly," Jana said.

"That child has already split the parents."

Jana asked, "Should I discourage Vincent?"

"Not at all. Suck him dry of all feelings. Make him pay off your credits."

Jana laughed aloud, and Didi stared, feigning truculence. "I leave early tomorrow. This friendship must not die; I want to contribute. But I cannot issue endless invitations. If you care, phone from time to time." She mock scowled. "Otherwise I shall assume you don't care."

Jana was reminded of Ghislaine and the certainties modern French women liked to proclaim. "I promise. By the way I'm going to the USA on Friday for my widowed mother's wedding. I will probably see Dirk. Any message?"

"The handsome M. Boonhausen. Pretty Dirk. Tell him he was delinquent in not solo-ing me but I forgive him. As a result I've met you." She took Jana's hand. "Use the kitchen as if it were your own tomorrow. Telephone when you return from Arizona. Tell me about your experiences, your adult experiences. Yes, I insist, you are an adult."

"Despite Roy?"

"Adults are vulnerable too."

Jana rose leisurely in the morning, went downstairs when all sounds had ceased, drank orange juice and contrived to make coffee in the tennis court the Labossières called a kitchen. Then drove back to the Chauvelets to shower and change into her working clothes.

At the office Jean-Claude said, "You have taken off a whole morning."

"Blame my social life. Don't forget I'm starting a long weekend tomorrow."

"I'm rather proud of myself. You will fly Air France first-class to Chicago. My friend Pierre Wijmegen is captain. You'll be welcome to the flight-deck and he'll lecture you on the complexities of flying a 747. He will also find you a flight to Phoenix."

"First-class! You're a star, J-C."

"The prices are so grotesque there are always empty seats. Good news, hein? But we have some more good news. I have signed what are ludicrously called statement-of-intent papers with Tarbes."

"That's brilliant," she said in English and kissed his cheeks.

He grinned. "I should complete more of these coups. Ginette embraced me too."

"But only because I need a new coffee machine," said Ginette. "I have to flatter him into spending money."

"Don't fib," said Jana. "You're secretly in love with him." And was alarmed to see Ginette blush.

"I doubt that," said Jean-Claude emolliently. "But one person who is in love with Gascon Air is Mme. Labossière. She spoke this morning and asked me to lease and maintain a plane on her behalf so she can take her private licence. I offered her the less expensive option of taking over the Cessna. Which means we can replace it with something newer."

"Do I get to choose?"

"I'm in a generous mood. You choose the plane and Ginette chooses the coffee machine."

Late in the afternoon a solemn man wearing what looked like expensive golfing casuals arrived for a *bapteme de l'air*. "A birthday present from my wife. Apparently I talked about flying a year ago and this is my wife's interpretation. I feel self-conscious."

"Many people do."

"Ah, you are not French. May I ask your nationality?"

"US."

"Why am I far more confident? I suspect Americans take flying more seriously. That the French might be careless, keen on panache."

Jana said, "Jean-Claude my boss is French and he's a better pilot. On the other hand with the whole of France to choose from he employed me. He too has mysterious beliefs about Yanks."

The man laughed and extended his hand. "I understand you are Jana. I am Thierry. One more question. Do you have an instinct for those who should not fly? I don't want to waste your time."

"To some extent. But it would not simply be a matter of yes or no. I'd discuss the situation."

"I am in your hands."

She introduced him to the main instruments, to the functions of the yoke, to dialogue with the tower and to the need for awareness. She taxied and took off, explaining events as they occurred, climbed to 5000 feet, flew a five kilometre box round the airfield and invited him to check his position visually.

"Is this interesting? Enjoyable?" she asked.

"Completely."

"You see the airport tower to the right. Using that as a reference I shall fly north-east - 045 degrees if you prefer - for ten minutes. We will be over forestry land and you may take control. Briefly."

"I look forward to that."

She had him holding 5000 feet give or take fifty, easing into gentle 15 degree turns, climbing on increased power, finding the reciprocal to previous headings. Finally she took over, flew downwind along the runway and spent all the altitude from 4000 feet in a continuous tight descent which brought her featherlight onto the tarmac stripes. He said nothing until the engine was switched off at Gascon Air's hardstanding.

"Tell me what we did over the past half-hour," she said briskly

He waved an irritated hand. "Ask me what I want to do."

"I think I can guess. Short answer: you aren't wasting my time."

"Would you be my instructor?"

"If that's what you want."

He stared up at the sky, enraptured. "What kind of an American are you? One of those snail-like Christians in a tight shell or a free spirit prepared to blaspheme?"

"Neither. But reflect. I live and work in France. By choice."

"Are you easily shocked?"

"Only by students who pull a gun in a dive."

His chuckled for some time. "Have dinner with me."

"You're supposed to have a wife."

"Suppose I lied?"

"OK, the answer's no. I know nothing about you."

"Find out at dinner."

"There's another reason," she said. "It's not always a good idea for students and instructors to mix socially. But not forbidden. Ask me after your sixth lesson."

He nodded and again looked up at the sky, his new playground. "Is it normal for a student to be aroused by his teacher? Physically aroused?"

"You're asking the wrong question. I'm close by and I'm a woman. Anything's possible. I and my second-rate looks may even be reacting to you. I was touched – and amused – by what you said. But fast forward. Put me in a dress, sipping Coke and irritating the wine waiter, and your high may drop down to a low."

His eyes took in everything, paused at nothing. "Why second-rate?"

"Nature's dubious blessing."

"Oh, that." He reached for the door handle. "Well, until the sixth lesson."

FOR ONCE it was paté and crudités instead of soup. Normally the Chauvelets showed little interest in Jana's working day but the prospect of flying to a wedding in the USA intoxicated them. As did the delicacies of US etiquette.

"And your father died, when?" she was asked. Followed by decorous discussion about the interval before remarriage.

Jana was progressively tested. Distinguishing between US Baptists and Roman Catholics left her hard-pressed in terms of vocabulary and religious insight. Eventually she was forced to retrieve the large Collins-Robert to compare a priest with a pastor.

Sylvie would have liked to know – financially - how Lisa's and Dave's residences would become one. Dithered, then clearly decided it would be a step too far.

Vincent watched these careful sallies and suggested Jana might issue a press release covering the trip. Ignorant of press releases his parents didn't respond. Vincent persisted, "Jana, you have often been kind about France. What are you looking forward to?"

"A dangerous question, Vincent."

"But you can tell us. France is not perfect," said Hugues smugly.

"Being served with ice water as I sit down in the humblest café. *Café filtré* universally available. Fast fast food. Good cable TV. Institutions that don't close for a two-hour lunch."

All three shouted simultaneously but, in the end, incoherently. It wasn't the first time Jana had reeled off this well-honed list and she wasn't surprised at the resentment.

"I warned you," said Jana. "When I said dangerous I meant dangerous for you – the French."

"But you are unfair. France is not the country for fast food," said Hugues, his mouth turned down.

"I agree. That's why you shouldn't do it."

"But we don't"

"In a Bayonne street I won't name there are three of the worst hamburger joints in the world."

Sylvie raised her hands piteously. "We don't eat there."

"But I have. Look. My hometown, Flagstaff, is crummy, dying slowly. But there must be a dozen burger joints in the centre where griddles are cleaned every ten minutes, the oil for the French fries is changed twice a day and the lettuce is crunchy Iceberg not the floppy stuff. If I want *sole véronique* at 15 euros I come to France, if I want five-buck hamburger, done rare to order, I go to Anytown, USA."

"Are you not happy, here?" Sylvie asked, concerned.

"Sylvie, I am ecstatic. You and Hugues are like deputy parents, I have everything my heart desires – almost!"

That left them uncertain until Vincent said, "Mother, father. Jana teases."

"Indeed, I tease. And I should have asked earlier. What uniquely US thing would Octavien like as a small gift?"

This at least distracted the older Chauvelets. Vincent said, "Something technical I think, even if it grieves his mama. It is his birthday soon. I imagined a visit to the Cité de l'Espace in Toulouse. Would a flight there be within my means? This must not be a favour."

"Gascon Air promotes juvenile education. Special discounts."

"Really! Ah you are teasing again."

"Vincent, I'd be delighted to arrange that."

INITIALLY she sat on the fold-down seat behind the captain. Later when the co-pilot went for a snooze she moved to his right-hand seat. "Hi," said the captain, "I'm Pierre. We won't bother with my surname. Even if you knew any Dutch it wouldn't help. France being France, we like to put our twist on foreign names."

"As with that famous racing driver Schoo-mahaire."

"Right on. Anyway, J-C – who shares initials with the deity – is a wonderful man. Met him when I was a kid in Lannion, when he flew the Rosy Granite Coast. Gave me cut-price lessons, helped me get work, even lent me his plane once. Since then I've taken the safe route. I can't see him sitting in a 747 with the auto-pilot on. He likes his independence, likes the commercial risks. Says he's lucky to have you. Shall I flip a switch and let you feel this eighty-ton monster?"

Jana said yes and did so. "It's like an eighty-gram cream puff. What's your working day like?"

"You mean do I yearn for just one engine? I suppose I do. I bought a Vanns in kit form, put it together myself and I take my son up at weekends. But I enjoy this too. I like meeting all the complicated rules; being exact; remaining invisible to the passengers. Bet you I can put this down on at Biarritz-Anglet-Bayonne on the same spot you land the Cessna."

"Bet you can," said Jana, amused by his competitiveness, probably picked up at Boeing when he trained for the 747. "I wasn't knocking civil airline work. I recognise the appeal. Heck, I'm pleased to fly anything."

"J-C says you're a natural but that's a lot more than tweaking a stall. It's checking the tyre pressures, living with regional ATC, attaching the cargo nets, doing the paperwork. Not resenting it; doing it properly."

"Hey Pierre, you're a romantic at heart."

"We all are, aren't we? Keeping company with the angels – but not too damn close."

When the co-pilot returned Jana went back to her luxurious seat-cum-bed in first class, nibbled caviar on freshly prepared toast, sipped at metallic Chablis and thought vaguely about Vincent and Octavien. Then slept. During the descent into O'Hare the Air France stewardess handed her a note from Pierre: Midwestern transfer, O'Hare to Phoenix, dep 16.40, arr 18. 55; ask for Jim Priaulx, ops manager, at their desk. See you in Paris some time?

She had time to kill and bought a Sun-Times with her Sprite before sitting down to text Dirk. The Sun-Times was quickly discarded, its contents remote and impossibly parochial. She felt the mobile vibrate in the pocket over her left breast. Use my name, Westair VIP lounge. Will call. D.

The Midwestern plane was an empty transfer and she sat alone ahead of the engines in relative tranquillity, listening to some Gerry Mulligan Boyce had insisted she download to her MP3 player. She enjoyed the quiet urgency of the West Coast jazz and wondered why it was all new to her. Knew the answer as she posed the question. Flying had driven away most forms of leisure. Given a day off she might well have... hired a plane! Am I predictable, a bore? she asked herself. Questions almost impossible to answer.

Dirk had reached the VIP lounge before her and stood up immediately as she entered, smartly dressed in his captain's uniform, a long way from Gascon Air. He held her tightly, kissed her on the lips, letting his tongue flirt in and out.

"Hey, you look great," he said, tanned, beaming.

"Not as great as you. Those duds, so authoritative. Why, Mr Boonhausen, you look almost adult."

"Got to keep it that way. Westair passengers hate young-looking pilots. Give me fifteen minutes to change then I'll fly you to Flagstaff."

She'd expected a deal with some other pilot. "You've got a plane?"

"An oldish Bonanza. Cheap rental. Get yourself a coffee and I'll be back."

Surely, he'd stay the night in Flagstaff. A short odds guess at her motel. When they'd last seen each other – at Bordeaux – he'd talked about fooling around.

Not that he raised the subject until he'd cleared with Phoenix tower. "You're OK with this? I sort of explained, back in France."

The wedding was at ten the following morning. That didn't leave too many options.

He seemed doubtful as if about to add something. Then the doubt went away as he glanced once again at the instruments, opened the throttle, released the brake and started to taxi.

To delay the questions she watched him fly, noted his hands reaching instinctively for the controls of a plane he might never have sat in before, his head moving positively to inspect the sky. Climbing now, he talked about his changed life, working with a mid-size airline, playing the company game, walking down the aisle and reassuring passengers. That out of the way he asked about France, generally at first then more intimately. Finally he was back to where he started when he kissed her in the VIP lounge: telling her how well she looked, how he'd missed her, talking vaguely about luck.

This was how he saw her. Her availability was assumed and was he wrong with that? There'd been one-night stands with others, there'd been Eliazar. Quickly his confidence grew - perhaps he thought he was doing her a favour. That rankled but she squared her feelings; she liked him, always had, and was in his debt – not just tonight but for helping her professionally during her struggles, for magicking her away from Arizona when she'd needed that most of all.

His good looks hadn't changed and his body was slender and hard. His mouth had felt exciting (yet familiar!) against hers. She knew he wasn't selfish about material things and it seemed he might be equally generous in bed.

After the short flight they were together in the back of a yellow cab, hip to hip, his arm around her shoulder. Money changed hands at the motel reception, the room was switched to a double and here he was on the phone, ordering pizza. Minutes later the night porter knocked on the door and handed over two six packs of Coors. Jana drank thirstily and he watched her, amused.

"Jet lagged?" he asked.

"Not til my hand felt the cold beer can."

"You've come a long way today."

Was he offering her a way out? Or inviting her to say she was fresh as a daisy, ready for action? A voice outside said "Pizza!" and made her jump. Then laugh. Time to act the good sport.

"Ever eaten an American Hot in the shower?" she asked, unbuttoning her blouse. "Two up?"

She woke at five disoriented in time and startled by the motel room. He lay beside her, one furry armpit exposed, snoring lightly. As reality took hold she was pleased to look at him with affection. Last night, once her misgivings were blanked out, the aim was not to disappoint him and spoil the gesture. Then unsatisfied desires grabbed her and restraint took a hike. Once wasn't enough and he laughed appreciatively as she reached down a second time.

A US male body, healthy, lacking the defects and neglect Americans disliked so much in Europeans. An ideal love-making device so long as high levels of hygiene turned you on. Hey, what about me? – incapacitated without a shower. Jana drifted off to sleep, woke at eight and hurried into the bathroom. Quickly he joined her, one hand on her haunch the other on her breast, turning her round and putting his open mouth over hers as the water tumbled over their faces. "I know, I know. There isn't time. But I needed reminding."

Hair dried, combed and – whisper it not in Gath – lightly lacquered she wriggled into a flowered print dress and pulled on high-heeled white sandals. Dirk struck a pose, showing off his dark brown slacks, cream slip-ons worn without socks, and a light green polo shirt tucked into his narrow belted waist. "Not formal but it is a wedding not a funeral."

Both were casually – even trivially – dressed for the occasion. The average age of the congregation was about sixty, the men wearing sombre but cheap suits and the majority of the women understated hats. The groom's side of the aisle had attracted about thirty people, the bride's about ten, perhaps reflecting Lisa's comparatively late conversion to the Baptist church. Dirk had been dubious about attending the service but Jana was glad to have him there since they'd been escorted to a pew near the front. There was no sign of a waiting groom and the reason became apparent when an organ processional, neither Wagner nor Mendelssohn, struck up. Lisa and Dave walked hand in hand from the rear of the church towards the waiting pastor.

Her mother looked uncertain though her light brocade dress in white and varying shades of violet was more festive than those who had come to watch. As she walked down the aisle she darted glances left and right looking for people she recognised. Seeing Jana her face collapsed, tears in her eyes. Jana too found control hard to come by and she reached out to touch her mother's finger-tips. This appeared to surprise Dave.

Jana had known from the first she would not get on with Dave. He had discouraged Paris and she worried about the fate of the capital raised from her mother's house. Seeing Dave in the flesh didn't help. As the service began he stood beside her mother, hands behind his back, like a politician waiting to butt into a debate. His responses to the pastor were rapidly sing-song as if for the dozenth time; a supermarket tannoy ordering operators back to their check-outs. Dave was short, his head shaven in the Bruce Willis style. Jana told herself this was none of her business and yet her protectiveness continued to grow.

The wedding service, which had lacked grandeur, abruptly came to an end. The pastor announced wearily, "Dave and Lisa would like to meet friends in the Sunday school to the side of the church. I'll remind you they are on a tight schedule but it is…" Here a desiccated smile. "… for the best of reasons."

The church was evacuated in less than two minutes, Jana and Dirk being the last to leave. Jana said, "The tight schedule is news to me. I had hoped to take the two of them out to eat. Oh, you don't have to act the fake husband now."

"I find that guy Dave kind of weird. I'll stay with you, see whether he talks as weird as he looks."

In the Sunday school they joined a line where first-time embraces were being exchanged. Lisa must have been waiting for them, dealing quickly with those in between, until her new and subtly odious husband had a word. Finally Jana was in her mother's arms and felt the fluttering anxiety. "Angel, angel. We've so little time. Dave, dear, here's Jana."

Speculation about Dave – shared with Dirk – had her facing a genuinely forbidding figure. Kissing seemed out of the question. Jana extended a hand, realised her mother's feelings mattered most, and compromised with a hand-shake and face brush. The US president greeting a minor state which lacked oil wells.

"Hello young lady," said Dave, still sing-song. "Glad you made it at last."

As if she lived just ten miles down the pike. "Sorry about that. It's been quite a hop. The last leg courtesy of my pilot. Mum, this is Dirk; he flew me up to Flagstaff from Phoenix, got me here on time."

Dirk embraced her mother noisily, reminding Jana how unfair the greeting business was for women. All that goddamn having-to-take-it. Feelings that were offset when she saw how Dave resented this collision with his new bride.

"Flew up, young fella?" said Dave shaking Dirk's insincerely proffered hand. "'s only four hours by car. Wasn't that extravagant?"

"Not at all, sir," said Dirk. "Flyers need to put in the hours. Fill up the log-book, you know."

Jana saw where this dialogue was heading and interrupted. "Mother, what's all this about a tight schedule?"

Lisa glanced worriedly at Dave who now mobilised a condescending smile from his limited repertoire. He said, "Not all of us can afford a plane. In just over an hour Mrs Kolcuk and I will take a Greyhound down at the station. Humbler than a plane but you could say we're bound for glory. Tell 'em Lisa."

The mere mention of Dave's surname, forgotten if she'd ever known it, would probably have perturbed Jana. Greyhound certainly did.

"Dave's been a great help," said Lisa carefully. "I needed the Lord's help and Dave helped me find it. We discussed a honeymoon; I'd sold the house, we had the money and we could have taken a vacation. Could have visited Paris." A sad shadow passed over her face. "But Dave said – and I firmly agree – that would have been showy. We have the Lord's grace and we don't need show. So why not spend time searching for what we do need: the Lord's word."

Jana and Dirk waited pregnantly.

Timidly Lisa addressed Jana. "We're taking a week's course of Bible study. Since we're Baptists - " The timid smile now extended to Dave. " – there's only one place to go and that's Wheaton, Illinois. The college there has wonderful courses. I've seen the literature."

"You're taking a Greyhound to Illinois this afternoon?" Jana asked.

"How long a journey?" asked Dirk.

Their questions failed to please Dave. "A piece of discomfort for our bodies. But healing for our souls, young fella."

Jana wanted only to cry out no, no, but Dirk was ahead of her. "Look, it's a shame Jana hasn't seen her ma for two years. How about we give you a chance for that? How about we fly you to Illinois instead? Our treat." He grinned wolfishly. "That way we get to know each other."

Dave was silent, mouth wide open, outraged. His pause proved fatal. Lisa's reticence became a glorious smile which no one, not even Dave, could have tried to suppress. "How wonderful, how truly wonderful. You've come all this way and there we were, in danger of running off. Even if it was for the best of reasons. Could you possibly do that? Use the plane? Wouldn't it cost too much? Oh Dave, aren't these young people generous?"

Then, with more than a hint of calculation, she added, "Surely this wedding gift is straight from the Lord."

Jana sought Dirk's face for signs of mischief but found it averted. The detour would cost him money but she knew he – and she too for that matter - would delight in the expense.

"There are coach tickets, bookings..." Dave's voice tailed away.

"Hurry home. We'll get a cab, pick you up, call in at Greyhound. Get a refund. If they won't play we'll make up the difference. Make it a real gift so you don't lose anything."

Dave had played his last card and had been muscled offstage. Everyone bid temporary goodbyes and Jana and Dirk went out looking for a cab. Jana said, "This is a crazy stunt you've pulled. The flight's 1500 miles and the Bonanza cruises at 190 knots, that's eight hours."

"You've forgotten the Bonanza's endurance. We'll need to refuel in Kansas."

She raised her hand to protest and he grabbed her wrist. "Think how long it would take by Greyhound. Jana, it's a real gift."

And so it turned out. What Jana had seen as a long, long flight charmed her mother and even touched Dave. "Half way across the US," he said in wonder as he entered the plane.

Buying in sandwiches, fruit and two flasks of coffee turned a potential ordeal into an extended picnic. And when Jana took over the plane for the second leg from Fort Hays, Lisa reached out from her seat at the back and touched her daughter on the shoulder.

Sustained conversation lasted only an hour. Thereafter the newlyweds dozed, looked out on New Mexico, dozed again, stretched their legs briefly in Kansas during refuelling, then dozed yet again over the northern part of Missouri. As they crossed the Illinois state line Dirk, with time on his hands, arranged a patch to Wheaton College, received recommendations for a modest hotel, arranged another patch to reserve a room for the extra night the Bible course didn't cover and even contrived to have Lisa and Dave picked up from the airport by the hotel owner ("They're Baptists and that's good enough for me. Ain't a favour when we're talking Baptists.")

The goodbyes were hurried and interspersed with techno-gobbledegook about attending to the plane and an early start the following day. Neither Jana nor Dirk had any intention of staying the night at a hotel catering for Baptists.

"A wonderful, wonderful day," said Lisa.

"Right Christian of you both," said Dave, glad to be resuming his dour authority.

Showered, lying on their motel bed semi-nude, eating slices of yet another pizza but, at least, drinking Sam Adams beer, they used the TV to rid their minds of engine drone. After an hour Jana was surprised by Dirk's inertia but decided to leave him to himself.

Finally he spoke. "You weren't expecting to have to sleep with me yesterday."

"Did I have to sleep with you?"

Manly fashion he tilted the bottle to his lips. "Isn't that how you saw it? Pressed for time and – goddamnnit – grateful for the flight."

Jana sipped her beer from a toothglass. "Did it seem like gratitude?"

"No, it was good. Very good."

"What's the problem?"

"What was going on in your mind."

"Not sure anyone of us can ask that."

He grunted, then waited. She held out then gave in, "Does it matter?" she asked.

"Yes."

Now it was her turn to wait.

"Just pondering if you'd feel grateful again tonight."

"I am grateful. I must transfer some cash but that won't change anything. It was your idea and it was terrific. Even if what you really wanted was to screw Dave."

He grinned. "Don't say it hadn't crossed your mind. I'm glad for your ma it worked out. But that isn't the point. Suppose I put my hand on you – just there. That would say something, wouldn't it? You'd think first then respond: thumbs up, thumbs down. It's the thinking that interests me."

She felt the side of his hand edging between her thighs. "Is there more?"

"Yeh. But that's tougher. Let's stay with this unless it pains you."

And now a sudden insight. "We aren't thinking long-term, are we?"

"That's it," he said, sighing.

"God, Dirk, you've changed."

"If getting older is changing I've changed."

She said, "OK, taking you up on that. Suppose I put your hand there. Then we did what you wanted but I explained nothing. Or, I explained everything but there was no sex. Which is better?"

"The explaining."

"Called my bluff, you devil."

"It's not a fucking poker game," he said angrily.

"A cheap shot. Sorry."

"So what's it to be?"

She leant forward. "I'm going to break the ground rules."

"Ah no, oh shit," he groaned.

"You arrogant shit," she said, astonished. "Imagining you know what's in my mind."

"It's too damn easy to guess. We'll screw and you'll explain. That there's no long-term."

"Long-term? You! What happened?"

"You should know. We're almost the same age."

"But that's the only similarity. Consider your looks, your pay, your uniform. Is the problem you don't see yourself as the main attraction these days?"

"What does that mean?"

She stared at his contorted face. "That life's changed for the worse. A shortage of willing broads. No more fun. No more variety?"

"Fun! Variety! I get that at Disneyland. What about something that lasts?"

"What makes you think I'd last?"

"Because you have lasted. You've taken shit and survived. You're… balanced."

After nearly forty years of startled looks, whispering, averted faces and – worst of all – sympathy, it wasn't the first word that came to mind. But was balance the end product? Had Dirk, careless in his relations with women, stumbled on a truth? Was she now properly equipped to live life? Was France, in effect, shining a light on a developed form of Jana Nordmeyer?

His face shone but with what? Anger? Frustration? Or – God forbid – awakening desire. She breathed deeply and forced herself to look at him objectively. Christ, he was still pretty – yet inescapably male. Why complicate things? There was a lot of pleasure resting on this motel bed.

Saying nothing, she moved on to him compressing her breasts against his tanned chest. Reached down and held him. "There's a pizza crumb at the corner of your mouth. See, I pick it up with the tip of my tongue. Now I swallow it. Think about that. What does it mean?"

He was staring at her as if she was the Second Coming.

"I like you" she said. "Always have. No more argument. Let's do something you call screwing and I call something else. After, if you want, I'll tell you why we mustn't think long-term – for both our sakes."

He whimpered but not for long. And she, thinking herself to be in control, dictating his therapy, found herself vulnerable, overtaken by new sensations which left her breathless, her chin shining with saliva. But sure, nevertheless, about the way her future must run.

"We both need another half," she said. "I've buried myself in flying as my only option. But there has to be another part of me. Not stamp collecting, not going to the gym; someone else who can break through the obsession. Not you, you're part of the illness."

He watched her calmly now. Got up, wet a towel in the bathroom and wiped his torso, then hers. He said, "You taught me a lesson. I wanted you back in France. Told J-C to sign you on. Put you on the back-burner when you came. Stud stuff. Figured I could do better. That last half-hour at Bordeaux I knew I'd been a fool. Earlier, if I'd asked, would you have come to me?"

"Out of desperation. And it would have been a disaster. Two left feet."

"Do you ever think about... love?"

"Not much," she said.

The return flight from Chicago was again with Air France but without Pierre and his difficult surname. Pierre wanted to see her in Paris and she knew it would never happen. Another flyer who was part of the illness.

CHAPTER TWELVE

Octavien flies

THE SUN was setting as she took off from Clermont-Ferrand and soon she had the unnatural Parc des Volcans out to port, cone-shaped extinct volcanoes saying the Auvergne was the Auvergne and these lanced boils were all part of the mystery. The instrument lights were showing up within the cockpit, above the switches and beyond the throttle lever where worn paint hinted at the Cessna's long life. Soon it would be handed over to Didi and with it a part of Jana's emotional attachment. For Jana Foxtrot - Sierra Delta Romeo and its chic wheel spats was William Powell as Nick Charles, The Thin Man, trim moustache and devastating put-downs. Seen once accidentally on late-night TV and remembered ever since. And she? Myrna Loy as Nora Charles, sleekly dressed and imperturbable.

Over the radio came Armelle's very correct voice asking for her Bayonne ETA. Jana read it off the GPS, "Who wants to know?"

"That American gentleman. Could you meet him in the airport bar."

"That American? Does he have a name?"

"He wrote it down but you must forgive my pronunciation. Do you know a Boo-ees?"

It took Jana several seconds. "An Afro-American I believe?"

"Indeed."

Jana hadn't seen Ghislaine for three weeks. There'd been phone-calls, brief and enigmatic regarding the man who professed to love her so much he was willing to tackle the intransigence of her mother. Ghislaine had mentioned using the asp if things went wrong. Since then she'd become remote.

To starboard the Dordogne flashed its sinuous reflection: useful during the daytime, less so at night. More important were the light patterns that identified the larger towns: Aurillac directly to port, larger and more distant to starboard, Brive-la-Gaillarde. The names still pleased her, especially set against the dull labels of her home state – Chandler, Prescott, Parker.

Finally the comfort of her homebase runway, Biarritz-Anglet-Bayonne, precisely east-west, confirmed by the Etang de Brindes, a small lake immediately to the south, always a relief in low cloud.

Boyce sat at one of the bar tables, crouched over a laptop, a barely touched glass of beer to his left. He spotted her as she opened the door, stood up athletically and greeted her with the rapid tattoo triple kiss. "You work late. Get you a drink?"

"A Sam Adams beer."

He grinned. "Just back from the States obviously? I'll have one flown over. In the meantime how about a Kronenbourg?"

His bustling confidence didn't suggest a man with girlfriend problems. He said, "I'm picking up Ghislaine late this evening and we're going to the jazz club. I need advice. Not personal stuff because I know you both chat and that's fine. But you need to know something about inner Boyce."

"Whoa. No need for a confession."

He laid his hand flat on the bar table. "A confession I'm happy to make. I guess you could say I'm in love. You know what? – I've never said that before. Ever. Cut to the chase I'll do whatever it takes for Ghislaine. However heavy. OK?"

Jana nodded. "I'm not giving anything away but I think she suspects that."

"Good to know. Thanks." He looked less confident. "Look, I'm no innocent. This is provincial France; I love the place but I know I don't fit in. Never will. If things work out with Ghislaine she'll pay a price. I think she knows that."

"Me too."

"My aim is to limit that price. Straight off she mustn't break with her mother. As you know I've offered to talk to Mme. le Lannic. Won't be fun but I have to try. Now I'm not at all sure about Ghislaine's feelings on this and I'm not looking to pry. But your French is better than mine and you know France better. Forget Ghislaine, if you can. What's your opinion?"

"If I gave it, you might act on it. I'd have interfered in her life."

He'd expected this and looked depressed. "She'll never know, I promise. Just be honest. Is that too big an ask?"

Before Boyce there'd been Vincent. Being asked such questions was no compliment, she realised. "I have reasons not to like Mme. le Lannic. I'm likely to be biased."

A crust thrown to a dog; he grabbed it eagerly. "You stayed there. Had an argument and left. But I wouldn't be here if I didn't trust you. I know you'll bust a gut not to be biased."

Jana spoke slowly. "From what I know of Mme. le Lannic I don't think you'll get very far. It isn't her fault, she's lived a tight rural life, screwed by the government and by the weather. She's learned to suspect anything new. Top of that I'm not sure your approach would be worth the effort. Your project probably worries Ghislaine. There, I've gone much further than I ever intended."

Jana had always seen Boyce as a guy who hid his emotions with laughter and ebullience. A black guy who'd got where he'd got in such a huge corporation had to be savvy. But now his shoulders said other things.

Folornly he said, "I wanted to act, not go with the flow. Thought she'd appreciate that."

"The American way," said Jana softly.

"Waddya mean?" A sore spot. Boyce worked hard at not being US.

"Steady. It's a cultural thing. You could say it's the USA's great strength but it has a dark side: a belief that any problem can be solved."

"Is that so goddamn wrong?"

"If there isn't a solution it's very wrong. Look, Mme le Lannic comes from centuries of farming stock, small farms, a bitter life, existence not guaranteed. And she's a widow – there's a lot of them around. Ghislaine's broken out, doesn't have dirty hands, got a job which gives her status in the village. There's stress between mother and daughter; Mme le Lannic sees her at risk but can't control her."

"Sees Ghislaine at risk?"

"Emotionally at risk. Ghislaine doesn't practise the old *omerta* game. Doesn't keep herself to herself. Has given up on village labourers. Meets men who are beyond her mother's comprehension."

Boyce looked trapped, his eyes were wide with consternation. "Throw me a lifeline, for God's sake."

Jana considered holding his hand but didn't. Too much US solidarity. "Boyce, you said it yourself, but in reverse. You're a successful suit and you see going with the flow as bad karma. But here you may have to. Take Ghislaine's lead. Don't force the pace. Be there for her; don't try and be ahead of her."

Jana drank off the rest of her beer in one swig and found herself shaking with anger. She gritted, "And next time choose a better grade of counsellor. Why me? What the hell do I know? My emotional track record is poor. I understand planes not other people. Ah shit!"

"Jana, sweetie." Boyce was almost on the verge of tears. "What have I done?"

She forced herself to think of him rather than herself. "Again, for what it's worth. Ghislaine's ready for you; the situation's yours to mess up. Forget loving her and trying to show it all the time. Relax with her. Genoa was a great but next time wear old jeans and go for a walk. Take her to McDonalds and joke about it: 'To know me you've got to understand the Golden Arches.' Pirate some software. Watch Friends in English and do her the subtitles."

It caught his imagination but there were still doubts. "Is that me?" he asked.

"Is SocleSoft you? Who knows? Perhaps it's the suit she likes and I'm telling you to commit suicide." Sometimes, she thought, it's a pleasure just to speak English in this country.

Finally, because he was clever and quick-witted, he got it. "Pretend not to care but actually care all the more. The light touch. As you're playing with me now?"

"It's yours to screw up Boyce."

But the secrecy lasted hardly any time at all. "You spoke to him," said Ghislaine over the phone as Jana drove to work the following morning.

"Look my dear, the guy is besotted. I told him one thing: his idea isn't good. I didn't want to but he forced me. If what I said was wrong mail me the asp."

Ghislaine said, "That wasn't all."

"No, and here's why I'm going to use the asp anyway. Counselling people's for the birds. It struck me he was too stiff, too much the company executive. I suggested he loosened up. In a flash I thought: perhaps G likes formality, being managed in bed. What the hell do I know? I'm a well-known failure at the love game."

Ghislaine said, "When we first met he had authority and he made me listen. That seemed enough. This thing with Maman is more difficult. I was flattered, of course, that he cared enough, that he had the courage. But Maman is never going to change and it's better she is not confronted. Boyce could not see this, he was not pragmatic."

"Too much damn honesty."

"Now, after your advice, he realises he was wrong. He is contrite. But there is more..."

Jana was waiting at a T-junction where it was notoriously hard to turn left. Hanging on to Ghislaine's *points de suspension* tested her patience. Ghislaine resumed, "He sees the whole thing as a disaster averted. Convinced he could have lost me. This is nonsense, of course. But it is touching. He's handed over power and did it willingly. We have moved closer together, I think."

BUT THE event rankled, perhaps because she continued to dwell on what Dirk had said the week before. To be seen as a source of solid advice was a burden and Vincent Chauvelet felt the backlash during the promised visit to Cité de l'Espace in Toulouse. Jana directed her attention towards Octavien, treating his father briskly and factually as if she were his tour guide.

Space exploration had never gripped Jana and only the landing of the shuttle enlivened a tableau of technology While Vincent tried to glorify a system for turning urine into potable water, Octavien had already noticed where Jana's interest lay.

Would Jana have volunteered to land the shuttle? he asked.

She shook her head. "It's only a small part of the mission. The rest is working computers, doing experiments and trying to stay comfortable. Not my bag. But if landing was a job on its own – I'd like that. See those dinky wings? So tiny! Tiny because they have to stand the heat build-up at thousands of miles an hour. But tiny's terrible when you need to control the plane for a landing. No second chances."

"It's dangerous. How can you like danger?"

"Haven't you been tempted to walk along the top of a wall?"

"My mother would discourage me."

"As she should," said Jana diplomatically. "But secretly, have you been tempted?"

"I'm not sure."

"Risk's funny. Certain jobs carry risks. But risk can make the job worthwhile. It isn't the risk we like but the proposition. Gosh, it was hard putting that into French. I hope it was understandable?"

"I always understand you, Mlle. Jana."

"That puts me in my place," said Vincent, trying to get back into the act. "This subject of risk. His mother protects him all the time and I accept that. But should I, just occasionally, expose him to the irrational? Nothing extreme, of course. Certain sports, perhaps."

"What was Hugues' view?"

"Considering he pushed paper at the Hotel de Ville he was daring on my behalf. He urged me into speleology which I hated. I settled for soccer. But Octavien is two people: left alone he would be intellectually adventurous and ignore physical activities. Yet if I recommended sport he would do it – but dutifully. So I hold back."

"Surely Octavien makes up his own mind," said Jana. "I get the impression he is doing it all the time. Look, there's a film show about Ariane. Why don't we rest our legs?"

Vincent's use of "dutifully" was clear-sighted and Jana watched Octavien throughout the film. Outside she drew Vincent aside.

"What are you suggesting?" he asked.

"Is space gripping him? I'm not convinced. Should we ask him?"

"I am sure you already know the answer," Vincent said shrewdly.

"I haven't primed him."

"Not today," said Vincent. "Perhaps on other occasions. But you are right. He's the reason we're here. You ask and I'll watch."

Octavien, typically, delayed answering, gazing at the two adults in turn, guessing at the preferred response. He said neutrally, "I am quite happy here at Cité de l'Espace."

Vincent broke in, keeping his face straight, "Octavien, tell the truth."

Brief sheepishness for form's sake, then a small smile. "The airfield. Our plane. Tutorials by Mlle. Jana."

Vincent shrugged.

"We landed at Muret-l'Herm" said Jana. "Only a small airport. There may not be too much going on there."

"Then we can talk about planes. I can take your instrument examination. You can explain our route home." He paused. "I like airports."

Jana looked at Vincent who said, "Why not?"

Jana had chosen Muret, twenty kilometres south-west of Toulouse, to avoid heavy landing fees at the main airport. Even adding the costs of the taxi it was cheaper and far less hassle. Muret looked like the sort of place a US accent might work wonders.

Soon Octavien was asking questions of the under-employed AT controller while Jana and Vincent sat drinking mugs of coffee, overlooking the deserted airstrip.

"It is what he wants," said Jana.

"I can't dispute that. And good education takes advantage of what is already there. But perhaps I should not think in those terms. This is leisure time. There is a French tendency to turn everything into a lesson."

As if it had been arranged for Octavien, two planes landed in quick succession and while the controller made his announcements Jana whispered explanations about flaps, changes in engine note and where each plane would turn from the main runway.

Gravely Octavien shook hands with the controller and thanked him with the sort of formality that so astonished Anglos. The controller said, "It has been a pleasure, m'sieur."

To the adults he said "An intelligent kid. Give him one more treat. Let him do the final when you leave."

As they walked past an open hanger a mechanic working on a Comanche engine looked up, saw Octavien and waved.

"Would you like to know what that man is doing?" Jana asked.

"Of course."

"Then ask him. Seriously, as you spoke to the controller."

Vincent and Jana stood five metres away in order not to intrude. Vincent said, "Do you remember repeating something Octavien once said? That he wanted to be an engineer like his papa. Now I am not so sure. Perhaps he has changed his mind. But is the attraction the subject or the prophet?"

"If it's a schoolboy crush he disguises it." Denied an exact idiom for crush Jana improvised with *tourner la tete*. Vincent looked at her sardonically: "*Tourner la tete* indeed."

Finally when their plane sat at the end of the taxiway, Octavien, his head diminished by the hugeness of adult headphones, said: "Cleared for take-off, Foxtrot – Sierra Delta Romeo" and heard a ghostly, "*Au revoir, mon petit brave.*"

At 5000 feet Jana levelled out, took off her windbreaker, folded it up and shoved it under Octavian's backside raising him to the level of the window. "And what was the mechanic doing?" she asked.

"Replacing an oil pump. He told me why it was damaged but the words were very technical. Said it was very important; that the engine might stop. He made me promise to tell my pilot – you Mlle. Jana – to check our engine."

"Quite right. I regularly check oil in the engine; on the ground with a dipstick, here, when we're flying, with the oil pressure gauge. If the needle swings to the left we could be losing oil. Also, I check engine temperature here. If we lose oil, friction increases and the temperature rises."

She was amused that the enormity of the next question made him tentative. "And then…?"

"I throttle back to stop the engine working too hard. Look out of the windows to see whether oil's escaping. Check for landing strips. Fly on, watching pressure and temperature like a hawk. If pressure continues to drop temperature usually rises and I have to think seriously of putting down somewhere. Sounds bad but there's no need to panic yet; at 5000 feet we have time."

She was conscious of Octavien's stare. "OK, the bad readings continue. I know where the landing strips are. Unless there's a problem I choose the nearest. I use the radio to tell ATC my situation. And now it's decision time: guess the big decisions."

He thought for a minute. "It must be the engine."

"Bravo! I could let it run so we reach the field quickly and land safely. But suppose it stopped before I reached the field. A plane with no engine is a glider and gliders are best handled at altitude, not close to the ground. Without an engine I get only one chance to land. By which time this thing – you'd hardly call it a plane! – is horribly hard to control."

Octavien's eyes glistened. "So you switch off the engine and start it again close to the ground."

"Bravo, again. But that can be risky in another way."

Octavien shook his head.

"I may not be able to re-start the engine."

"Oh!"

"And oh from me," said Vincent from the rear seat.

"It's oh from me too. Emergency landings aren't fun especially if there isn't a proper field. But it helps if the pilot has done plenty of hours in that plane, has a feel for the machinery. The best option is probably stopping and starting. That's what I'd do if the readings weren't terrifying and the engine still sounded smooth. In between I'd have to glide but we'd be quite high and I'd be able to control it more safely."

She stroked Octavien's head. "So why don't planes terrify me? One reason is the way they're made. Cessna started in 1927 and they designed this plane way back. They designed it, tested it, then sold it. A good plane but improvable. Soon hundreds of customers were, in effect, testing it, making suggestions. New versions of the plane were brought out and the process started all over. Fact is Cessna are just as concerned about this plane as I am. Any carelessness and they could be sued to death in the courts."

Octavien was silent, looking at the instruments, the sky around them, the endlessly varying ground beneath. His voice was slightly shrill through the earphones. "Those are good reasons. But fear can be just fear."

Vincent stirred at this unexpectedly adult statement. "That's true," said Jana remembering Matthieu and his inexplicable problems. "One way of preventing that is having the student repeat procedures, over and over, until habit replaces fear."

"But the student may fear flying itself."

And now the memories were far more intimate. "Then he or she should be discouraged. Flying isn't for everyone."

"Certainly not for the majority," suggested Vincent.

"I want to fly, but it frightens me," said Octavien.

"That may be just ignorance," said Jana. "Learning the basics can drive that type of fear away. Why don't we find out. Vincent, would you allow Octavien to fly the plane for a few minutes?"

"Is that legal?"

"No."

Vincent laughed. "The perfect answer to a Frenchman. And the best encouragement. But is Octavien willing?"

Octavien nodded forcefully.

Jana said, "First watch my hands, see how gentle they are on the yoke. The plane wants to climb; my job is to stop it. Watch again. I turn the yoke gently to the right, hold it for perhaps two seconds, then return it gently to where it was. Look at the compass and see if you can remember - as you should - our previous bearing. *Voila!* We've changed our direction. OK? Now, as pilots say, Octavien you have the plane."

Back at the Chauvelets there was an iced cake decorated presciently with a model plane, even if it was a Dassault Mystère. In his responses Octavien steered a diplomatic path between the space centre and the flying.

As Jana washed up Vincent said, "He tries hard not to hurt my feelings."

"A remarkable child."

"The pair of you get on so well together." Vincent said.

Jana remained – intentionally – bent over the low sink. "Flying," she said. "It's a boy's world."

"A world delivered with such grace."

There would be more of this, Jana realised. And each time the implications would be emphasised. She thanked God for the caravan outside and the empty first-floor landing at night. As the adults sat down together and the *pineau des charentes* was broached, she couldn't rid herself of the impression that Hugues looked at her in a new speculative way.

CHAPTER THIRTEEN

Enter Christopher

JANA trawled the Internet for a newer second-hand plane to replace the Cessna. A company in Dijon offered a range of Robins, now made in New Zealand but previously in France, some dating back to 1985. Robins filled the French skies but Jana had never flown one and in any case had a secret prejudice for US companies. "Price reflects average condition and some older (but classy) avionics," tickled her. The Robins were not strong contenders at Gascon Air and Jean-Claude had already shortlisted another Cessna which he and Jana would look at when they had time together. Jana's main aim was to keep her mind occupied.

Switching to a site of worldwide sources she clicked on a virtually new Piper Mirage. The price, at just over a million dollars, and the location, Englewood in Colorado, were both a little rich for GA's modest purse. She moved on, irritated by the way "worldwide" often defaulted to the USA, irritated too by unimaginative French sites and their offhand links.

Her heart wasn't in it. The previous night there'd been more flurries from Vincent. A long and boring discussion ostensibly about Octavien's education had been interrupted at regular intervals with invitations to comment. Jana had nothing to say. For one thing she had never needed to understand the complexities of the French education system and often used US analogies which meant nothing to French parents. For another she knew this was not really a subject open to third parties but a long drawn-out spat which had helped break up Vincent's marriage. Nor was she taken in when Vincent seized on her feeble contributions, thanked her profusely and promised to relay the information to Octavien.

Such evenings raised problems. Vincent was likeable enough and since Jana had suffered his wife's autocratic tongue her sympathies were with him. Octavien's ultra-formal seriousness was charming but was also her Achilles heel. Discouraging Vincent might hurt Octavien. It was easy to see where this would end. The elder Chauvelets obviously thought Jana was a good influence on son and grandson. Sooner or later Vincent would make a request which Jana would have to turn down; this would be resented and she would be looking for new lodgings.

Perhaps the logical solution would be to move before there was any cause for resentment. But on what grounds?

Listlessly she continued trawling and came up with a 2007 Cessna 182T, an evolution of the Cessna they were discarding, showing only 150 hours on the clock. Ads for second-hand aircraft were often coy about prices but this one was specific: $33,950 down payment, $2188 per month, the balance of $305,550 in a year. Jana had always avoided getting to know Jean-Claude's finances and doubted whether he could run to this. The vendor was in Arlington, Texas, but perhaps it was worth mentioning if only to gather a more accurate picture of how Gascon Air was underpinned. For her own protection.

But now Ginette was holding up the phone. "A gentleman with an accent," she said.

As Jana put the phone to her ear the caller was already talking: "Surely my accent isn't that bad?"

"I'll trade you," she said. "How about mine?"

"Good gracious, American! Let's make best use of our French failings and talk English."

"So long as you don't talk superior."

"My dear young lady I'm a poverty-stricken Brit from Essex just scraping by. Superior to no one."

"I like the 'young lady' and we love poverty here at Gascon Air. I'm Jana Nordmeyer one of the company's two pilots. What can I do for you?"

"Names. Nordmeyer sounds like an explorer or a cross-country skier; can't match that. I'm Christopher Day. I've lived in or near Bayonne for twelve years. Started out helping Brits buy French houses in the days when houses cost peanuts. Now, to quote Damon Runyon, I do the best I can."

"Damon Runyon?"

"Ah, you must be a very young young lady. Runyon: sports writer in the fifties who wrote short stories about New York low life. Should have won a Nobel but his stuff was far too funny. Back to me. French property prices have zoomed up so I now help out monoglot Brits scared witless when the *taxe foncière* demand drops through their letterbox. Normally I wouldn't need Gascon Air's services but yesterday I acquired an old-fashioned client, a house buyer."

"Are most Brits monoglot?"

"Ms Nordmeyer – Jana – don't distract me. This is my national shame. You tell me why perfectly normal people living in Cheltenham or Harrogate uproot themselves and end up in the south-west eating Marmite and playing bridge without a scrap of French. They provide me with a living – a very modest living – but make me feel like a pimp. Where was I? Yes, the new client. Quite quite monoglot. Even worse, in a hell of a rush. Property to see and it's all to be crammed into two days. A huge circular journey which would spell death for my fifteen-year-old BX. I have his authority to hire a plane but that's the simple bit."

"You need to know how near we can get to these places in the plane."

"Bless you. Obviously I've come to the right place. Agents or vendors will pick us up when we land and we need to keep their drive to a minimum. I'll need to visit Gascon with my list and fit it to your maps. Assuming you like the sound of the job."

Jana said, "We've done this in miniature so, sure, it's our type of work. But you – and especially your client – must realise we'll be landing on aero-club grass strips, no facilities other than a windsock. That could be part of the charm. Why not sell it as an adventure?"

"Aha, *le marketing*," said Day. "Though I'm not sure my lot are great adventurers. Can I see you soonest?"

Jana was waiting for him in Gascon Air's reception area. Her limited experience of the British had not been encouraging: their jokiness frequently interfered with normal communications. The chat they'd had already confirmed this to some extent.

Her view took in the car-park and Day's arrival was immediately obvious. His Citroen BX was covered with chalky dust and may have been red underneath. One rear light was repaired with gaffer tape and the rusting roof rack was garlanded with elastic spiders. As he emerged, it was clear the car proclaimed the driver. His greying hair almost touched his shoulders but not stylistically, it had simply been neglected. A long-sleeved lumberjack shirt had been laundered far beyond throwaway and the primary colours had dissolved into grey. The jeans too had lost most of their blue. His boots, however, looked expensive and new. Jana wondered uneasily whether she might have to ask for proof of his finances.

Close-up, as they shook hands, Jana saw the tan of a longtime resident. "The maps are in there," she said. "I'll get you some coffee; I promise you it's OK."

"US style? The stuff I now call *café allongé*? That's good news. I've never been an expresso man."

Although the coffee was close to boiling he sank a third of the mug and sighed appreciatively. "First things first. You see me as a scruff and suspect I could be null and void. Here's a thousand-euro cheque as a retainer to get us off the ground – and isn't that a nice metaphor?"

Jana mumbled her denial but he laughed comfortably. "Don't give me that. You looked totally cast down. I simply can't afford to dress up when I'm working. Translating French culture isn't just paperwork; everything's new to these *arrivistes:* power fuses, stop-taps, chimney pots, jets in gas ovens. I toyed with painting Monsieur Touche-à-Tout on the side of the BX but that would mean I'd have to wash it."

"Jack-of-all-Trades?"

"That's it. By the way, the thousand euros came from Mr Grandage, a man you're quickly going to dislike. No Francophile he. A property speculator. But this Brit beggar can't afford to choose. I'm wasting your time. Here's a rough map covering the nine houses; let's see what you've got in the way of landing strips."

The addresses lay within the Bayonne – Bordeaux – Cahors - Toulouse rectangle. Jana taped half a dozen AT maps together then used an overlay to mark the reference points. "The two addresses in Villeneuve-sur-Lot are going to be tricky," she said. "They're on either side of the town and the strip's north. It's not worth looking for another strip for such a short flight."

"No need to worry. Mr Grandage will have those interested jumping through hoops. All that matters is fitting the visits into forty-eight hours. He has a horse running at Newmarket the following day."

"Seems a waste. He'll be flying over some of France's most beautiful territory and it sounds as if that won't mean a damn."

"Well at least it'll mean a damn to me."

His sudden assertion surprised her. She looked up and saw bushy eyebrows from which tails of hair curved down to touch his eyelids. Until then he'd been jocular, now almost truculent.

He said, "Sorry about that. I love France but it's my fate to deal with people who've moved here for all the wrong reasons. For sunshine, cheap wine and empty roads. And then they drizzle because France isn't Esher."

"Or Arizona."

"Really? Are there Americans here who whine? Not you, surely? An interesting job, a wonderful part of the planet, French good enough for pilot talk. Besides, you don't look the part. Mind if I ask why you're here?"

"A love affair that went wrong. Plus I suspected France would be kinder than the US."

"Kinder? Oh, I see. Is it?"

"Mostly."

He paused. "Am I keeping you?"

"Give me your take on France."

"It's the home of irony and I'm living proof. I was converted on an exchange holiday to Amiens. Junked history, did modern languages at Cambridge, lectured at Sussex, married a Leavisite. Far cleverer than me, very stylish, much sought after. We parted amicably and she's now spouse to a full prof at Balliol. We didn't have too much but she got it all – with my best wishes. That's several ironies rolled into one. But here's another. I looked for work in France because I couldn't afford to live in England."

"And it went well?"

He smiled faintly. "More marginal than not, but I've clung on. And I enjoy life despite the monoglots. I looked for teaching at first but it's the wrong way to go. Many Brits down here are lazy so there's manual work available. I profit from their laziness and their ignorance. A pimp of sorts."

Jana stood up. "Come and sign a couple of papers and then we'll look at the plane."

Jean-Claude had returned. Jana explained the charter and introduced Day. Jean-Claude asked, "How many people in the party of M. Grandage? – pfui, that name, he sounds like a Frenchman."

"Him and his wife."

"Does he enjoy his comfort? Perhaps the Seneca would be better. These landing strips would be no problem, Jana?"

"The strips are all 2500 minimum."

"Let us temporarily reserve the Seneca. Tell your client, M. Day, it is a twin-engine plane, faster, more capacity."

Having allowed Day to sit in both planes Jana escorted him back to his car. Opening the door he said, "I've been ordered all over the place by M. Grandage - " He used J-C's frenchification of the name and they both laughed. " – I wasn't looking forward to this escapade. But I have a feeling you'll make it bearable."

They shook hands and Jana watched him drive away. Why were his shabby clothes offset by his expensive boots? she asked herself.

LUC Labossière's class did not respond well to Jana on the pleasures of flying. For one thing they were a year too old, and blasé with it, given the level she pitched her talk. She should have taken heed when one of them gave a languid but precise account about how aerofoils provide lift. Thereafter most writhed in their seats and resisted participation. Goaded by Luc they finally did respond but not as he might have hoped. Jana was taxed with accusations about aerial pollution and other environmental matters. Puffed up with self-righteousness they then moved on to the war in Afghanistan and Luc was forced to bring things to a close.

France had taught Jana resilience in the face of anti-US opinion and she was inclined to shrug off the animosity, even applaud the class's political awareness. Their rudeness she attributed to youth. But Luc, wanting to defend his students' behaviour, looked for other subtler explanations. Was the "structure" of her talk "not quite right"? he mused.

Jana also knew the French loved to criticise foreigners face to face, often about language, occasionally about culture in general. Certain words Luc was presently using, especially "structure" and its variants, suggested he was entering an arid phase. "Hold on, Luc," she said. "You're way over my head. I'm only a joystick jockey. Most of my talk is over the VHF. Not much call for oratory there."

Released from formal politeness Luc hunched his shoulders pleasurably at the prospect of debate. Ignoring her call for pax he advanced a thesis in which words like "context" and "self-consciousness" took on a life of their own. His speeches – no other word - were dense with allusion and each part of his argument interminable. Occasionally she'd flown loquacious academics to conferences. Then, as now, she had let the flow of words lull her, hoping to pick out key references that summarised the meaning.

When he realised she wasn't responding he repeated himself. Flying, it seemed, demanded intellectual resources; he, Luc, a non-flyer, was quite sure of this. This Jana grasped but when "modality" was twisted into forms she never suspected sense went backwards. A sliver of daylight emerged as "intellect" and "articulacy" were interwoven; Luc insisted that Jana had the capacity to communicate at a higher level. But undermined this flattery by pointing out that she presently risked "texturalism".

They had moved from the classroom into Luc's office. As he talked her eyes slid over his well-stocked bookshelves and she recognised the source of her failings. Not so much that her meagre collection of books (mainly technical) didn't match his, rather that she had never found any such need. If books were a measure of sentience, was she in fact sentient?

Suddenly Luc ceased talking and his expression turned from pedagogue to social animal. He smiled, "I have been lecturing I fear."

A grotesque truth, writ large, but Jana smiled back. "I'm an obvious target, a soulless technocrat. An unbeliever abroad in the Vatican. French people feel obliged to improve me."

He laughed with apparent sincerity. "I suspect you speak more concisely than I do. Which reminds me. Didi has arranged a dinner and hopes you can come."

The opportunity to be slangy was irresistible. "Come on, Luc. You know I wouldn't fit in. I'd be a transatlantic stumbling block."

That at least silenced him. As if she'd hit him with a baseball bat. "You are saying we are too…"

"Sage?" Jana offered.

"French or English meaning?"

"Take your pick."

"That we could not adapt?"

"That you'd *have* to adapt, Luc."

He saw the condescension. "Forgive me. That was terrible. But I don't understand. You and Didi are great friends."

"The bond between us is flying. Maybe we should have but we never touched on texturalism."

The scope of what he'd done worried him. Had he accidentally trampled over Didi's great friend? Jana too saw his position and offered help. "Just lie about it, Luc. Tell Didi I can't make it on the day."

"But you are – secretly - our main guest. Didi knows you have a full agenda. I was told to choose a date that suited you."

"You could tell the truth but that might hurt Didi. Or make it dinner for three." She smiled. "But you'd be adapting if you did."

For all his forensic skills and devotion to teaching Luc now stuttered and Jana, with Jean-Claude waiting, had to hurry away. She drove the van with mixed feelings. Even though she liked Didi there was something shockingly satisfying about behaving destructively like this. But there was also a price. She'd defined her own limitations; certain events were closed to her. It was all quite, quite non-US but then she wasn't living in the USA. After ten minutes her mobile started to vibrate. It could have been Jean-Claude asking her to make haste but that wasn't J-C's style, he never nagged. She let it vibrate.

THEY WERE on their way to Grenoble in the Seneca and the Alps were starting to emerge on the horizon. Jana had the plane and Jean-Claude had slid down in his seat, oblivious to the north-south divide of the Rhone, perhaps on the verge of sleep. But not quite. "You look disturbed," he murmured.

She told him why.

"You don't usually lack confidence."

"Confidence wasn't the issue," she said. "I could have busked my way through the evening. But Luc had just given me one of those high-grade French enemas about the power of thought. To put me in my place. I imagined the dinner and all I could see was more of the same. It was an honest reaction. France is said to approve of honesty."

"With clichés it's best to be careful. There's often another that says the opposite. French is also the language of diplomacy, a fancy word for lying. But being a born and bred Frenchman, capable of handing out enemas of my own, I am drawn to other meanings. Was it more than just a dinner? You were scheduled

to be the main guest. That doesn't sound like an evening of So-
cratic dialogue."

"Scrabble? Charades?"

He said, "Those don't sound like Didi. She's already had two
sessions with the Seneca (She won't need any more) and she
talked about you. She admires you. More than that, she knows
you. I doubt she'd bury you in Derrida." A smile started to
emerge. "Aha, I see a sliver of light. It explains why Luc couldn't
clear up his mess."

She waited then caught his mischievous look. Then realised.
"Would they do that? It's so old-fashioned."

"If movies are any guide it happens regularly. There's even
an English word for it."

"Matchmaking," said Jana.

"But it doesn't translate. We say *jouer l'entremetteur*, which
is what pimps do. Jana, your roots have betrayed you. The Labossières have money and influence; no doubt they could make
it work. But I'd love to know who they picked for you. I regret
not being a member of the selection committee."

 "Have I been insensitive?. Surely this is interference."

Still he smiled seraphically. "Interference! What a crass way
to talk about friends. How about humanitarian aid?"

"We can't be sure."

"As a Frenchman I am a hundred percent sure."

"Pour the coffee, J-C."

ATC directed them to the 3000 feet grass strip at Grenoble
almost at right-angles to the 10,000 feet tarmac runway. The
broker led them to the eight-year-old Cessna Stationair. It had
an obvious family relationship with their 172 but they both took
childish glee in its greater modernity. When Jean-Claude started
the engine the major instruments appeared as displays on two
electronic panels.

"The display is more blurry," said Jana, "but much cleverer.
Altimeter thousands are separated out quite differently, made
more prominent."

They took off. For ten minutes Jean-Claude tweaked the Stationair's tail in steep dives, canyon turns, sideslips and stall re-

coveries. When he handed the plane over Jana duplicated the exact sequence and he applauded ironically. "Soft hands and a good memory."

"Can we afford it?" she asked.

"No," said J-C, grinning.

"But that won't stop you, will it? It's 235 kay, isn't it? Remind yourself that's dollars not euros. Say you'll walk away if they won't knock off 20 kay. Promise! Don't go soft on me, now."

As it was, a harder, almost unrecognisable J-C emerged during the negotiations, talking about soft markets and flight from capital (whatever that was). The broker, a Pole with savage French, spat out his disagreements but eventually walked a hundred yards away to phone the owner. If anything his surliness had increased when he accepted J-C's offer of $205,000. Perhaps the figure had cut into his commission. Since the Seneca was needed in Bayonne the following day, Jana offered to take it back, leaving J-C to complete the transaction and either fly the Stationair back or return by train.

"By train? You're joking?" said Jana.

"I could perhaps hook a thumb."

"That's more like it."

About to step up into the Seneca Jana looked at her mobile. Seven missed calls all from Didi. Now would be as good a time as any.

The phone emitted a low scream. "You wretch. After all this time; just as I'm about to do pi-pi."

"Don't forget to lock the bathroom door."

"You Americans... so practical."

Disconnected sounds ensued. "Where are you?" Didi asked.

"Standing on a grass strip at Grenoble, waiting to take the Seneca home."

"Why not call me while you're flying?"

"Depends whether it's a long or short call. Fine if it's short, telling me to go shit in my hat. Less so if you're feeling philosophical. After a time an automatic signal from the phone can screw up communications. Or so it's said."

Didi said, "What's this hat-shitting."

"Saying fuck off, but more politely."

"My angel of the grass strips, why would I tell you to fuck off?"

"Not you, your spouse."

Sounds of flushing. "I should make all my phone calls here. The acoustics are so resonant. It seems Luc blundered."

"Not necessarily."

"Then you believe I'd invite you here to make your life a misery?"

Jana said, "Another possibility. A matter of social engineering. Let's say sexual engineering."

Didi was quiet. "A shrewd guess. But would that be so awful?"

"Does the other half know he's a guinea pig?"

"It is not an experiment!"

"Does he know?" Jana insisted.

"He might guess."

"Is he an academic?"

"No."

"Then I'll come."

Yet again she flew into strong late afternoon sun, the penalty for operating from France's west coast. To keep herself alert she turned up Channel Sixteen, called up unnecessary met forecasts, checked and re-checked RT strength. Human voices helped her concentrate in a flight corridor where most traffic was flying to or from the same bearing.

Jean-Claude was right. Matchmaking was a regular feature in domestic US movies, and, presumably, in real life. But probably it depended on being part of a social circle. At college she had avoided other students as self-protection; in the Air Force there were no social circles she knew of. Living in a caravan in Tucson and working lengthy hours had turned her into a solitary. Beyond that there was Roy. Only in France had she found groups.

Her instinct had been to turn down the invitation. Being forced into such a game was bad enough, doing it before an audience was strictly for extroverts. And yet, and yet… France had transformed her, made her more courageous. Daily awkwardness was no longer a menace. A foreign language took the edge off embarrassment and blurred minor disasters at the dinner table. Also, dining with Didi was unlikely to be dull.

She left Valence behind to cross the Ardeche National Park, a wild area which could have contained a crashed plane for months. Crashing wasn't something pilots thought about other than as gallows humour. During their many flights together Roy had often broken this unspoken rule, perhaps because he subconsciously feared becoming a pilot. At first he seemed to be making conversation; now she saw it was a recurrent theme. Once he'd asked how long it would take to reach the ground with a dead engine from 6000 feet. He'd considered what she'd said for a couple of minutes, possibly wondering how you passed the final seconds of your life. Said nothing.

Jana could now think calmly about Roy, especially those early months when she'd been his hero and her needs had taken a back-seat. Eliazar and other one-night stands had shown that sex was fleeting and only part of what she yearned for. Mostly flying absorbed her but today, alone in the plane, crossing an uncaring part of France, she felt vague stirrings. Busying herself with the Seneca's routines wasn't enough.

CHAPTER FOURTEEN

Dreaded Grandage

THE SENECA was needed for Christopher Day's charter the following day. Given Grandage's character reference, Jana arrived an hour earlier to prepare things but Day was even earlier. He wore another plaid shirt flayed by detergent but slightly more colourful.

"Proof I need the money, eh?" he said. "Can I help?"

"I'm going to fill her up. After that I'll clean the interior."

"Do pilots use a brush and shovel?"

"When they work for eensie-weensie airlines."

He said, "Let me brush and shovel while you do something more technical. Change the sparking plugs, say."

"Spark plugs."

"I was close enough. Look, can I cadge a ride to the petrol pump? I've never seen a plane refuel."

"Cadge?"

"Bum."

"See! You can speak English if you try."

He snickered quietly, pleased at her feistiness. Stared at, he wiped off the smile, deliberately over-acting – a naughty schoolboy.

The plane eased over to the pump where Jana handled the hose and applied the credit card. Through the windscreen she saw him watching her. Back in the cockpit she glanced sideways and saw him shake his head.

"Did I do something wrong?" she asked.

"Damn feminism, I always get it wrong."

"What the Sam Hill are you talking about?"

"A long story."

"Tell me while we clean out the plane."

The way he reached into the cockpit's inaccessible corners proved he was used to labouring. He hummed an unrecognisable tune as he worked.

"You were saying," she reminded him.

"How about just the ending? The rest doesn't do me any favours."

"Tell the story."

His voice became brisk. "I liked being married but... well, in short, my wife took off. Fair enough. However, I like women's company. I made a sort of vow to stay calm, not get suicidal. After all divorce guilt is usually evenly divided."

"You said she moved upwards. Was that planned?"

He seemed startled. "Her... new spouse wasn't why we split up. She remarried with my blessing. If I'd been sour I'd have been sour about myself. I dropped out of her circle and came to France, as I'd always wanted. My first girlfriend here was PCF, an activist with the railway workers and not terribly likeable. That didn't stop me. I made her an offer she couldn't refuse: Tell me about women's causes, I said. Convert me. The French love supplication, love being asked to teach."

"Most know enough to suspect the English!"

Day was almost upside down in the footwell. His voice echoed. "I was sincere, I swear. I read stuff she gave me, went to her rallies. She took to me. After two months she invited me to join her forever in international socialism; to stop working for Anglo invaders. I was grist to her mill, whatever that means. But it didn't last. She wanted more than a feminist *naïf*. She wanted my political soul and I'm not sure I have one. We had a blazing argument over the *authentique* recipe for cassoulet. And don't tell me there isn't such a thing – I know better"

Jana said, "Even a spoonful's too heavy for me. I take it you came out on top, shouted louder than she did?"

"French leftwingers eat very badly." He rose up, his face flushed from being inverted. "Got some Windolene? Mr G might want to look out at la belle France."

They finished with time to spare. Jana made coffee for the vacuum flask and they drank the remainder between them. She said, "So you're easy meat for women intellectuals?"

He scratched his hair, still uncut. "Women I get on with see me as a foreign clown, no great threat. It's a role I play well."

"Sheesh! You Brits!"

"Oh don't worry," he said laughing at her outrage. "I never wanted to play in your backyard. I know how humility goes down in the USA."

Why was this obscurely insulting?

He went on, "Feminism demands application in the Hexagon. It's less about behaviour, more about theory. These days I open my mouth and I'm into syntax error – within seconds. No matter my heart's in the right place, I misuse the key words." He paused. "I was lucky I didn't try you out."

Why the hell, she asked herself, does that humility thing piss me off? "I doubt I'd have understood you. Feminist grammar's not my thing."

He was looking at her again from under those incurving eyebrows. He said, "I've come this far so I'll finish my confession. I warmed to the idea of a US woman flying planes and working in France. Each fact was a triumph. But what do I know? I kept my mouth shut. What jarred was seeing you at the petrol pump. It seemed all wrong: like watching a neurosurgeon cut toe nails."

Jana didn't care to encourage silence. "Muddled thinking, I'd say."

He sighed. "That too. Time for me to patrol the car park."

He still wore the expensive boots and she'd forgotten to ask why.

GRANDAGE'S flapping navy blue shorts reached his knees and his leather sandals came with black socks. He carried a blazer with brass buttons and referred to his wife as "Mother." Day introduced him and as he shook hands he looked suspiciously at the side of Jana's face, as if he expected it to cost him money.

"So, you're the pilot, eh? Yank, too. 'ow do you get on with the French?"

It was a voice that expected to find fault. "Oh, you know. They bring up Afghanistan and I refer them to Omaha Beach. It works out as *match null*. No problems, really."

"Do you let 'em push you around? I wouldn't. I'm from Dewsbury."

"Dewsbury," Jana faked recognition and Grandage accepted it complacently.

"I suppose Mr Day has told you: I'm 'ere to make money. Nine properties in two days. May buy the lot, may buy none. You know the timetable, you know the places. I'm told we'll land mostly on grass. That a problem? Or do you need a ten-lane highway like in Los Angeles." He paused in reminiscence. "I bought some property there too."

"No problem with grass, sir." The honorific slipped out and Jana checked whether Grandage thought he was being sent up. He took it as his due and she went on, "Just one point. Most strips are unsupervised and I take a low-level downwind inspection before we land. Just to make sure sheep aren't grazing."

"That's your business," said Grandage glancing at the Seneca. "Who's going to sit where? Mother can go in t'back, of course."

"It's your nickel, Mr Grandage," said Jana. "Why don't you sit up front? Mr Day can sit behind with your wife and act as stewardess. There's a bag with coffee, croissants and OJ in back if you fancy breakfast. Meanwhile you get to see the wonderful countryside."

"I'm not here as a tourist," grumbled Grandage. "Just for the euros. But I don't mind seeing where I'm going."

They flew north-east to a flying club strip near Marmande, halfway between Bordeaux and Agen. Grandage was persuaded with difficulty to wear the headset and when Jana announced her runway inspection before landing he crankily asked if the announcement was necessary. "Like all that blather on the big planes. Who cares about wind speed?"

Wearing the headset was standard practice, otherwise Jana would have stripped it from him. Instead she restricted herself to ATC dialogue and safety announcements, biting her tongue off on the downwind run when she noticed a Renault Espace with *agence* markings parked on the adjacent road. During the approach it occurred to her that Grandage might also object to excessive taxiing and decided to drop the plane down within the first ten metres of the strip, much closer to the rudimentary car park.

Day handed down the two passengers and escorted them to the Espace where he acted as translator and saw them aboard. Jana watched him say something to the driver and hurry back to the Seneca.

"Anything wrong?" she asked.

"I had to apologise for the shitehawk." His face was troubled.

"Not your fault."

"I need to control him better. He's so bloody rude."

"Don't try. Remember, he's got dough. And I've known worse."

"It shouldn't happen." He shook his head. "My own sodding countryman too."

"Remember, I've got the plane to fly. I can tune him out. Think of him as ballast."

"Ballast, yes. Buy you a drink after?"

"If I don't buy you one. Quit suffering."

On their return it was clear the torment wasn't over. Grandage had found fault with the house's swimming pool and although he'd been impeccably informed beforehand by Day it was clear he'd sniped all the way back. Now he turned to Jana.

"Time bloody well wasted. Eh Mother? In Dewsbury we'd never have had this happen. And now I suppose the timetable's all at fault."

"Nope. We're on schedule," said Jana with false brightness. "Relax Mr Grandage. Have yourself some juice and coffee."

"Juice! Oh, you mean orange juice. You Yanks! Never mind orange juice, let's get on with what you're paid for."

"Seats belts on. Headsets. Start engines."

The cockpit glowered with atmosphere. Jana tried another angle, "Are you enjoying the beautiful French countryside, Mrs Grandage?"

"Ay bless you. From up ere I can't tell t' difference between France and the Vale of York.

The *petit déjeuner* turned out a failure when UHT milk was served up. "We don't reckon anything to that muckment where I come from. Milk's milk."

"Sorry about that, sir," said Jana who was beginning to see satire in this form of address. "I was scared real milk might spoil."

"I tek it you've heard of ice."

In contrast with the gloom inside, the scenery offered France in all its glory as they entered the south-west corner of the Queyron national park. "The country's so big," Day said to the quartet at large but with Jana particularly in mind.

(Stick things out. Britain's better than this.)

"Far better than nine-tenths of my home state, Arizona."

(I'm bearing up.)

Grandage sighed, mainly through his nose.

Like many grass strips the one near Villefranche-du-Périgord was hard to pick out from the surrounding greenery and Jana circled a couple of times at 5000 feet. She wondered whether Grandage would regard this as incompetence but he was unobservant about anything outside human relations. This time no one was waiting but Day too had noticed and was already using his mobile.

"M. Gilbert apologises. Says he's ten minutes away."

This brought a sniff.

When her passengers had been collected Jana faced at least an hour's peace and she lay down on the springy turf beside the Seneca. She thought about Christopher Day, theoretically a free spirit, harassed by a man who was paying him money. She liked Day's concern for her. She dozed and was woken by voices raised in disagreement. Lazily she cranked up on her elbow and saw a recently disgorged people carrier. Mr Grandage was dissatisfied with the vendor's price.

"It's the figure I emailed," said Day. "Gilbert wouldn't have dared change it. There'd be problems with the *notaire*."

"It's too high for that house."

"I take your point. I thought it was fair but obviously I'm wrong. That's why I emailed you a full spec and that's why we're doing the tour."

Day's defence was inarguable and left Grandage with nobody to blame. He made a small snarling noise, glanced round and saw Jana still lolling on the grass. "And that doesn't please me either, young woman. You're not being paid to sleep on the job."

"Whoops. My apologies, sir," said Jana as if addressing a USAF drill sergeant. "I promise not to do it at the yoke."

"Everything's a laugh with you, isn't it."

But Jana's attention was elsewhere. Day stood still, his shaggy head thrown back, his eyes fixed on the sky. His voice sounded wearied. "Mr Grandage." A long pause. "It seems you and I will never agree. Nothing Miss Nordmeyer or I do suits you. Let's call this exercise to a halt."

"What's that?"

"Fly back to where we started."

"And leave me and mother stranded?"

"I wouldn't do that. I'll call another pilot and have you picked up. Or we'll fly you back to Bayonne."

"And have me pay for this wasted flying?"

"First, it hasn't been wasted. You've seen two of the properties. Second, I'll bear the costs."

"You!" Grandage's eyes gleamed behind black framed glasses. "You haven't a penny to your name."

Day smiled. "But that isn't your concern any more."

Jana intervened. "Don't do it, Mr Day. I can bear the hassle."

"Hassle!" shouted Grandage. "What are you talking about, hassle."

Day smiled again, grimly. "If you don't understand, Mr G, nothing I can say would make things clearer."

This time he sneered. "Can't take a bit of straight-talking, eh?"

"What's it to be, Mr G. Shall I call someone or shall we fly you and your wife back?"

"So I'm the villain am I? A businessman trying to earn a living. How about the race meeting, day after tomorrow? Which I could miss."

"That's why I'm bearing the cost."

"Which'll bankrupt you."

Day took two steps forward and Jana shouted, "Stay still. It isn't worth it."

But Grandage himself had lost his bite. He retreated several steps. "A poor kind of businessman you are."

"I'm getting tired of this," said Day. "How about we leave him here and fly off."

It would have been contrary to Jana's code as a pilot and she needed to point this out. But she noticed Grandage, turning this way and that, gazing at the demonstrably remote surroundings. The people carrier driver had left and only a narrow country road hinted at an urban existence beyond wave after wave of tightly packed trees. Grandage, like most bullies, whimpered. "You wouldn't do that?"

"I might but I suspect Miss Nordmeyer has professional obligations."

The phrase meant nothing to Grandage. "Can't we talk this out? Like human beings?" Meanwhile Mrs Grandage sat placidly on a low wall, unperturbed by threat and counter-threat. It seemed this wasn't the first time.

Day asked, "What's it to be Miss Nordmeyer?"

"Forget what's been said. Do what we all set out to do. Open our mouths as little as possible from now on."

"That suit you, Mr G?"

His relief was obvious. "Just a bit of hastiness. Let's keep going."

It was hard to decide whether bullying Grandage was any less likeable than obsequious Grandage. His feigned interest in flying, the string of clichés about the landscape and a sudden implausible love of France strung up Jana's nerves for the rest of the day. Her problem lay in reacting seriously to what he said, treating it as if it were important.

Where possible she watched Day to help her cope. His expression remained obscure and his clipped answers suggested a mind elsewhere. The visits lasted into the early evening and when the Grandages were finally ushered back into their rental car at BIC with promises of an earlier start the following morning, Jana said to Day, "I'll take a rain check on that drink. Tomorrow, when we've got rid of them for good, would be better. Champagne time, even."

He leant back against the dirty Citroen, looking at her but somehow not seeing her. "I'm knackered, absolutely knackered. I couldn't stand what he tried on. I thought dinosaurs like him were all dead."

There were things she wanted to say, wanted to know but he hung there, silent as a battered scarecrow. Reluctantly she let him be. "It will be easier tomorrow."

"Gawd. This is a hard way to earn a living."

The next day's flights were less tense. Given fourteen hours' rest Grandage had returned to his abrasive self, perhaps ashamed of the weakness he had shown. Insults and complaints, lacking their earlier sharpness, rolled on but it was like listening to a recording. When Grandage wasn't looking they caught each other's glances and smiled faintly. In the end Grandage himself realised he had become a blunt instrument, settled back in his seat and allowed the scenery to drift past. Back in the car park, clumsily, like someone unaccustomed to such gestures, he handed Jana a fifty-euro note.

She thanked him with extreme formality. Said, "The houses. You said you might buy all or none. What's the verdict?"

He was surprised. "Four out of nine. All good prices. I'd have haggled over two others but the French don't do that."

"Worth the trip?"

At first he didn't realise why she'd asked. Then, slowly, he did. "Oh yes, worth the effort." After a long pause he angled his shoulder away from her. "Thanks."

Only when the rental car had disappeared did they allow themselves sighs and laughter. Day said, "If he could have said thanks backwards he would have."

"I take it you didn't call your ex-wife mother?"

"Sounds incestuous."

Jana held up the note. "At least we can drink comfortably on this. I see it as a tip for both of us."

"The drinks were supposed to be my treat."

"What was it he said? Not a penny to your name. And what about the big gesture? Paying for the plane hire. Financial suicide."

"It had to be done," he said simply.

She felt a small shudder and hoped it didn't show.

THERE was a bar he wanted her to see, near his garret flat in the centre of Bayonne overlooking the Nive. She followed him in the van, playing down any sense of anticipation. Parking was a nightmare. She ended up half a kilometre away but the bar was worth it.

"It started out as a brasserie but the all-day eatery side is long gone," he said as they stood on the checkerboard tile floor and looked down impractically long vistas. "I doubt it'll survive. It's just too big even though it gets pretty lively at the weekend. But look at all this dark panelling – real wood not rotten chipboard. And the brass rails. Once the bar surface would have been a huge sheet of zinc. What I like are these horse boxes, but then we Brits are always keen on privacy. Oh, and the tables: more thick wood with cast-iron legs; you'd never disturb any drinks if you bumped against them, they're just too heavy. And even if you did the marble inlays are wiped clean in a second."

Jana nodded. "There are one or two bars like this in New York City but they're retro, not original."

"Would you like a beer? They've got *pression* Grimsbergen."

"Leffe too. Get me a Leffe."

"Grimsbergen's better. Let's have a glass of each and do sippers."

Sippers! She raised her eyebrows. He said, "A navy term. My dad was navy. Sippers is sharing your rum ration with your shipmates."

Shared glasses! Seemed kind of daring.

As they sat down with their beers their feet touched beneath the table and Jana looked down to check the lay-out of the cast-iron legs. "Now there's a thing," she said. "I've been meaning to ask. You dress like… well, let's say, unstylishly. Except for your boots."

"They look like a luxury. And in France they cost the earth. But, remember, I'm not just a property pimp. If the *chauffage centrale* goes wrong, call Chris, he's cheap. We didn't plant the oleanders and the barbecue's this afternoon; Chris'll do that. My feet are hard worked. I started out wearing trainers and needed three pairs a year. Now I bite on the bullet and the boots make sense."

"And the clothes?"

"What do you want? Jude Law? Actually there's method in my madness. Wear old clothes but always turn up with them newly washed. Says two things: I'm efficient and I'm low cost."

"I like the way you cleaned out the Seneca cockpit."

He looked slightly embarrassed. "Want to try the Grimsbergen?"

When she nodded he turned his glass so she faced an untouched part of the rim. She tried not to think about this, one way or the other. "Grimsbergen is different. Want to remind yourself what Leffe's like?" she asked.

And of course he took her glass straight off the table top. Hygiene or whatever; neither was an issue. They both slid back in their seats. He asked, "Both are good. Tell me, do you still get a buzz out of flying? I'm not talking job well done. More the abstract side. Or is the question pure cow-pat?"

"Mostly it's quiet satisfaction. Job well done, as you say. But there are special moments, like when I'm giving lessons. When I have to put into words something that's instinctive. When I need to reach out to someone else. Why do you ask?"

"I was watching you." He laughed nervously. "Taking my mind off Mr Dewsbury for quite long periods. There's this paradox: you're relaxed but attentive. As if you're in a trance but obviously you aren't. Your hands move independently, your eyes move mechanically. The Spanish have a word – *enchufado*. It means plugged-in, not just electrically, but metaphorically. 'At one with', if you like. You're not just plugged into the plane but into the invisible stuff outside as well."

Jana coughed and it must have been noticeable. He was concerned, "Have I said something wrong? Something stupid?"

The dryness continued, together with a desire to talk, to confess. "Nothing wrong, nothing stupid," she said in a voice that wasn't hers. "You're a good observer, that's all."

"I've gone too far, haven't I?"

She shook her head and felt her hair swing in confirmation of her gender. Saw him as a man, saw sympathy in those down-curving eyebrows. "I decided on flying when I was a kid. I knew then - as now - I'd always need somewhere I can go to. Away from this face. What you saw in the plane was Jana Nordmeyer without the port wine stain, beyond the curious looks. Coward's way out, perhaps, but it works most of the time."

His eyes were wide now, the concern deepening. "And have I wrecked things? Cut you off from that… place?"

She forced herself to laugh lightly, knowing this was not always controllable. "I'm glad you saw me that way. At my best. But look, things are getting heavy. We're here to enjoy the beer in this museum of a bar. Are you in France for good?"

The question startled him. "Nobody's asked that before. I've never asked myself. I suppose I am. Back in Blighty I'd be forced back into teaching. There'd be no way I could keep going on odd jobs there. To tell the truth I've grown to like this second career if I dare call it that. The job's got status. When M. Touche-à-Tout gets called in it's because he can do things others can't."

"A superior son of a bitch."

"That's right. I should invent my own jargon. As if I were a doctor. Or, for that matter, a Roger-Wilco flyer."

Jana said, "Your Commie girl-friend wanted your soul. I'm surprised she didn't see you as a member of the labouring masses."

They were over the hump and he was laughing freely. "Commie girl-friend! Trust an American to bring me down to earth. PCF activist has much more zing. Wonder what she's doing now?"

Daringly she asked, "Was she never replaced?"

"Not really. I have curiosity value but no staying power. One thing puts off French women is I'm better read. In French literature, that is. That outrages them. That and being published in the little magazines."

"On what?"

He didn't seem keen. "Oh you know, Perec, Butor, the experimentalists. Bit like shooting fish in a barrel once you've learned the code."

And Jana hadn't learned the code. "How about France in general?"

"Oh, that. Head over heels in love. A hopeless case for anyone who's keen on language." Abruptly he changed his tone, sensing he might well be drifting away from her. "But then, you've slotted in. Your French is good. You must be happy here."

"I'm at peace." But was that strictly true? "I'm flying. My boss is great. I have a couple of friends – woman friends."

"Nothing… else? Hey, let me order you another Leffe."

Men had been entering the bars in ones and twos as they talked and the noise level had risen. Two fresh glasses of beer represented the end of one chapter and the beginning of another. Jana toasted him: "Suppose Mr Dewsbury had called your bluff?"

He steadied himself. "Fact is, I wasn't bluffing. I meant what I said."

"Was he bluffing, then? That stuff about being poor?"

"Don't forget I'd had a long talk before I phoned Gascon Air. Money fascinates him and he made it his business to find out I hadn't any. That's why he could start out behaving like a true bastard."

"But how would you have made good?"

"There are ways," he said vaguely. "In the US they call them loan sharks."

"But that would have left you in the doodoo."

"Way I saw it, it had to be done."

Jana waited for him to say more, saw he wouldn't. "There's something I don't get about all this. OK, you're a shining white knight and the guy was a real prick. But it wasn't life or death. You could have suffered a few more hours."

"I suppose I could," he said, tracing patterns in the spilt foam.

He looked blank and, in the end, it was blankness that gave him away. "You didn't do it for yourself." she said.

He might have continued pushing foam round for ever if a young, confident French voice hadn't intruded. "Mademoiselle, discourage your boy-friend from wasting beer and have him order me a Brothers Grim."

"*Salut* Norbert," said Day. "Meet Mlle Jana Nordmeyer. An *aviatrice*. Norbert's the most important person in my life. He keeps the BX running."

"A *pression* quickly, Christophe. I will charm Mlle. Nordmeyer in your absence." He sat down opposite, placed his hands with their black rimmed nails flat on the cooling marble and smiled in that unquestioning way young Frenchmen have. "Christophe and I were speaking French. Are you OK with that?"

Jana pushed her thoughts – complex and self-entwining – to one side. "M. Day said it all. I fly planes out of Bayonne and your controllers have this Pyrenean accent. If I couldn't stumble along in French I'd have hit a hilltop long ago."

"And that would have been a tragedy," he said, his smile widening. "American too. And you are far too modest with this talk of stumbling. I understand now. Christophe talked about an inspection tour of houses with a customer. You were his *aviatrice*. May I assume your relationship with Christophe is purely commercial?"

Jana waved a hand. "Monsieur – what am I to call you? I don't know your surname and I'm not sure you deserve a first name. Let's say Monsieur Ix.

"You must call me Norbert."

"But I wish to put you in your place."

"But why? Am I not charming?"

"Perhaps. But that adjective you just used is very ambiguous."

"Adjective?"

"Commercial."

"I do not understand."

Day was now standing at the table holding a glass of beer. Choosing to use English Jana said, "Would you like to tell your friend – the charming Mr Ix – why it's dangerous to describe our relationship as commercial."

Day edged Norbert along the bench seat with his backside. "Norbert, dear friend. French can be a *faux ami*. A commercial relationship between a man and a woman can mean, how shall I put this, a carnal contract."

Norbert exaggerated his apology. "Not for a moment... I spoke only of a fee for transporting Christophe. And I had a reason. I wanted to establish whether Mlle. Nordmeyer is free. No, there must be a better word than free."

Day reverted to English. "This satyr of a garage-man means 'spoken for'; are you familiar with that? I've had trouble with the French translation. The dictionary says *déja prise* which is even more alarming. As if you'd been carried away on the saddle of an Arabian horse."

But Norbert caught the two French words amidst the English. "Thank you, Christophe, for simplifying. Is Mlle Nordmeyer already taken? If not, I, Norbert, would like to..."

"This is getting rather distasteful," said Day.

"Oh, I don't know," said Jana. "Monsieur Ix – I still call you that for the same reasons – the answer is no. I am not spoken for. Luckily there is a French solution. Let's be happy with our present *ménage à trois*."

Norbert took her hand and histrionically kissed the fingers. "And you talk about stumbling French. A *ménage à trois* has the possibility to become one fewer. I look forward to that. And it will happen. I am richer than poor Christophe; I will give you champagne not beer."

Jana drew her hand away gently. "You assume I'll give in."

"Champagne and my charm? Resistance will be futile."

"There is a better bet than champagne. Imagine, Norbert, the two of us together, enclosed in a small space, neither able to escape. For a whole hour."

Day laughed. "Oh Norbert, for the first time I hate being poor."

"What is this desirable situation?" Norbert asked. "Ah yes. I understand. Not just an *aviatrice* but also a *professeur*. I will find the money. Not just to be alone with you, my dear Mlle. Nordmeyer, but with danger as well."

Norbert got up, went round the far end of the table and squeezed out over Jana's lap. "I will order more beer and go to the *pissoir*. Where I will comb my hair. In preparation."

Day looked after his friend. "I hope you're not put out. He's a nice chap, really. Does all my repair work on the cheap."

"He's good fun," said Jana. "In a French sort of way. But he interrupted us."

"He did. And you were right."

Jana found herself stammering. "Will there be a chance to find out why?"

"I may be poor but I'm good at meals."

"Text me the ingredients you need."

CHAPTER FIFTEEN

Surrogate parent

VINCENT was away at a professional conference in Bordeaux. It was also his week to have Octavien. The obvious solution would have been to re-arrange the schedule with Yvonne but he preferred to leave his son in the hands of his parents. More specifically, with Jana.

Jana returned home eightish having delivered two mechanics to a broken-down road grader just north of Orange in the Rhone Valley. As the Chauvelets watched television she ate a cold meal at the kitchen table with Octavien placidly doing his homework at the other end. She marvelled at his adult sensitivity; having noticed her weariness, he bent again over the work and continued to fill in his exercise book.

Relishing slow spoonfuls of raspberry tart, Jana said, "The pattern on those pages, it's called quadrille."

He nodded. "I've seen that word. This one is different: pages with large squares."

"All kid's exercise books in France have designs like that. As if you drew graphs all day. Or did math."

"Or as if we were all babies." He imitated his teacher: "Fit your written letters inside the squares."

Jana laughed. "I suppose we can't knock it. All French people write the same way. What are you working on tonight?"

"English."

"Can I help? Or is that forbidden?"

"It is very simple. I read a summary of an English book and answer questions. Robinson Crusoe. I don't like summaries."

"You might find the original hard. It was written ages ago."

"School shouldn't be easy."

"Octavien, that sounds very German."

His face lit up. "I'm told Germans work harder."

"In my experience, the country works harder than the US." An image arose of Christopher Day looking heroic in front of his customer. "The Anglos in Britain seem to think the same. But you must finish your homework."

"Oh, I finished that long ago. Questions one to nine. I do more to show Mlle. Tenancier I am serious."

"Is she in any doubt?"

"I learned a new phrase this week. Teacher's pet. Perhaps I am a teacher's pet. Certainly I am not my classmates' pet."

Jana added milk to her coffee. "Octavien, you are way above my level."

She found him staring. "I think you joke. But we could talk."

"Flying?"

"About Papa?"

"He's not here. That's not nice.""

"But we cannot when he *is* here. He is unhappy."

"He and Mama are no longer together," said Jana.

"It's hateful being young. Papa is unhappy but will not explain why. I cannot ask Mama. Grandpère and Grandmère say it is not my concern. And you say it is not nice."

"Papa is happy when he is with you."

She said, "You and I are friends. That pleases him."

This facile answer left him suspecting an adult conspiracy. His next question was harder. "Mlle. Jana, you do like papa, don't you? You find him agreeable?"

"We talk together a lot. Often about you."

Octavien shot out his wrist and looked at his watch. "Time for me to go to the caravan. Good night, Mlle. Jana."

EARLY afternoon and she was halfway to Bagnole-sur-Cète to pick up the two mechanics who, presumably, had repaired the road grader near Orange. Just visible to port were the elegant sails of the Millau bridge. Pressing against her left breast was the accusatory weight of her mobile phone - switched on!

Had she been flying a Boeing or an Airbus over US airspace she would have been breaking Federal Communications Commission regulations. Outside the US and when flying a light aircraft the regulations were more fluid. The consensus was against mobile phone use but the restriction was speculative. No one was entirely sure whether phones can or will interfere with avionics. In the past Jana had discouraged passengers from making lengthy calls and had kept her outgoing calls to less than a minute. Now, with the Cessna's autopilot and GPS switched off, she was ignoring the rules. As it happened almost all the flight passed without incident and it was only during the final approach that the phone tingled. With her left hand she took it out, ignored the phone's screen, flipped it open, said, "Jana here. Be with you in five minutes." and dropped it back into her pocket.

She taxied to the small admin hut, swung the plane round and switched off the engine. Quickly she was out, opening the plane's passenger side door and ushering in the mechanics. "There's a six-pack of Heineken in a coolie box. It's all yours. I just have to make a phone call."

Standing on the windswept turf at the side of the runway she took out the mobile. "*Chris Day à l'appareil,*" said a quite unfamiliar voice and she breathed quickly through her open mouth

"It's Jana."

If she'd been expecting warmth there was only disappointment. "You were flying when I called, weren't you? Isn't using a phone illegal? All those warnings on civil planes."

"I… took precautions. Minimum risk."

"Minimum risk? There should be no risk at all. Why didn't you warn me? Or ignore the call?"

Ignore the call? Christopher – are you dumb? "Everything's under control."

"You're suggesting things do need controlling."

He hectored and she had no defence. "I'm a long way from home. In the Rhone valley. I wanted to take your call."

"Jesus Christ, Jana."

Gradually her ability to reason started to take over, as it did when she was at the yoke. She recognised why he was angry and spoke slowly, softly. "I promise you my electronic stuff was turned off. There was nothing the phone could affect. I wanted to take your call."

A long silence ensued. He mumbled, "Sorry about that. What the hell do I know? You're near the Rhone; that seems a long way away. Will you be back in time for dinner - here?"

It *had* been worth the risk. "Early evening. Text me the ingredients as I said. I'll only switch on the phone when I'm out of the plane."

As she got back into the Cessna the two mechanics, beer cans now open, watched. Given there'd been no engine noise they must have overheard her.

One raised his can. "Here's to love."

She grinned, still revelling in what Day had said. "And here's to less emotion."

These days most of her evening meals were provided by Sylvie Chauvelet and she was out of touch with grocery shopping. In a discarded British newspaper picked up at Bayonne airport she'd read an article which rated French supermarkets. Carrefour had come out top, which was why she was driving to the other awkward side of the city. The evening aisles were almost deserted and she felt the cold of the chill shelves on her lightly clad body. Shopping had never been a delight since it was usually the prelude to cooking for one. Today was different. She chose knobbly tomatoes, said to be available only in France and of guaranteed flavour. A must for any Francophile.

Again parking space near his flat was impossible and she left the van on a cleared area in a failed industrial site. To have changed clothes would have complicated the evening and she could only be thankful Jean-Claude had dispensed with the shabby Ruritanian uniform. Make-up wasn't an option. She'd been unadorned when they first met and he'd have to take that into account. Hiding her face would seem like a plea. She combed her hair quickly walking away from the van.

Hand-written scraps of paper were Sellotaped to the door jamb of the terraced house. The stairs were narrow and Jana brushed past doors leading to other horribly adjacent house-holds. The last set of stairs was narrower and steeper but carried an encouraging laminated notice - *First, last, everlasting DAY!* with an arrow pointing upwards. There was no bell-push and her knock sounded old-fashioned.

"Congratulations," he said, opening the door. "You aren't even breathing hard."

"Who is everlasting DAY?"

"Donne's love poem: An Anniversary." He guided her through the door. "Now you've made me feel pretentious. John Donne, the for-whom-the-bell-tolls poet."

"Are all your guests poetic?"

"There aren't enough for the statistics to mean anything. The few that make it this far tend to be French."

Poetic and other literary clues abounded once she was able to look round his living room. Everywhere shelves in bare wood - arranged round the solitary window, turning it into a deep re-cess, above the door and on top of the two kitchen cabinets. From floor to sloping ceiling. Never a gap.

Shelves were more conspicuous than books – the latter mostly second-hand with ragged spines that made the titles hard to read. Mixed in with disintegrating French paperbacks, the sort with beige bindings and a minimum of information on the cover. Books that needed no publicity, books for readers who knew everything about the contents. Here and there hardbacks, the spines faded or darkened by age, lacking dust jackets.

Jana looked closer at an orange spine: the Penguin imprint. Orwell. "This one's in English," she said. "That's cheating. Didn't you do modern languages?"

She sensed him watching which was what she wanted. He said, "You wouldn't expect me to read Homage to Catalonia in French."

"I suppose not. Of course, English is a modern language too."

He carried her plastic bag to the tiny square sink. "Score you nine out of ten for the tomatoes. Did you squeeze the veal before buying?"

"Why would I do that?"

"Remind me when we're eating. Wine? Good grief: you'll end up in Carey Street. Let's hope the cooking matches up."

Already she needed to ask about Carey Street and a life dominated by books. A richly foreign host.

He said, "You've had a long working day. I'll get you a glass of white Bordeaux – at about a fifth of what you've spent – and you can put your feet up in my only easy chair. Read a book. Do a zizz."

A zizz! "Aren't we here to talk?"

"Not while I'm cooking. I need to concentrate. Talk comes afterwards."

For a time she watched him working in the partially separated kitchen. His hands moved quickly as he cut, peeled, mixed and tasted. She sipped the wine, remembering his anger on the phone and what it had meant. Eventually she pulled out the Orwell book, reading slowly, trying to pick out details that might prove useful. Very briefly she dozed, waking to see him setting out cutlery.

To leave him direct access to the kitchen she sat at the far side of the table where he put a plate in front of her. "Simple tomato salad. You chose the best toms and I had the best onions. Mild, slightly sweet; can't get them in England. The chopped green is basil. That little dish is olive oil and vinegar mixed." He stopped, alarmed. "You wouldn't be wanting the yellow stuff that comes in a bottle."

"Give me credit. I've lived in France for two years."

"I should have remembered your French. Is the onion OK?"

"Exactly what you said it would be."

Now, covertly, she resurrected the details of his face that time and space had muffled. The eyebrows were still dominant, potentially ferocious. Thatchy hair overhung his ears. A sinewy muscular body which must have been an asset when he faced

Grandage. His sense of determination was at odds with his face-tiousness.

"You've done twelve years in France," she said. "Were they difficult?"

"Only while I was shedding my life as a teacher. And finding what I could do without. Losing music was agony but my ex got the hi-fi and the CDs; I've never had the cash to replace that lot. As to the books – second-hand books – I've played the gradualist game. This lot cost - what? A thousand euros, but spread over time. Sometimes I break off reading and play a Cosi aria in my head. It comes back in bits. Tell me about being a pilot."

One memory remained eternal: utter exhaustion and a forklift under the spotlights during the graveyard shift at the timber yard. "Damned hard. And the good old USA made it harder. I just had to be obsessive. Luckily I rarely had any doubts. Except now."

"Now? Here?"

"Away from work. When you're out plumbing or painting some guy's woodwork you've something to come back to. It's on these shelves. I've no back-up. Sure, I have books. A Cessna handbook, an airstrip guide, aviation law. Out of the plane what do I do? I think about flying *et c'est tout*."

"Next course. Two minutes."

He got up, took her plate and was back within his own deadline. "Veal scallops in a modified Bolognese. Buttered new potatoes. Green beans. A glass of your far-too-expensive burgundy. The hardest trick is putting it in front of you on the dot. Otherwise you could be alone in a slow restaurant. Hmmm. Good plonk."

"Plonk. Zizz. Carey Street," she said. "Why don't you speak American?"

"I'm inviting you into my life. Sideways, if you like. Look, this lack of back-up. You say you're bookless but flying for a living is serious. Should you be looking for diversions? I'm just an odd-job man, I need a hinterland."

"I've got older, I think I do need a hinterland. My dad edged me towards poetry a little and these shelves make me envious."

He said casually, "I could help you with that. Provided I don't appear pushy."

When they'd finished, he washed up and she dried. Then he put out a board with a crottin de chavignol - knife but no side-plates - and poured more wine, "I could lend you a book or two. But that's no fun. How about I read you poems and you read back?"

Throughout he'd spoken briskly - the way Brits did, hard to follow, as if talking to a group. Now his voice was quieter and gentler.

Sharing sounded good. "But start me on the ground floor. Poems with a beat, musical Sousa marches."

Instinctively he knew. A dozen verses of Chevy Chase, Dover Beach, Hardy's The Darkling Thrush, Keats' When I Have Fears. Then "as a formal introduction to me and mine", the Donne:

> *All Kings, and all their favourites,*
> *All glory of honours, beauties, wits,*
> *The sun itself, which makes times, as they pass,*
> *Is elder by a year now than it was*
> *When thou and I first one another saw:*
> *All other things to their destruction draw,*
> *Only our love hath no decay;*
> *This no tomorrow hath, nor yesterday,*
> *Running it never runs from us away,*
> *But truly keeps his first, last, everlasting day.*
>
> *Two graves must hide thine and my corse;*
> *If one might, death were no divorce.*
> *Alas, as well as other Princes, we*
> *(Who Prince enough in one another be)*
> *Must leave at last in death these eyes and ears,*
> *Oft fed with true oaths, and with sweet salt tears;*
> *But souls where nothing dwells but love*
> *(All other thoughts being inmates) then shall prove*
> *This, or a love increasèd there above,*

When bodies to their graves, souls from their graves
remove.

And then we shall be thoroughly blessed;
But we no more than all the rest.
Here upon earth we're Kings, and none but we
Can be such Kings, nor of such subjects be;
Who is so safe as we? where none can do
Treason to us, except one of us two.
True and false fears let us refrain,
Let us love nobly, and live, and add again
Years and years unto years, till we attain
To write threescore: this is the second of our reign.

Listening, Jana needed to adjust. Two other people were involved: the poet and Day himself. Words full of whispered love-talk but indirectly served up. She made him re-read the Donne to hear one line a second time ("Running it never runs from us away"). Then a third time to help her guess what the poem meant to him and whether it had further meaning for her. The notice at the bottom of the stairs had been there for some time, was laminated for Christ's sake! It wasn't a personal invitation. Yet the way he read this stuff…

Three times was enough for Day. "It's just self-centredness on my part," he said. "Time for you to earn your keep." As an American she faced Whitman but the windy shapes of Out of the Cradle Endlessly Rocking were beyond her. He agreed. "That was unfair. You were right about Sousa poetry – the marching beat. How about Eliot; he was US even if we sort of absorbed him. Try New Hampshire."

The shorter lines helped.

Children's voices in the orchard,
Between the blossom and the fruit-time:

And she herself was encouraged to repeat lines, to get the rhythm better. Then, to her intense disappointment, he closed the book and pushed it away. "Very cosy but this isn't the point. What matters is you finding a book and opening it. I take it you went to uni, all Americans do. They taught you about radial engines. Were they satisfied with illiteracy or did they force-feed you adverbs?"

"How the hell do you know radial engines?"

He sighed. "It's the point I'm trying to make. As it happens I not only know they exist I know what they are. The cylinders aren't in line they radiate out from the crankshaft like a star. Why do I know? Because I read books, and for all sorts of reasons. Surely you read books at uni."

Shamefacedly she explained the rigidity of her high school courses and the haphazard way logistics became the basis for her Air Force degree. When she missed out detail he interrupted with questions that forced her to go back and amplify. He appeared fascinated by the minutiae of the US educational system.

"Why on God's earth do you need all this dull stuff?" she asked crankily.

"Facts, I need facts."

"You sound as if there's an agenda."

"Oh, there's an agenda," he said. "Without it you'd be suspicious, with it you'll see me as manipulative. I lose both ways. But let's take a detour. Here's a bookish question: is it possible for men to be honest to women. I don't think so."

"How would I know? Has any man ever tried?"

"Probably not. Men fear flying without charts." He grinned. "Shit, that could be Coleridge and I don't like Coleridge. What I'm saying is this: talking to women men are rarely original. Whereas books – good books – have to be original. Allusive too. Books hide motives and ask readers to work things out. Honest characters are the death of literature."

"But we're not in a book."

He raised his voice slightly. "You've got imagination, haven't you? Write yourself into one. Ask yourself: are you better equipped to stand honesty than, say, Captain Ahab or Yossarian? Or Gatsby for goodness sake? There's a chap who had problems with honesty."

Ah, yes. Stripped of its context, that enemy of sleep: honesty as a defect.

"Have some crottin," he said, cutting the small pat into halves. "Do you mind cheese called horse-shit? But you knew the word, didn't you?"

"I'm a super-hygienic Yank. Never dared try it. But I can't be out-grossed by a Brit."

"Out-grossed!" His face lit up. "Concise and direct. Dare I use it?"

"You don't mind if Yanks chop up your sacred language?"

"I once risked an A-level on that very matter - arguing with my English teacher about a US word now out of fashion. Cinch – Why don't we accept it? Short, memorable, no English equivalent. My English teacher was a Henry James freak and didn't see things my way. I always liked downtown but baulked at tad."

"Cheese is good," said Jana. "Doesn't kill the wine. But back to honesty and your agenda. I see the risks. I've suffered a lot from dishonesty. Honesty, too, if it comes to that. But here I am, sitting in comfort, gee-ed up by John Donne, sipping what Sinatra weirdly calls 'burgundy brew', a real day's work behind me. Try me with honesty."

He stood up from the cushions he'd occupied on the floor and reached for something that had once been a fattish book and was now a fluffy pile of pages. "Let's try one or two definitions. Here's what you know: honesty: free from deceit, frank, sincere and the rest. But how about morally right? That's the one that worries me."

"Almost carries a health warning. Honesty as a duty. Hold back and you fail as a human being."

Carefully he eased the reassembled dictionary carcase back on to the shelf. "We're getting too damn philosophical. How about a little test? Could you explain why you're here tonight. Everything."

Unconsciously she drew her hand up the back of her neck, pushing her hair into confusion. Again and again. Thinking.

Having retired to his cushions he got up again, picked up the bottle, noticed their fullish glasses, put down the bottle, sat at the table, rested his chin on his hands and engaged her. Made it impossible for her to look elsewhere. "We can't, can we? It's tactics. A man and a woman alone in a room, together, willingly. Anything may happen or nothing. Neither of us knows. Nor does it stop short; to be truly honest there'd be no omissions, we'd have to include everything we hoped for. With common sense and politeness screaming retreat, retreat."

His eyebrows had come together in a form of anger. "There's a US saying: how do you like them apples?"

Without a US accent the question didn't click, sounded foreign. Picking ideas out of Homage to Catalonia had been poor preparation.

Carefully she said, "Yet there's always a secret urge: honesty as a kind of social suicide. Just for the reaction."

He nodded approvingly, causing her to breathe out, exhilarated.

Neither had touched their wine but this time he rose decisively and stood over her with the bottle. She raised her glass slowly to prolong his nearness. Pile-less corduroys rubbed bare at the knees, a lap of untucked shirt forming a valance. As he poured the wine the single bulb that lit the room picked out a tangle of golden hair on the back of his hand.

"Lend me a book with some of this in it," she said.

"This what?"

"This kind of talk."

He sat down to think it out. "There's a Boris Vian... But then of course you read French. L'Herbe Rouge - it's rather hot-breathed. Purely verbal but that's the way with French authors. A woman makes a plea to the narrator and it's sort of... Nah, it won't do."

"Why not?"

"There's no balance between him and her."

"Are we balanced?" she asked, her eyes round. "While I'm doing all this learning?"

He leant back in the kitchen chair, irritation passing over into possessiveness, pride in what she was. "Just now you're in my playground and that's a fact. But with books you only need time and some concentration. Your toys are quite different. Grown-up toys."

"The Seneca doesn't mean much up here."

He said, "It's not the Seneca, that's an inert thing, a bag of nails. It's the way you tease it into doing things. Flying steadily at nought feet down a grass meadow, head arched sideways on a tour of inspection. Climbing and turning at the same time. Following a line parallel to the way you came in. Finally, turn and down, your eyes ahead of the plane, hands doing this and that to other things."

"You notice."

"I also read books. See my latest, definitely not second-hand."

It was on one of the lower shelves and had a virgin dust jacket. A traditional How to Fly manual that she herself, a teenager then, had bought in an earlier edition. Thirty thousand printed.

"You're not thinking of learning…"

"I don't have the money. I needed to know more about you."

"You only have to ask."

"Oh, I will. Perhaps if you teach Norbert I'll ask him. He seems infatuated."

She'd forgotten Norbert. "Suppose he gets Jean-Claude as instructor?"

"Norbert's not philosophical about being turned down…"

Jana glanced at her watch. "I don't want to fall asleep at two thousand feet. I'd better go."

They kissed chastely, but mouth to mouth.

AS SHE turned into the driveway she saw light in the lounge. Vincent sat there watching a Bud Boetticher western dubbed into French, a bottle of cognac on the floor beside the easy chair. He pointed to the bottle but Jana shook her head. Not a time for liquor.

"I wanted to talk but it's late," he said. "You are tired."

If that's what he thought he'd misread her face. But perhaps her face was reverting, away from a thrilling new world back to the old one. "Go ahead," she said, dropping down into Hugues' easy chair.

"You've been talking to Octavien."

"I do that regularly. If you mean recently he raised a subject and I discouraged him. Didn't think it was right."

Vincent took a largish sip of cognac and she wondered how long he'd communed with this bottle. And why. He said, "Is happiness a forbidden subject?"

"It was an incidental subject," she said, noticing the asperity. "There was a wider subject I stepped away from."

"That subject being me."

He was hoping to provoke a reaction. Her silence meant he had to go it alone. "Eventually you did talk about me."

"Octavien had the wrong impression. I corrected him."

"May I ask about this wrong impression?"

She spread her hands. "I'm unhappy with this talk. It's telling tales out of school. Perhaps you can understand. I'm not sure Octavien was speaking to anyone other than me."

"He's a child. And you and I are... familiar."

"He's a thoughtful child and has his own opinions. He trusts me and I'm honoured that he does." There was more she would have added but the clumsiness of the French for "trust" inhibited her.

Vincent was becoming exasperated. He'd hoped to slide tangentially into his plan and it wasn't happening. Now he faced taking the initiative and feared what lay ahead. Jana didn't envy him. This was an exploration of honesty between a man and a woman seen in a new light

"You like Octavien, this is agreed," he said, speaking deliberately.

"True."

"May I ask how much you like him?"

But Jana was ahead of this crablike approach. "I've had little experience with children. He knew there was a conflict between you and Yvonne about his future. But he was even-handed and I tried to be too. Later he became franker, developed new opinions. I didn't imagine I could guide him but he appreciated being able to talk to another adult."

None of which Vincent wanted to know. Having set his stalking horse in motion he was disappointed to see it accepted as a real horse. Jana had refused to accept Octavien and Vincent as interchangeable.

"Let me put a purely hypothetical situation," he said.

Despite the tenseness she fought hard to avoid smiling at this very French conversational device.

Vincent continued, "Purely hypothetical. Without reference to anyone or anything else could you imagine being Octavien's parent?"

He'd tried hard. Straining to be indirect, substituting "parent" for "mother", eliminating himself. But in doing so he left Jana with a painless exit. "Well no, I can't. I fly for a living. It's not just a job I love it's a way of escape. I need to fly and flying is erratic. Not the life for a parent."

With only one option left, Vincent sighed. "Jana, am I not attractive to you?"

"Attractive?" She let the word hang in the air. "We have talked. I hope I've helped with Octavien, I sympathise with your marriage problems. You are a good man and a good father. You were thoughtful about my comfort with the caravan. I was grateful for that. I enjoy your company." Could she apply a killer blow, despite superstition? "As to becoming closer there is, I fear, someone else."

The last thing he had expected and, immediately, she was glad she'd unleashed it. Various expressions passed mutely over Vincent's face but the one that grabbed her was the hint of outrage. Shockingly he'd imagined he was the best she could hope for. That his practicality would overcome her disfigurement and that she ought to be grateful. That the stain was a price he would pay to stabilise his domestic affairs.

"Another?"

"Very recently."

"Tonight, in fact?"

She nodded. Should she soften the blow? "There is no certainty."

But he didn't dare explore that.

In her bedroom she tossed the day's clothes into the laundry basket with some reluctance: she had worn them earlier that evening, they were part of the experience. As she put on the oversize tee-shirt she wore in bed she knew Day would find such a garment quite alien. A pyjama man if ever there was…

With the light out she wished she had a photograph. His face flickered evasively. Concentrating on the eyebrows she lost the shape of his mouth. He stooped, didn't he? Or did he? She despaired that her sight, so good at fixing landmarks from the air, didn't work at half a metre. Especially trying to fix that moment when he'd rested his chin above his triangulated arms to address her and no one else. Even the words – which she would have loved to fondle and analyse – were dissolving. She had only impressions: a gentleness, intense almost irritable explanations, neat hands in the kitchen.

The harder she reached for him the vaguer he got. They had sat apart. There had been little mutuality. But the blur comforted her, welcomed her, as she prepared for sleep.

CHAPTER SIXTEEN

Jana assessed

JANA'S previous visit to the Labossières had been brief. She'd arrived after midnight following dinner out with Didi and had left quickly the next morning. Now she had time to appreciate their comfortable way of life. She lay on a lounger on a huge terrace furnished in pinkish local stone, the Pyrenees as a backdrop. The location, south-east of Bayonne, was high enough for her to trace the minor road that led down to the bridge, over the Nive, into Cambo-les-Bains, up the Col de Pinodiéta and, beyond the mountain, southwest to Pamplona in Spain. There was Crystal in her glass and somewhere in the house Luc played and re-played part of a slow passage from one of the nocturnes. The lounger was upholstered in soft leather that could easily have been shaped into a fashionable Parisian jacket; as it was the leather folded round her body. She had arrived early at Didi's insistence and been told to "behave lazily" during the final preparations for dinner.

The massiveness of the house and its luxurious appointments perversely invoked the canted roof of Christopher Day's garret, its tattered library and the simple devices for supporting life. Snuggling against the cushioning she wondered whether to bring Didi up to date. Explaining Day accurately and subtly would be difficult; nothing about him was certain. And there was also the matter of behaving fairly towards tonight's unidentified male guest set aside for her. The cushions didn't encourage decisiveness.

A delivery van left the rear of the house along the half-kilometre of driveway. What expensive titbit had it left behind? A specialised paté, a dozen ripe peaches? From the side of the van Jana saw it was part of an even greater indulgence: bread and baguettes from the last baking at the village *boulangerie*. Brought to order. That would amuse the impoverished Day.

And where would he be at this very moment? It had been a warm early September day and his work tended to be ruled by the weather. Some difficulty with a swimming pool, a defective ice box? Solving the technical stuff wasn't the difficulty, the hardest thing was staying calm as tipsy customers offered suggestions then had to search for cash to pay for his services. "Luckily the French have invented a verb: *patienter*, to be patient," he had said. Deep down he didn't appear the patient type. Initially he had withstood Grandage but then he'd cracked. Angrily. Cracked on her behalf, of course.

"Smiling to yourself, you look quite smug," said Didi arriving beside her and reaching into the ice bucket for the champagne.

"Who wouldn't be? Here I am in the - " The word for lap escaped her. " – on the knee of luxury."

"I sometimes feel a tinge of guilt even though I've earned most of this house. It pleases me to see you enjoy it."

And Jana responded to the affection. There was no way she could hold back. "Lie down on that other lounger. I have something to tell you. It may mean something, I don't know."

She described Day as objectively as she could. Careful to temper her enthusiasm, emphasising his foreignness, the little she knew and his marginal role in French society. "Would I sleep with him? Of course. But it isn't the only qualification. In France I have slept with another man and that is all it was - a physical experience. Afterwards it was like coming away from a swim. Being with Christopher is a wider world." She paused. "I could change a little and perhaps I need to."

Didi's glass of champagne sat untouched on the table. "My first reaction is to be terribly French." She laughed. "But then I am French. From what you say he too is restrained. To shower you with books would be crude seduction. So there's poetry and pouf, an end to that. Eventually you will share his bed and find whether he wants to be generous. Perhaps he doesn't wish to be and that will be an agony. But it must be done."

"I've survived other agonies," Jana protested.

"The question may be: what would you give up? Flying? Not at all. In any case that is surely part of your attraction. But how about your solitariness? That may be the gift."

"So French, so clever." Jana sat up, temporarily discarding luxury. "You do understand. At first I felt I must not tell you."

"Why? Oh, yes. Poor Gérard. Life and especially love are not fair. Use him tonight. Compare him with your M. Day. No, forget that kind of pragmatism. Enjoy his company. He is good fun and – ultimately – philosophical."

And so it proved. As partner in a fledgling publishing company Gérard was well-travelled and immediately gained Jana's interest by detesting French television. "I have never understood," he said, "why the news broadcasts on six channels must be timed for eight o'clock. Suppose one arrives late? Such Teutonic rigidity. Didi says you fly for a living. I'm fascinated but I want to ask intelligent questions about flying. Help me."

They were sitting side by side at the dining table, he on her good side. She liked the way he turned his whole body when he spoke, liked his open-necked formal shirt with its multi-coloured stripes. She said, "Let's pretend you've already asked that question. Flying is often misunderstood, it can be dull. That part needs a certain temperament."

He was keen to engage. "But surely the key is that dull activities – checking the sky, looking at the instruments, knowing what to expect – must become instinct. Breathing is dull but its dullness does not irritate us."

Jana said, "There is a reverse side. People who are good at repetition may have trouble solving situations that aren't routine. Also, non-routine events are rare; we may be numbed by routine, we may expect routine. I'll bet there's less routine in publishing books."

He was eating paté with a knife and fork which he put down to smile at her. "The innocent belief that tomorrow will bring a masterpiece. Routine teaches us this doesn't happen. We too must learn to stay alert, avoid being numbed. But not all discoveries arrive as manuscripts. You are American, you speak excellent French and you work in a country where attitudes towards your government are – shall we say – mixed. You have a story to tell."

"But no skills to tell it."

"Those skills are overrated. And there are such people as editors. I make this conclusion: you speak the language well because France interests you. Thus the French – who are given to self-love – would appreciate your point of view."

Day had said something similar. "You may be right," she said. "I am not often homesick. France has been kind."

"Kind? Ah yes, I see. But that is surely our minimal qualification for membership of the human race."

"It's at a discount in the US."

"Hmm. Your story takes on other aspects. Look, I must not impose myself but it is worth taking notes, keeping a diary perhaps. If you agree I could provide some guidance."

He looked less like a publisher and more like a harassed accountant: thinning fair hair combed back, rimless glasses, slightly protruding eyes, pale complexion. Earnest but likable.

"What guidance?"

"Forget opinion, stick to facts, passages of dialogue, descriptions of things, people and events you may well forget." He smiled reminiscently. "Nothing, absolutely nothing, about the weather."

"But I fly. The weather's large up there."

"I had forgotten. Then you must make weather sound very technical. Cumulo-nimbus up to ten thousand metres, wind from the north-east, 21 kph."

"What on earth are you two talking about?" Didi called out from the other side of the table. "Sounds like flying. In which case you should be talking to me?"

"Gérard suggests I become an author."

"What an excellent idea. The American Ex."

One of Didi's legal friends raised his hands in mock protest. "But I don't think St-Exupery was terribly good with planes. I can't imagine him flying a jet. How about Jana as the American Jacqueline? Or is Jacqueline Auriol *vieux jeu*?"

"Not to me," said Jana. "I read her book. I suppose if you marry the son of the French president you get to fly all the planes you want. Even so she was a test pilot and you can't buy that. But forget labels. To produce a book I'd have to learn how to write. Gérard says he'll guide me but I need more than just guidance, I need teaching. It will be back to the chalkboard."

"Nonsense," said the legal friend. "Anyone can write now. Soccer players. Pop-stars, even right-wing politicians. Practice as you fly over the Auvergne."

"Practice what? Come on, you all qualify as intellectuals and all intellectuals write. What's the difference between writing and simply putting one word after another?"

Luc intervened. "A marvellous question. Let us have a competition. Answer in fifty words. The best response wins a bottle of Didi's 1990 Latour."

"That will require a very good response," said Didi firmly.

A *poulet de Bresse*, boned and reconstructed round pork and oyster stuffing, arrived at the table, served by a chef apparently hired for the evening. The eight guests replenished their glasses from three opened bottles of Hermitage. "One thinks guiltily about Ethiopia when dining chez Labossière," said Gérard.

As the meal eventually moved on to couches, coffee and digestifs Jana noticed a kind of democracy which drew everyone in. Muted personal talk, of the sort she and Gérard had exchanged, was forbidden as was prolonged discussion about individuals. This wasn't surprising. Given what she knew about Didi, guests who were shy probably disappeared from the Labossière circle.

Amazingly everyone other than Jana responded to Luc's challenge though she couldn't recall anyone making notes. It wasn't a judgement for the faint-hearted since contestants had to read their contribution aloud – or, in the case of an *avocat*, quote it from memory – and face stringent criticism.

"They're hard to follow," Jana said to Gérard.

"The fifty-word limit. It condenses the style. You're hearing written not oral French."

Contestants were only allowed to vote for the work of others, resulting in an easy majority for Luc himself.

"Please read it again. More slowly," said Jana. Which Luc did. Writing was characterised by rhythm, he claimed. His single sentence was deliberately rhythmic to prove the point and included a five-word quotation from Verlaine. Jana asked if she might keep everyone's entry and the *avocat* with the good memory wrote his out for her. The pieces of paper were passed to her without self-consciousness and conversation resumed on a completely different topic.

When it was all over and they were sauntering confidently to their cars, it was late enough for a pleasing chill in the air. Hidden by the bulk of Jana's van parked at the rear of the house Gérard kissed Jana inexpertly on the corner of her mouth. Separated from tabletalk formalities he proved briefly inarticulate. "We may meet again, I hope," he said. In a further anti-climax they clumsily exchanged mobile numbers.

As the van hissed along the driveway she asked herself whether the stain had obliged him to kiss her as "a minimum qualification for membership of the human race." Out on the main road she pulled into a layby and opened her mobile, switched off during the dinner. No missed calls. Christopher Day was now a smear, the only remembrance his over-washed shirt. Might she tease him into posing for a photograph? He'd recognise the ploy. Luc had said rhythm was the essence of writing; was uncertainty the essence of ill-defined affection?

WITH AN extra plane to cover the Tarbes contract Jean-Claude now needed another pilot. Normally such appointments (there hadn't been many) were informal, the result of a recommendation by someone he trusted. This time he favoured a different approach. They sat together in the office, a full complement of three, drinking Ginette's coffee.

"Gascon Air is a business not a hobby," J-C said to Jana. "I must start behaving as if I owned the company. However gruesome I must attend to administration. I have two possible candidates. We will interview them as if the three of us were the human resources department. Which of course we are."

"I won't watch them, I'll watch you," said Jana.

"You think I cannot administer? A mere bush pilot with my office in my back pocket. I shall be totally forensic."

Jana said, "Won't the interviews be a farce? We need a pilot not a manager. Simply have him fly you to Montauban and back."

"Our pilot must also represent Gascon Air. I need someone *sympa*, who comforts anxious passengers while pulling out of a spin."

"Does that mean I'm *sympa*?"

"My dear Jana, if you are not sure you are miraculously stupider than I thought."

"What's my *qualité* when I'm introduced?"

"Perhaps *eminence grise*. But why grey? I have never truly understood."

Jana asked, "Let's do the interviews in the Seneca?"

"Excellent idea."

"He and him!" Ginette pointed out. "Are they both masculine?"

Jean-Claude said, "My employees are so clever, so penetrant. Thus they spoil my little joke. I wanted to surprise Jana. One of them is, in fact, a woman."

Jana said, "In that case I need official status. A job title."

Jean-Claude looked round the cramped room. Since they'd acquired the Stationair, Ginette had asked Cessna for a 1 x 1½ m wall-poster of the plane. Alone she had laboriously rearranged the shelf units to free sufficient wall space; the poster was now pinned alongside an enlarged version of the Gascon Air musketeer logo. "Now our marketing has redesigned company headquarters I agree, we must be formal," said J-C. "How about *présidente-directrice general*."

"And you?"

"Oh, *fondateur-proprietaire*."

"And me?" asked Ginette.

"*Chef de pub*."

"Dishonest. I'd rather be *réceptionniste*."

The first interview started in the stationary Seneca but the questions continued quite naturally after take-off. Jana judged Jérome's appearance from the Seneca's rear seat and decided his close-cropped light brown hair aped US aviation practice too closely. But then he had over 2000 hours as a flight instructor with one of Bordeaux's well-endowed *aéroclubs*. Perhaps he was popular because he looked US.

As the flight continued Jana realised J-C had been right to insist she flew too. In a tiny company compatibility was essential and Jérome himself underlined this. Used to a stream of wealthy students he had developed a heavily correct way of speaking which Jana found irksome. If he got the job this would need to be rectified. She held her fire as J-C requested a predictable set of manoeuvres and emergency procedures, all performed immaculately. Questions only began to form when Jérome approached the grass strip that had been first port of call with Grandage. Jérome's routine, she noticed, matched hers; he too had stretched his head towards the side window, scanning the terrain to port during his downwind pass.

Suddenly she realised she was watching him as Chris Day must have watched her from roughly the same position. What did a three-quarters rear angle say about a person's intelligence? Unconsciously she reached for her mobile to check for texts. Took her hand away, ashamed.

Jérome taxied back to the eastern end of the strip and Jana asked, "Were you confident the strip was long enough?"

"Well, I know the Seneca's rotate and - " He laughed lightly. " – I felt you wouldn't ask me to commit suicide. I haven't landed on too many unattended runways but I spent time a couple of years ago learning how to estimate their length. I'd say this is 850 – 900 metres."

"Good enough," said Jana. "It's 876, so you can be pleased about that."

J-C turned in his seat and raised his eyebrows. Jana nodded.

J-C said, "Let's fly minimum height towards Toulouse and I'll check your RTC procedures in more crowded airspace."

Out of Arizona

Smoothly Jérome looked at his altimeter, set the Garmin and did as he was told. With time to spare Jana asked, "Jérome, suppose the roles were reversed and you were checking out J-C. What tests would you ask him to fly?"

"The western side of Toulouse is busy, crossing the civil routes from Marseille, Milan and Turin." Starting to loosen up, he half-turned. "However the area I know best is north-east of Bordeaux near the Paris corridor. It's not CdG but that's where I take my students to test their nervousness."

J-C said casually, "Mind if I switch off your port engine?"

He reacted immediately. "At two thousand feet? For an emergency landing? That wouldn't be simulation, it would be almost the real thing. I'll do it if you insist but in my own defence I'd have tried out the Seneca on one engine at five thousand if we'd been flying for real." He thought for a while. "But then I should have asked your permission to do that, shouldn't I? Black mark there."

The intercom between the three of them was silent. Jana recalled J-C had demanded a somewhat similar test in the Seneca. Would she have remembered to ask for such a check? J-C turned slightly and she shook her head.

"My *partenaire* thinks I was unfair. Climb to whatever height you wish."

Jérome flew the plane for a couple of minutes on one engine. Then glided unpowered, with the air whistling menacingly over the wings and fuselage. He grunted, "As I thought, she glides best slightly pitched up. At less than 150 feet the nose obscures the approach. You have to memorise what's ahead. Difficult but then nobody has ever said otherwise." He re-started the engines. "I'll go down and do what you asked for."

At two thousand feet he switched off the port engine himself, trimmed the plane, then put it into the shallowest possible descent. At five hundred feet he said, "Assume we're gliding. I am looking two, three kilometres ahead; nothing possible at the moment. I'll alter the trim to raise the nose, to make things more authentic. The plane would be dropping at twenty feet every ten seconds. Still nothing at three kilometres. Still nothing."

"Can't trust the altimeter down here." He glanced at his wristwatch which must now be acting as a stopwatch. Jana had not noticed him press the button. "Gliding at just under four hundred feet. There's something beyond two kilometres; a barer area, fewer trees but large rocks. Now we're under three hundred feet. Nothing ahead. Two hundred. Just dense trees. Tree tops are better than ground level rocks, but only just. Decision time. Full flaps, nose slightly up. Body braced." He started the port engine.

Jérome shook his head. "Doubt we'd have survived. At least trees are better than houses." Nobody had asked him to but the plane was climbing now. An instinctive reaction - felt by all three of them - away from low altitude.

"Good, Jérome, good," said Jean-Claude quietly.

"The operation was a success but the patient died," said Jérome.

Jana put her hand on his shoulder. "A pilot simply lengthens the odds. None of us can beat gravity."

At five thousand feet he levelled out. Hollowness made Jérome's voice sincere. "I'd like to fly with Gascon Air." he said. Jana tightened her diaphragm to suppress her feelings. J-C's face was expressionless.

Back in the office Ginette, who must have taken to Jérome, was eager for their judgment. "Good pilot," said Jean-Claude curtly.

"Talks rather formally. But we'd knock that out of him," said Jana. She was reminded of her professional obligations. "Good pilot."

"Our other hopeful arrives at two o'clock. I need a sandwich," said Jean-Claude. "Will I see you at the bar?"

"Give me a couple of minutes to check my phone," she said, pointedly walking away from the door that led to the airport.

A text: Phoned. UR flying. Call.

"Jana here." She'd forgotten the sound of his voice.

"Couldn't bring myself to call your mobile. Who knows what desperate manoeuvres?" Yes, that was the voice. Higher pitched than she remembered. But familiar and now getting into its stride. No sentimental Yankee-style felicitations.

"I'd switched off," she said. "Just as well, really. An hour and ten minutes ago the Seneca went into the tree-tops just south of Villeneuve-sur-Lot. No survivors. But not for real. We were checking out a new pilot. A simulated attempt at an emergency landing."

"Sounds as if he failed."

"It does, doesn't it?" She wanted to be as clipped as he was. "The fact is both Jean-Claude and I would have done the same. There was no way out."

He was silent for a few seconds. "Seems eerie. Talking to you and you so brisk. I'm not sure…"

She wanted him to finish the sentence. "It was a bit like that at the time. Never mind. You texted."

"Yes. I'm poor. You know that."

"I know. I'm not poor, just impoverished."

"But I'm rather old-fashioned."

"Does that mean we're finished?" She tried for a light teasing tone but it didn't come out that way.

"Only if you insist."

"I'm not insisting."

"Glad about that." How she wished she could match the easy way he spoke. But then Brits were supposed to be the worldmasters. He went on, "I'm offering you a treat but, as usual, it's qualified. Born out of poverty."

"A visit to the *déchetterie*?"

"How the hell do you know the French for dump?" he asked, laughing. Oh joy at that! A target carefully chosen, hit dead centre.

"You don't give me credit. Every village has a sign pointing the way."

"So they do, so they do. There are more ways of learning French than from a book. As you have proved. My apologies."

Jana said, "Don't go soft on me. I appreciate your schoolmaster side. My job is to have my ass kicked. So what's the treat?"

He laughed again. "I'm having difficulty keeping up. Normally I run rings round Yanks. For one thing they're too polite. But Frenchness has rubbed off on you. My treat, then. Truly low key."

"I'm your slave, slavering."

"I have a job, rebuilding a boundary wall at a Brit's holiday home. He's away, the house has lovely views, we could chat – profoundly, of course - while I work. I could run to sandwiches. Afterwards go for a pint."

"But there's more, isn't there? What you're saying – I can tell by the tone – you haven't returned to home base."

"How about more poetry? From me but mainly from you. And a different approach. Do you see yourself as a romantic?"

He didn't mean sex. "I've always said romantic flyers end up self-interred. But how do flyers become flyers? The wish to fly is romantic. Let's say I've had my moments."

From sounds over the mobile it seemed as if he were moving slightly, getting more comfortable. She liked that. He said, "Here's a fact. Poetry isn't best served by being romantic. Too many people favour the first gush principle – the first entranced read-through. Poetry is a tough discipline; it profits from re-reading and re-thinking."

"So I should rehearse?"

"Exactly. Is rehearsing too finicky? Too close to the classroom?"

"I think it's a great idea." Her reply hung in the air, incomplete, needing to be finished off with his first name. Yet he the Brit – in true Brit style – hadn't released that sanction. How could she make it happen?

He said, "Trawl the internet for poems. Find them yourself because that's so much better than regurgitating stuff I've chosen. Print them out. Go through them a few times." He sighed. "I feel I'm bossing you about."

"Don't think that for a minute."

Jean-Claude had eaten his snack and drunk his coffee. "A long call. Your expression is bright, optimistic. I will not ask any questions."

"If it works out I'll tell you. You deserve it. I'll get a *jambon cru* and a Sprite. Another coffee for you. Then we'll talk about Jérome."

They faced each other across the plastic surface of the fixed table. He said, "Jérome yes. But your face is more important. I am happy. You could work with Jérome?"

"He's cool. And cool is the sign of a good pilot. I've been thinking. I'd never have thought to ask you for a one-engine test. Would you have asked me?"

"I am your boss, I am infallible. The answer has to be yes. But deep inside my psyche…."

Jana asked, "How about the stopwatch?"

"Here, I can defend myself. My watch is plain analogue; I am not a *sportif*."

"You escape so well, J-C. Next you'll be defying gravity."

"On a good day, why not?" He sipped his coffee. "So we were both impressed by Jérome. The question is should we examine Martine the same way? The obvious answer is yes. But consider this: suppose Martine lands the plane safely. It could happen; I cannot exactly duplicate the conditions." He looked at her quizzically. "You and I learned to be factual, non-emotional about flying. Today I for one experienced a frisson. Might we feel differently about a safe landing?"

"My God, J-C, that's Jesuitical. But you're right. For what it's worth both examinations should be the same. And then we must lay bare each other's soul."

"And you say I'm the Jesuit!" he said, laughing. "I agree. No more agonising. A few words about Martine. I've known her for five years. She's an instructor with Aéroclub de l'ENAS at Balma north of Toulouse and has at least 1500 hours. Divorced, thirties, two sons, almost a petite *bourgeoise* since she was married to a man who did something serious in a bank. One thing that will interest you: she went solo very very quickly."

"I browsed the subject recently," said Jana. "The consensus says that soloing quickly isn't necessarily the mark of a great pilot. Certain people simply react better to exams than others. What is interesting is her CV. Before she was an abstraction;

easy to ignore in favour of Jérome. Now she's a person and we have to be fair."

They were ready to leave the bar. He asked, "Another woman pilot, how do you feel? You must know you are held in affection, not just by me but by Ginette and Armelle. And the ATC staff I talk to. I shouldn't say this but your gender is one of the reasons."

"I've been lucky," said Jana. "In the US we're told not to believe in luck. Only in what we deserve. Gascon Air is a sort of home. If I have to work hard to be re-accepted that's no bad thing. If Martine joins us I'll make her welcome. Even if she thinks I'm an over-privileged Yank."

Martine arrived on time to the minute in a Robin and they walked out to meet her as she taxied to the hardstanding. Emerging from the cockpit she paused with one foot on the wing foot-plate, looking her best. Dark hair close cut, short yet muscular, an excellent bum tightly presented. She embraced Jean-Claude. "Sorry about the Robin, the ostentation. I have a lesson at five and I like to be punctual." She put out her hand to Jana. "And this is the famous *américaine*. My dear Jana we know about you even as far away as Balma. All good things I assure you."

Given that Toulouse was her home patch Jean-Claude took the other direction: picking up on what Jérome had said and directing Martine to the so-called Paris corridor north-east of Bordeaux. One thing immediately struck Jana; Martine adopted a different voice for radio work: clipped, almost gender neutral.

"It's true," said Martine. "My first instructor - I quickly got rid of him - was a rugby enthusiast. He had certain views. He alerted me to others of his kind in aviation. In this part of France I decided not to be a woman over the airwaves."

"I never had that option," Jana said laughing.

"Oh no. With good French your accent is an asset. As your countrymen say: if you have it, flaunt it."

The geography Jean-Claude had chosen meant they could use the same grass strip yet again. "I must remind myself to be vocal," Martine said. "Would you ask me to land on an unsuitable runway? I think not. Here the Seneca's approach will be 90 mph and that runway is long enough. But I will pretend. As I close the throttle a sheep wanders across the far end; I can still land but I must be brutal with the plane. There. Just beyond halfway."

Both Jean-Claude and Jana became less talkative as they contrived parameters for the emergency landing. When J-C asked if he might switch off the port engine Martine said authoritatively, "I cannot agree to that. I think I understand; you are asking me to pretend to land without power within the next five kilometres. I have flown this plane less than an hour. That is too dangerous, we are too low."

"If you could prepare for this – in your own way – would you do it?"

Her fingers tapped the yoke. "Let me see. I cannot promise. May I take over?"

She climbed to five thousand feet. There she made no attempt to glide the plane, believing perhaps that the test would be only theoretical, that there would be no actual low-level gliding. Instead she devoted almost four minutes to flying the plane on one engine. "It is more stable than I imagined. Yes I will do the exercise. But you understand I will re-start the engine if I feel it necessary."

This time Jana was careful to see if Martine activated her stopwatch. She did not do so nor did she pay much attention to the altimeter. Her assessment of the descent rate was entirely visual. As with Jérome, there was no comfort from the ground below when Jean-Claude broke off the exercise.

At five thousand feet J-C said, "That was excellent Martine. I apologise if I was extreme."

Martine shook her trim head. "It was useful. We should all be taken to the edge on occasions. I would do things differently a second time but that is irrelevant. On such occasions there are no refinements.

"Is it fair to test your memory, Martine?" J-C asked. "Could you find the grass strip again without using the Garmin?"

"How surgical you are, Jean-Claude" she said, smiling brightly. Nevertheless she re-traced the course precisely, as Jana suspected she would.

"What's the secret?" Jana asked.

"I fear it's a mystery. The images reappear and are recognisable but they are not a logical sequence, they are in reverse. Something I am blessed with. I can take no credit."

Back at the hardstanding she embraced Jean-Claude with some fervour. Then she embraced Jana. "I sensed you all the time, Jana. A presence. Not critical, but benign. I would like to work with you both. Flying is my life as it is with you."

As the Robin left the Bayonne runway, Jean-Claude shook his head. "Mon Dieu this is going to be difficult. I'm glad it will be a shared decision."

"I will need a full twenty-four hours."

"I may need longer."

As she drove home Ghislaine phoned her. "We have not spoken for some time."

"I should hope not. You have a more important acquaintance. Is all going well?"

"A miracle has happened. Maman has met Boyce. The cold war has become a truce. Tepid, but a truce. We wanted to celebrate and you are the only person who understands our little problems. Boyce wants to cook you dinner."

"I am... slightly enmeshed."

"Good. Bring him too. Assuming we are talking about a him."

"Only slightly enmeshed. I am having to proceed delicately. He is poverty-stricken and worries about charity."

"My dear Jana, you are speaking so quietly. This is something different?"

Jana said, "I hope so. Superstitious Anglos say: I will not tempt fate. In effect, not take anything for granted. Do you understand?"

"Ask him to invite us and we will bring the food. And the wine."

Jana gestured even though Ghislaine was at the other end of a radio transmission. "I have already done that. Next time I will have to move on."

Ghislaine asked, "But we will meet you soon?"

"We must. I need to prove I have friends. Good friends."

"A walk, then. Ice skating – no this is the wrong season. Why not lying together on the beach."

"I will move heaven and earth. But very gently."

CHAPTER SEVENTEEN

Not so cruel wall

YET AGAIN only three places were set at the Chauvelets' dining table. Vincent had taken to having his evening meal alone in the caravan and conversations languished. This had continued for some days and Jana found it progressively more depressing. The solution was obvious but she suspected the aftermath would be painful as it had been for Mme. le Lannic. There was some hint of this when she simply announced their names: "Hugues. Sylvie." Their heads jerked up, their faces wary.

"This cannot go on. I am disrupting your family."

They glanced at each other, trying to decide who was better prepared for the discussion neither of them wanted. Sylvie said, "There is Octavien."

"He is part of the problem. Occasionally he wants to explain his troubles to me. I shouldn't be his confessor. "

"Your company is instructive," said Hugues vaguely.

Jana tried to imagine how loss of rent would affect them. There was money coming in here and the interior of the house was bright and spruce. Not surprising since Hugues had a local government pension; received wisdom said retired public servants did well in France. Before Dirk, they had existed without the extra cash and had not apparently suffered. But perhaps this wasn't the point. The French, especially the elderly French, had a certain attitude towards money which US Jana had never truly fathomed. She had first noticed it at street markets where black-dressed widows could spend a minute grasping and squeezing two dozen, three dozen peaches before grudgingly taking the two that met some impossible standard. Ah, said foreigners, they buy well but Jana wasn't sure. The process was too visceral, too inborn to be casually described as bargain hunting. And the tendency re-appeared in a different form at what Jana would have called garage sales where dilapidated items of furniture, well beyond usage, carried ridiculously optimistic price tags. As if the vendor's memory of the purchase price was still as sharp now as it had been thirty years ago.

Certainly the Chauvelets had embraced her conversationally, fed her well and seen she was comfortable. Sylvie's tears had been quite real when Jana had spent that single night in the hastily rearranged store-room, suggesting genuine shame. But even then Jana had been uneasy; had Sylvie also been thinking about the need to lower the rent? And when they became aware that Jana might be the answer to Vincent's domestic problems was their quiet enthusiasm based on parental or economic reasons?

But if their motives were obscure Jana's were focused. She'd found it hard to forgive that look on Vincent's face - You'll never do better! – and her cold treatment had driven him into the caravan. Octavien? Regularly he was capable of reaching out and touching her. She knew too she represented a benign force neither father nor mother could match. But in the end would either Vincent or Yvonne have thanked her for emphasising their defects? Yvonne had rejected what she saw as Jana's influence on her son and may have been right all along.

Across the table the Chauvelets had the resigned look of aristocrats under scrutiny by the *tricoteuses*. There was little to be gained plastering over her decision to leave.

"I shall be truly sorry," she said, turning departure into a fact. "You have been open-hearted and kind. Even more important, living with you has helped me understand France. Made me less of a stranger."

Neither saw this as anything other than a theory. "Where will you live?" asked Hugues.

"I think this time I must find a little apartment."

"You will be lonely."

And well she might. The role of paying guest had held loneliness at bay and had improved her French. But Chris Day's way of life – romantically, perhaps – had seemed more honest, more appropriate. And, of course, less constricted.

Only one gesture had eased the claw of Mme. le Lannic's pathetic clutches. "I will of course pay a month's notice and the remainder of any unused month." The Chauvelets sighed.

THE BRIT'S villa overlooked Ondres Plage to the north of Biarritz. That part of the coastline was notoriously undistinguished consisting mainly of driftwood-covered beaches with a backdrop of scrub. But someone had found a small hump and built a contoured bungalow with views that hid the immediate foreground and concentrated on yachts five kilometres out, en route for Arcachon and La Rochelle. The final part of the access road led up a sandy track and Jana, distrusting the van's ability on loose surfaces, walked the hundred metres. The distressed wall was quickly visible and she saw him watching her. There was no greeting. Their mutual inspection was silent, she to refresh the blurred details of his face, he for reasons she could only imagine. Then, as if by agreement, they both looked out on the Bay of Biscay.

"Did you ever sail?" he asked.

"Once. In Chesapeake Bay. A guy I met in USAF. Three days. Next best thing after flying."

"Quieter."

"Less intuitive."

Day said, "I'll take your word for it. We were saving for a Contessa 32 when she gave me the thumbs-down. I thought it would bring us closer. Looking back I can see it was my thing, not hers."

"Perhaps it was better you never got the boat. You'd have hated to have lost it in the settlement."

"You seem to know a lot about me."

"I do a lot of guessing."

He pointed to a pile of irregular stones. "I have an image about how four of those are going to fit together in the wall. Can't afford to lose that info. Make yourself comfortable. I've got a LiLo here for you."

"What's a LiLo?"

"An airbed."

"But you're kneeling," she pointed out. "We wouldn't be going equal shares. How'm I going to find out what dedication feels like?"

That made him snigger. "Ten minutes and I'll let down the LiLo. Then you'll feel the stones underneath."

"Just so's I don't get the Yankee free ride."

"Let me guess. It has another meaning. How about tailwind."

"You never need my translations, I always need yours."

But he'd already started working.

Sometime over the years she must have watched a bricklayer and appreciated the neatly interlocking procedures. But this was different. He picked up a stone and rotated it this way and that over the cavity it might fill, holding a second stone in his other hand, checking that against a future cavity. Generously applied mortar acted as a filler as well as an adhesive.

"Slow work," she said.

"Makes a nice wall, though."

Work already complete confirmed this. "How did you learn?"

"Ten years ago I quoted someone a fixed price to keep me honest. Then did the job three times slower than I would now. It was a wonderful tutorial. And starvation's the best teacher."

"The French call that last bit an *apophtegme*."

He nodded. "A five-dollar word. It's what I love about the French. The way they revel in bags of syllables. Don't get me wrong, I'm impressed by *apophtegme*."

"Dumb Yank knows big word?"

He straightened up. "How about another big word, two of them – self-abnegation? You go in for it now and then, but it doesn't come naturally. Doesn't match your job or your nationality."

"Is that a compliment?"

"On the whole I don't do compliments. Proper ones are too much hard work."

"Nothing wrong with a memorable one,"

He was concentrating and didn't reply immediately. "You're fishing. Not worthy of you."

"I'm not exactly over-supplied."

"Being able to ask you here today: it said something about you, it was a compliment."

She lay back on the LiLo trying out the compliment's meaning and staying power. "What do you need to know about me?" she asked finally.

"Anything you care to mention. But it's the sound of your voice; I like to encourage it. Of course I could be naïve, the victim of a sucker punch. I'm impressed by your flying but then who wouldn't be? Flying's like walking on water. But perhaps I'm over-impressed?"

"Weasel question gets a weasel answer. Yes and no. Given a load of money, a patient instructor and unlimited time you could learn to fly. What couldn't be guaranteed is you'd survive the first week on your own. It's a matter of outlook. Watching me fly you don't see the bits that matter. Chances are you were hood-winked."

He put down the stone he'd just picked up. "Even more important, did I over-impress you? The books, the book knowledge, the quotes. The stuff I was doing when you were learning to fly. With me there are no invisible bits. What you see and hear is what you get."

"We're talking about firsts for both of us; we've no standards to judge by and we were both bowled over. Over-impressed. Think about it in a month's time. Always assuming…"

"Is that real pessimism," he grunted. "or false pessimism?"

"Take your pick. It's my default state."

"Imposed by a cruel world?"

"I suppose."

After a long stare with his mind on something unexplained he busied himself with his stones, moving them about noisily. Time stretched out and half a dozen had been positioned and mortared in before he abruptly recited:

> *Think in this battered caravanserai,*
> *Whose doorways are alternate night and day.* "

Know that?"

"I should and I hate myself for saying no."

"Don't say that. Please. Not to me. Reflect on that American-ism – it must surely be US – don't get mad, get even. Say to yourself: Does he know the Seneca's cruising range? It's all a matter of playing at home or away: my speciality or yours. Where was I? Old Omar." He repeated the couplet. "Does it tickle your fancy.?"

"I like the rhyme and the rhythm. What's great is I've no idea what a caravanserai is and yet it doesn't matter."

"A big poetic truth. Almost never ask what a poem means; it's rarely what matters most."

"Second line's neat."

He said, "It is indeed. How did you choose the stuff you've brought?"

"First-line appeal."

"Anything else?"

"No love poems," said Jana.

"Aw. Read me the one you've rehearsed the most."

"Do you need title and the author?"

"You wouldn't want to see me embarrassed, would you? Having to ask?"

"Dorothy Parker's Ballade at Thirty-Five." Jana read it.

"Best thing about it?" he asked, resuming his work.

> *I was tender, and, often, true;*
> *Ever a prey to coincidence*

"Secret reason for liking it?"

"She's close to my age."

"Lie down on the LiLo. Close your eyes for ten minutes."

"What will you be doing?"

"Laying more stones. Off and on looking at you."

The experience was almost oppressive. Is he looking at me now? Has he learned anything? Good or bad? Is my face com-posed – whatever that means? She dozed for a few seconds, woke up with a jerk and wondered if he'd noticed. But he seemed buried in the work. Was this the image of him she wanted to carry away? Kneeling doggedly, miles away from literary games. Should she be more active; was this passivity some kind of test?

Without raising his head from the wall he asked, "I've asked you before. Are you all right with my teaching?"

"I'm charmed."

"Charmed? It's just that I tend to rush things. Get things wrong."

So he wasn't as assured as she imagined. He doubted his appeal as she doubted hers. "Nothing's going wrong at this end. Promise."

And now he did look up.

At ten he came from behind the wall, used it as a seat and opened a flask of coffee. This brought him nearer. "My ex was high-born, let's say upper middle-class. In the early days she called me a clodhopper as a joke. I didn't mind."

"Clodhopper. Boy, how my vocabulary's expanding. I'm guessing clumsy, with your hands and the way you speak. Totally ridiculous. The stones in the wall tell a different story and I love the way you fly off at tangents. Like landing at Christoforo Columbus, Genoa. Good for the liver."

"Hmmm. A professional compliment I take it. My social skills wander but you've never complained. You go with every change."

"Pure self-interest." She took a deep breath. "I think you were going to say something about this." She touched her cheek. "But decided it wasn't the moment. Why not now?"

"If I've held back it's because what I'm inclined to say seems so obvious. I can see it might discourage feeble-minded males at dances and in offices. But once the gap is crossed is it still a concern? Do you think that colour's always part of my frontal lobes? I assure you it isn't. There's much more to pay attention to."

Jana spoke carefully. "It isn't a factor with, say, half a dozen people I know in France. But my conditioning is very deep. One half-assed word or look and I'm back at grade school wondering what comes next. A form of paranoia, dormant a lot of the time. Then it gets up and bites me."

She told him about Mme. le Lannic. "I guess it was childish getting out of her house there and then. So I'm childish."

"You don't see me as a second shoe, I hope?"

She laughed, rather excessively. "Why are there so many footnotes to our conversation?"

"Because you tempt me – for your own good, of course. Second shoe: an unpredictably imminent and probably unpleasant sequel to something that has just happened," he said, sticking his thumbs underneath his braces. She was meant to laugh at the academic tone and did so - with relief.

"Another poem, please."

She retrieved her printout and read Over St John's Hill.

"Did you know Thomas before?" he asked.

"Nope."

"How did you find the poem?"

"Trawling, browsing. Riding piggyback on other people's likes. The start hit me right between the eyes."

"Read it again."

> *The hawk on fire hangs still;*
> *In a hoisted cloud, at drop of dusk, he pulls to his*
> *claws*
> *And gallows, up the rays of his eyes the small birds of*
> *the bay.*

"What matters?"

"More childishness I'm afraid. It's my world."

"Jana, Jana." How rarely he used her name. An un-US trait and therefore more thrilling when he did. "I can't stand these apologies. Imagine if you will you've got the stick – no, it's a yoke isn't it? – between your hands. At all times. You never apologise for being a pilot, don't now."

"But I'm a beginner with poems."

"That's merely an accident in time. It has no qualitative meaning. You're using beginner and ignorant interchangeably. For me ignorant is pejorative, almost wilful. And that isn't you."

"What is your name?" she asked suddenly. "What can I call you?"

"Whatever you like. Why not Clodhopper?"

"Please. It's important, vital. I come from a first-name society. I know it doesn't go down well with Brits but I'm not a Brit. I need the connection."

He recognised the intensity. "See! That's oafishness on my part. I knew the US loves first names but I'd willingly – intentionally - ignored that fact. My culture's better than your culture, yah-boo. I'm sorry, and I need to say that. My name? How careless I've been. Like most kids I've never liked it; it made me sound fragile, likely to break in the middle."

"So it's Chris because that's shorter and you don't want to spend time on it. Could you bear it if I used it in full? My privilege. Christopher."

His eyes opened. "Sounds different. Must be the accent. Say it again."

"Christopher."

"Who would have thought…? It's yours."

"It's yours, Jana."

Now he laughed. "That may take more time. I often want to say your name yet my upbringing prevents it. It's yours, Jana."

"And with your blessing."

"In purely secular terms – with my blessing. Jana."

"No, that's not right. There's a period that spoils it. Should be a comma. With my blessing, Jana."

"This could run and run." He looked down at the ground. "Let's hope it does."

The coffee had been drunk but she no longer wanted to be apart from him on the LiLo with the wall dividing them. She offered him help. She would hold up two further stones, allowing him to judge six shapes at a time. Haphazard at first but a rhythm emerged. They spoke far less and his rate increased. By twelve her arms ached horribly and finally he noticed.

"Shit, Jana."

"That was good. No period."

"Time for sandwiches. We can use the house. Perhaps there's some coffee."

He rooted around in the huge elegant kitchen but could find only tea. "You could share my Sprite," she said

"Those trade names. They arouse suspicion. What's Sprite like?"

She handed him the opened can, saw his lips touch the slot she had sipped on. "Why, it's just pop, lemonade," he said. "Why don't they sub-title it for Brits?"

The built-in table was end-on to a picture window that faced the sea. A wind had sprung up, bellying the sails of four yachts, keeling over the hulls at the angle beloved by all amateur painters. "Don't they look terrific?" he said. "But so slow."

"Stylish with it, though."

As he unwrapped the baguettes she noticed how carefully he'd layered the components of the salad so that each bite brought a cross-section of flavours. The apples and peaches he cut deftly and fanned them out on a plate. After munching a couple of mouthfuls he said, "Gahh, I'm thirsty. Better make do with water. You had the foresight to bring Sprite; I can't leave you gagging."

"I've got another."

A brief silence descended as each considered the implications of having him drink from the opened rather than the unopened can.

"Those were two good poems," he said.

"You were leaning over my shoulder as I trawled. There was no way I could come up with Hiawatha."

"Aha, a literary snob in the making. Whoops, belay that. I jest, I jest. Tell me the stuff you didn't choose."

How could he be so sharp? To reach in casually and squeeze her sensitive parts? "There were hundreds. How can I remember?" But she was sure he knew she was lying.

"Time for another poem."

"I need a quick sip first," she said, opening the second can.

Afterwards, he picked it up, "OK if we continue being sacerdotal?"

The word was beyond her but not the sense. She said, "Perhaps literary snob is right. I started wondering what French verse sounded like. I rehearsed this a hell of a lot, trying to get rid of the accent. Baudelaire: Au lecteur

> *La sottise, l'erreur, le péché, la lésine,*
> *Occupent nos esprits et travaillent nos corps...*

He made her read it twice more, saying nothing, listening hard. Then he meditated. After which he asked her to do it yet again.

"Ballsy of you but that's incidental. I read French verse but that must be the first time I've listened aloud to it since I came to France. A shocking admission. The lines are no great shakes but they themselves are just lines. You made me realise what I've been missing. A great idea and I'm very grateful. Oh, and the accent wasn't a factor. That was French."

She blushed to an uncomfortable level, knowing this often exaggerated the stain.

He slapped the table. "Time for me to earn my keep. A bit of Shakespeare which I happen to know by heart. Needless to say I cheat. This is prose not verse but sometimes you'd hardly know:

> *...A good sherris-sack hath a twofold operation in it. It*
> *ascends me into the brain, dries me there all the fool-*
> *ish and dull and crudy vapours which environ it,*
> *makes it apprehensive, quick, forgetive, full of nimble,*
> *fiery, and delectable shapes..*

Mentioning Shakespeare caused a painful, nervous echo. Trawling she'd discovered two sonnets which even she had recognised as hugely familiar. The temptation had been powerful but reason won out. She hadn't been asked to parade her emotions. Only to prove to him they could talk to each other usefully.

He added, "Falstaff, Henry Four, Part Two. Everyone's favourite. Salutary for me. I saw the play in London and heard crudy pronounced cruddy not croody. Things like that matter to teachers. Now I'm no longer a teacher and they matter even more. Words, dear Jana. Forget the baguette - words are what we're feasting on."

Wanting more of this she knew, tactically, what was demanded. "Time to get back to the wall. I've had an idea."

Between them they carried a simple bench from the patio down to the repair site. On this Jana set out half a dozen stones for closer assessment without the need to reach down constantly or hold them for long periods.

"Logistics. My major at college. Actually, in this case, ergonomics."

Talk was less wide-ranging, more functional as fatigue replaced the morning's enthusiasm. She asked him what would be a reasonable target and he made a mark in the ground. They calculated this would require thirty-six more stones. Only twenty-four had been laid that morning and the total seemed ambitious. As he took a stone from the bench she replaced it and stood side by side with him viewing the options from the same orientation.

Once he'd applied the mortar she looked ahead at the next move. A few false starts and her eye became as good as his leading to a smoother, more productive flow. For minutes on end the pleasure of standing by him, occasionally touching him by accident disappeared into a sense of unity. The wind increased and her hands became sorer.

At one point, bent with weariness, he pointed to a stone he had just mortared and said, "It won't do, will it? The top surface slopes too much."

It would have been the twentieth stone and there'd been grim reassurance in passing that staging post. But she saw his concentration and gripped his arm. "Take it out quickly, Christopher. Before the mortar dries."

Occasionally he hummed music she presumed to be classical and she would have liked to join him. The chance came when she recognised Homeward Bound and she accompanied him an octave up. He stopped, wiped a streak of grey mortar across his cheek and smiled thinly. "Sorry about the highbrow stuff. Paul Simon from now on, eh?"

The sixtieth stone was laid as both of them tried to remember the lyrics of Night Game. She felt his hand on her shoulder, the pattern of his ribs pressing against her upper arm. "Pretty good for a white-collar worker," he said.

"How many more days?" she said, pointing at the wall.

"Two, perhaps three."

"On your own, I guess. I've got a living to earn."

They washed themselves in the house. He'd parked his old Citroen at the rear and drove her down to the van. "Two vehicles," he said. "Two separate spaces. It seems a waste."

"What's the Brit talk? Knackered. You look knackered, Christopher. You talked about a beer but you don't have to."

"How knackered are you?"

"Not too bad, considering."

He looked out through the windscreen. "I had this idea. We drive to my bar, just like two members of the French working classes. We find out what the owner's having for dinner tonight and we latch on to two bowls. We order beers. If we smoked, we'd smoke. We'd sit down, stretch our legs and luxuriate in being tired." His grin was faraway. "We wouldn't have a shower first. Would that be some kind of North American heresy?"

"Enter a stinking witch. Lighting a Marlboro."

"I take that as a yes. There is of course a snag. Sooner or later, probably by osmosis, Norbert would find out. He'd shove his hip against yours, try to fondle your breasts, talk about the readiness of his cock. He's my mate, God forgive me. But he doesn't have to be yours."

"I'll drive him mad with desire and leave him locked in the can."

They ate stuffed heart at the bar ("While my kids survive on old *pain de campagne*," said the owner) and went Dutch on the payment. Jana then begged a cigarette – a Marlboro no less – from one of the old men cloistered in the corner, touching his cheek and making him simper.

"It's all right," she told Day. "This is a once-a-year thing. But you described an exact scene and it's been that kind of experience. Think of me as a working-class tart."

Smoke rose in a soft ball above her uncombed hair and he watched as if it held prophecy. He said, "I've never thought manual labour was ennobling. Still don't. But I'd have rather done what we did today than toured a *bastide*. I'd call you a good sport but I'd be scared you'd scratch my eyes out."

"No I wouldn't Christopher. I know you just a bit. Enough to recognise you're saying it… well, knowingly." It was the first cigarette she had truly enjoyed. The first in which she had recognised the cigarette's seductive properties.

"Can you manage a final poem?"

"Aren't I due one from you first?" she asked.

"Indeed, but who's counting. Let me see what pops up. Remembering how important it is to avoid Hiawatha. How about Robert Frost, in honour of your nationality. It's called The Bear."

She listened, forgetting to smoke. "I'm such a novice. First pass I make about thirty percent. Do it again, please."

He did so. "And I'll do it again," he said. "See if you can pick out a line."

This time she concentrated fiercely, stumbled over the half-remembered words and he gently provided the couplet.

> *He paces back and forth and never rests*
> *The me-nail click and shuffle of his feet*

"It's going to sound corny but I thought you'd pick that line," he said. "And for the obvious reason."

She said, "The me-nail click." She pulled the sheaf of papers from her breast pocket. "I need to study a little. Your pieces change things." Her lips moved as she tried out one after another to herself. Impatiently she put out the cigarette. "Yes, this is the one."

But her choice had to wait awhile. As if on cue Norbert arrived, went through his mechanic's routine with her, ordered more beers, sat down and looked expectantly. Seeing the stub in the ashtray and knowing it wasn't Day's he spent a minute trying to force his packet of Camels on Jana.

"One's enough," she said. "It's only a minor celebration."

Norbert looked from one to the other. "Celebration?"

"I helped Christopher repair a wall. We worked hard. Now we're relaxing."

"Christopher, you said Christopher."

"Fellow's an Anglo but he does have a name. I'd have liked to call him Christophe but you got there first."

"Not Chris?"

"Christopher."

Norbert leant across the table his face nearing hers. But she knew it would be all right. He kissed her three times, alternate cheeks. Abstractedly he picked up the Camels and proffered them again. She shook her head.

"But once you did?" he said

"Years ago. In the USAF."

"Jets? Fighters?"

"Both. Seems like a long time ago. I didn't make the grade and that made me spit." She smiled at each in turn. "I'm more reconciled these days."

"When you start taking flying lessons, Norbert, Jana will tell you all about it," said Day.

Norbert gestured at the sheets of paper on the table. "What is this? Am I interrupting?"

"As we worked our bodies we declaimed poetry. This will be Jana's last poem."

Jana said, "It's in English but I guess Christopher can translate. I should explain, Norbert. I know so little about poetry and I simply looked for good lines. This has a very, very good line but I was disappointed. For the Brits it's very famous. Almost too famous."

"You were hoping to be chic?"

"I was indeed. However, there's something in it for Frenchmen. The poet is Wordsworth – very hard for the French to say – and he is looking across the Channel in the late eighteenth century. Here is a small part of the poem:

> *Bliss was it in that dawn to be alive,*
> *But to be young was very heaven!--Oh! times,*
> *In which the meagre, stale, forbidding ways*
> *Of custom, law, and statute, took at once*

The attraction of a country in romance!
When Reason seemed the most to assert her rights,
When most intent on making of herself
A prime Enchantress--to assist the work,
Which then was going forward in her name!

Day took the sheet to help with the translation and gradually the words returned from him to Jana in a cloudy but elegant form. Second time around Day's reading was more confident, closer to poetry.

Both independently had wondered about Norbert. But he listened and frowned.

"It is bizarre," he said. "Christophe is Rosbif and I know he cares about France. You are American and I think you too are francophile. But Anglos in general do not seem to care at all. Often we are hated. But this man, this poet. Remarkable."

As Norbert spoke Day scribbled. Now he handed over the scrap of paper. "On behalf of Anglos everywhere. A translation, a little gift."

And now Norbert himself read out the French. Loudly. To the annoyance of others in the bar. He kissed them both again. "I must go," he said abruptly.

"A sensitive lad at heart," said Day.

"I think I must leave too," said Jana. "And for the worst of reasons. I was pleased to make my gesture of filth but now hygiene takes over. Dear Christopher, can you forgive me for needing a shower more than your company?"

"I'll walk you to your van."

Again she'd parked on the building site. She took out her keys and leant back against the unopened van door. "What can I say? That I enjoyed myself? That I was buried in what we did? Thank God for France."

As she had hoped he leant against her, pressing her against the side panel. "It was a risk. I've been damn lucky."

"Oh no. But never trim those eyebrows." It was supposed to be a joke but her voice sounded reedy, tremulous.

"The money thing. It probably sounds fussy, out-of-date. Back in the early days I helped a US chap buy a house in St-

Jean-du-Luz. He had no idea of the system, didn't understand the size of the *notaire's* fee. Accused me of ripping him off. I got copies of all the receipts and added everything up. He knew he was wrong but he wanted to lash out. Said he was just checking because Brits had a bad record, seeing Yanks as a soft touch. No hard feelings."

She touched his temple.

Day went on. "No hard feelings. Trouble is he was right. Ten years ago you could still buy a good house down here for thirty-thousand euros and Brit middle-men were notorious. I got out of that work some time ago and I swore I'd simply do cash business from then on. That I'd charge fair prices even if it meant starving. That there'd be no hard feelings. I tended to stay clear of your lot too. Until now."

He kissed an eyebrow. "Your being US is important even if I haven't quite worked out why. A US flyer. Yeah. But will the money thing divide us? Am I being precious, British?"

"Hell, I'm the last person to advise on hang-ups. But here's a thing. I have a friend, Ghislaine, a pharmacienne. She has a boyfriend, Boyce, an Afro-american manager with SocleSoft France. I like them both. They've had a personal triumph and wanted me to help them celebrate. I mentioned you. They said bring him along. I mentioned the money thing."

Jana hooked two fingers in the vee of his open-necked shirt. "I'm not asking you to choose. I'd drop them in ten seconds flat. The question is: should I?"

"No, you shouldn't. Let's meet them."

"With me paying, as I very much want. Happily. Ecstatically."

"With you paying. I could say no, of course. But where would that get me, where would it get either of us? It seems like taking advantage and yet in this day and age there are supposed to be no advantages. The days of foolish chivalry are over. If I want your company – and I do – yet can't get over this little thing perhaps I don't deserve you."

"Kiss me Christopher." As he did so she tried to combine the touch of his lips with the firmer less personal contact of his body. Making them a part of the same sensation.

"I'm moving from Ahetze soon. Getting an apartment. In Bayonne. I'd like it if you could help."

"There's nobody better in Bayonne." They kissed again and she stopped trying to come up with theories.

CHAPTER EIGHTEEN

Freeing up

ANGLET, jam in a sandwich of towns clumsily thrown together to create the airport name. It proved the better bet. Day said everyone remembered Biarritz and Bayonne, never Anglet. Take a place south of Montaury university and the Mirambeau clinic, he told her, and she'd be close enough to the planes to complain of the noise. In the end they went south of the airport and found a newly built block of ten apartments among the detached houses off *Départmentale 254* but shielded from the autoroute.

"It's so US," she said, walking down the access hallway. "Inside here I could kid myself I'm living on one of the new lots round Tempe."

"Wherever that is," he joked.

"Know me, know Arizona."

"I keep trying to imagine Arizona. Remote, mountainous, not much grass, healthy. But of course it's more probably never-ending suburbs clustered round half a dozen big towns. Towns surrounded by nothing. I don't see you as suburban US. You're too cosmopolitan."

"So you do do compliments."

"For you I break the rules."

Once she'd walked round the apartment, looked out of the windows at the smug surrounding bungalows with their pale orange walls, and worked the shower she wanted to start living there even though it was unfurnished. Loading up the van in the Chauvelets' drive took less than an hour and Day's presence ensured an air of finality. Vincent had talked half-heartedly about moving out and leaving her a free run but she pointed out this wasn't practical. He would want to visit his parents and the problem would remain. When he played his final card – Octavien – she said she'd take him out for treats, but only on his own. Vincent either trusted her or he didn't.

Day took her to Emmaus for a few sticks of furniture to tide her over. He said, "People tell me it's the French version of Goodwill which may mean more to you than me."

As she wandered round the Emmaus warehouse with its refurbished chairs and wardrobes, she recalled her mother's warnings to her as a child. "Break that," Lisa used to say, "and we won't get anything near as good. It'll be down to the Goodwill for some junk." Goodwill had been step zero on the suburban ladder. No doubt stepfather Dave would see it as the step down Jana was doomed to take. Her mother's most recent letters read like a form of dictation from Dave and there were questions – softened by Lisa but still evident – about Jana's attitude towards matters of faith. He has your best interests at heart, her mother added apologetically. During Jana's return phone calls neither cared to discuss this, unable to dredge up the key euphemisms.

Not that Jana embraced Emmaus wholeheartedly. She was sufficiently transatlantic to reject the idea of upholstered furniture others had sat on. Fastidiously she limited herself to a kitchen table, two chairs and a clothes rail like those used in garment districts. The bed, when it arrived, would be a major investment. In the meantime she was making do with a light sleeping bag from Super U, cushioned by the loan of Day's LiLo. After insistence by Day, who had more experience, she bought a rather battered kitchen cabinet which proclaimed its age with circular ventilation discs built into the sides. The apartment came with a fitted range and they went to Darty for the fridge.

From the centre of this stark cavity Day said, "It'll be aesthetic judgements from now on and you're better off making those yourself. All I know are book shelves. If there'd been an Ikea you could have decked out the flat cheaply and with style. But France came late to the Swedish colossus and there are only three stores in the country: Rouen, Tours and Pacé east of Montpellier. Got to dash, got a pool to clean."

Ideally they should have tailored their quick goodbyes to the embraces employed by couples married for five years. But mutual warmth made it difficult. "I'll text," he said wanly, bowing to the likelihood she might be flying. Both hated text's juvenility.

Re-housing herself had required several short absences from Gascon Air. Grateful for Jean-Claude's understanding, she reported on her altered emotions.

"The tall Anglo who looks like Don Quixote," J-C said, recalling the two Grandage flights. "French passion rejected. I am disappointed. I felt you would have favoured one of my countrymen since I, alas, am unavailable. No doubt this Christophe accepts your little ways."

One matter remained unresolved. "Who's it to be: Jérome or Martine? How long has it been?"

"How I hate you," he said. "And myself for creating the perfect dilemma."

"Let's tell the truth? Say we can't choose. Would they accept piecework, with the flights split?"

"Both are looking for permanent employment," he said. "But it is a way out."

"Or get them to toss a coin."

The following day, at short notice, a senior manager from the engineering company Vincent worked for, needed to fly to Toulouse and back, pilot to wait for the passenger. All at full flying rates with premium parking thrown in. Unprecedentedly this dedicated executive rejected the seat next to the pilot, preferring to spread out his papers at the back. Jana was free in effect to fly solo.

At 2500 feet she stealthily removed a compact from her shoulder bag to examine her face - quite simply to identify just exactly what Day had seen. This required a rare knack: an ability to sneak up on herself. Otherwise the reflection was unhelpfully familiar. Turning her head abruptly from side to side, half a dozen times, she managed to ensnare a startled look. Was this her?

Too dangerous. She put away the compact and resumed her ten-kilometre arc of awareness. But her mind still roamed. Deliberately she reduced Day to his worst features: an education which had dissolved into self-entertainment, the gradual shedding of all responsibility, ambition renounced and an unhealthy fascination with manual labour. Appalling failings, at least by US standards.

And what was he to her? An intermittent mentor who mentioned affection but didn't dispense it. Who ferreted into her mind and emotions but who never lowered his own drawbridge. Who had doubts.

How had he affected her? The plane was still a safe refuge but she was now vulnerable to someone who was not easily explained and whose instincts as well as his passport were foreign. And then there was... But traffic density was growing and the other more objective Jana was itching to take over. Time to contact Toulouse ATC.

On final approach she spoke over the intercom to her silent, absorbed passenger. "I'm told there'll be a car waiting. I'll get you within twenty-five metres."

"Too much of this and I'll lose the use of my legs."

"Busy day?"

"Not so busy. Rather life or death. A yes or a no."

With the plane stationary and the engine off she opened his door and made a half-gesture towards handing him out, indicating the grab-handle and the foot stirrup. Instead he shook her hand. "I'd like to be more exact about how long I'll be gone."

"Do you want my mobile number? Call me and I'll have the engine running?"

He was almost as short and dapper as Sarkozy but far more charming. He laughed, "By then it will all be over. I need to be back quickly but I'll telephone those who need to know. I don't want you glumly attached to the plane. Give me your number and find a place to relax."

He was gone and the tarmac was empty. Distantly an Airbus roared into take-off. The framework of my life, she reflected.

This was the private part of the airport, lacking the facilities of the main concourse. The café was unofficial, slightly scruffy, but there wasn't a tourist in sight. She slipped her mobile open and called Day.

"I'm doing the other thing I'm good at," she said. "Killing time. I'll break the call if you're busy."

"I'm good at waiting too," said Day. "Watching Renaults in a supermarket car park. It's an old dear whose central heating I fixed two years ago. I take her to the Auchan from time to time. She meets friends at Flunch. Then I push her trolley round the aisles, drive her home and unpack her groceries. She's fit enough to take the bus but she's a widow. Gets lonely."

"Looking at Renaults? I'll bet my licence you brought a book."

"Silver Poets of the Seventeenth Century. To remind me of the duds. Shall I read you something?"

"I'll need the rest of my life to check out the masterpieces. I must get into the habit of carrying a real book, not an airport paperback. As a favour give me a couple of Englishisms I've never heard before."

"Well there's rhyming slang. Say one thing, mean another. Supposedly the way Cockneys talk in the East End of London but I have my doubts. Picked up some new ones recently, one very historical, very US. 'I'm going for an Alger.' Alger Hiss standing for piss."

"Doesn't speed up communication."

"The aim's obscure. Perhaps you lose the game if you're forced to ask."

Jana ordered another latte and the waitress looked puzzled. Masking the phone she said "*Café au lait.*" then switched back. "Sorry about that. The French can't be bothered to learn basic Italian. Actually rhyming slang sounds a hell of a lot of effort. No need for that. Just bring me up short talking normally. About your plonk and your zizz."

"Oh gosh, something to order is quite hard. Will Australian do? Pointing Percy at the porcelain?

"Pointing…? Got it!" Jana said. "You still OK for time? No sign of your old lady?"

"This is a good way of passing time."

Jana said, "Here's a question. Have you got an accent? I'm like most Yanks, in awe of Brit speak. I'd hate to be told I've been talking to – my dear! – a member of the working classes."

"Originally Essex, sneered at by all other regions. Nasal, most consonants gone missing. The upmarket broadsheets call it 'estuarine' which says it all. I dropped it pretty damn quickly at Cambridge. But what about you? You don't speak 'out West' at all, just common, garden US." He paused. "Always a pleasure, always a surprise, always reassuring."

"That makes me lucky."

"Got it, flaunt it," he said genially.

"Perhaps I speak differently talking to you."

"So I'm luckier still."

How could life be bettered, sitting on a ribbed aluminium seat, drinking over-milked instant coffee, surrounded by concrete slab buildings and inhaling the smell of aviation fuel? "Christopher, is it OK if I fix up with Ghislaine and Boyce? Say no and I'll never mention those names again. Honest."

"They're your mates Jana. They know you; they can tell me things. Don't deny me that."

"I'm not into denying stuff, Christopher."

They rang off. Suddenly, sitting down confined her. Jana stood up, stuck her hands deep into the pockets of her chinos, her arms stiff and trembling, and walked round the jumble of undistinguished buildings. Took a second tour. As she embarked on a third her passenger called. A mere word-snatch: "Twenty minutes." A lilt suggested things had gone well. Confirmed when he bounced out of the Mercedes, leaving the door swinging, and strode over to the plane. She indicated the rear but he shook his head, "I must sit in the front. It's criminal not to pay attention to my wonderful homeland."

She'd checked the flight order. "So M. Danieli. It was a yes."

"How perceptive, Mlle le Pilote."

As she closed her door he took a flat brown bottle from his jacket pocket. "I don't usually drink spirits but today there was a need. One mouthful, I promise. That will be quite enough. It's not cognac, just anonymous brandy from the Hérault. There will be no cabin rage. Only a lightness of being."

In fact barely a teaspoonful since he was more diverted by her preparations for take-off, reading labels on the switches and listening to the RT. Their heading took them into the afternoon sun and she lent him a pair of sunglasses.

He said, "I have this urge to talk about what I've done but I cannot. The situation is commercial and sensitive. However, my story is not as interesting as yours. Tell me about that long examination of your face."

"And I thought you were buried in bumf."

"I looked up and was fascinated. Am I allowed to ask? Was it love?"

His high spirits were irresistible. "I hope so."

"A Frenchman?"

"Alas an Englishman. But I assure you he loves France."

"And the mirror?"

She felt slightly coy. "Romantic nonsense. I had this whim: to capture the sense of me that he had seen. Very difficult. What I see gets in the way. There's my voice too. Half an hour ago we were on the phone. He said pleasing things about the way I speak. Away from home we have a poor idea of our accent."

"It goes well with your French. Let us speak English and I will judge how it sounds to him."

She explained. "He encourages me to read him poetry aloud. I have some Wordsworth, very famous lines about the rebirth of France." She read him the passage from The Friend marked by the scribbled notes used for the translation. He asked her to repeat it several times.

Jana added, "I understand M. Wordsworth had second thoughts about the revolution. But I don't think it matters. When he wrote this he was telling the truth."

He asked to see the printout and asked about the scribbles. She told him about Norbert's reaction and he nodded. "I can understand. My English demands I talk about heat-treated bogies, profit and loss. This word bliss – the context is usually sexual. But here it is something different."

"A celebration."

He nodded happily. "Indeed. Bliss for you? No I think not; you are still exploring. Bliss for me? Perhaps. For a very short moment. Then I face a special board meeting when I return. Board meetings drive out bliss. But I think we can say this is a good flight. I am glad I asked about the mirror. Glad I heard your English as he hears it."

At Biarritz-Anglet-Bayonne there was another Mercedes. As she turned to open her door he held her arm. "Your friend, this Norbert, has a translation of the bliss poem. Is it a private matter? Could I see a copy?"

"Of course."

"Does one tip a pilot? Somehow that seems crude even though I would be ridiculously generous."

"No tip," she said. "But you could celebrate your news with a kiss. French style. One, two, three."

"Not one, two, three, four?"

"Assymetry's better than symmetry."

"And if you fly me again could I ask for the special service? The readings?"

"I even do Baudelaire. In the original."

His lips fluttered over her face and he was gone, a rare passenger capable of opening his own door and stepping down with a modicum of grace. The Mercedes pulled away at excessive speed and Jana got out the clipboard to record the mundane numbers that defined a round trip to Toulouse.

THAT EVENING Jana drove out to a branch of But, the national furniture chain, Ginette had recommended: "Inexpensive. Not too stylish, I fear. But the range is wide."

"I need to buy a bed."

"Doubtless," Ginette said, looking mischievous. "There are two rules: as big as you can afford, as big as you can accommodate."

At the store a youth unaccustomed to wearing a suit but, nevertheless, wearing one shuffled over, his lack of confidence palpable. "Mademoiselle desires?"

"May I lie on the beds?" Jana asked.

"But of course. The plastic is there to protect. It is better without the shoes."

Only when she sat down on the mattress did she recognise her disadvantage. The youth seemed to share her misgivings for he stepped back two paces. Bare of linen, duvet or blanket the area she lay on was enormous.

"It is quite firm," she said.

"That is good for the back."

Was it? Wasn't the mattress intended to enfold as well as support? Why on earth had she no worthwhile experience of beds? Ah yes, Tucson. Let's forget that.

"Is there a softer mattress?" she asked.

He pointed to other beds down the line but these were significantly cheaper, increasing Jana's uninformed suspicions. Brochures mentioned mattress cells capable of remembering the pressure they'd absorbed but in the end Jana's decision came down to one of her choices being in stock, two others not. Back at the apartment the new mattress got jammed in the stair-well and sheer self-interest compelled one of her neighbours to help her manoeuvre it to the first floor. The foldable base proved to be lighter and far easier to lift. Now she lay down in her own bedroom and wondered whether it would seem coarse – or at least presumptuous – to announce the arrival of her bed.

"Hi, it's me. Just a quickie. Could you write out the Wordsworth translation or must I call Norbert?"

Day reckoned it would come. He'd work on it the moment he put the phone down. But why?

Jana explained.

He sounded tired. "Sounds as if you're getting a better class of passenger."

"I've promised him Baudelaire if he flies with us again."

"Good on yer."

"Sounds like Australian," she said.

"Indeed."

"One more thing. I went out to But an hour ago and bought a bed. Bigger than a double; a king, perhaps a queen."

"That's good news. Very good news." But his tone of voice was at best neutral. "Got a date for Ghislaine and Boyce?"

"I'll call them after this. See you Christopher."

"Jana."

Was it wrong to make loaded suggestions, to hurry things along? Was this the US way? Elsewhere in the world was there a natural rhythm at odds with Arizona?

UNABLE to decide between the two pilots Jean-Claude decided Jana's suggestion was the only way out. But that wasn't the end of it. "I will make the offer about ad hoc payments to Jérome. But would you – as a special gift to me – call Martine."

Jana was outraged. "You rotten coward. You're head of this Mickey Mouse organisation. You're supposed to take responsibility, especially when things get difficult.

J-C smiled engagingly. "Heads may delegate."

"OK, I'll do it. But I'll need to sweeten the offer."

"How?"

"That will be my secret." And she deliberately waited until he himself was flying the Stationair before calling Martine.

Jana said, "I have told J-C how cowardly he is. But I share his difficulty. You are both extremely good pilots. And if that landing had been real, if you'd buried us in the conifers and broken my neck I'd have left this world peacefully, knowing there was no other option."

Martine gurgled with laughter. "Mlle. Nordmeyer how charming. How well you beautify that unpleasant possibility. My compliments to you and Jean-Claude for a demanding examination."

"Both you and the other candidate reacted differently, yet entirely legitimately. An impossible choice. What do you think about dividing the work?"

"Suppose you allocated certain days to each of us: Sunday to Wednesday for one, and Thursday to Saturday to the other. Then after an agreed period, reverse the allocation. That would help me plan my lessons."

"Excellent. I'll put that to Jean-Claude. I may well insist."

Martine laughed again. "I said I wanted to work with you both. For Jean-Claude that didn't need saying. I was in fact addressing you. I look up to the United States whatever our political and cultural differences."

"I'm flattered. J-C seems to share this view."

Martine said, "And I've not even seen you fly. Yet I have this feeling. And I accept the arrangement"

"Martine, Martine. I have seen you fly. I remember you saying: 'I cannot agree to that.' You wanted the job but not if it meant compromise. You'll teach me, that's for sure. Good pilots should never be modest. I look forward to your savvy."

"Mlle. Nordmeyer - "

" – Jana!"

"Jana. You have a special style, a generosity that is rare in this country. It is perhaps sentimental but you warm me. I will be happy with Gascon Air – with you."

Jana turned to Ginette. "Can you get J-C on the VHF. I can't remember the Stationair's call sign. In any case you're quicker."

Ginette handed Jana the microphone.

"J-C it's Jana. Excellent idea from Martine. Each pilot gets three or four consecutive days. After a month they switch sequences. She'll join us on that basis."

"Jana from J-C. Great work, persuasive *partenaire*. I'm sure Jérome will agree. You see, I was right to be cowardly."

"J-C from Jana. This will sound corny but I need to say it. Talking to Martine: I'm happy to be in France, happy to be flying with you. Odd, but there it is."

"Jana from J-C. Do I sense the influence of Don Quixote – the Anglo Don?"

"J-C from Jana. Just Martine. And France. Over and out."

Ginette who disliked being surprised or impressed said, "This is not the Gascon Air headquarters. It is the road to Damascus."

Jana shook her head. "The conversion occurred months ago. Today was just a reminder."

"How?"

"Martine said something nice. This is a country where compliments count."

Ginette reflected. "Most of us, we'd rather argue. But I'm happy too. *Bienvenue à la France.*"

CHAPTER NINETEEN

Quartet linguistics

DAY had achieved the rare feat of parking his Citroen within a hundred metres of his front door and begged to be picked up rather than lose the place. Jana who regularly suffered from cramped parking in these dense Bayonne streets agreed.

He was waiting in the street when she arrived, swung quickly into the cab and started fumbling for the seat belt. Most passengers did that since the mounting point had been illegally improvised a decade ago. Automatically she reached across to pull the belt forward and found herself looking into his face at ten centimetres. Neither said anything, simply looked; she noticing a gentleness at the mouth corners, slight amusement, familiarity. "Others get to do their own seat belts, I hope," he said. They kissed and it was different. More skilled in some way.

He said, "You look... Christ, I need the right words... as if you're in tune with the world."

"Those words will do. A coupla days ago a Frenchwoman said something sweet: unexpected, original. Made me glad to be in France." She rested a hand on his shoulder. "And now there's all this Brit stuff too."

"You're in clover."

"Hacking my way through the explanatory footnotes. Talking to you is like multiple choice at junior high." They kissed again, showily, as if someone had a camera running. A horn sounded in the narrow street and they both sighed.

"So where are we going?"

"A place Ghislaine knows called la Bonne Femme, south of the town."

"I know it. Same vintage as my favourite bar. Furniture and fittings from the fifties. Chalk-board menu. Doubt we'll need desserts. And Ghislaine has some news?"

Jana explained how she had met Ghislaine, how Ghislaine had met Boyce and how Boyce – against the odds – now wanted to melt Mme le Lannic's granite heart. Adding, "Which may have happened. Or half-happened."

"Boyce sounds like a Boy Scout. A goody-goody" he said.

"Oh, he's a Boy Scout. While Mme. le Lannic's probably votes le Pen."

He said, "So we can sit back?"

"Not at all. Boyce is Francophile. Says it's not Ghislaine's body that races his motor but her nationality. He'll expect you to support him."

Day's hand rested on the back of Jana's seat. Now he ruffled her hair. "I can understand a taste for the exotic."

"Come on! Boyce may be exotic but I'm not. Even in rural Gascony. I'm Yankee standard. Broads like me – in the undamaged state – are always on tap: in the movies, on TV and in the French imagination. Just as long as we keep our mouths buttoned up." She grinned. "For reasons I don't get, I seem to have bucked the system."

"Complete bollocks. You're so rare you're almost endangered. A Yank living comfortably in a foreign country. You don't knock Uncle Sam and you aren't keen to get back. Not in my hearing anyway. You're adaptable. Doesn't sound much but that's why people like having you around." He stroked her back. "That and a few other details."

"But couldn't I say the same about you?"

Day shook his head. "Good grief, no. Brits abroad are commonplace. Most are eccentric. Playing the village idiot."

"Not you."

"I'm not so sure. Poverty and eccentricity are often confused. I don't mention the weather, don't have a telly and I read a lot. A useful member of society? I think not."

Jana pulled up sharply as a tiny diesel car driven by a pensioner steered unexpectedly left. "Stop bad-mouthing. Give me something else."

So he murmured the sonnet she'd thought too risky to include in her list.

So long as men can breathe, or eyes can see,
So long lives this, and this gives life to thee.

"You left it out." he said.. "It's world famous and you were looking for smashing first lines. No doubt you had your reasons."

"It seemed too forward. The words worried me back then. I didn't want to be pushy."

He nodded. "How remarkably British. Do you always adjust yourself to foreigners?"

"Come on, I'm just a home-town Arizona girl. France was a huge stride. Brits? First thing I had to get used to: you're straight."

"And are you a hundred percent sure?" he asked laughing. "Should I ask myself the same question. Actually, I mustn't tease. I've tossed you bags of responsibility. Being a sarky bastard I was always bound to be devious."

"Sarky?"

"Get with it, Nordmeyer. By now you ought to be able to guess. OK. I apologise. Shall I do that sonnet again or its twin? The one I think is a bit over the top."

"Choose the best line out of the second one."

"Hmm. Perhaps the best couplet. Mind you it tests your feeling for irony:

I love to hear her speak, yet well I know
That music hath a far more pleasing sound

He acknowledged her silence. "They're only words, you know, written by a balding Brit who may have been gay – like the rest of us. Pretend you're hearing them in your earphones with a strong Gascon accent."

"My attention might stray."

Day said, "Professionally tough but pure jelly inside. But that's the power of words. Mind you, how about words and music? The double whammy. Look, indulge me a bit: Imagine I'm a mature soprano at her peak. Singing the ultimate adult love song - *Porgi, armor*. Mangled by me but you may get half an idea."

He muttered the aria against the rattling diesel, then summarised. "The countess is convinced her philandering husband no longer loves her, asks God to ease her pain and tell her how to win him back. No, it's not us, thank God. The song's philosophical, reflective, even upbeat and it's saying: your heart may get broken but it's worth the risk." He stopped abruptly. "I'm tutoring again. Why don't you shut me up? Tell me about planes."

"Oh Christopher, never stop tutoring."

"Planes!"

"You know they can stall?"

"Sure. A bad thing. Don't know why."

"Too steep an angle of attack is major. The wing stops being a wing, there's no lift. The tail pitches back and ohmigod! Bad if you've run out of altitude. Then there's another stall, much worse. Just one wing's affected and you drop out of the sky like a sycamore spinner. Survival's hairy or plain impossible. You get the idea. Stalls are best avoided."

"Are you happy in this slippery world?" he asked.

"I follow the rules and stay airborne. Except, that is, when it's fun, when I induce a stall as I land, right at the last moment. The stall horn sounding as the tyres touch the runway. I kind of like that. Smacking gravity in the face."

He massaged the back of her neck. "Newton gave it a name; you added the experiment. Out there in the void. All done in techno-talk with an American accent; it's part of your oomph."

At la Bonne Femme he put a twenty-euro note in her hand. "Sorry about being so furtive. I'm trying damn hard not to be embarrassed."

She pulled his face down. "Shit, it's just dough. Why don't you charge for the poetry."

They were the first to arrive and were asked – in that procrustean French way – whether they wanted aperitifs; as if the alternative was unthinkable "Let's be sentimental and order *pastis*," he said

Sipping, she said, "I used to drink lots of this, convinced it went with the territory. But there's a tiny problem. The flavour: it's kid's drink. Yet the French see it as sophisticated."

"Ah, but watching *pastis* turn milky – that's not childish."

"I'll give you that."

Ghislaine and Boyce burst on them in a flurry of embraces and hand shaking. Noisy animal spirits.

"It's Chris isn't it?" asked Boyce, opening his purple satin shirt down to his navel.

"Except with Jana. She prefers to go the whole hog."

"Christopher," said Ghislaine, tasting the effect. "Yes, better. A saintly quality."

"Hey, I'm a Brit. We burned Joan of Arc."

"And now you buy the *ruines* the French don't want."

Boyce broke in, "What are you drinking. Ah, the local sarsa-parilla."

"For sentimental reasons," said Jana.

"Never too early to start blubbing. Two more Ricards please."

Everyone wanted the daube and the meal was quickly ordered. Boyce asked for, and got, a bottle of mature Madiran. "Also for sentimental reasons," he explained.

Jana said, "Who's going to tell the full story?"

Ghislaine gestured. "It's Boyce's project. Me, I thought it was a suicide mission. What's more – and this is shameful – I wasn't sure it was worth the effort. I was wrong, very wrong. When it happened I found myself in tears. I deserved that. Thank you Boyce."

"No problem, hon. I was a fool and I jest rushed in," said Boyce in English.

English was a breach of etiquette but Ghislaine shook her head at Jana. "My English is getting better. Boyce wants to be expressive. You two – Jana and Christopher – will recognise that."

Each looked at the other warily.

"Well, don't you?" Ghislaine asked sharply.

"Thanks to Christopher I'm learning poetry," said Jana. "Doubt that I'm getting expressive but it's a big step for a dumb *aviatrice*."

Day sighed. "Jana specialises in what she calls sad sack and I try to stamp it out. But Ghislaine guessed right. Jana talked about planes and I was smitten. The accent's low key and it's got authority. It works just as well with poetry and now it's my accent that sounds dull and nasal."

Ghislaine watched them both, head switching this way and that. "I see, I see," she said. "What do you and I talk about, Boyce?"

Boyce grinned. "Who takes notes? Something like: ain't we lucky?"

"Boyce exaggerates," she said, secretly pleased. "But back to Maman."

Boyce resumed. "Ghislaine went top of the innings, and that was good. Said we'd be happy with Maman as part of the plot. But if she forced us to choose… I'd got my play all written out. Instead of sitting in the car counting Superbowl winners I went down the side of the house, got out the mower, cut the lawn. With both of them watching me through the picture window. Came in and handed over a flan which just happened to be Mme. le Lannic's favourite."

"Perfectly planned, just like D-day," said Jana.

"There's more. G got up to make the coffee and I talked fast as a Tennessee auctioneer. About a trip G and I took up to the border village called Iholdy where, it seems, Mme. L was born. And where she is invited next weekend. I just monologued, not stopping for a second, didn't dare.."

"And as I arrived with the coffee pot," said Ghislaine, "Maman turned and said: Iholdy, Iholdy. Just that. I cried."

"My job was done," said Boyce. "A token bite of flan, a sip of coffee and I took a Stilson from my shoulder bag. I'd been told a tap washer needed fixing upstairs. Left them to it."

Ghislaine sighed. "We hadn't allowed Maman time to think. Or react. Now I added emotion. My tears helped and I even squeezed a tear out of my dear mother. After some encouragement Maman invited us to dinner. A very stiff affair. Boyce has been trained: he stays silent or talks about sheep farming in the Pyrenees. Gradually he's replacing Maman's kitchen shelves. We visited Iholdy and she didn't like it a bit; condemned it as primitive. We proceed."

Against all this Jana recalled the gaunt face, the dormant fear and the repeated whisper *Impossible*! Ghislaine asked. "What is this poetry? Very romantic, I assume."

Jana laid memory to one side. "I helped Christopher repair a wall. Not exactly romantic but very symbolic. However, it turns out he is also subversive. He told me to find poems I liked. By myself! The *aviatrice*! I read them while he rested from his labours. Which was strange and pleasing. Here is one." She took out the worn sheets and read the Baudelaire. Again Ghislaine's head switched curiously from her to Day and back.

"Did an itty-bit of poetry back in high school," said Boyce. "Bit dangerous for a bro who wasn't into sport so I didn't look for high grades. But I liked it; some of it swung. I got the music from what you read. Now I need the script so I can get the sense."

Ghislaine turned to Day. "You were once a teacher."

"It worries me, but – thank God – it seems to work, for both of us. Jana rehearses the lines and she's good on rhythm. When she reads I hear new sounds, something fresh. It's the accent of course. Perhaps I should say Jana's accent."

Boyce looked up from the Baudelaire. "Doubt you'd say the same about mine."

"Everyone says you're a raving Francophile. That may be all you need."

Boyce addressed Ghislaine. "I'm tempted but I'd need practice. My French has gone as far as it can. This takes it further. It says things that are beyond me. Are software development managers allowed? Would you laugh?"

Gislaine pinched the back of his wrist. "Of course I'd laugh. And jeer. And sneer. My God Boyce you are being very simpleminded. Surely you know me better."

"Would it appeal?" He shook the sheets. "These are others' words, others' ideas."

Ghislaine said, "And we drove here in a car someone else made. You like the idea and I'm charmed. No, that's too weak. I would be swept away. But you must choose the poems."

By now the robust *daube* had been served and stood hissing with heat, in a brown casserole on their table. Wine had been splashed into glasses. Ghislaine entertained them with risqué anecdotes about the pharmacy's customers, while Day talked of Lea & Perrins Brits too timid to do business face to face with the water company.

"Aren't you glad," said Boyce in English to Jana, "you know the *subjonctif*? That you aren't going to end up as fish bait from this kind of character assassination?"

"Perhaps we're fish bait behind our backs?"

"Nah, I see it this way. We're both US and it's obvious. Plus we've been tamed. We're house Yanks. If anyone wants we can talk Brad Pitt or Obama. Otherwise we can find our way to the can without stumbling."

Ghislaine interrupted. "Tamed socially, perhaps. But not in every sense."

"One advantage about being black - I don't blush."

As Day had predicted no one had the capacity for dessert. Coffee marked a civilised delay but it was clear Ghislaine and Boyce were aroused by the discovery of poetry and keen to try it out. In the street outside the embraces were ever more flamboyant. Ghislaine whispered in Jana's ear, "Your Anglo. He has the ability, I think. And the words."

"I think so. I am so happy about Boyce – and Maman."

"Being vulnerable frightened me. But now I accept it, willingly." Ghislaine added, "Christophe went quiet. Why?"

"I just don't know. He can be quirky."

Jana waved off their car, her mind on Christopher. Day had continued to watch and smile but had contributed less and less throughout the meal. A dying away dating back to a small turmoil when Ghislaine kissed Boyce across the table and made visible play with her tongue. Now Day stood by Jana, hands in pockets, face expressionless.

Dare she ask him back to her apartment? But he got there first. Abruptly he instructed her to drive to the Adour's south bank, where the *bateaux mouches* embarked. "Park facing the Pont Saint-Esprit," he said. Near the town centre with the *mairie* only half a kilometre away. A high wall of five-storey residences towered over the van and smelt of decay. Not an optimistic environment.

Her voice was artificially bright. "Boyce certainly took to your idea. Perhaps he could use a translation of the sonnet."

"They are – as you transatlantics say – an item," he said distantly.

"How about us?"

"It isn't a term I go for. I don't want you absorbed. I want you free and independent. In charge, as you are in a plane."

None of this was comforting. "Is it wrong of me to want to be absorbed? A part of me at least?"

"It's not for me to say," he said. Then, more decisively: "I was pondering back in the restaurant and I know what makes you unique. You were dealt a shitty hand without the temperament to fight back. You aren't naturally tough and uncaring, are you? But somehow you found a form of protection that left the good bits untouched. You're a woman like any other, yet not like any other. You're skilled, open-minded, laconic and – let's not miss out the old Adam bit – just a bit like Shirley MacLaine. In the old days."

Many people had lied to Jana, often to be kind. She'd watched their faces as she watched Day's, for eyes that looked over her shoulder, for false informality, for a fixed smile. There was none of that. If anything he looked pained, trying to get the words right.

"You want us to keep meeting?" she asked.

"Yes."

"These things I have, will they last? For you?"

"Definitely." He spoke firmly.

"What do you want from me?"

"Faith."

"Faith? In what?"

"In my feelings for you."

There was so little to grab hold of. Her questions skated this way and that. Looking for stability she concentrated on the stone arch of the Pont Saint-Esprit. The French are good with bridges, she thought, but the US is better. She spoke slowly, "The way you put it: faith's going to be tested."

"It will be."

"What can I depend on?"

He sighed. "Nothing much. We're just two human beings. What could be more fallible? You'll need to be wary, see clearly. Balance my feelings against your doubts."

"And what are your feelings?"

"Jana, Jana." He cupped a hand against her left cheek. "I know enough about words not to use the big ones. The meanings differ so damn much. I want your company and no one else's. I know, I know, saying all this leaves awful holes. But it is the truth."

"Christopher, kiss me for fuck's sake," she said in a low desperate voice. The yearning was obvious in his body against hers. But it was as if they were avoiding contact, not achieving it. When she drew away he looked hopeless, under a death sentence.

"I've got the new bed," she said, laughing feebly. "Can you stay the night?"

But he said nothing and kissed her again. She clung on. Eventually the silence got to them both and she drove him home. Now when she kissed him there was less tension; the embrace had a purpose – to say a temporary goodbye. She could afford to be gentle. As she drove off she saw him in the side mirror standing in the middle of the street, a dark shadow between phalanxes of shining car bodies.

THE FOLLOWING days were unnervingly conventional. She called him and recognised the welcome - perhaps relief – in his voice. They saw each other twice a week. Again she brought raw materials and he cooked a meal. He read poems and prose passages then attended urgently to her comments. Both talked about their childhoods. On arrival and departure there were lingering embraces. He started visiting her at the apartment, bringing books and suggesting CDs she might like for her new player. When she bought a small couch he lay on it and she let him fondle her hair. The evenings were tranquil, intelligent, almost elegiac. As if they were at the amicable, somehow bearable end of an affair. She reminded herself constantly that he had implored her to have faith. This she had – at least while he was present. Alone, imagining the future, was another matter. His instruction was never far away: forget the big words.

During one quiet moment she managed to ask him if Ghislaine kissing Boyce – demonstrably, vulgarly at the restaurant – had disturbed him in some way. He smiled reminiscently. "I suppose so. Not because I'm a prude, I hope. It's just that I prefer walls between public and private. But, perhaps that's what makes a prude."

After a month she received a phone call from Eliazar, released briefly from his work at La Spezia and now in train for Bilbao to arrange the funeral of his mother. Obsequies and sex, it seemed, could share folders.

"Aha, you still breathe that way, *anglosajón*. I am at the river bank with my vehicle, my temple of love. You will come or you will not come. I will be philosophical."

Would sex with Eliazar betray the faith Day had asked for? Seeing herself naked in that airless Spanish motorhome touched on her needs. It had been a long time.

Eliazar noticed the pause. "As before, no obligation. And I will be *ingenioso*."

"I'll come."

At two the following morning she drove stealthily away from the motorhome. Purged? Eliazar deserved a less hygienic epitaph. Replete? That would do. But he'd changed. Normally he prepared her for love-making in a detached, languid way. It shouldn't have pleased her but it did. That had gone. Possibly the Italian women in and around La Spezia weren't as amenable to his Latin manner as she had been. For the first time she noticed a committed hunger. His promise of a third climax ("You will be glad.") was welcome if unexpected.

Since their rutting had always been for the fun of it, she had treated the evening as an experiment, a testing of her feelings elsewhere. But his tight grasp caused her to wonder whether tonight had been especially good value.

"You have a young body," he said obscurely.

"Is that good?"

"All men want a young woman. Those who say not, lie."

She smiled. "You haven't asked whether I enjoyed it."

"You did. But not with me, with someone else. Yet I do not complain."

Someone else! As she drove away she was struck by his fatalism. During the evening she had imagined Day transplanted into Eliazar's knowing body, but it hadn't worked. For one thing Eliazar worked silently whereas words were Day's lifeblood. Eliazar was physically confident, she doubted Day would be.

The comparison now seized her as she reached the road and was able to relax her concentration. There were no similarities. Tonight, as before, she'd been untouched. Yet watching Day slice onions or something equally mundane she had come upon other versions of herself. Enhanced and expectant.

Being faithful – a variant of what Day had urged – was her gift. There would be no more Eliazars. The pain and the not knowing would be borne. In bed, under the largest duvet available from But, she stretched out like a starfish, taking advantage of her solitary occupation of the mattress. She ached slightly from what they'd done together and accepted this as disinterested comment.

Arriving at Gascon Air the following morning half an hour late, bog-eyed from lack of sleep, she lifted the empty coffee pot. "Is this J-C's doing?" she asked Armelle whose coffee-pot awareness was not as acute as Ginette's.

"It is your boss's doing," said Jean-Claude from the office door. "And there is more bad news. You have no time to make coffee. Didi waits in her Cessna, engine running. She wants to be taught stall recovery and I, apparently, am inadequate. I offered her Martine in an hour's time but she has set her heart on you. Not that she needs any more tuition on stalls."

"But without caffeine, I'm only Ja," said Jana piteously.

"No task too small for the *proprietaire*," said Jean-Claude. "Take your time reaching the Cessna and I will urge my middle-aged bones over to the café."

Didi watched tolerantly as Jean-Claude hurried over to the plane with a polystyrene cup. "And I always imagined I was self-indulgent," she said.

Jana said, "If you want professional instruction you'd best allow me my coffee. Otherwise I may climb to nine-thousand feet, bollix us into an asymmetric spin and leave you to resolve it."

"There's an American word – feisty. I've missed you. Have you ever mastered an asymmetric?"

"It half happened during USAF flight training. But I was at twenty-five thousand feet and I had the Mojave desert to play with. Even so I lost seven thousand feet."

Didi eased the Cessna off the runway, did the business for optimum climb rate, looked around. "Gérard sends his regards. He's become engaged. I cannot guess at cause and effect."

"If you're hinting at kiss-and-tell I won't play." Jana shuddered at the taste of the coffee. "I wish him all the luck."

"She's a synchronised swimmer. Like Christine Lagarde. You appear to have been avoiding me."

"Not intentionally. I am sort of à *deux*."

"I know that. I have met Chris - Christopher."

Jana sipped more coffee. "Hence this wasted hour of instruction."

"Not totally wasted. Practice stalls have never satisfied me. As the books say they lack menace. Are you clever enough to be more realistic?"

"Perhaps. But let's grab some more altitude."

They experimented for quarter of an hour but Didi's skills and quick reaction times snuffed out the problem within seconds. Jana laughed, "The solution's obvious, allow the stall more time. But should I really ask for that? In a plane that's flying through cereal no pilot's tempted to hang around. I need to find out if the thinking has moved on. After all the Cessna is elderly and that could be a limiting factor. Why not do me a nice tight box and tell me what you want to tell me."

Didi turned. "I swear I didn't intend to poke my nose in. But who knows? I want you to be successful, to be happy. For those things I might interfere. Gérard was a lesson."

"Poor Gérard."

"I didn't conceal anything from M. Day. I said you were my flying instructor. That we were friends. My only invention was the work I offered. I pretended my gardener was on holiday and I needed a shed moving. Which was half true. The shed had to be dismantled first and I estimated the work would take several hours. I offered him lunch on the patio and we chatted."

Jana nodded.

"Not about you, my sweet. And certainly not about the two of you. I wanted to know him a little. It seemed innocent. Now, as I tell you, it seems less innocent. Am I forgiven?"

"Not yet. Let's see what you found out."

Didi said, "Ah, yes. This was clumsy. Let's forget this discussion. I'll fly you back to some real coffee."

Jana shook her head. "I need to take the risk."

Didi banked the Cessna smoothly, lengthened the curve, assumed the reciprocal to within two degrees without correction. Was flying competence a form of reassurance, Jana asked herself. "Tell me then."

"Much of it you know. Literature, music, divorce, the retreat from formal employment. A genuine love of France. You're seen in parallel; a foreigner who has integrated. He was careful, very careful, but couldn't entirely suppress what he felt. But in the background there was a burden I do not understand; something is holding him back. A reluctance. Almost an illness."

Jana nodded. "But not when we first met."

"Meeting you forced the issue perhaps. I'm guessing, of course. But his problem – if it is a problem – is internal not external. You cannot resolve it for him. More important: your role must be that of a presence, a regular presence. One that accepts but does not question."

"More or less my conclusion. Is he… attractive?"

"Oh, my dear…"

ON A BRILLIANT early autumn afternoon when southwesterlies off the Bay discouraged casual tourists they took sandwiches and a flask and drove over to the Brit's house to inspect the wall, now complete. "It looks professional," Day said. "I'm proud but puzzled. There is a limit to suck-it-and-see with certain skills. Plastering for instance. But this works."

"Being useful was your ticket to living here. You had to learn."

He looked at his hands, sand coloured with rough skin, the fingers incurving in repose. "Who could best put them into a poem?"

"Carol Ann Duffy," said Jana. At the Thursday market Day had spent a euro on Duffy's Rapture, stained with used cooking oil - a cheap but valuable present for her. She said, "The lesbian stuff doesn't matter. She does good detail when she needs to."

His head jerked. "You read it?"

"Didn't you want me to?"

"I pass on books. Not forcing them down your throat, but hoping all the same." He didn't – perhaps couldn't – finish.

"I read it all, several times," she said. "Sometimes I heard your voice."

Clumsily, without planning, he put his arm round her shoulders and hugged her. One of the rare moments she lived for. Even so there were doubts. Had she secretly begged for the hug, knowing what made him tick?

A gust of wind blew over the top of the wall tousling her much tousled blonde hair. "Let's use the wall," he said and sat down, leaning back against the rough stones and stretching out a hand to guide her.

As they crouched together, anorak arm against anorak arm, she knew he would kiss her if she said more about Rapture. But wouldn't it be a form of nagging - not the simple presence Didi had recommended? And might he see through the ploy anyway?

"Planes - something romantic."

"You can turn and shed height at the same time. If you're a great flyer – and I am - you tell yourself you can see a descending corridor through the air. But it's not just movement it's noise too. Pilots love engine sound. It's security and control."

He took her upper arm and she felt the response to what she had said. He whispered, "Weeks ago I wanted to stay ignorant about your profession, to protect your mystery. Now I need to know more. I imagine you doing authentic things. Travelling down that – What was the word? Corridor! Excellent! – down that corridor of air."

They were – briefly - a couple. Her presence working as it should.

"I saw Didi recently," Jana said. "You did work for her."

"Moved a shed. A friend worth cultivating. She's rolling in it and thinks the world of you."

"I solo-ed her and there's always a sentimental attachment. Actually that's unfair. I like her a lot and she's a great pilot."

"I see why you get on." He smiled, almost to himself. "It felt odd. She asked me to take you round for dinner. I don't take you anywhere, do I?"

"There's your favourite bar?"

"I was talking more generally. I just spout, I don't dream up outings. And we're not even-Stephen, I spout and you listen."

"Spout? You mean poetry and the rest? Sounds like a put-down. What's wrong with a bit of John Donne and the occasional necking?"

"Occasional! You're right. I'm under-performing." Accidentally she'd manipulated him. Yet, perversely, it was the embrace she'd always wanted, always expected from him. Gentle, contemplative, exploratory, untroubled; moving over her face and easing towards the clothed warmth of her shoulder. Bringing her close to wonder – Ah no! One of those big expressions he'd taught her to distrust. And yet... weren't these touches, these slurs, these wafts of breath the physical show of loving?

"Oh God Christopher," she sighed. "If you want us to be even-Stephen – crazy Brit word – let it start here."

"I always take, never give."

"That's not what it feels like."

She knew enough not to prolong things and risk anti-climax. Knew she must break away after a minute, stroke his face, engage his eyes, and find an excuse that worked. "I need to see you." A tiny giggle. "Supported by your wall."

He appreciated the artificiality. "Talk to me," he said. "About being a student."

"Not my happiest time. Grade school was bad but the badness was obvious. 'Miss Cottingham, can I catch what Jana's got?' Junior high was worse. As if prettiness and conformity were the only essentials. I was an empty chair in the classroom, a used plate at the cafeteria. Senior high worst of all. All that testosterone washing around. Geeks and Neanderthals looking for a willing body – any kind of body. Denied Miss Make-Up or Miss Large Boobs they came to me, thinking I'd be grateful. They were nasty when I turned them down. Being picky, they said, I'd die a virgin."

Day sighed. "But didn't some kind of familiarity eventually develop? Weren't some of them capable of seeing beyond the face?"

"Say herd of lemmings, say class of kids. Once you're poison ivy the typecasting stays. No one questions mass judgement."

"My God, how did you survive?"

Jana shrugged. "I was sixteen when my parents asked me about university. By then I wanted to join the USAF. I concentrated on math and physics - hard subjects to shut out everyone else. Levers to be pulled. I looked for, and got, impossible grades which made me even more unpopular. Physically I was dirt, academically I was miles above them. Nobody seemed to think this was fair."

"Not pleasant listening to this," he said. "And there's something lacking. Last time we were standing up, able to see the Bay. The sea was part of the work and the talk. Mind if we move? Can you stand the wind?"

"Goofy question."

They stood up, picked another spot round a curve in the wall. "The least I can do is sit upwind," he said.

"A verray, parfit, gentil knight." she said. "I've waited light-years to say that. But it's cheating isn't it? Memorising it, knowing its time will come. The trick is to do what you do. Absorb the stuff throughout your life and let it pop out, whenever."

He shook his head. "It's a standard ragbag of eng-lit tricks. What moves me – truly – is having you quote Chaucer. Why can't I come up with something moving about – I don't know – ailerons."

"Wanting to is all that matters."

He turned towards the Bay. "A hard day for sail. Just a mini-tanker for company."

Hiding his face?

Again the sandwiches were carefully assembled and wrapped: slices of Montbéliard sausage interleaved with transparent discs of white onion. "I've never been hundred percent sure of your tastes," he said abruptly.

"I guess we talk too much about other things."

"I guess we do

She was reassured he had only brought one coffee cup.

"We've been too solemn about the poetry. There are other sources, not just tubercular romantics. Lorenz Hart for instance:

> *Wait till you see him, see how he looks*
> *Wait till you hear him laugh.*
> *Painters of paintings, writers of books,*
> *Never could tell the half.*

He said, "We're told it's OK to substitute her and she. But Hart was gay and the song sounds better using he. Hart's one of your national treasures but he dates back. When words were as important as tunes. But I'm pushing again."

"For an educated guy you worry too much. Too much even-Stephen. Flaunt and push. Two of the reasons why I'm here."

"Normally I don't need encouraging. But sometimes I'm a teenager reborn, a step away from blushing. I've said it before: used properly American sounds adult. I must defer."

"You're being silly but you give silliness a good name."

As he faced her profile she felt his breath. He kissed the side of her nose. "More silliness," he said. "I have to go away for a while."

"Sounds as if you've just decided."

"I have."

"Is it to do with us?"

"It is."

"Will you phone?"

"I can't be sure." He kissed the disfigured cheek, a dozen butterfly touches. "Do you mind not knowing?"

"I'll miss you. You know that. I'll cling to the idea there's a good reason. Leave me a list of poems – to prove you're still alive. Oh shit, Christopher, you don't deserve me blubbering."

"Jana. Jana."

CHAPTER TWENTY

A question of language

NOW NINE, Octavien had won a schoolwide essay competition with three-thousand words on "Technology and society". The cheap scroll and ribbon were typical of French literary awards and the elder Chauvelets decided to compensate. But their offer had been too casual. Octavien had rocked them by asking for another Mlle Jana flight and Jana had further disturbed the family by refusing to take Vincent in the plane. Had even insisted that Vincent be elsewhere when she picked up Octavien. Her sternness was out of character and the grandparents' blank faces should have cut her to the heart. But Day had been absent for nearly two weeks, there'd been no phone calls and she was having difficulty hanging on to her shredded emotions. The child sat subdued and low down in the van seat and she suspected Sylvie and Hugues must have worked hard – probably acrimoniously – trying to dissuade him.

Normally Jana had no difficulty finding a way into Octavien's thoughts but not this time. Questions about the forthcoming flight, its direction and whether they should land for a snack produced only monosyllables. Perhaps getting into the cockpit would do the trick.

"Pretty good, winning that prize at nine," she said conversationally.

This broke though the silence, only to elicit more resentment. "Not at all. I heard my teacher talking. She used English words – age weighted. I did not understand. Now I do."

"How complicated things are in France. No US school would dare do that. It's probably unconstitutional."

"You are joking Mlle. Jana?"

"My country-folk are the most competitive on earth. But they need clear goals. Age-weighting would be kicked out as left-wing nonsense."

He smiled, almost furtively, looking out of the van window to hide his face.

When they arrived at Gascon Air Ginette had been primed and handed Octavien a wall-poster of the Stationair. "A memento of the day," Ginette said. "I will keep it on my desk until you return."

Octavien thanked her gravely then bent over the desk and kissed her three times on the cheeks. Jana was astonished. Despite her experience of French families she had never entirely grasped kissing etiquette. It was her impression that only toddlers – at their mother's instruction – greeted adults this way. Octavien surely was far too old or far too young. But why should such a controlled child feel the need?

Having installed Octavien in the Stationair and secured his seat-belt Jana feigned the need to return to the office. Ginette saw Jana's raised eyebrows and laughed.

"That embrace," Jana asked. "Why? How? What?"

Ginette shrugged. "It happens."

"He's nine."

"I have been embraced even by teenagers," Ginette said, rather smugly. "Three things were different, though. Often a child will offer his cheek. Octavien instead took the decision. Also he kissed me three times; that's more usual with adults."

Jana said, "You said three things."

Ginette smiled mischievously. "Ah yes. Nine-year-olds do not kiss with that intensity. It is, after all, just a salutation. It should not be – shall we say – sexual. Be careful, my innocent *américaine*. That boy may not only be in love with planes."

At Jana's suggestion they flew north along the coast, aiming to circle the two large lakes south of Arcachon. In a detour which she did not explain they passed over Ondres Plage where a Brit had recently ordered wall repairs. And there it was, the stylish bungalow with its surrounding paddock and curving wall. Octavien, however, stared down on the coastal shallows where a jet-ski bounced madly.

"Would you dare ride one of those?" Jana asked.

"I wish them death and destruction," he said, unexpectedly. This freed him to start talking again. "You have a boyfriend. He is English. Is it good to speak English from time to time?"

Much had been packed into those sentences. Not least the belief that he was entitled to discuss her private life.

"Perhaps you'd better define boyfriend."

He wasn't embarrassed. "A man whose company you like."

Too pat, too limited. Was she being sent up? His face was impassive. She said, "I like Jean-Claude but he is not my boyfriend."

"But could he be?"

Now, surely, she was being sent up!

"Are you curious or teasing?" she asked.

"Do I have to say?"

"If you want an answer."

He sniggered. "Am I a monster? Mlle Rebuffat, my science teacher, says so"

"You are playing a game. Taking advantage of your age and your intelligence. It is not exactly pleasant…"

Below the port wing the strip of coastline was streaming by, unheeded. He asked, "Do you like me?"

"Octavien, that's a dangerous question. I'm sure you know why."

"Mlle. Jana you are cleverer than Mlle. Rebuffat. I think you can answer the question."

Jana considered buying time with a call to Arcachon tower but didn't put it past him to recognise the ploy. "I do like you. You are immensely clever, you have the curiosity of youth and you are fun to talk to. And my heart breaks because your parents' problems make you sad. However you are a problem yourself. You are developing – at great speed – but you are not yet a person. I have to be careful; I must not influence you. Especially when your questions go in all directions."

He remained mute for ten minutes, obediently looking out as they circled first the Etang de Biscarosse, which had featured in Didi's final lesson, and then the Etang de Cazaux et de Sanguinet. After that they toured the open expanses of the Bassin d'Arcachon with its giant sand dune to the south-west

It appeared she had unintentionally silenced him. "There is a small airfield south of the *bassin*," she said. "Shall I check whether there is a café with ice cream?"

"Would there be people there? Could we go where there are no people?"

So, yet again, she flew down the Grandage grass strip. Then the weather had been hot if windy; now it was chilly autumn. Octavien nevertheless wanted to "feel the grass under my trainers." He accepted Jana's spare windbreaker which rendered him more rather than less solemn and they walked to the far boundary wall to look back at the Stationair from a distance.

"This is a small adventure, landing in this nowhere." he said.

"Flying is best when it's simple."

"I am sorry I teased you."

"It was flattering. Teasing means being friends."

"Friends." He sighed. "When I was very young. I ridiculously asked papa if I could marry you."

Ginette had warned her to be alert but his voice lacked guile. "It was an innocent way of saying you liked me."

"I think I wanted to say more," he said carefully.

Maintain the same tone of voice, that was the key. "That can happen. It is natural."

"Perhaps you do not understand… "

"I think I do Octavien. It didn't shock me."

"But it was wrong, surely," he stammered.

"I assume you wanted to touch me. In effect, your papa said you mustn't. So you didn't. Wanting to touch me wasn't wrong."

"Papa said it was."

"I'm sure your father said it was wrong to try. But the desire – between men and women – is not only natural, it's essential. The human race would die out without it."

"And still… you are happy to sit on this wall?"

"Do you intend to touch me?"

"That would be wrong."

"Then I am happy. I am even grateful."

She expected him to ask why but, without showing any emotion, he took out a handkerchief and wiped his eyes. It was hard not to put an arm round his shoulders even though that would be wrong – wrong in the way Octavien now recognised wrongness. Instead she followed his gaze towards the Stationair. "The wheels have covers," he said.

"Called spats. They add streamlining but sometimes I think they make the plane look like a toy. Not serious."

"I cannot dislike the plane. Your plane." Again he wiped his eyes. "You said you were grateful."

"Octavien, look at me, please. As a favour. Tell me what you see."

His eyes shone wetly. "A face I think about when I am sad." A fleeting smile. "And when I am content."

"Describe the face."

"It has a mark that says it is your face."

"Others think differently. They look away. They don't care for my face. When I was younger I was like all girls, I wanted to be pretty. Obviously I wasn't pretty. That was hard to bear. Yet you didn't look away. You seemed not to see the mark. I'm grateful for that."

This left him thoughtful and he turned towards the Stationair. "Spats. A strange word for a plane."

"A much shorter word in English. The French word is confusing for English speakers – half-gaiters."

"It makes the plane human." Then he jumped up. "The time! The time! My grandparents insisted - only an hour. They told me to look at my watch."

Jana laughed. "I won't charge them for our talking. I promise."

Seated in the cockpit she asked if he could remember the procedure for starting the plane, twitting him affectionately for the events he had forgotten. Then, deliberately, she slipped back into technicalities. There'd been too much emotion.

But there was still something at the back of his mind. "I asked about your boyfriend but you did not answer. Perhaps I was impolite. Does your boyfriend see the mark?"

Octavien's worries had allowed her to forget Day's absence. Now she needed to control her voice. "He is angry about those other people. That makes me grateful too."

"Can you tell me about him? Am I allowed to ask?"

Perhaps she could keep talk to routine detail. "In England he was a teacher of French and German. Married and then divorced. He has always loved France and has lived here for ten years. At first he helped his countryman buy houses here, now he does casual labour for them. I helped him repair a wall." It was no good; no detail was mere routine, That last sentence had carried far too much feeling.

"Not like the movies."

"Not at all. He is quite poor, so no posh dinners."

"He is handsome?"

"For me, yes. But I am prejudiced. He is tall, thin and does not care for his appearance. His hair is long and his shirts have been washed too much. They are almost invisible."

Octavien laughed. "Again, not like the movies. And his... qualities?"

"He has many books, all bought second-hand. He tells me about them, reads me passages. I now like to discover books. Before I was lazy, I flew planes and little else." Having passed through the barrier she found the urge to re-live things stronger than the need to hold back. "He insists I use the computer to discover poems. I rehearse them, then read them aloud to him. I read poems aloud while we repaired the wall."

"You were content? Obviously."

"Touched and content."

"And will you...?" His voice trailed away

But she'd gone too far, resurrecting the gap between pleasure and doubt. The plane, as so often in the past, became the diversion as she checked instruments, read off the GPS details and swept the sky from left to right.

Finally she responded. "There are uncertainties. I do not know. He is protecting me from something. I am afraid."

He sighed and the sigh's expressiveness made her giggle, slightly out of control. Caused her to sniff. "This was to have been your treat."

"It still is."

"Let me tell you something that isn't uncertain. Have you read books about the age of chivalry. Dumas, the musketeers, where knights fought for a woman's honour?"

He nodded.

"When I met my boyfriend it was like the Count of Monte Cristo. A man who had rented a plane turned out to be a bully. He insulted me. My chevalier, who was with me, could not endure it. Although he is very poor he offered to pay for the flight so that I could escape the bully. This happened in the twenty-first century not the Middle Ages."

"I would have challenged the bully to a duel."

They both laughed more loudly than this deserved. In the distance she could see the home field tower.

LIKE other mobiles, Jana's announced texts by trembling, often against her breast. However, waiting for texts had become too fraught; at any time of the day and night, sometimes at half-hourly intervals, she took out the phone and stared angrily at the empty screen. Felt a fool doing so. During Octavien's prize flight she rationed herself but resumed the moment he disappeared down the Chauvelets' driveway. Driving to work the following morning she made three checks within the first twelve kilometres, hating her irrationality, ashamed she no longer trusted the technology. Most of all she loathed the back-lit orange screen for remaining blank.

Heavy rain that had started during the night was still falling. An arcing smear on the van windscreen, directly on her line of sight, could be traced to a wiper blade torn in the middle. She could easily have dropped in at a large Intermarché en route and bought a replacement blade. Yet she preferred to endure the irritation, allowing it to mesh with Christopher's absence - the more painful infliction. Misery, her mother had once said, looks for friends.

The rain was heavy enough at the airport to discourage all but necessary flights and Gascon Air staff sat around the office, failing to look busy. Coffee was drunk to excess and time jelled. Reduced to reading her old log-books Jana finally put on her waterproof jacket and walked over to the terminal building book-shop. Most titles were new and obviously lightweight, many were whodunnits translated from English, but there was a range of old faithfuls and she came away with Zola's Le Ventre de Paris.

She'd imagined it would be instructive but the first few words (*Au milieu du grand silence, et dans le désert de l'avenue, les voitures de maraichers montaient vers Paris...*) drew her in. An hour later she slightly resented being handed the phone by Jean-Claude.

"An Englishman," J-C said, causing her briefly to gulp. "Not easy to understand. I asked him to speak English but his accent tires me."

"My name's Baines," the voice said. "With an i, not that it matters."

More nasal than Day, on the verge of complaining. She'd heard a similar voice once before. But when? Grandage, of course, but not quite as pronounced. Lacking the authority too.

"A world of difference," Jana said. "Who'd want to be i-less Banes? Hi, I'm Jana Nordmeyer, a Gascon Air pilot. What can I do for you?"

"American! Start by comforting me. I take it I was passed on because of my bad French. Heck, I try so hard."

"Mr Baines, this is France. Language is a form of torture. Imagine the pain I went through when I arrived from Arizona."

He laughed. "But you're from can-do country. Don't Americans force everyone to speak English – that is, American?"

"Not if they want to get paid."

"Good point. Look, all I want to do is book a flight. Not today, obviously, not with it…" He paused.

"Pissing down. Go on, Mr Baines."

"I'm having problems understanding the system. With this *bapteme de l'air* arrangement it seems I've got to – must - take hold of the joystick. And work the thingies. I'd be terrified. All I want is some scenery."

"You're not wasting my time. There's no flying until mid-afternoon. If you want to chat, an Orangina buys me for half an hour. I'm a cheap date."

"Would you really? That's very kind." She noticed the lengthened, flattened vowel: ka-ai-nd. "I could be at the airport bar in twenty minutes."

"Let's play a game. No descriptions: you work out which is me and I'll do the same for you."

Jana handed the phone back to Jean-Claude who shook his head. "More foreigners. Why not a German – or an Albanian – for a change?"

But for Jana it was a chance to chase echoes.

Chinos and a military shirt with twin breast pockets made her easy to spot, especially since she'd unrolled a map on the table. But he proved to be unnerving. The same ragged grey hair as Day, the same height (albeit carrying more belly), casual clothes that were neither French nor US and a half-hearted smile which Day also tended to affect.

"Ms Nordmeyer," he said, extending his hand.

English by an Englishman. "Jana," she said, offering hers.

"Oh, sorry. Adrian."

An Englishman with a dubious gayish first name. Typical.

"Well, actually, Adie most of the time," he added.

Even more dubious.

Still standing he looked down. "You bought your own Orangina. Gawd. It's true what they said."

"What did they say? And who were they?"

"Americans. Two floor traders in a bar in New York. Wouldn't let me buy a drink; just to make a point. Brits, they said, are the meanest people in the world. The biggest panhandlers. Barman, here's fifty bucks for this Brit's tab. Tell us when it's gone. It won't take long."

"Did you stay?"

"I took them at face value."

A stupid Yank, clever Brit story. Even so she laughed. Day tended to slip in one of those after too many Grimsbergens. Then he apologised profusely. Amazing how tolerant love made her. And how pathetic to find herself here, like a kid in a candy store. All expectant, covertly listening to the way Adie said things.

"Buy the next," she said. "As a favour, you pay but let me order."

He didn't sip the Grimsbergen but drained off half the glass. Just like Day. Gasped with pleasure. "You know your beer."

"An expert trained me. But let's clear up your problem. The *bapteme de l'air* is a restriction on aeroclubs. They can't offer flights as such, just thirty-minute hops for people who might take a course of lessons. Hired flights are Gascon Air's business. If you've got the dough we'll fly you."

His glass was empty; he leant back against the banquette and looked wholly content. "France is so bloody complicated but that's what I love about the place. No problem about the dough. Will you – personally – fly us?"

"How many is us?"

"It ought to be three. A married couple – also Brits – I'm pals with. They live here and you're not going to believe this. They have a dog. The prospect of crashing doesn't faze them, but leaving the dog behind to fend for itself does. So the husband stays behind as dog-sitter. Just two, then. But will you be the pilot?"

She smiled. "Is that important?"

He smiled back. "It is."

"Perhaps I ought to ask why."

"You'd imagine I was lying. Or there was something in it for me."

"Try me," she said.

"You might feel insulted."

"I'm Arizonan, working in France. I'm among expert insulters. Try me."

He shook his head doubtfully. "Perhaps you're too young. Oh, what the hell? Cast your mind back to the Falklands War. Remember your secretary of state? Name of Alexander Haig, a former Army general." Haig – another stretched-out vowel. "Our equivalent was Lord Carrington and, yes, he was a genuine lord. The two had dealings. Afterwards Haig said Carrington was the most duplicitous bastard he'd ever known. You see where I'm going. I think that revelation tells us a lot about Americans. And, of course, about Brits. But not, I hope, about me."

"What it says is Haig was an international imbecile. Being duplicitous went with the territory."

He straightened up, bowed his head. "I'm sorry. I've been playing clever-clogs and you're one yourself. Let's start again. I liked the sound of you straight off. But you also fit one of my prejudices. Americans fly naturally: as pilots and as passengers. Everything fits together. That's why I want you as pilot. Incidentally, after the Falklands Carrington resigned on a matter of principle. I wonder what Haig made of that."

"Probably thought the lord was a wimp. I'll be delighted to fly you. But where to?" She gestured at the map. "And for how long?"

"When I wasn't so paunchy I loved the hills. Along the Pyrenees would suit. A couple of hours or a bit more." He glanced at the food display cabinet. "Gosh, I'm starving. Can I buy you anything? To get me off the meanness hook."

"Chicken salad baguette and another Orangina." As he stood at the counter she heard him speaking perfectly serviceable French. Yet he'd pretended he couldn't. Why did Brits insist on – seemingly enjoy – underselling themselves? When he sat down, she asked him.

"It's more fun. Nothing more boring than boasting."

As simple as that.

She said, "You have an accent don't you?"

"Yorkshire. Why do you ask?"

"I have an English... boyfriend." It never seemed the right word; not strong enough. "We seem to use different dictionaries. Zizz, LiLo, plonk: weird words. He was born in Essex but got rid of his accent when he went to college."

"University. College is something else. Did he go somewhere swanky?"

"He didn't say that. He wouldn't in a million years. But I always assumed Cambridge was swanky," she said.

"Very. Like your Ivy League. Actually Essex the county is part swanky. A bit like New Jersey. Newark at one end, Princeton at the other."

"You know the States, then."

"I'm a retired hack. I've been around."

She asked, "Why hack? Sounds like more underselling?"

He grinned. "Absolutely. Not an ounce of social status."

"And you're sort of proud of the fact. Just like Christopher."

Now he laughed aloud. "You look puzzled. And so you should. You're actually asking what's it like to be a Brit? You've got to understand we never mention social status – lacking it or wanting it. Although we have to be careful. Job interviews, for instance. You say Christopher went to Cambridge; he won't be unaware."

"He's lived in France for ten years. He builds walls, repairs furnaces."

"Furnaces?"

"Heating, hot water"

"Ah. One of your weird words. Is he wildly francophile?"

Ah, the pleasure of talking about it. "Totally crazy. He's away for the moment and I miss him. In baseball terms you're my designated hitter. Going to bat on his behalf. Your accent: I hear the differences but it's still English English. More or less the same hair-cut too."

"Lucky chap."

"See: lucky chap not lucky guy. Two thousand miles' difference." she said.

"You're a romantic, Ms Nordmeyer.?"

"Jana."

"First names - I'm not really entitled," he said.

"Entitled, schmeiteled. You have my permission."

"Careful. Being British is the only charm I've got. Change the way I say things and what's left?"

But she was leaping ahead of him. "And you know about first names! I had to twist his arm to get Christopher. Not Chris, I wanted it in full."

"Perhaps he fears being mucked about. Perhaps everything's perfect as it is."

Mucked about! "Is it wrong to shoot higher?"

"Not wrong but it's peculiarly American. Mind you, my guess is he's adapting – and willingly. You're not from the Home Counties and that's what good old Christopher likes. For that he's having to pay a premium. Go ahead: muck him about."

"He likes hearing me speak. Asks me to read poetry because of my accent. My accent! That makes him a crazy, surely?"

"Not on your Nellie." He'd joined the club; he was doing it on purpose.

"Nellie?"

"It makes him entirely sane. Or it makes me totally crazy."

"You Brits!"

"Jana, you warm the cockles of my heart. I was wrong about romantic. You're passionate. As I said, he's a lucky chap. Or a lucky guy."

As she drove the van back to her flat the mobile teased at her breast and she pulled into the next available driveway. Drove in forwards, not caring about the house's owner. Let him bring out a shotgun.

Read the text.

CHAPTER TWENTY-ONE

Acts of faith

HER APARTMENT had remained half-furnished. Books provided the main signs of occupation, some she'd bought but mostly those he had taken from his shelves and forced into her hands. Gifts that brought their own burdens. Raggedy paperbacks that were too intimate, so much a part of his character; she feared she might not do them justice.

He had an answer. "Don't read them cover to cover, dip in, taste them, chuck 'em into a corner if they don't suit. Don't treasure them as things. Books are what they leave behind, they're not interior decoration. Hardbacks made me uncomfortable even when I had money. Too big, too stiff, too unnecessary. You can stuff a paperback into your pocket. If it falls out buy another. Better still don't replace it; rely on what you can remember."

They had been standing in his apartment at the time, looking for a specific title. She said, "You're such a liar – yet sweet with it. All these shelves prove you accumulate."

"In effect the shelves are a card index. Reminders that a book exists. If I had the energy I'd glue the spines to the walls and save bags of space."

"So what's this one about?" Her index finger came down on a faded red hardback. "This isn't a paperback."

He didn't even look closely. "She by Rider Haggard. A kid's book really, recommended by my grandmother. Quite spooky. A woman who's a hundred – two hundred? – years old but has kept her looks. A marvellous two or three pages at the end."

"No sentimental attachment?"

"They all have that. But I'm attached to the contents, not to the paper and cardboard. Take it, it'll scare you out of your tiny Arizonan mind."

To some extent it had. And he'd been right about the ending; the manic scream was now embedded. She made a point of returning it, saying he shouldn't be without it. He'd laughed and kissed her, admitted she was right. Now that she'd read it the paper and cardboard had taken on physical value. He admitted that.

As he returned She to the shelf he said, "I was wrong about some books. I hang on to the poetry. If a poem's good enough I never get to the bottom of it. And I can't memorise everything here. There are collections and anthologies too, hundreds, perhaps thousands of poems. I need the flickability."

His text - Your apt. 21.00. - had been short enough to be ominous. He'd never been concise and if the news had been encouraging he'd have hinted. Surely. As she waited she invoked superstition: nothing she did was out of the ordinary. Her work clothes had gone into the laundry basket and she'd put on an old housecoat. She'd washed her hair, combed it and let it dry untended. Made a shopping list for the following day. Polished the mirror in the bathroom where a dried-on blob of shampoo had irritated her since the weekend. If she'd been able to eat she would have prepared an evening meal. But her throat was dry and her taste buds deadened so she chewed a precisely segmented apple.

Housecoat, hair and shopping list were supposed to damp down anticipation; inevitably they made it worse. Finally she gave in, sat down. If the worst comes to the worst what will I lose? Very little by prevailing standards – especially those of her home country. In the USA, she told herself, love affairs were defined by copulation. Nothing else counted. Yet here, drawn to a foreigner in a foreign country, she'd never even laid side by side. A love affair?

Roy had been different. Despite her lack of experience, turning off on to that logging road had been a natural and mutual decision. True the car had prevented them coupling ("I'm in my forties," Roy had said. "It's so goddamn juvenile, so uncomfortable.") but neither doubted what was to come. Her breasts, bare in the chilly air, had been at his disposal. When his hand, flat between her thighs, eased upwards his questing thumb told her what would happen once central heating and soft furnishings were available.

Day had never seen her breasts and his hands had never rested between her legs. Nor had they talked about physical love. He'd even been slightly comical. A movie Englishman - the opposite of the hairy-chested US hero, avoiding the "big" words and sparing with her Christian name.

And yet, and yet... that contradictory mix of comfort and thrill might well have added up to the state of love. He'd chosen words for her alone; the sentences were unique. He'd helped her to shut out the staring world. Never mind if his feelings stopped short of yearning or longing, that only the tone of his voice provided feeble confirmation. That passion was reserved for the poetry only intermittently concerned with love. Might he be changing? Moving towards a greater articulacy?

I'm in a movie, she said: one that has been poorly conceived and has gone straight to video. How weak and ill-defined this story would seem compared with a ninety-minute romance about New York commodity brokers or Ivy League academics. Her plot had none of the certainties or latent treachery typical of modern cinema.

And where was the common ground? Day shared almost nothing with Jana's past life. He'd chosen his burdens, hers had been inescapable. And for him there'd always been recourse to what others had written.

Shocked by this growing bitterness, she sat up straight. Use your brain, J, use your brain. Ask questions. Look for reasons why. Why did he revel in what she'd done, insisting on seemingly boring detail? Why the rhapsodies about her accent for God's sake? And what about their silences – in his apartment, at the wall? Silences as unifying, as any of the talk.

Half an hour before he was due she opened a book and – as he had suggested – tasted it. Updike's The Poorhouse Fair which he'd recommended: "In his twenties, yet he writes well about old people." But after a page or two it was inevitable she would turn to poetry. She looked for something knotty and impenetrable with barely perceived rhythm and words that came together oddly. Understanding wouldn't be the goal. Someone, not Day, name now forgotten, had said no one should ever read Ezra Pound. His politics were barbaric and his verse opaque. She ran through the index of an anthology she had picked at a *marché aux puces,* killing time in Bordeaux.

Pound was listed once. It wasn't what she'd expected or what she needed:

> *I make a pact with you, Walt Whitman -*
> *I have detested you long enough.*
> *I come to you as a grown child*
> *Who has had a pig-headed father*

But its directness seized her. Especially since she had taken against Whitman following her aborted attempt to read him aloud to Day. She slipped into the short, easily grasped cadences and was only interrupted by the sound of Day's Citroen, now in need of a new silencer, arriving in the car park. Standing she noticed he was ten minutes early. But when she went to the window she saw him continuing to sit in the car, a motionless shadow apparently seeing nothing.

Opening the apartment door to him she was convinced their separation had already begun. His trousers were navy blue moleskins never before seen. His generously cut white shirt looked almost new.

"You look startled," he said.

"Your clothes."

"You've only seen me shabby. Shabby, with theories about shabbiness. What I wore was an insult. A very English insult."

They held hands and then, awkwardly, kissed. But it wasn't an inadequate kiss; it would have passed muster in that well-scripted movie about the two academics greeting each other in Harvard Yard, the leaves of Fall brushing round their shoes. In those stories it was always Fall.

"You guessed, then?" he said, searching her face.

"There were clues," she replied, hating herself for being calm. She'd intended to behave civilly but that had gone out of the window when his calloused, wall-building hands touched hers.

"Clues. Like one of those boring detective stories we Brits specialise in. I should have smoked a pipe."

Despite herself she laughed. They were still holding hands. Abruptly he kissed her again and it was hell's own job preventing herself from folding her body against his, taking one of those roughened hands and holding it against her breast. Should she have done so anyway?

He said, "You smell of something I'm supposed to respond to."

"Sit down for God's sake. It's just shampoo. You know about shampoo, don't you?"

He took the couch. "Heard about it. But soap's good enough."

No one – not even her dad – had used soap. She said, "You've got good hair. Worth attending to."

"Gill said that."

"Gill?"

"My ex."

"You've never mentioned her by name. Anyway, she was right."

"All that matters is to get it clean, isn't it? What more does shampoo do?"

"Makes it fluffier. Makes individual hairs follow natural waves."

"Fluffier!" he looked astonished. "An improvement? Or just pointless detail? Like giving a grizzly bear a manicure. I mean I've never bothered about style, can't afford it."

"You're at a cocktail party. Once you're into your stride about Thomas Pynchon there are no problems. But before that. People might think you were the hired help."

"Or the village idiot." He nodded, allowing her to lead him down this side alley. "A kind of arrogance. But when we met you were willing to talk to the village idiot. Oh, just a minute. I was a customer wasn't I?"

"I hope I did more than front-of-house."

"You let me help clean the Seneca's cockpit. That was definitely flattering. I've been meaning to ask: given my shirts and my haircut what did you see? Later on I was Horatio at the bridge with Mr Dewsbury but that was over in seconds. We went for a drink, now it seems so accidental." He paused. "Isn't there a movie called The Hulk? No romance in that, surely?"

She'd wanted to go on talking about shampoo and cocktail parties, anything that seemed ordinary. But as he often did, he'd strung together two unexpected facts and taken off in another direction. She needed to breathe more carefully, more deeply. "You do jump around, but I think I get your drift. You're like all men, hopeless when it comes to male attraction. If I asked for an example you'd come up with a sportsman, somebody with muscles, a pretty-boy TV celeb. Never in a thousand years would you point to... let's say, Bill Clinton."

"Clinton!" He repeated the name, rolling it round his mouth. "Isn't he rather elderly, rather obvious?"

"Across a crowded room, being obvious is what counts."

"But his face, it's not - "

" - a Greek god? Clean-cut and classical? Most women hate sleeping with sculpture."

"But Clinton has a track record. He's untrustworthy."

"You mean a bit wicked? Goodness gracious! How many men have fantasies about tarts."

Day shook his head. "Gosh, you're quick. I suppose at this point a man would say: ah, but that's different. Surely I didn't come over like Clinton?"

That was quite funny. "You certainly didn't," she said, laughing. "But you share one thing. You both have a sense of humour."

"Was that it? Cap and bells?"

"No, of course not," she said, almost angrily.

He heard the way her voice changed. "Sorry. But forgetting the psycho-stuff what did you see? A scarecrow getting on for fifty. Acting facetiously, I think you said. A non-US package: a Brit who didn't wash enough, teeth not A1."

"Don't be ridiculous," she said. "When we met I hadn't just got off at CdG. I'd been in Europe for a couple of years. You listened when I spoke, spoke back in a way I could trust, looked into my face, saw what there was, went on talking. To me alone. No revulsion, no pity. I must have ticked a box or two, so you drew me into a world I only knew dimly. You seemed... aware of me."

She brought a dining chair close to the couch where he lolled, turned it round and rested her forearms on the chair-back so she could look down on him. But he wasn't outfaced.

"And now?"

"I think there's something between us," she said. "And it's grown. To the point where you're facing a dilemma."

"Do you still trust me?"

She frowned. "I trust you to do what you think is right. But not necessarily to pick what is right."

"So, I've read a lot of books, I'm good with my hands but I'm an emotional blockhead?"

"Blockhead isn't good American."

"Asshole?"

"Too strong."

Day shook his head. "I've run out of vocabulary."

"And I'd never blame you. I think things are complicated and, of course, I don't understand why. We've gone our own way in the past and we're neither exactly flexible. Which sounds like a good time to tell me what you have to say."

"How do you react to this as a proposition?" he said.

How English, she thought. A dull form of words to soften a blow which probably couldn't be softened. But no. Go on. I'll not analyse. Just keep talking. Please!

He went on, "You're good at working things out; I suppose it goes with your job. What I have to say is miserable territory and it will hurt – hurt both of us. Suppose I said nothing? Suppose we just walked away from each other?"

Jana shook her head. "The pain's already there and you started it. I at least, need closure. Yeah, yeah, it's a terrible word. I'll bet it grates your nerves as it grates mine. Those parents with the lost kid, clinging on. Finally saying it to the TV cameras. Closure! Who came up with that? A funeral home? Telespeak for handling grief and sorrow? You can't preserve grief or contain it. Yet I'm hung up on that very word. Breaking up, I have to know everything. A silent goodbye wave would kill me."

"We do fit together, don't we?" he said, leaning towards her. "It's a shit word and we both recognise its shittiness. A curious take on unity. What was it you said? There's something between us: I think I've just unearthed a little more."

"And yet…?"

"And yet. A lot of sad stories start that way. I didn't think you'd walk away in silence. It's never 'Do not go gentle' with you. There's always that mental toughness. I envy it."

"Time to grit our teeth."

"Just so," he said. "Let's start the sad story. Which means going back to my marriage and why it failed. Or why it didn't fail. Take your pick."

"Do I need to know Gill?"

"Probably. It explains Christopher's curse. I didn't deserve her so she too, like all of us, is ultimately a mystery. Daughter of religious parents; not religious herself but guided and sympathetic. Better degree than mine, eng-lit. in her case. English rose looks, shoulder-length brown hair. Gentle, soft-spoken but not vapid – a rare combination. Would have remained my wife until her dying day."

"A paragon?"

"The word's too haughty, too glossy. She tended to bring out the best in me and in others. I have this crazy idea you'd have got on with her but that's probably my egotism."

"How did you meet?"

His eyes lit up. "In church! With neither of us looking for God. A good St Matthew Passion so it must have been Maundy Thursday. Music makes me vulnerable. She was two rows down. Brown hair shining. I didn't give a toss what the Evangelist was singing: just cared for the musical sounds and that head of hair. Why? What's wrong!"

Jana said nothing.

"Oh, shit Jana. Why is there so much damn discomfort? You're thinking Bach's better than the Cessna. You're quite wrong. You bring a working world with you. Meeting you was like meeting someone famous – someone worthwhile, who'd done great deeds. Back in that church Gill and I were simply amateurs. It's no great thing to like music."

"OK," said Jana neutrally. "Keep going."

"Marriages fail because of money, infidelity, boredom or the realisation that the two people just aren't suited. I was different. Mine failed on the road to hell or perhaps in hell. And I arrived in the time-honoured way. I thought I knew best, I acted for the best and possibly I may even have been right. Is that clear? It shouldn't be."

He's trying to amuse me but it'll take more than that.

Day said, "When I look back – which I normally avoid – what kills me is my moral position. I've never discussed this with anyone and there's a good reason. You'll want to help but almost inevitably you'll be driven by emotion. That won't work. I need hard-edged truth."

Not only was this not amusing, it was worrying. Until then she'd been sort of half confident, quarter confident. Love triumphs doesn't it? But that was what rom-com said. Inside a conviction was growing. If Gill hadn't come out tops, what were her chances? Listening, even sharing, might not be enough. She shuddered. "Tell it the way you think best. Just don't knock yourself."

"Did you know simple tests show pain is easier to bear if you repeat swear words – extreme ones – over and over. Perhaps self-knocking works the same way."

"Not when you've got an audience who needs to know."

That stopped him. Left him with his mouth open and she was pleased. He might not get it all his own way.

Now he frowned and that was good too. He asked, "Any ideas yet about where this is going?"

She shook her head "I keep guessing but getting nowhere." It wasn't the truth; the future was entirely blank. One thing, she didn't want to help him. Didn't think he was entitled.

He sighed. "If I sound ironic it is an English failing. You know, I'm supposed to care for you yet I've left you uncertain. That's almost as bad as direct betrayal. I could gabble it all out in ten seconds then leave it in your lap. But I'm not dragging it out to be sadistic or literary. It's my story but I need you to see it as I see it. Need? That the right word? I think it is. Or am I scrabbling for approval?"

"That's pretty pathetic, Christopher. I haven't said you're posing. Just don't leave me in the dark while you punish yourself. It's not a great combination."

"Trouble is I can't stop myself untying what I have to say. Seeing how it works, how it might have worked better. And this isn't the time." He shrugged himself into a more upright position. "Where was I this last fortnight? Fontenay-aux-Roses, just outside Paris. Spending time at a neuro-psychiatric clinic called Les Pervenches. I looked up that name: a flower we call periwinkle. For what it's worth it's also slang for a female traffic warden."

"Why was I there?" he asked. His bravado was that of a teenager not an adult. "I'll tell you why but let's not make this a Saturday morning matinée: to be continued in our next. Did I find what I was looking for? The answer's no. Was I expecting to find it? Not really. A fool's errand, then? Almost, but not quite."

She didn't respond; continued to straddle the chair, leaning on the hard back which pressed uncomfortably into her forearms.

"So what was it? Self-delusion? Indecisiveness? Desperation? Desperation's best. I went to Paris even though I'd sworn I wouldn't. Because of you. Because you'd re-tutored me - reminded me about a woman's company. I wanted a future with you but knew that would be up to someone else. At Fontenay-aux-Roses – a place which doesn't live up to its name, by the way – I was hopeful. And I'd done without hope for ages."

"After all," he said lopsidedly, "My degree proves I can do rational thought."

"Christopher. Christopher."

He took her hand. "It's not One Flew Over the Cuckoo's Nest. I haven't lost my marbles. Oh! Is that another footnote?"

"It is but I get the idea."

"More about Gill. I'd been married just over a year, we were both teaching and I was full of intellectual fizz. Ideas well above my station. I started putting together research for a doctorate. A linguistic theory of Feuerbach – as if that matters a damn now. Hard work even though my German's pretty damn good academically. But it lacks that underlying sympathy I have for French. Hard work and a huge range of source material. A lot of evenings not spent watching telly."

Telly – a word the Brits used a lot. Sounded like a kid's word and perhaps that was the point. Disguised contempt.

"Work that turned out to be too hard," said Day. "I should have backed off when I found myself looking forward to the weekends. But you don't back off when you're in your twenties. I don't recall much of what happened except I ended up with what they used to call a nervous breakdown. Six months off work with strict instructions to stay away from Feuerbach. How awful it is chewing over all this."

"You were hurt. I want to know how."

"But it's going to hurt you. Anyway, to be brief, my breakdown had side effects. Stress, low self-esteem and – the part that directly affects us."

"You've got to forgive me," he said, looking up from the couch, his face vacant. "In my spare time I'm a wordsmith; you know that. I've got two options now: technical medical or the dirty joke. Neither are pretty. There's also the literary route but when Henry James was faced with something similar he bottled. Wonderful with human delicacy but on that occasion there was nothing for Old Hank. I have to do better and I'm going for backwards-forwards military talk. In short: Erection, Absence of." He shrugged. "Among the world's disasters it's no big deal."

Silence was Jana's only option.

"These days it gets a fancier name with more syllables: erectile dysfunction. Happily reduced to ED. Causes are psychological and/or physical, prognosis is open-ended. Adding to this bowl of cherries I am one of the twenty percent who can't be reached by Viagra and its siblings. Even so the worst part was low self-esteem. It's still there. You'd have seen it occasionally if you'd known where to look. At the wall, for instance."

"Tell me! I'd like to know. Truly."

"You helped me choose stones. I appreciated your nearness, but low esteem said I didn't deserve it. I tried to out-argue myself and time passed. I looked up and realised you were knackered."

"Knackered! Sheesh at this distance it was a willing martyrdom. I'm honoured to have suffered for the cause." She spoke lightly. "Low esteem must have been taking a break when you saw off Mr Dewsbury."

"Damned unlucky, Mr Dewsbury. I don't care a damn about him but I did and do care about Gill. An open-ended prognosis – weeks, months, years - but Gill wanted children. Like most newly-weds we'd been waiting until we'd saved enough. She talked brightly about IVF but the Christopher Day she married wasn't her new old man. Quite simple, really. I saw myself as an invalid, not the head of a growing family, and there's a grain of truth there. What isn't in doubt is how low self-esteem made me all persuasive. I talked brilliantly against IVF: 'a mechanical process', 'good for the lab not for the bedroom', that sort of thing. I hinted – unforgivably, I can see that now – that I might turn against a child born 'artificially'. Did I believe that? I have no idea but I suspect I didn't want to know. I was having difficulty behaving like a thinking adult - taking responsibility for a child seemed like a nightmare. Over tears that are an agony to remember, I insisted we divorced. I told you it was 'amicable' but that's dangerous shorthand. Was I manipulative? Absolutely. Was I right? All I can say in my own defence is she's had two daughters with the Balliol prof. Is she happy? Like me, she isn't the same. She blames herself for the divorce, says her part was cowardly. I'm not sure how secure her marriage is."

Jana pressed his hand against her cheek. "I'm sorry for both of you. At least I haven't changed."

"That warms me and terrifies me."

"And what about the commie? The railway activist if you prefer?"

"Sympathetic. Tried to help. Said she could do without."

"But you dropped her?"

"I can't be sure. The daggers-drawn argument about cassoulet did happen – silly as it sounds. She hated being bested."

"I take it we're now more or less up-to-date."

He sat up fully. "All that was ten years ago. The side-effects have since eased. As you can imagine I've read up on ED and developments in psychiatry. Not with any great hope since I don't care for splints or the more frightening stuff."

Splints?

"Over the last couple of years the ED focus has changed. The press has dug out a controversial ED figure and he's made the running. Figaro flirts with him and Le Monde calls him a charlatan. Perfect for business, international business. He's a Russian called Khantsev and he holds court in Paris. Wouldn't have been my cup of tea if it hadn't been for a middle-of-the-road article in Libération with a headline that caught my eye: Monsieur K – Has he got something? Good journalism; long interviews with literate patients. Perhaps I was half convinced."

He looked into her eyes. "Then I met you and I re-read everything. Went over the doubts, assessed the risks. Knowing I'd never sleep if I didn't take it further"

There was nothing to say.

"I phoned Khantsev. He sounded tired. Had I read Le Monde? he asked. I said I had. 'I am not a fucking magician,' he whined. ED takes time and many get impatient. Two hours each day over two weeks, some of it deceptively basic. 'People are so ignorant,' he said. They resent the IQ test but for most it's the first time. Then there's an updated Rohrshach 'turned into software because computers make people happier'. The prognosis? He shrugged and pointed to his successes. 'There's a simple explanation; I spend time on data and discovery.' Not that there are any guarantees; if the prognosis is encouraging it's the result of accurately measuring the patient's attitude. And that, as always, is subjective."

"So you saw him – without too many expectations?"

Day nodded

"Not through the French health service, I take it?"

"Does that matter?"

"It means you paid. Paid right royally, I suspect. And yet you've no money."

"So I borrowed."

"Ah yes. Loan sharks you said. A good truthful US term while the French are more polite. You're not the only one who uses the dictionary. *Usurier* doesn't tell the whole story; sounds more biblical."

"All right, all right. I'm in hock. Let's get back to the Khantsev."

"Should you have seen him?"

"Yes, I should," he said gruffly. "Was I a fool? Of course I was. And why? Because my life had changed. I turned up at BIQ airport with Grandage's lists and, at ten metres I saw a blonde head, hair hacked, bending over maps of the northern Languedoc. A head that matched the shape of something I lacked. Beyond that, foolishness was always round the corner."

It was a diversion, perhaps a plea but she wasn't having it. "You've made up your mind. It's Gill all over again but without the discussion about mechanical processes. No persuasion. I get dumped and you go back to your solitary life loaded with debt. Likely to have your arm broken for non-payment."

"You get dumped. Yes."

It was one thing for her to say it, quite another to have it confirmed in a hard, non-emotional voice.

"Do you like messing up women?"

He gestured. "Stop being aggressive Jana. Go through it all again on your own. Tell me how I arrived at this horrible point in my life. And why. Make us coffee and be as honest with yourself as you're being tough with me."

She made the coffee but even as she ran water into the percolator she knew the sort of things he would say.

He held the mug in both hands like a crystal ball. "I say 'dumped' and it churns my guts. I tell myself there's no point in dressing it up; I'll be a bastard whatever. Talk bluntly so there are no misunderstandings. And then the images creep back. The back of your head as you stare out of the plane, understanding what's out there. You, asking me to read the Donne again because there was a line you liked. Remember? It wasn't a line I could have predicted: *Running it never runs from us away.* And you, supposedly a poetry ignoramus! Again, you're drinking Leffe, legs stretched out, making tiredness look desirable. Why not just be friends? I ask myself, and I howl at the moon. The idea's fucking ludicrous."

As in the past he drank off a great gulp of hot coffee, proving perhaps there were more important things than pain. "Do I like messing up women? No I don't. I messed up Gill and I mustn't mess up you. I look ahead. See myself hanging around the edge of your life – incomplete, emotionally dependent – a disappointment at best, a curse at worst. You probably disagree and I'm privileged you do. But what part of you is doing the thinking?"

At last, she told herself, it was time. "So you're dumping me because you care for me. The old Viet Nam excuse: to save the village we had to destroy it."

"The right touch of realism. But take a careful look. Your instincts are based on how we've been together. I love that, I share that. But that's yesterday. You're a healthy, attractive – oh so bloody attractive – woman. You mustn't become a drab from years of nursemaiding, of making excuses, of suppressing what's natural. To be completely selfish I don't want to be the cause of that."

"But that's how you see it."

"It is. But I've had more time. I know you have a generous heart. I know we fitted together. You may see staying by me as a return for what you imagine I did for you. But what I did is tiny, and what you'd be doing is enormous. And in the end, probably useless. The chances are you'll change, and not for the better. I won't have the Jana I started with." He put down his mug and squeezed her hand. "Can you imagine the self-hatred? I tell you, I'm good at low self-esteem."

She felt like a violently shaken bottle of Coke. A fizzing, barely contained concentration of energy – but without direction, without function. He had planned it and had the better logic. She needed to step back, to make her own truths work for her. To execute an emergency landing that would be successful

"You've had more time. So give me more," she said.

"It's wasted effort."

"Now that's unfair, Christopher. Writing me off as a thinking being. At the moment you're wiping the floor with me. But if you're honest you must give me a chance. And if you're truly honest you've got to listen to what I say. To accept that I might have something you hadn't considered."

He hadn't imagined there might be a shred of hope. "You're right. It's a relief, a big relief, to be told there may be something else. However unlikely. I grasped at the dubious Russian so any light would be welcome. Otherwise it's pretty damn dark. I'll come back tomorrow."

"Oh, please God, no. I don't want to spend the night alone, working out what to say. I need you to remind me how important it all is. Stay until it's done."

For the first time the certainty and the stubbornness on his face slackened; there was even a hint of doubt. "I'll stay."

She said, "But we need to pull back. Take a break. Do something different."

As he looked around he saw the anthology, open, face down, on the arm of the couch. She knew he could no more ignore that open book than stop breathing. "Pound? That's a rich stew. Normally, that is. But not this oddity."

"I wanted a rich stew, poetry that was beyond me. More like music than words. I'd heard about Pound but that was easier than the rumours."

"I can see that. Something obscure, eh? Too hard to make sense. Something to hum, to keep away painful thoughts." He flipped through the index. "Pound was a good choice. But this unrepresentative bit is all there is." Miraculously the relentless voice was returning to the precise murmur he reserved for poetry. "Should I see if you have something that fills the bill?"

"I'd like that very much. How about a sandwich? I'm running on empty."

"I thought I'd never eat again."

There was only corned beef. In her impatience she gashed a finger opening the can and her slices of onion were three times as thick as the ethereal wafers he had provided for the picnic. But she needed to be back with him and with the books. As she came in she started to apologise for her clumsy onions but he uncharacteristically reached out without asking, took a sandwich and tore half of it away with his teeth.

He'd been searching other books on the floor, "I remember getting you these St Exupery quotes, hoping there'd be something about flying. But it's overblown. I mean: 'a coma of blue lightnings when night has fallen'? Pretty much a velvet cushion, eh? He's better about boats:

If you want to build a ship, don't drum up people together to collect wood and don't assign them tasks and work, but rather teach them to long for the endless immensity of the sea.

He continued, "Tell you what, whoever owned this book first didn't like Ex either. They left this quote as a bookmarker:"

Once you have learned to fly your plane, it is far less fatiguing to fly than it is to drive a car. You don't have to watch every second for cats, dogs, children, lights, road signs, ladies with baby carriages and citizens who drive out in the middle of the block against the lights.

"That's William T. Piper, president of Piper Aircraft."

"Poetry, Christopher. Poetry please."

"Right. Here's Pound. From the Cantos. Not particularly obscure but it's all we've got:

> Dark blood flowed in the fosse,
> Souls out of Erebus, cadaverous dead, of brides
> Of youths and of the old who had borne much;
> Souls stained with recent tears, girls tender,
> Men many, mauled with bronze lance heads.

"I'll read that again."

"Hmmm. Better than the sandwiches," she said. And then, as she knew he would, he went through the rest of the book stopping at things he fancied and reading them aloud. For a moment the earlier horror was at rest. Finally he closed the book with a snap.

"We're just making things harder for ourselves," he said. "Jeez, what the hell's that?"

Blood was oozing through the handkerchief she'd wrapped casually round her finger. "Nothing. Just the corned-beef can. Let's get on with…"

But he got up, took her hand, removed the handkerchief. "Cotton wool. Women always have cotton wool. And Elastoplast. Shit, you call it something else."

"Band Aid. But it's nothing, really."

"I'm not having you bleeding in front of me, like some goddamn saint."

And so she surrendered and watched, ironically, as he bandaged her.

"Hold it up, slow the blood flow," he said. "You look odd. Did you imagine I'd lost my feelings for you?"

"Odd? Is that surprising? No, I didn't think that"

He was trying to speak more quickly. "Of course, I still have feelings. Where were we? Making things harder for ourselves."

"Indulge me, Christopher. What did the Russian recommend?"

"Are you sure…?"

"I'm sure."

"Can I ask why?"

"There were times when you said you were persuaded. Perhaps I can guess at them."

He took a sheaf of papers from his back pocket. "I took notes. I'm not sure he approved. But damnit I was there because I wanted to believe, against the odds if need be. I had time to reflect: just two hours with the master and the rest of the day to kill. Reading Eliot on the Ile de la Cité and Jean-Claude Izzo back in my ramshackle hotel room in the Marais. I wondered about humiliation – surely it's only a threat for adolescents. Adults should be above it. I thought about you a lot and wished I had a photograph."

"Ah!" she said involuntarily.

He looked up quickly. "You as well? Don't all Americans carry them in stacks? But then, do photos exist? For either of us."

The notes rustled in his hand. "The initial stuff was pretty banal. ED patients – Sufferers? Victims? – tend to be self-centred. No surprises there. So Khantsev's sessions take the form of a dialogue. I was required to think of myself as half of a couple, never a singleton. First off I had to define the other half – you – in detail. That was harder than I thought; Khantsev's consulting room is pretty lush, soft-leather chairs and couch, original paintings, hi-fi, even a telescope at one of the windows. For me it was never other than sordid and I had to force myself to imagine you there. But he never let up. He created scenarios, asked for my reactions and then interrupted me with 'How's this affecting Jana?' Occasionally he tested my feelings about you, checking for resentment. Resenting what? I asked. 'Towards Jana for being normal,' he said. Ten minutes later he'd have you and me in bed together, you comforting me. I was disturbed; we were doing this without your permission. But it worked in one sense. Loneliness adds to ED and he made sure it was never just him against me. You were there too."

His coffee mug was now empty but he appeared to notice it for the first time. As he reached for the armrest to pull himself up, she took the mug out of his hand and refilled it. He said, "His wretched Powerpoints were useless; used as backdrops to emphasise nearness. Men and women, supposed to be ultra-normal, holding hands, leaning forward over restaurant tables. Except they weren't normal. Khantsev caters for the carriage trade and his models all wore Armani. The women look strangely like Binoche."

When he laughed at this reminiscence it emerged as a bark. "He was careful to make sure I never saw other clients. I never left the clinic the way I came in; his receptionist guided me out via a different staircase. Again it's not so surprising. My cousin had a vasectomy at the local hospital in Croydon. He was consulted as part of a group that stayed together for the surgery and for the stitches removal. A common-interest social group, he said, all ready-made. I wouldn't expect the same bonhomie from ED."

As he flicked through the handwritten sheets he stopped and massaged his chin. "Having you there in the room was, as it were, more problematic the second week. One theory is that ED men are emotionally downcast if their partner is out of step during love-making. 'Emphasising the male's inadequacy,' as he put it. Jana must learn to slow down, he insisted. Sounds like part of a dirty joke now; then it was hardly bearable. As if I were sharing you with him. I pointed out that not everyone (And, of course, I was thinking about myself, no one else) had the capacity to raise the subject with their lover. 'There will be no need,' he said. 'I will do it for you. Naturally Jana will be attending all future consultations.'"

Day shook his head. "I need to apologise but I'm not sure why. Taking your name in vain, perhaps. At times I thought I'd been reborn a teenager; at others I felt outraged. And now"

It was all horrifying. "Don't apologise. Remember, you were there on my behalf ."

Again the harsh laugh. "I'd almost forgotten. He believes music could play a part in resolving the mismatch. I assumed he meant music as a turn-off: Orff, early Mendelssohn, Buxtehude organ music. But before I could ask him to elaborate he started listing stuff others had mentioned, Blur and U2, which meant nothing to me. I didn't pursue it."

"Hilarious."

"Now it is, not then."

"I mean I hate heavy metal bands like Metallica but who on earth would lie in bed with that blasting out?"

"I'm not sure he's convinced about the music. Certainly he allowed me to drop it. But he has strong feelings about how a man should react if the love-making, in his words, 'reaches an advanced state and then fails.' The partner should be given 'manual relief.' This was his most radical idea. He says it re-establishes the union."

They were both silent and for the first time Jana looked away. In a welter of theory and talk, an image. What does that do for me? Would I want it? Allow it?

Day almost whispered. "Received wisdom says the mouth gives the best relief. Khantsev says no, never. The separation of bodies is likely to make the male more self-conscious."

Another image which Jana dwelt on during the next silence.

Day's head was now erect. "I may have been... unjust. Often he's cleverer than I've made out. He recognises lists like this can be discouraging. And that there's an inherent flaw in rendering sexual behaviour into words. He talked about films: two delib-erately normal-looking people following his recommendations. 'Provided they emphasise normalcy," he said. Then he laughed. 'But there are risks. Legal risks.' He asked me if I had any sug-gestions but I fear I hadn't.

"As I said, optimism came and went. There were times I could persuade myself that some recommendations deserved considering. Others had responded and if Khantsev is to be be-lieved it worked for them. But that was then. Afterwards came the personal diagnosis: his guess as to why I am what I am and whether I'm capable of changing. There was virtually no out-right encouragement. For what it's worth there are no psychiat-ric barriers. The key is time, aeons of time, which of course gets him off the hook. Otherwise I must look for progress in the worst disappointments. Laying aside the most obvious question: should one's life be governed by this alone? And for fuck's sake should anyone else's?"

Tears finally pricked the corners of her eyes. "Oh Christopher."

He sat opposite her, a half-eaten sandwich in one hand, the rest of him reaching for something offhand, something ironic. "The straightforward solution is obvious: until I have a clearer view of myself I mustn't get involved. Or at least avoid anyone who matters. But this was you, Jana. You matter, and talking to Khantsev proved how much. Taking out the loan: I couldn't not do it. It's just dough, as you once said."

And now she was beginning to see the dilemma from his viewpoint. When her mobile sounded she needed to prevent herself screaming.

"Chérie, I believe you are Gascon Air's only poetic pilot," said Jean-Claude cheerfully

"I believe so," she said.

"My apologies for calling so late. But a satisfied customer - aware of this astonishing qualification – demands your services tomorrow. A seven o'clock departure, again for Toulouse. He calls himself Baudelaire but I think he lies."

"Does he need confirmation?"

"I will text him."

"Bless you J-C. Tell him to bring his own choice of verse."

Day had stood up and was about to leave. She said, "No Christopher. Not yet. One way or another it all ends in this apartment. Stay the night as a favour to me. I'd invite you to share my bed but you'd suspect I was taking advantage. Go ahead anyway, use my bed. The couch is too small for you but not for me. I have something I need to discuss but there's not enough time left tonight."

He shook his head. "I'll do whatever you say. But if you're honest – and you always are – you'll see the dead ends. Plus a truly vicious twist. I know you and care for you more than anything. But let's suppose, by some freakish argument, you managed to increase your value in my eyes. It wouldn't help; rather the opposite. There'd be all the more reason to turn away."

Despite everything she smiled faintly. "How about diminishing my value? And how about blackmail rather than persuasion?

I'm sorry for holding you here. It's not for dramatic effect I assure you. I need to dig out some information, read it and decide whether I should pass it on."

"Blackmail? Hardly a stepping stone to happiness. Doesn't blackmail, by definition, bring resentment?"

"It does indeed. Perhaps it all depends on how tough we both imagine ourselves to be."

At dawn she came knocking on his door and he emerged, sluggish, blinking, to see her trim in starched and ironed campaign shirt, clean chinos and her short-cut blonde hair held back on one side with a large decorative clip. "Juice and coffee on the table. I'll toast you a couple of baguette slices if you like. Lousy night?"

"A lousy night. You look damned professional. Forget that. Rather lovely."

"It's the qualifiers that make the Brits British. At least I'm not quite lovely."

"How much time have we got?" he asked.

"Enough."

"What is it you want to say?" He was trying to match her crisp talk but sounded tentative.

"I need to back-track. Yesterday we were head-to-head. My emotions were fried. You didn't deserve what I handed out. I honour your reasons for breaking up. What you're saying is I shouldn't be burdened with someone you regard as defective. I think I know how you feel towards me – no, let's check that. Brits may not use the big words but I'm a sentimental Yank. I am as sure as I can be – as an interested party – that you love me. And I certainly love you. Losing you will be like having my heart ripped out."

His orange juice had gone down in one and he was reaching for the percolator as she spoke. His hand, crooked to take the handle, halted a foot away – someone else's hand, unneeded for the moment. "Better late than never," he croaked. "I love you, Jana."

"But not enough to take risks?"

"One way of putting it."

"And so you've decided. I'm to be released from loving you because you're imperfect. I'm free to roam, free to find someone who is perfect."

"We're not talking cosmetics. It's an imperfection big enough to taint us both."

"It's a male thing and so I must take your word for that. But there's an assumption here. That in your view I deserve perfection."

"Jana, you're playing with words."

"You're right. When I was a young girl my parents had me examined by a medical specialist. Here's his report with the bit that matters highlighted:

Jana is afflicted with a naevus flammeus better known as a port-wine stain. Such stains persist throughout life. The area of skin affected grows in proportion to general growth. Port-wine stains occur most often on the face, as in Jana's case. From being usually flat and pink the stain's color may deepen to a dark red or purplish colour. In adulthood, the lesion may thicken and small lumps may occur.

Day took some time to read this. Jana said gently, "The key words are the last two: 'may occur'. So I may pass the rest of life very much as I am now. Not hopelessly handicapped as I look for that perfect mate. I may even find him. Should I tell him what may happen to my face or play the odds? But if the worst does happen should I rely on his humanity or can I expect to be dropped. Dumped."

Now she handed him a photograph cut from a newspaper. "And just so we know what we're talking about here, have a look at this. This man's a Welsh politician - you may know his name, I've forgotten it, not that it matters. He's in his fifties and his *naevus flammus* has continued to develop. This is what 'small lumps' can look like."

He looked at the cutting for some time then put it to one side. From sitting tensely on the edge of the chair he had slipped back and was watching her with his mouth half-open. She went on, "There's a parallel here as I'm sure you've noticed. Aeons may pass, you say, before your situation is resolved. If it ever is. It would take a great deal of love from any partner to ride that one out. I think I have that love. And from what you've done on my behalf – however wrong-headed your final decision – I think you could help me with my defect. And if my face goes horrible you may have learned enough about yourself not to drop me."

His breathing through his half-open mouth was now audible but he hadn't noticed. "Oh Christopher, it is blackmail of a sort. Or we could be trading one defect for another. You may have noticed something else, too. One thought I'll have to live with is whether I'd have shown you that letter if you hadn't tried to be honourable last night. Let's try and forget that for a moment. Think of me as adding to your hope. It doesn't make sense you going it alone when I would give anything to help you and be allowed to love you. If that big word you're so suspicious of means anything at all this surely is it, for both of us."

Now his head dropped, perhaps to hide his face. He said, "I'm not asking for comfort but... I'm not sure why any woman could love me. There's what I did – for the best of fucking reasons – to Gill. But what the hell are the other attractions? I've dropped out of the struggle, accepted defeat, there's a negativity. And you – you've fought on, you're certain. There's a wit."

"And yet you've defended me and thrilled me. Opened your mind and opened mine. Shared your work with me. And oh! that lanky, thoughtful body – how I love it. Christopher, in the end it's a trivial gesture, but if it helped I'd never enter another cockpit."

"Christ Jana! No!"

HE STILL looked like Sarkozy and she found him pacing the hardstanding, head tilted back as if he were scenting the early-morning air like a gundog. The second she appeared he quickened his step, took her in his arms and kissed her cheeks.

"M. Danieli you will scandalise the airport."

"Giacomo, please, Jana. But please, no more French. Let us speak English the whole of the flight. An important journey but not like the last, where my balls were unpleasantly exposed. I shall enjoy the flight and your company."

"No more talk of balls."

"Jana, you are a prude. I have a confession. I received Jean-Claude's text but I had no time to find any poetry. I must depend on your resources."

"I have some."

As before he stepped athletically up into the Stationair and watched her closely as she did the pre-flight. "Like a priest," he observed, "but a living, desirable priest engaged in a far less arid profession."

Her relations with the control tower staff were more relaxed these days and she was able to offer Danieli the same inexpressible benison she had once offered Octavien:

"Biarritz tower, Foxtrot Hotel Kilo Echo ready for take-off," he said, then grinned childishly, quite unlike Octavien.

The still rising sun flooded down the runway from the east, shining it like ice. She eased the throttle, heard the engine note change and released the brakes. Felt the transfer from ground to air with her finger-tips and climbed to three thousand feet.

Danieli sighed. "Still a beautiful sensation. I can feel the plane hanging in the air. We must mark it with some poetry."

"The book's in the musette on the back seat."

"Bravo" he said. "It is in English, as if you knew my mind. Is the marker significant?"

"It is. Practice that poem in your head. Then read it aloud."

"But tell me what it is."

"A sonnet by Shakespeare. Very familiar to the Anglos to the point of being banal. Read it with passion Giacomo. Especially the third line from the end.

"You mean: When in eternal lines to time thou growest?

"Grow'st. It's one syllable. Otherwise the line doesn't read right. You wanted poetry – so take it seriously."

He read it again, correctly, concentrated on it for ten seconds. "Thank God I know English. It's beautiful. Like this day, this sense of suspension above the ground, like the expression on your face."

"Like all those things."